# ON FIRE

# ON FIRE

*A novel of the 1950s*

John Ogden

Book Guild Publishing
Sussex, England

First published in Great Britain in 2007 by
The Book Guild Ltd
Pavilion View
19 New Road
Brighton
BN1 1UF

The speeches of the Commissioner for South East Asia and
the Commander-in-Chief in Chapter 2 are taken from
Rene Cutforth's *Korean Reporter* (Allan Wingate, 1952).

Typesetting in Baskerville 11½ on 13 by
IML Typographers, Merseyside

Printed in Great Britain by
CPI Antony Rowe

A catalogue record for this book is available from
The British Library.

ISBN 978 1 84624 155 0

*Now all the youth of England are on fire*

William Shakespeare
Henry V, Act II

To my brother officers who shared
their memories of these days with me

*On Fire* is the first book in the trilogy
*A Military Education*

I am not I. You are not he or she.
They are not they.

Nor is a pound sterling a pound. The 1950
pound would be worth at least £35 today. The
exchange rate then was US$2.80 to the pound.

# Contents

*Characters and Maps*

# Chapter 1

## Palmy days

'Now girls.'

George Bulman was sitting behind a trestle table covered by a green army blanket. On the blanket were three trays marked in, out and pending. In the pending tray lay two paperback novels. The other trays were empty. George did not waste time on paper work. He read everything once and then gave it to the serjeant-major or one of us to deal with. 'Good training for you,' he would say. George was noted for the economy with which he despatched his duties and for his courage. In the later stages of the Second World War he had won the Military Cross twice: first in Normandy, then in crossing the Rhine. We were devoted to him.

We were sitting in George's office in our hutted camp at Hang Seng in the New Territories of the crown colony of Hong Kong. Major George Bulman was the company commander of X Company, 2nd Battalion, The Prince Regent's Light Infantry. It was 1951. We had been in Hong Kong for two years, part of the British forces stationed there to defend the colony from the People's Republic of China, the new communist country. There was no serious confrontation. The Chinese rarely rattled their sabres at us. They were far too occupied trying to sort themselves out after years of civil war. But we were there to stop them if they should try to annexe the colony. We were cold war frontiersmen.

1

George's girls were his company officers. We had gathered for his regular Saturday morning briefing, a round up of administrative and training points he wanted to review. It was one of the ways he trained us. He always ended these sessions by planning an opportunity to defeat another company on the sports field. In peacetime, George's battlefield was the sports ground, his enemy the other company commanders in the battalion.

The divide between our ages seemed considerable. George was in his early thirties, well built with a moustache, a chest full of medals and sleek black hair. To us he had vast military experience and seemed twice our age. We, his subalterns, were not as green as we had been. He had seen to that. But we had no battle experience. The exception was Dermot Lisle, the second-in-command of the company, who had fought in Italy in the war and had also won the Military Cross. Dermot had only recently rejoined the battalion from a staff job at the War Office in London. George treated Dermot with respect though he could still address him with a 'now, my girl'. Not even Dermot could touch George's experience and authority.

For ten minutes George reviewed the week's work, what we'd done well, what we could do better. Then he turned to Dermot.

'Congratulations again, Dermot,' he said, 'on our success in the battalion small-arms meeting. I loved watching the faces of my fellow company commanders as you collected yet another cup.' Then, turning to the rest of us, he said, 'Now what's our next coup to be?'

Dermot was an ace shot. He had represented Britain in the last Olympics. He was also a fine trainer. I had grown up with guns. In the short time Dermot had been with us he had improved our shooting, including mine. He was full of gaiety. His very presence made one feel better. If he hadn't had such a snub nose he would have been handsome, too.

'Well, Burgo?'

Burgo Howard was a year younger than me. Blond and a great athlete, he had made a reputation at pentathlon, the military sport that combined running, fencing, riding, swimming and shooting. He had been successful, too, in Hong Kong at khud running, which involved running up and down the peaks. He had trained the battalion team to beat all the other regiments in the colony.

'Well, Burgo? What about challenging Y Company to a final khud running competition?'

'They wouldn't accept,' said Burgo. He had a penetrating stare, which he now directed at George.

'They might if we gave them a handicap,' said George staring back at Burgo.

'No, Y Company just hasn't got the runners. Anyhow the season's over. Why Y Company?'

'It's time I had another bet with Horace Belcher.'

Horace Belcher commanded Y Company. He was rich, handsome, a great horseman and a polished polo player who drank too much. He also liked gambling. George and Horace often had bets. George did not always win.

'Any ideas, Miles?'

'We might beat them at cricket,' I said.

'Might isn't good enough. I want a quick, surprising and decisive win. Cricket takes too long and could end in a draw. Toby?'

Toby Errington was nineteen. He was a National Service officer who had joined us six months ago. Tall and able with a dreamy air, he had a place waiting for him at Oxford. He was not a natural soldier and his uniform never seemed to fit him properly, which had led to him being nicknamed 'Manky'.

'What about darts?' he said.

'Darts? Darts! Stap me! I hadn't thought of darts. There's an idea. Could we beat them?'

'We could if we said the team has to have an officer. Y Company are good but they aren't as good as us and they haven't got an officer who can play.'

Toby's platoon loved him. Not one of them could beat him at darts. He chain-smoked, and excelled at crosswords and chess.

'Do you think Y Company know how well you play darts?'

'Surely Horace won't know?'

'Of course he won't. Excellent. Darts it is. You and I, Manky, shall work this up.'

At that moment Company Serjeant-Major Budd knocked on the door, entered and saluted. He was short and had a red face. He had probably been waiting outside the door to hear what was going on. The walls in the hut were flimsy.

'Yes, Budd?'

Budd and George had been together in the war. Some said that Budd had started as George's soldier servant. In the war he had been his platoon serjeant and then his company serjeant-major. He had won the Distinguished Conduct Medal. George often called Budd by his name rather than addressing him as serjeant-major. Budd did not seem to mind. They had a close relationship.

'When you've finished, Sir, the platoon serjeants report everything "All Sir Garnet" and are ready for their officers.'

'Thank you, Budd. We've not quite finished. Tell them we'll be through in five minutes.'

'Sir,' said Budd. He saluted and left. He seemed happy with this answer. He rarely interrupted George on such a poor pretext but, as we had gone on longer than usual, he may have thought something important was being discussed and he would not have wanted to miss it. The meeting being mainly about sport George had asked only the officers to attend. He held that our first duty was to lead and win on the playing fields. If we led well there we would do so on the battlefield and the men would follow us. Had there been a

4

hint of a more tactical or administrative nature to our meeting George would have ensured that Budd, Colour Serjeant Crum and the platoon serjeants were present.

He knew that anything he said in his office could be overheard in the company office, where the serjeant-major and the company clerk sat, and would be round the company within the hour. George liked this. He told me it was good for communications. The company thrived on gossip and was much more likely to believe what George said if the company office had spread the news around in advance. He said his orders then merely reinforced what they had already heard. This also meant that he rarely had to be the first in telling any bad news. The news would have already spread by the time he had to confirm it. He said it made life much simpler. If he wanted to talk to you without being overheard then he would take you on a walk in the open, well out of earshot. This infuriated Budd, who felt he had a right to know everything, but it worked. It also added to the mysteries of George's style of command.

'What's arranged for the weekend?' asked George. We took it in turns to organise weekend activities. This weekend Burgo and Toby were responsible. They explained what arrangements they had made.

'And you, Miles?'

'I'm going sailing,' I said.

'Are you?'

'It's in the leave book. I'm away for the weekend. The colonel's approved it.'

'Don't capsize. And don't get married. Anyone got anything else to say or ask? No? Good. That's that. I must go and find Horace Belcher.'

We broke up. I walked down to my platoon lines where Serjeant Whettingsteel, my platoon serjeant, greeted me.

'Has the company commander,' he asked, 'really challenged Major Belcher to a game of darts?'

'It's not to be a personal match. It's a company team versus Y Company. Each team has to have an officer.'

'That's cunning. I haven't heard that Y has an officer who can play darts like Mr Errington.'

'Nor has Mr Errington.'

'The serjeant-major says he's going to lay a smokescreen in the serjeants' mess. He's going to say he doesn't think we've got a chance and that the company commander's got this one wrong. When he thinks he's laid his subterfuges he'll take a few bets himself.'

'I'm away sailing this weekend. Will you all be all right?'

'Don't you worry, Sir, you go and enjoy yourself. We'll be fine. There's swimming organised and a game of football. Mr Howard is holding a fencing class. There's the cinema, too. You can over organise them. They like a bit of time to themselves. Tomorrow, me and my little brother are going to Kowloon to the services club there. We'll be fine.'

Serjeant Whettingsteel's younger brother was in my platoon, too. He was a corporal. They were known as Big Steel and Little Steel. Little Steel was thinner but taller.

George was keen that we kept the men occupied to keep their spirits up. Hong Kong had little recreation to offer the troops apart from the obvious fleshpots. It was also expensive. So we arranged a lot of activities ourselves. The men's spirits were good. This was also due to their being very fit and to the weather being bearable at this time of year. But they could easily get bored.

We were fortunate in having a hutted camp. When we first arrived we had had to delay landing from our troopship as our tented camp had been flattened by a typhoon. Another regiment took two days to get it standing again. Lying in a flat plain of old paddy fields, the camp was impossible to drain properly. For a year we suffered occasional flooding. The colonel occupied us every minute of the day to take our minds off the discomfort. We became very fit and still were. Then the battalion moved to our present hutted camp, on the side of a hill, which we had watched being built. The huts had fans. We thought them a great luxury. A newly arrived regiment was now suffering in our old tented camp.

Big Steel and I held our final weapon inspection of the week before our Lee-Enfield rifles, Sten sub-machine-guns and Bren light-machine-guns were locked away in the armoury for the weekend. By the time Big Steel had reported everything 'All Sir Garnet' – the regimental expression for everything being correct and in order – the duty bugler was sounding the cookhouse call, floating it seductively over the camp. Big Steel saluted, dismissed the men and they went to their Saturday dinner.

For the last few minutes Dermot Lisle had been with us, checking the armoury. Together we walked along the road that took us round the parade ground to the officers' mess.

'How do you find Big Steel?' Dermot asked.

'I couldn't be luckier,' I replied.

'He was with us in Italy. I remember him well.'

'It's time he was promoted. Was he in your company?'

'Yes, at the end. And Little Steel?'

'He's ready to be promoted, too.'

'They'll have to wait.'

'Good. I don't want to lose them.'

'How long have you had your platoon?'

'I got it just before you re-joined.'

'What were you doing before?'

'I was ADC to the governor.'

'Enjoy it?'

'Very much. I learned a lot but not much about soldiering. I'm glad to be back. I like soldiering.'

'How did you get that job?'

'The Governor, Ivan Blessington, is married to my cousin Sonia – well, my mother's cousin really. He asked for me.'

7

'So you were a captain temporarily?'

'For a year.'

'Who's ADC now?'

'Hugh Jermy. He's my best friend in the regiment. We joined together. And we were at school together. I'm sailing with him this afternoon, and staying at Government House tonight. Were you ever a major?'

'For a bit at the end of the war. I've been a captain ever since. You'll have to wait some time before you're a captain again, Miles.'

'I know. Do you think you'll have to wait long to be a major?'

'Yes. But the colonel has told me he wants me to have a company as soon as he can arrange it.'

'How well do you know Colonel Guy?'

'We've only served together fleetingly. For much of the war he was away from the regiment and commanded a parachute battalion.'

Guy Surtees had only just taken over command of the battalion. Well decorated in the war he had arrived with a great reputation. Everything we had seen so far justified it. He had the air of command about him and he was fun. Commanding the battalion was taxing yet he made everything look easy. He must have been disappointed in us occasionally but he never lost his temper as some senior officers did just to make, I thought, an effect. You knew where you stood with him. He never connived, prevaricated or plotted. We had been fortunate in our commanding officers. Colonel Guy was to prove exceptional.

We reached the officers' mess. As soon as we had dropped our hats and belts in the cloakroom, Dermot went into the anteroom to have a drink and I went into the dining room. I had ordered an early lunch so I would not lose time in catching the ferry in Kowloon to take me to Hong Kong Island. Two or three others who aimed to catch the ferry

8

were already eating. I dropped into a chair and looked round the room while I waited to be served.

On the table were the three great silver candelabra and the four silver vases given us by the Prince Regent, our great patron. We were not an old regiment, having been raised in the early years of the Napoleonic Wars to form part of a brigade of light infantry that was being trained by Sir John Moore. At the time we were experimental and avant-garde troops. We remained elitist about this. Our ways of working and our discipline were still based on Moore's humane and revolutionary thinking. We were jealous of our light infantry standing. After Waterloo the Prince Regent had adopted us to claim a close connection with a regiment that had been in the midst of the battle. He used to say to the Duke of Wellington, 'I was there, wasn't I Duke?' The Duke always replied, 'I have often heard Your Highness so remark. Your regiment certainly was.' Towards the end of Queen Victoria's reign, General Sir Garnet Wolseley – later Field Marshal Viscount Wolseley and noted in the kingdom as 'our only general' – became our Colonel-in-Chief. The regimental expression 'All Sir Garnet', to indicate everything was in order, came from him.

The regiment had distinguished itself in the two world wars, raising many battalions. Now we had two battalions when most regiments had been reduced to one in the post-war rundown of the army. The reputation of the regiment attracted recruits, but it was friends in high places, muddle at the War Office and the outbreak of the Korean War that had prevented further reduction. The officers and serjeants still lived in some style. We were proud to do so. It was swank, of course, but we felt we had something to swank about.

The Star ferry chugged across the narrow waters between the mainland and Hong Kong Island. Water traffic seethed between anchored ships, most of which flew the White or Red

Ensign. The harbour never failed to fascinate. The water round Hong Kong had a chameleon-like ability to change colour and mood. Sometimes it was blue, sometimes green, sometimes white. Varying in intensity and shade, it could be translucent or opaque. I loved gazing at it. As we closed with the shore, Hong Kong side, I looked at the curve of the shoreline and the beguiling town behind it. I could hear the bustle and constant chatter of the place. In those days Hong Kong was no more than three storeys high, except for the new offices of the Hong Kong and Shanghai Bank, which towered over everything. There was a delusive sensuality and exoticism about Hong Kong. Despite all its colour, money and freedoms most of its people led a harsh life. Increasing numbers of refugees pouring over the border made it harsher.

At the ferry terminal I took a rickshaw for the mile or two to the Royal Hong Kong Yacht Club. The club and the boats were on a tiny island a hundred yards offshore. I was late. I rang the bell for the boatman. I could see many of the yachts were already out in the harbour preparing for the start of the race. The boatman knew me but took his time.

'Captain Jermy, ready, ready. You late,' he said, shaking his head.

He rowed me out to where Hugh was sitting in the boat we shared, moored to a buoy. I scrambled aboard leaving my overnight bag with the boatman to put in the locker room at the club. Hugh had rigged the boat. All we had to do was raise the mainsail and sail off. Mainsail raised, I untied the warp holding us to the mooring buoy and let go. A light breeze took us out into the eastern end of the harbour. Hugh was on the helm. We moved fast through the slight swell, heeling a little in the wind. The bustle and intensity of Hong Kong disappeared behind us. We were suddenly in another world.

As well as having the looks of Adonis, Hugh was talented, versatile and popular. He was the first of my year at school to

10

get into library, the group of senior boys who held monitorial rank, responsibilities and privileges in our house. He was the first to win his school colours at cricket. He was competitive. Some people crave a drink, sex or a cigarette. Hugh craved success, success at whatever he was doing. He was careful about what he took on but once committed he had to succeed.

We had started sailing together when young. When we were seventeen he decided we would enter a sailing regatta held at Burnham-on-Crouch. In the first race we capsized, largely my fault. I was frightened. Not so Hugh. He was cool. While I gasped for breath and spat water Hugh got the boat upright, climbed back in and pulled me in. He refused all offers of help from the safety motor launch and we bailed the water out. We sailed on, caught the tail of the fleet and were not the last past the line. Every day for a week with Hugh at the helm we improved our position until, on the final day, we won. Or rather Hugh won. He had to win.

Racing a boat occupies mind and body. It's all absorbing and the race was as invigorating as ever. We were second across the line, which pleased me, but I could tell Hugh was irritated he had not come first. We did not talk until we were back on our mooring. Taking the sails off, Hugh said, 'What's the news from Hang Seng lines?'

'Horace Belcher was drunk every night last week.'

'That's not news.'

'I can't vouch for Wednesday. I was on border patrol.'

'Catch anyone?'

'No refugees. We got a gang of smugglers. They were carrying petrol in jerry cans on long poles. We caught them lifting the cans over the wire. The police were pleased. It's a lucrative trade smuggling petrol into China. The gang was carrying a lot of money.'

'Are the Chinese patrolling the border at the moment?'

'Not that I could see. I think they encourage the smugglers and couldn't care less about the refugees.'

'More digging and wiring I suppose?'

Our main task was to prepare defensive positions on the border against a Chinese attack.

'It never stops.'

'Nothing new?'

'There's some speculation about when we'll move to Singapore. Heard anything?'

'No more than it's the battalion's next station.'

'There's also talk about being sent to Korea, not Singapore. Colonel Guy says we should be prepared for it. He says our training here is far more suited to fighting on the hills of Korea than in the jungles of Malaya.'

'I've heard nothing about that. That would upset your plans with Kitty, wouldn't it?'

'I haven't got any plans with Kitty.'

'She told me that when the battalion moves to Singapore she would follow.'

'That's what she's saying.'

'Kitty loves you. Do you love her?'

I had grown up with Kitty. Our fathers had been in the regiment and neighbours in the country. We had been brought up within two miles of each other though I was the elder. We had always been close friends. Her mother had died when she was young. My father had been killed in the war. Her father was like an uncle to me, my mother an aunt to her. My mother's cousin, Sonia Blessington, was Kitty's godmother. Together Kitty and I had learned to ride – she was better than me – dance, swim, fish, play tennis, sail and, even, shoot. In later years, when at our boarding schools, we had drifted apart. When the battalion sailed for Hong Kong Kitty was in London. She fell in love and got engaged. It went wrong. Sonia suggested she came to Hong Kong to get over it. She had arrived three months ago. She had grown into a beautiful woman. I was still at Government House as ADC before I had handed over to Hugh. We had seen a lot of each other, got very close again and fallen into each other's arms. I was in a fearful fix. Hugh knew all this.

'Do you love her?' he asked again.

'Yes, but it's impossible.'

'I don't see why?'

'I can't possibly marry her. You know no one in the regiment gets married much before he's thirty. The army frowns on it until one's twenty-five. I'm only twenty-three.'

'She says she's going to marry you, that you were made for each other. She's very determined.'

'She always has been.'

'I'd enjoy it while you can. Love doesn't last long, in my experience.'

We had taken the sails off and had been sitting idle for some time, the boat stowed. The boatman came alongside to take us off.

Sonia and Kitty were having tea in Sonia's sitting room at Government House when Hugh and I arrived.

'Come and sit down and tell us how you did,' said Sonia, who was looking as svelte as ever. 'You don't look wet.'

'Hugh sailed us into second place,' I said. 'There was only a light wind. We didn't even get our feet wet. There'll be more wind tomorrow morning. What have you been doing?'

'We went to watch the polo. Your team played rather well. What's the name of your team captain?' asked Kitty.

'Horace Belcher.'

'Yes, Horace. He played particularly well,' she said. 'He's an exceptional horseman.'

'He lives for horses, gambling and drinking.'

'Anchovy toast?' asked Sonia.

'Please,' I replied.

'Where does soldiering come in?' asked Kitty.

'Soldiering allows him his pleasures,' I said.

'If I were a man I'd want to be a soldier. You have a wonderful time. Here you are in Hong Kong, all sailing and polo. What more could one ask?'

'Night patrols, digging trenches, cleaning weapons, guard duty. Would you enjoy all that?'

'If you do I don't see why I couldn't. I suppose if I can't be a soldier the next best thing would be to marry one.'

'Cake, anyone?' asked Sonia.

'Thank you,' said Hugh.

'I sometimes think,' said Sonia, 'that my darling god-daughter wants to have her cake and eat it.'

'Oh, I do,' said Kitty. 'Doesn't everyone?'

'We may sometimes want it but we don't always enjoy it if it's given. Don't you know that saying of Saint Teresa's that more unhappiness is caused by prayers being answered than not?'

'Oh, Sonia, can't a girl have dreams?'

'Just so long as she knows they're dreams.'

'I think I'll have some cake. I need reassurance.'

Between mouthfuls she said, 'Will someone take me sailing tomorrow?'

'I have to attend the governor tomorrow morning,' said Hugh. 'There's a race at eleven. Why don't you go with Miles?'

'Is that all right, Sonia?' I asked.

'It's a lovely idea. I'll come and watch and we can all have lunch at the yacht club. That's settled. Remind me who's coming to dinner tonight, Hugh?'

'The chief of staff and his wife, some of the younger taipans with their wives, a few government officials, Mary Plant and us. Twenty in all. The list is on your writing table.'

'How can we make it fun?' said Sonia. 'I know. Let's dance after dinner. We've got some new records. And why don't we play tennis now, the four of us? There's plenty of time before we have to dress.'

We changed into tennis clothes and played two sets of tennis, Sonia and Hugh against Kitty and me. Sonia and Hugh played well together. They seemed to have a closer understanding of each other's play than Kitty and I did. They won both sets.

Two years in Hong Kong, including a year as ADC, meant that I knew everyone at dinner. The men all wore white double-breasted tuxedos, except for Ivan Blessington who wore a single-breasted coat made of heavy cream silk with a dark blue cummerbund. The women wore short dresses, many clearly from Paris. I sat between Mary Plant and the wife of a taipan, a Hong Kong merchant prince. Mary belonged to the fishing fleet, a young woman out from England angling for a husband. Sonia knew her mother. The merchant prince's wife had married successfully from the fishing fleet a year or two before. Sonia had probably invited the younger merchant princes and their wives so that they would introduce Mary to suitable unmarried men in the colony. It was an eternal game.

'Good evening, Juliette,' I said to the merchant prince's wife on my right. 'Haven't you been home since I last saw you?'

'No, we go next month. I can't wait.'

'Sea or air?'

'Air, thank God.'

'You're lucky.'

'I know. The company's doing well and it's paying.'

'How long?'

'Six weeks.'

'Long enough. You'll be pleased to get back.'

'That's what other people say. I can't think why.'

'Six weeks in England will make you realise how well off you are here. England is so dull and drab.'

'I still long for it. When were you last home?' she asked.

'Two years ago now. We'll be out here for at least another two years, though we're due to move to Singapore soon.'

'Fighting the communists?'

'Yes.'

'Will you enjoy that?'

'It'll be a change. I've enjoyed Hong Kong, though.'

'You were lucky to have the Blessingtons here. Aren't you a cousin or something?'

'I am and they've been very kind to me. But most of the officers and NCOs in my regiment have enjoyed it. It's a wonderful station.'

Another course was served and Juliette turned to talk to the man on her right.

'Did I hear you say there's a wonderful station here?' said Mary Plant on my left. 'Do you mean Hong Kong has trains, too?'

'There's a station in Kowloon. The trains go to the border. I meant Hong Kong is a wonderful military station, somewhere to be posted. How long have you been here, Mary?'

'Two weeks and I'm mesmerised.'

'You'll either love Hong Kong or you'll hate it. I love it. I don't think Juliette, on my right, really cares for it. If you're going to settle here make sure you love it first.'

'What do the Blessingtons think?'

'You'd better ask them. They're professional nomads. They can settle anywhere. I rather think Ivan Blessington likes it. Sonia finds it a little difficult because of Phyllida.'

'Phyllida?'

'Their daughter. She's at school in England. It's too far for her to come here every holiday. Sonia goes home to see her.'

'By sea?'

'No, by air. It takes three days as opposed to four weeks.'

'She must be rich.'

'She is.'

'Are you?'

'No. Her side of the family was cleverer with money than mine. I'm not a catch.'

16

'Pity. You're rather nice. But I don't want to tread on Kitty's toes.'

'Kitty and I have known each other since childhood.'

'Oh, is that all?'

When the women left us I moved to sit next to the chief of staff.

'How are you enjoying your days digging and wiring after the luxuries of Government House, Miles?' he asked.

'I like soldiering, general.'

'You'll get some proper soldiering in Malaya, soon.'

'Do you think we'll still go there? Colonel Surtees thinks we're likely to be switched to Korea.'

'As far as I know your movement order still stands. I don't see the War Office changing plans, though they are perfectly capable of it.'

We laughed and talked about sailing.

Later, after the first guests had left, Sonia said, 'Don't go. We've got some new records. I've had my sitting room made ready for us to dance in. What about it?'

Soon we were all dancing. The lights were low. Noel Coward followed Judy Garland who followed Fats Waller. I danced with Juliette and then Mary. Then I could not resist asking Kitty.

'Happy, darling?' said Kitty as we danced.

'Mmm,' I replied.

'This is having my cake and eating it.'

'Is it a dream?'

'Isn't that the name of the song by Debroy Summers? Don't you remember playing it in the school holidays?'

'You were rather distant in the school holidays.'

'That's because I was growing up. I'm not distant now, am I?'

'At this moment you couldn't be closer.'

17

'Do you think too close? Will people talk?'
'They are already. Mary seemed to know about us.'
'Weren't you proud?'
'I was surprised. She's only been here two weeks.'
'I told her. I didn't want her stepping in,' said Kitty.
'Who else have you told?'
'Sonia.'
'She knew.'
'How do you know?'
'I told her. Anyhow she'd guessed.'
'I love Sonia.'
'So do I.'

After an hour the party broke up and the guests left. Ivan went to his study.

Sonia said, 'Let's have one last record. What shall it be? Here we are. Lena Horne singing "The man I love". Now, Miles, I want to dance with you.'

We danced. Hugh danced with Kitty.

'Kitty does love you, Miles.'

'Do you think it's on the rebound?'

'Whether it is or not, she loves you. She's much more settled and calmer. She's got over that man she was engaged to.'

'Sonia, what am I going to do?'

'You're going to marry her, aren't you?'

'How can I? We're so young and I'm a soldier.'

'What does that matter?'

'I can't get married yet. Do you think she'll wait for me?'

'How long?'

'Three years.'

'Three years. That's a long time. Well, you've known each other since childhood. I suppose another three years won't matter. Why three years?'

'The army doesn't give one marriage allowance until you're twenty-five.'

'Why do you need that? I thought you had money of your own.'

'No. Mummy says my father spent it all.'

'He spent a lot but there must be a lot left. Oh dear. I see.'

The record finished.

'Bedtime for me,' said Sonia. 'That was fun.'

'Bedtime for me, too,' said Kitty.

As I lay in bed in the dark thinking about what Sonia had said, the door of my room opened and a shaft of light played across the walls. There was a rustle of clothes dropping on to the floor. A moment later Kitty slipped into my bed, naked.

'Oh, my darling, how I've missed you,' she said. 'Promise you'll roger me all night.'

## Chapter 2

# *Frantic days*

'We're going to win the darts match, aren't we, Manky?' said George Bulman.

It was the following Saturday. We were sitting in George's office. The in and out trays remained empty. There were still two paperback novels in his pending tray but the titles looked different. Having reviewed the week with us and then conducted a lengthy discussion on the sporting facilities in Singapore, George had turned to the pursuit of Horace Belcher and his humiliation at darts. George was now assessing the risks and anticipating the hazards as he did with all the sporting events we entered.

'Short of one of our team having an accident or catching clap I can't see a major problem now,' replied Toby Errington.

'Remind me who's in the team.'

'Colour Crum, Lance Corporal Rothwell and myself. Butcher Jones is reserve.'

'Perhaps we should put you all on light duties?'

'No. But you could buy us some beer. Colour Crum plays better with a pint or two inside him. Rothwell too. They say it steadies them.'

'If that's your advice, I accept it. Now—'

George's voice trailed away. A tap on the door had interrupted him. 'What is it?' he said.

For some minutes I had been aware of a kerfuffle in the

office in the next room, where the serjeant-major sat with the company clerk. I had heard raised voices, which sounded as if the serjeant-major and the colour serjeant were having an argument. I could not hear what it was about and it wasn't loud enough for George to have sent one of us to ask them to quieten. It was unusual. Something was up.

Serjeant-Major Budd entered and saluted.

'What is it Budd?' George said sharply.

'We're for Korea, Sir.'

'What on earth do you mean?'

'Colour Crum reports that it's just been announced on the Hong Kong wireless station that the Second Battalion Prince Regent's Light Infantry, previously designated for Singapore, has been ordered to proceed to join the United Nations forces in Korea, Sir.'

'Farouk me for a chocolate soldier!' said George. 'Who said that?'

'Colour Crum says he heard it on the wireless just now. You know how he keeps the wireless going in the company stores all day to see if there's anything of interest. I thought you would want to know pronto.'

'Did they say when?'

'No, Sir. Just what I said Colour Crum said.'

'Yes, indeed. Korea, is it? I'd better talk to the adjutant. See what he knows. Don't go. You'd better hear what the fellow has to say.'

He picked up the telephone.

'Exchange? Put me through to the adjutant.'

There was a wait. I wondered what sporting opportunities George would find for us in Korea, apart from shooting.

'Percy? Is that you? Have you heard the news from the Hong Kong wireless station that we're off to Korea? No? Well it has just been announced. Are we? You mean you know? When did you know? Only half an hour ago? What's that? The colonel's gone to see the general? Why the general? Oh, he's gone with the brigadier, has he? When do we go to Korea? Soon? That's better. The colonel's called an O group for midday? Now you tell me. What do you advise we do meanwhile? Stop bothering you, you say? Well I'd advise you to stick a little closer to your wireless set, that is if you've got one in the orderly room. You might hear some more up-to-date news. Hello, hello. The bugger's put the telephone down.'

George beamed at us.

'It seems,' he said, 'the news is true. Send for Colour Crum to be congratulated. It's good to get one up on the orderly room.'

Colour Crum appeared immediately. He must have been listening outside the door. He was a large man, a little over-weight but with a confident air.

'Colour Crum, you've surpassed yourself again. We've got battalion headquarters rattled. Better cut along to the quartermaster's stores and see what's going on there if you haven't thought of that already, which you probably have. Perhaps the first thing we should do, serjeant-major, is check the men's kit, see they've got everything if we're off to war.'

Budd and Crum saluted and left.

Still beaming George turned to us and said, 'To it, girls.'

'So it's true we're off to Korea?' said Big Steel when I met him in the platoon lines. 'The lads are excited about it.'

'Are they now?' I said. 'I wondered how they'd react. What about you?'

'I'm excited, too. I'm looking forward to having a bash at the commies. I thought we'd be going. There's been plenty of rumours. What do you think?'

'I had always thought we'd go to Singapore. So did the company commander. I'm puzzled they've changed our orders.'

'They say there's been a terrible battle and the Gloucesters have been over-run. They probably need a mob like ours to sort it out.'

'Why is it the sergeants' mess always knows more about what's going on?'

'Your news is generally more accurate when it comes, Sir. We just keep our ears closer to the ground.'

'You mean the orderly room serjeant gives you titbits that the adjutant withholds from the officers.'

'Not just the orderly room. Quartermaster's stores knows a lot, too.'

A runner came up to me and saluted.

'Company commander's compliments, Sir, and would you come and see him immediately, Sir.'

'Maybe you'll get some more accurate information,' said Big Steel. 'I'll start the kit check, while you're away.'

I followed the runner back to George's office.

'Thanks to you I've lost a pretty sum,' said George. 'I only bet we'd go to Singapore because you said the chief of staff confirmed it.'

'That's what he told me, George,' I replied. 'Maybe he misled me on purpose, but I doubt it. This looks like a sudden change of plan. Big Steel says there're rumours that the Gloucesters have been over-run in a terrible battle. How much have you lost?'

'Only a tenner to Horace Belcher. It's not the money. It's losing to him. He'll be unbearable. We must win that darts match. No, the reason I called for you is the colonel's back and he wants to see you as soon as possible. He wants you to do something. You'd better go now. Be a good fellow and let me know what it is.'

I walked across to battalion headquarters wondering what it could be the colonel wanted me to do. He very rarely sent for one. Promotion? No, I'm not the next in line. To take over one of the support company platoons, like the machine guns or the mortars? No, I was not trained. I went into the adjutant's office and saluted. Percy Smythe, the adjutant, glanced up from a pile of papers strewn across his desk. He looked as though he was not enjoying his Saturday morning. He was tall, carried his uniform elegantly and spoke with a slight lisp.

'The colonel wants to see you, Miles. Go straight in. I'm having a miserable time working out strengths and drafts and releases, who's to go to Korea and who isn't. No sailing for me today.'

Oh dear, I thought. The colonel is going to tell me I'm not going to Korea. That would be awful. No. He's going to tell me to drop Kitty. I knocked on the colonel's door and walked in. Colonel Guy was standing at the window gazing out beyond the camp. In the distance I could see the sea. It looked white today. He turned. He was my height. He looked straight at me with his large eyes and smiled. He always smiled, whatever he was doing, and he always looked you in the face.

'Miles, I take it you've heard the news we're going to Korea? Good. I've always expected this, as I think you know. One of the difficulties about Korea is we know so little about it. Brigade has given me some briefing notes but they don't tell us much. I'd like you to go and see your cousin, the governor, and ask him if you can use his library at Government House. As you well know, he's a bibliophile. He told me recently that he'd rebuilt the library that the Japanese destroyed. He showed me round. He's very proud of it. I'm sure you'll find something interesting on Korea. At five o'clock on Monday I want to talk to all the officers about Korea and, as part of this, I want you to brief them on the country and the people. Take this paper from brigade. It needs flesh and anecdotes. Bring it alive. Understand?'

'Yes, colonel. I'd better ring Hugh Jermy now to ask the governor if I can do this.'

'Good idea. Say it's at my request. If you need to stay at

24

Government House for the night you can but be back here by Sunday night. I'm going to let the battalion enjoy itself this weekend. It'll be our last opportunity. Then come and see me on Monday morning and run through with me what you're going to say. You'll need some visual aids, so see what maps the intelligence officer has.'

Hugh Jermy was waiting for me in the ADC's office at Government House.

'The governor's waiting for you. He wants to talk to you himself. He's delayed lunch. Sonia and Kitty have gone to watch the polo. There's just the three of us.'

We sat down in the small family dining room. Ivan Blessington was a lean man. He looked at me with his slightly hooded eyes and I immediately felt he was looking straight into me. I had learned that his look was merely the expression of his intense intellect and curiosity. It could be frightening until you realised this.

'So you want to know all about Korea, Miles?' he asked.

'Colonel Surtees said you have built a fine library, Sir, which you had shown him. He said you were bound to have some interesting books on Korea.'

'Yes, we've a few. After the Japanese the Americans know more about Korea than anyone else and they've been writing about it for over fifty years. But no one knows much. The present situation stems from Roosevelt, Stalin and Churchill making no firm agreement about what was to happen to Korea after the defeat of Japan. The original idea was that she should be free and independent. Then at Yalta, in February 1945, Roosevelt proposed a period of trusteeship first. He was keen on trusteeships, though Churchill thought Roosevelt naïve. Stalin agreed originally, but only verbally. At Potsdam, in July 1945, in all the haggling over territorial claims Korea got left out. When the war with Japan ended suddenly in August there was no agreement about Korea and it fell into joint Soviet-US occupation. Overnight the Americans took a decision about a boundary. A Major Dean Rusk and a Colonel Bonesteel (yes, those were their names) were given thirty minutes to decide on a dividing line. They found an atlas and plumped for the 38th Parallel, which they saw ran north of Seoul, the capital, and divided the country neatly in two. Quite arbitrary, but I'm not sure what else they could have done. To everyone's surprise the Soviets accepted this. This is where the country's division began and where the trouble started. It didn't go down well with the Koreans. I know all this because I was at Yalta and Potsdam, and then in Washington.'

Ivan Blessington had been a fellow of All Souls. I had often wondered why Sonia, who was so full of life and gaiety, had married him. I saw again why he was so good at his job, but I was still puzzled by what Sonia saw in him.

'The best place to start,' Ivan went on, 'is generally *Encyclopaedia Britannica*. In the case of Korea I'm not sure it will tell you what you want to know.'

'Why?'

'So much has happened in the last few years I doubt it's up to date. Few Englishmen, of course, know anything about it.'

'Who was the first Englishman to go there?'

'In modern times Curzon was one of the first and he wrote a book about it. We have it.'

'And earlier?'

'Korea was an ancient kingdom. Until the late middle ages they were far in advance of Europe, like the Chinese. They know this and it hurts. They resisted the first European incursions and defeated the Japanese in a great sea battle. But then the Chinese defeated them and they became a vassal of China and closed their borders to everyone else. That's why it's known as the "hermit kingdom". In the nineteenth century, Japan started to wake up and China weakened. She was unable to protect the country any longer

26

and Korea became a natural target for everyone. All the great powers established embassies there but the Japanese made the running. In 1904 they walked in and in 1910 they formally annexed the country as a colony.'

'Why didn't anyone stop the Japs?'

'Russia tried and failed. Remember her humiliation in the Russo-Japanese War? The only other country that could have done so was America. But they had done a deal with the Japs over spheres of influence in the Pacific. You know, "you have Korea and we have the Philippines". I suspect we connived at this.'

'I thought America didn't believe in empires.'

'Don't you believe that. They are building their own empire of influence. They don't like the British Empire, or rather European empires, and the British is the only one really left now. Wherever America goes she likes things to be done her way.'

'Do the Koreans speak Japanese, then?'

'The educated classes can. Some went to school in Japan. They can also read and write Chinese. Many will have ten or twenty thousand characters. But they speak Hangul, an ancient language It has a unique alphabet, invented at the King's bidding in the fifteenth century.'

'Can they speak English?'

'A few – a very few will speak American English taught them by American missionaries who have been there since the turn of the century. It's the missionaries who know most about the country.'

'What's the name mean?'

'The name? Korea, you mean? We Europeans call it Korea from the Koryo dynasty. It means "land of high mountains and sparkling streams" an accurate description. The Japanese call it Chosen, a corruption of the Koreans' own name for their country – Chosun, which means "the land of the morning calm", another accurate description.'

'Is the country industrialised?'

'Hardly. The Japanese built the railway and started to industrialize the country in the north. It is still an agricultural economy based on rice. Most of the country is owned by an upper class and worked by the peasants. It's very poor.'

'Are they religious?'

'That depends on what you mean by religion. They're shamanistic. They're Confucian. There are many Buddhists. These beliefs appear to build on each other, to be indivisible and result in an extreme hierarchical class structure. I doubt if the missionaries have converted more than half a million to Christianity in a population of thirty to forty million for the whole of Korea.'

'Why did the north invade the south?'

'Their leader Kim Il Sung had been trained by the Chinese communists, and supported and armed by the Russians. He thought he could just walk in and there'd be no resistance. If the Russians had not been boycotting the Security Council at the time he would probably have got away with it. As it was, America managed to get the United Nations to agree to fight back.'

'What are Koreans like? What could we expect to see?'

'What are they like? Foreign, very foreign. If you think Hong Kong is a foreign country think again. Korea is the most foreign country you could go to. China, Japan and Russia appear foreign immediately you arrive because you can't read the signs. You'll find Korea more so as it has had no contact with the West, which the other countries have had. Go and have a look at the books. Study the photographs. The people won't have changed much. We can talk more over tea or dinner. I hope you're staying the night. Sonia and Kitty will want to see you, especially if you're off as soon as I hear.'

Hugh and I walked along to the library. I had asked him to help me. He was not just a good sportsman; he had a good mind too. When I had proposed that he should take over from me as ADC to Ivan Blessington I had not considered how he and Sonia might affect each other. I wondered now whether they might not be mutually attracted. Sonia was so poised, beautiful and sophisticated. Hugh was such an Adonis. Then I decided she was too clever to prejudice her position and Hugh was too ambitious to endanger his. I thought no more of it.

When I was the Governor's ADC I had spent some time in the library as it was a good place to be by oneself, but I had not noticed the section on Korea. We found it next to that on Japan and started to take the books out and look at them.

'Look what it says here,' said Hugh. 'It's from the *New Korea* published in New York in 1926. "Korea is today infinitely better governed than it ever was under its own native rulers, better governed than most self-governing countries and better governed than most British, American, French, Dutch and Portuguese dependencies."'

'The author must have been a fascist,' I said. 'Let me read you this from Curzon's book. "It's dedicated," he writes, "to those that believe that the British Empire is, under providence, the greatest instrument for good the world has seen and who hold, with the writer, that its work in the Far East is not yet accomplished." What do you think of that?'

'Those were the days. What else would you expect Curzon to say?'

'Don't you believe him? That's there's still work for the British Empire?'

'We've lost India.'

'Yes, but everywhere else?'

'Of course.'

'We shouldn't have handed India over so hastily. What a bloodbath. What a mess.'

'Look, it says here that the population of Korea under the Japanese rose from thirteen million in 1910 to twenty-seven million in 1945. So the Japanese can't have been that bad at administering the country.'

'They wanted to increase the population. More "yellow peril". Haven't you heard that the Korean guards in the prisoner-of-war camps were crueller than the Japanese?'

'Look at this map,' said Hugh. 'Four fifths of Korea is mountainous. The rest is rice paddy land. How can you fight in country like that?'

'The Chinese seem able to, so we'll have to. What does it say about the climate?'

'Comparable to northern China.'

'Not much help.'

'It says "the whole country has one month with a mean temperature below freezing. Seoul, the capital, has two months. On the Manchurian border it's five months."'

'I hope we don't have to fight on the Manchurian border. Anything else?'

'It rains a lot in the summer.'

'Looks formidable. Look at the pictures in this book. Mud huts roofed with thatch. And the clothes. Positively medieval.'

'I want to go, too,' said Hugh.

'You can't abandon the Blessingtons after two months. You'll have to do your time here. They like you. Remember, I recommended you.'

'They'll understand.'

'I doubt it. It would inconvenience them dreadfully. They've got used to you and they like you.'

'I must go. It's my chance to win a medal.'

'Oh Hugh, you're so ambitious. You are more likely to be killed or wounded than win a medal.'

'I must go.'

'We'll be there for a year, more, possibly. There'll be plenty of time for you to follow.'

'What if the war ends?'

'From all the rumours we hear, that seems unlikely.'

Hugh went off to his ADC's duties. I went on searching through the books and taking notes. Then I sat down at a table and recorded the points that Ivan Blessington had made at lunch. A picture of a strange and foreign land began to take shape. I wondered if any of my brother officers would believe me. A servant brought me some tea. It was getting dark when Sonia and Kitty came to find me.

'Oh Miles,' said Sonia and hugged me.

Then Kitty put her arms round me and held me tight.

'I'm going to become a nurse, darling,' she said. 'I'll come to Korea or, if the beasts won't let me, to Japan. You'll get a tiny wound and I'll nurse you, how I'll nurse you. Oh, darling, I can't bear the thought of you going but I can't stop you, can I?'

'Kitty,' I said, holding her tight.

'I'm going to leave you two together,' said Sonia. 'You are staying the night, aren't you, Miles?'

'Please. Ivan has been so helpful. But I must finish what I'm doing. On Monday I've got to brief the officers on Korea and I'm still not sure what I'm going to say. Stay a minute, Kitty.'

What I really was not sure about was what I was going to say to Kitty. I was going to Korea. I had to. I wanted to. There was no question about that. Where did that leave me and Kitty? Would she wait for me? This would test whether her love for me was merely on the rebound. And it would test my love for her.

'Kitty,' I said, when Sonia had left, and I was holding her in my arms. 'I do love you so.'

'I know you do, my darling. And I love you so much.'

'I have to go.'

'I know you do. I was so hoping you were going to Singapore and I could follow you.'

'Yes. Will you stay here with Sonia?'

'I don't know. Will Sonia want me hanging around? I really would like to be a nurse but I suppose that's impractical. Maybe there's something I could do in Japan. Or perhaps I should go home and look after daddy and wait for you there.'

'I can't ask you to wait for me.'

'Why not?'

'I could be away for a year or more.'

'People wait for each other far longer than that.'

We hugged each other harder.

'Why don't we get married now?' Kitty suggested.

'We've never talked about marriage.'

'Come on. We were made for each other. I love you. You love me. We're going to get married one day. Why not now?'

'Supposing I was killed?'

'At least we would have been married. I would prefer to be your wife, even if a widow, than not be.'

'We're very young.'

'What does that matter?'

'I can't afford to look after you and supposing I am killed?'

'I'll inherit Sherborne one day from daddy. Your mother has money. We'll be all right. They'll look after me.'

'Oh, Kitty I do love you so. Let me think about this.'

'You think about it, darling, but I know the answer. Fate is making this decision for us.'

Kitty wrestled free and left me. I had been tussling with the question of marrying Kitty for some weeks. I had discussed it with Hugh, and then with Sonia. I did not see how we could. Did going to Korea make any difference? Was Kitty right or was this just another example of her impetuosity? I tried to settle down to my notes again but I had lost my train of thought.

There were only twelve to dinner: a taipan and his wife, two Chinese couples who had senior positions in government, the captain of a warship and the household. When the women had withdrawn, the conversation turned to how long Hong Kong could survive as a British colony. Ivan Blessington said indefinitely. Whether he really believed it I do not know. He argued that while China could walk in and take Hong Kong relatively easily, though suffering great casualties, Hong Kong was more useful to China as a free port and trading entrepôt under British control. He also thought that China had enough on its plate in Korea not to expose itself to the hostility of the world over Hong Kong, as well. He then told us we had suffered a major reverse in Korea. The Chinese Volunteer Army had attacked, in great strength, the British brigade holding the line of the Imjin River. Two of the three British battalions had been able to withdraw almost intact. But the Gloucesters had been surrounded and over 500 had been captured. The battle appeared to have caused the Chinese massive casualties and their advance had ground to a halt.

The naval captain asked Ivan what he thought the outcome would be.

'I can't see,' Ivan said, 'how either side can win. China can go on throwing troops into the battle but the Americans control the air so they will always stop them. The Americans, or should I say the United Nations, cannot afford the casualties necessary to drive China out. I don't believe Truman will allow MacArthur to use nuclear weapons. That could lead to world war. So it looks like stalemate. If the United Nations forces could re-establish their line on the 38th Parallel and stay there, then they could say they had repulsed the aggressors and, even, won. China, however, would take its time to accept that situation.'

Ivan's assessment turned out to be prophetic. After the guests had all left Kitty asked me what we had talked about after dinner.

'The war in Korea and whether China will walk into Hong Kong.'

'So?'

'Ivan says the war could drag on for some time but China won't walk into Hong Kong.'

'And us, darling?'

'I'm thinking about us most of the time.'

'Just you do that, my sweet.'

'I've an idea about tomorrow,' said Sonia. 'Why don't we take *Surprise* out, drop a hook in a bay and have a swim and lunch? What about it, Ivan?'

*Surprise* was Ivan's yacht. She was a forty-eight-foot cutter, built in Australia after the war, and the apple of Ivan's eye. I think Sonia had bought it for him, to have more fun.

'That's a lovely idea, Sonia,' Ivan replied. 'Yes, we'll go after church. Hugh, would you arrange it? What about you, Miles?'

'I'll get up early and finish my briefing. I'd love to come.'

'Good, we can talk about what you're going to say about Korea on the boat.'

Later, Kitty came to my room and we made love furiously.

'Well?' said Sonia.

We were sunning ourselves, in our bathing dresses, on the foredeck of *Surprise*. Kitty and Hugh were still swimming. The sea looked aquamarine. Ivan was in the cockpit talking to the Chinaman who looked after the boat.

'Well what?' I replied.

'Are you going to marry Kitty?'

'I can't see that going to Korea makes the position any different. If anything it makes it more difficult and more unfair to Kitty.'

'Kitty will wait.'

'How can I ask her to? Long engagements are death.'

'Marry her then.'

'Sonia. Stop bullying me. Think of Kitty. I've a one in six chance of being killed, one in three of being wounded. How can I ask her?'

'She'd prefer to be married to you.'

'How can she know?' I protested. 'You make me sound selfish. I'm trying to think of it from her point of view as well. I know she'd marry me tomorrow if I asked her but what sort of life would she have? Everyone would think it was a shotgun wedding. I'm going to discuss it tomorrow with Colonel Guy. I have to. He'll be less partisan than you.'

'I just see two people in love and I want them to be happy. Perhaps, in this awful world we're now living in, happiness is impossible. I'm too romantic. How've you left it with Kitty?'

'We're going to see each other on Tuesday. We've arranged to have dinner at the Imperial in Kowloon.'

'Neutral ground. I see. Thank you for telling me.'

'You know that Hugh wants to go to Korea?' I said.

'Ivan's guessed.'

'What did he say?'

'He said Hugh should want to go to Korea and he's pleased that he does. He'll let him go in time. But Hugh must serve his time with us. Otherwise it would be too disruptive and look panicky. I don't want to lose him either. He's good company. It's bad enough you going. Ivan will telephone Guy Surtees about it. Ivan says he'll ask Guy to send another Prince Regent's officer when he's one to spare or reward. He's also going to ask the general if he can have a Goorkha, too. There's enough work for two ADCs and we wouldn't have any upsets if one had to leave in a hurry.'

'That makes sense.'

'Don't say anything to Hugh. Let Ivan handle it.'

'Of course not. Ivan's very good at that sort of thing.'

'Yes,' she said, 'Ivan's very good at that sort of thing, as you say. I'm going to have another dip before lunch.'

She dived into the sea and raced Hugh round the boat while Kitty climbed out and joined me on the foredeck.

On Monday morning Colonel Guy bugled for me. Percy Smythe looked as if he had been in his office all weekend.

Papers were still strewn all over his desk. But he was affable and told me to go straight in to see the colonel. Colonel Guy was looking out of the window at the sea, which now looked jade green. He told me to sit down and I took him through my briefing, as much Ivan's as mine. He said he liked it and made a few comments to clarify some of the points, emphasise others. He then told me not to rush its presentation.

'Could I talk to you about a personal matter, colonel?'

'Yes, Miles. What is it?'

'I'm debating with myself whether to get married. It's Kitty Fisher, General Fisher's daughter. We've known each other since childhood. She came out to stay with the Blessingtons three months ago. She's Lady Blessington's god-daughter. We've been talking about getting married. I'm not sure about whether we should. And I know I would have to ask your permission.'

'How old are you now?'

'Twenty-three.'

'You're young. You've plenty of time. The regiment thinks it a bad idea to marry too young. Soldiering in your twenties is about travelling light, being unrestricted in where you can go and what you can do. Your family is your platoon. You're still growing up. Marriage is a great responsibility. Then there are children to think of. There's also the question of money though I suppose both of you have that?'

'I've no money of my own, colonel.'

'Haven't you? You surprise me. Your mother has, hasn't she?'

'Not as much as she had, she tells me.'

'Don't let's discuss that. You need to be very sure about getting married to go through with it. If you have any doubts it's best delayed or put off altogether.'

'Thank you, colonel.'

He smiled. I saluted and went out into the adjutant's office.

'You look down in the dumps,' said Percy Smythe. 'Didn't he like it?'

'Oh, no. I mean, yes. He said it was fine. I was thinking about something else.'

'Plenty to think about, don't I know. The advance party is off tomorrow. We go on Friday. Horace Belcher commands the rear party and then transfers to the staff. He's been with the battalion for three years. Colonel Guy says it's time for a staff appointment for *him*. Overdue, I'd say. Anything I can do for you? No? Off you go then. I'm looking forward to your *spiel* this evening.'

I walked back to the company lines. George was in his office. Three new novels were in his pending tray and, for once, there were papers in his in tray. He was reading *No Orchids for Miss Blandish*. He looked up.

'Are you married, then?' he asked.

'What do you mean?'

'Prodigious pretty girl, Kitty. Fine horsewoman, too. *Stupor mundi*, I'd say. My first colonel's wife told me never to marry a girl you meet in the colonies. Always take her home first and run her round the paddock there. She might look different in England. But you've nothing to worry about. You've known her since childhood, haven't you? She's a smasher.'

'George, we're too young to get married, don't you think?'

'Ah, you've seen sense. Yes, you're far too young to take on those sorts of responsibilities. Now, I'm glad you've come in. I want to go through these rolls with you,' he said, pointing to the papers in his in tray. 'Allcock, Beasley and Jones 91 haven't enough time left to serve to go to Korea. Sit down and we'll go through the rolls and see what changes we need to make.'

'Have you heard?' I said. 'Horace Belcher's to command the rear party and then transfer to the staff?'

'Good riddance,' said George. 'The bugger's reneged on

the darts match. He's no more than a pissed, poodle-faking, polo-playing punk. Now sit down.'

I met Kitty in the foyer of the Imperial Hotel. She looked tired but ravishing. We went into the bar.

'Darling, I know what you are going to say,' she said, as she sipped a John Collins. 'Sonia and I have talked about it endlessly. You think we're too young and that it's unfair to marry me before you go to Korea on Friday. I agree. I hate it, but I agree. I'll wait for you.'

'Sweetest Kitty, I love you so much. But you mustn't wait for me. You must feel yourself quite free. Even if I wasn't going to Korea I'd still say this. It's all happened too quickly.'

'I wonder if you really do love me, Miles, when you say that. Sonia wonders too. I shouldn't have said that. Damn.'

'I know Sonia doesn't understand my point of view. I'm just trying to be honourable and not hold you to anything.'

'I don't want you to be honourable. I want you in my arms, in my bed, screwing me. It's unbearable you being so po-faced and honourable about it.'

'Think what might happen to me in Korea.'

'You mustn't say that. You'll be all right. Look, we love each other. I'll wait for you.'

'You mustn't.'

'Don't be an ass. I love you, Miles, my darling. Can't you get that into your head?'

'Oh Kitty, I love you, too.'

'Then we'll wait, for each other, won't we?'

I knew I couldn't hold out.

'Yes, we'll wait.'

We looked at each other. I took one of her hands into both of mine and held it. She placed her other hand on top of mine, leant forward and kissed me lightly.

'Now that's settled you can buy me dinner,' she said.

In the dining room we sat opposite each other. Under the

38

table I wrapped my legs round hers. I didn't want to eat dinner. I wanted to eat her.

'Where will you be when I'm in Korea?'

'I've been thinking about that. Here is nearer than England if Sonia will let me stay. I'd like to be as near you as I can. How long do you think you'll be there?'

'Eight months, ten months, maybe twelve. The battalion we're relieving has been there ten months. Say a year.'

'This time next year. Could we be married in England?'

'Could be.'

'I'm so happy. And I'm broken-hearted, too. A year. A whole year. I think I'm going to cry.'

'Tears are the refuge of plain women and the ruin of pretty ones.'

'Who said that?'

'Oscar Wilde.'

'Oh, darling, I do love being with you.'

'Will you write?'

'Every day.'

We sat over dinner, not eating much, until we were the last people in the dining room.

'Come back to Government House with me.'

'I can't. I must go back to camp.'

'Can I come with you?'

I shook my head.

'Can we stay here? I want you to roger me.'

'I've got to get back.'

'Oh Miles, I think I'm a bit drunk.'

'I'll take you to the ferry.'

We walked to the ferry, her arm through mine, had one final hug and then I let her go. She did not turn back. I could tell she was crying and didn't want me to see.

Burgo, Hugo and I shared a cabin on the troopship. After we had embarked, handed in our weapons to the armoury and

39

stowed our kit, we were called to assemble on deck. The commissioner for South East Asia had come aboard to see us off with Ivan Blessington and the commander-in-chief Far East. We were getting the full treatment.

The commissioner stood in front of us, tall in a crumpled tropical suit and a panama hat that had seen better days. He took off the hat and held it in his left hand.

'The people you will be fighting,' he said, 'may be from the Peoples' Republics of China and North Korea but the weapons they are using are Russian. Their training is Russian. This is the same enemy who threatens France and Britain. You are joining an historic expedition. You will be fighting as if on the soil of France or on the beaches of Britain. You'll be fighting for the British Empire alongside Commonwealth forces. The Korean War is part of a Russian attempt to conquer the whole world and make slaves of us all. This aggression is being resisted not only by individual nations but by the free peoples of the world under one organisation of which you are part. It's up to you to show the world the valour and unconquerable spirit of the British people. God speed.'

'That's pretty clear,' said Burgo. 'He did it rather well, don't you think?'

Then the little general took the commissioner's place. He left his hat on. He was a light infantryman. We knew him well. He knew us too. He was on his way to becoming a field marshal. He looked us in the eye.

'Shoot quickly, shoot straight and shoot to kill,' he said. 'Don't go away unless you are ordered to do so. Stay and fight it out. Even if the enemy gets behind you or round your flank, stay put. So long as you have ammunition, water and a little food – stay and fight. This is your opportunity to enhance the reputation of your great regiment. As a light infantryman I salute you.'

A great cheer greeted his words. The RSM told everyone to keep silent.

'No nonsense there,' said Burgo. 'I'm glad he got in that bit about enhancing the reputation of the regiment. It's one of my favourite phrases.'

The RSM called for three cheers for the general, and then for the commissioner.

I went across to say goodbye to Ivan Blessington.

'Miles, I'm so glad to see you. Sonia sends all her love and says she will write. She hopes you will write too. I'm delighted you and Kitty have an understanding. Sonia thinks you should have got married immediately but I think you've done the right thing to wait. God bless you, my boy.'

He may be a stick-in-the-mud, I thought, but he turns up trumps. For the first time I felt tears in my eyes.

I saluted him and returned to Burgo.

'We should be going now,' he said 'but the latest rumour, relayed by Colour Crum, of course, is that there's a typhoon brewing.'

Tugs pulled the ship off the docks. We anchored in midstream and lay there for a day, waiting for the typhoon to move on. We gazed at Hong Kong and Kowloon and all they meant to us. Hypnotically the water kept changing its colour.

## Chapter 3

# *We arrive in the Land of the Morning Calm*

Five days later we landed at Inchon. The navy took us ashore in the ship's launches, which fought against a strong tidal stream. Those returning empty from the shore shot past us. The sun was in our eyes so we could see no more than the dark shape of the land ahead. Once ashore the battalion assembled platoon by platoon, company by company, and rested while the stores were landed. The men stood at ease. The officers gathered together. Cigarettes were handed round.

'Where are all these mountains you told us about?' asked George Bulman. 'Place looks as flat-chested as a maiden aunt.'

'Sure we're in the right place?' said Burgo.

'That's the Navy's problem,' I replied.

'It'll be ours if we're not,' said George.

'Look at the tidal range,' said Burgo, pointing at the steep, muddy shore. 'The tide must rise and fall thirty feet. We could be in the Channel Islands.'

'Not with this stink,' said Toby.

Blowing gently off the land was a scent of warm rotting vegetables and human faeces.

'Here come the taxis,' said George.

A column of fifty American trucks drove up. We clambered aboard and set off on a tarmac road. It must have been the only one in Korea. I sat in the front of a truck with the window down. The warmth of the engine added to that of the sun. In the distance I could see a long line of hills.

'You a limey?' asked the black driver.

'Yes,' I said.

'Poor bastard,' he replied. 'You boys took a lot of casualties on the Imjin.'

'So we heard.'

'This country's a son-of-a-bitch,' he said, gesticulating at the scenery with his right hand.

'What do you call this truck?' I asked.

'Betty. She's mah one and only Betty,' he said, slapping the wheel.

'I mean what kind of a truck is it?'

'Betty's a dooce and a half.'

He slapped the wheel again. None the wiser I shut up. We had been travelling east. Now we turned north. Walking down the side of the road in the opposite direction was a column of what had to be Koreans: men in loose-fitting white robes and trousers; some of the women in clothes the colours of the rainbow. They carried bundles on their backs. Some had them on their heads. They held bundles in their arms, as well as pots and pans. One or two carried babies. A few pushed carts packed high with possessions. They looked tired and old. A few children ran at their feet.

'Refugees,' said the driver. 'They're everywhere.'

So we found. Even at the front, every now and again, we would find a group struggling south through our lines. They reminded me of the pictures I had seen, when young, of the hordes of refugees streaming down the roads of France in advance of the Nazi blitzkrieg. It was a mid-twentieth-century phenomenon.

After an hour or two we motored across a bridge spanning

a broad river into a built up area, or what had been a built up area, much of it rubble and ravaged by war.

'Seoul,' said my driver.

'Where?'

'Seoul, the capital of South Korea. It's changed hands four times so far in this goddam war.'

'It looks like it,' I replied.

He had pronounced Seoul as 'Sole', as most foreigners do today. Colonel Guy and Ivan Blessington had pronounced it 'Sool', which is how the English pronounced it in those days. I could see there was a lot I would have to get used to in fighting alongside Americans. The Koreans pronounced it 'Sa-ool'.

We motored into Seoul until we came to a wide avenue at the end of which stood a large, almost colonial-style, stone building lying imposingly in front of us with a mountain for a backcloth. Further behind were more mountains.

'Jap governor's house,' said the driver. 'Better built than most of the buildings. Could be why it's still standing.' He laughed.

As we passed it I saw it was a shell. The windows were empty and the interior devastated. Curiously the mature trees lining the avenue were untouched, as was a line of younger trees growing along the centre of the avenue. We passed some tanks stationed by the crossroads. The buildings to the left and right looked gutted.

'Fire,' said the driver. 'They always burn Seoul before abandoning it. Surprising there's anything left to burn.'

He laughed again.

We drove out of the city following the long column and re-crossed the river.

'What river is this?' I asked

'Han River, same we crossed before.' He laughed.

It was warm now. The trucks kicked up vast clouds of dust. We had lost the tarmac road before we reached Seoul. The

44

soldiers in the truck in front of us were covered in red-brown dust. I looked at my clothes and saw I was, too. The driver laughed.

'This,' he said, 'is a good road.'

The road began to climb between mountains, which were unlike anything in Europe. They shot upwards like pyramids, not a gentle slope in sight. They rose almost vertically to a pinnacle, then fell as steeply to paddy fields and then rose vertically again. It was just as the books at Government House had described and which I had found so hard to depict in my briefing.

'These are only hills,' said the driver. 'Wait till you see the mountains, man.'

He laughed again. I hoped we would enjoy Korea as much as he was.

After another hour or two we came round a bend, ran down to the bank of a river and stopped.

'This,' said the driver, 'is as far as I go.'

'And the river?'

'Still the Han, man.' He gave a final laugh.

On the other side of the trucks from the river was a tented camp, laid out in straight lines, as if for a general's inspection in England. Lined up in front of the tents was a battalion of the Duke of Marlborough's Regiment, known as the Duke's Own. We were relieving them. Standing there too were Dermot Lisle and our advance party.

'Get your men together,' Dermot said. 'Corporal Rothwell will show you your lines. I've taken over the company stores the Duke's Own are leaving behind.'

We lined up beside the truck, opposite the Duke's Own. Two years in Hong Kong had made us into a fit and sun-tanned battalion. So we were not greeted, as we might have been if we had come direct from England, with cries of 'Get yer knees brown'. Before the Duke's Own had gone to Korea they had been camped next to us in Hong Kong so the

45

regiments knew each other. After a few shouts of 'Here come the Fat Boys' alluding to the Prince Regent, to which we were inured, coupled with 'The fucking Trojans 'ere at last', another regimental nickname, there were shouts of 'Didn't know it was Christmas' and 'Bring yer mum, too?' from the Duke's Own, as we were carrying a lot of kit. Our lads shouted back 'Fucking 'ell, it's the Fook's Own' and 'How's the Fook's Own?' pronounced with a northern accent, as the Duke's Own was a north of England regiment. The NCOs on both sides put an end to it. A couple of young Duke's Own officers, whom I had known at Sandhurst, strolled across.

'Hello, Miles,' they said. 'Nice of you to come.'

'Couldn't wait a day longer. Where's the enemy?' I asked.

'Enemy? Why, we've sent him packing. You don't need to worry about the enemy.'

'But where is he?'

'Somewhere up there.'

They pointed north.

'We were told there was a battle raging.'

'That's all over. They ran away.'

'Sounds unlikely.'

'You'll have a lovely, peaceful summer here. Except when it's raining.'

'Thanks for the briefing,' I said.

'Enjoy yourself.'

No sooner had the battalion formed up with its stores than the Duke's Own started to clamber aboard the trucks. Within thirty minutes of our arrival they had left and we had the camp to ourselves. I had never known a quicker hand-over, if you could call it a hand-over.

'We're to spend the night in this camp,' said Dermot.

'In this camp? With the enemy just up the road?' I said.

'No one knows exactly where the enemy is. They've retreated out of sight. The rest of the brigade is dug in to the north. We're to sort ourselves out for a day or two. Then we'll join the brigade. Tonight we're to settle in.'

'Suits me,' said George. 'Make sure everyone's comfortable. I doubt it will stay as cushy as this for long.'

I went to find Big Steel.

'We've some reinforcements,' he said. 'Lads from the Duke's Own who've still got plenty of time to serve. They left seventy behind. We've got four. Tidmarsh is one of them. We had to send him to the Duke's Own a year ago to make up their numbers when they went to Korea. Good to have him back. He's got a stripe now. We trained him well. I've split them up between the sections.'

'They'll need green berets and regimental badges.'

'Colour Crum's got everything in hand.'

'Have you checked we've got everything?'

'Yes. And I've got them cleaning their rifles.'

'Let's have a weapon and foot inspection in three-quarters of an hour. We must keep a routine going or it will be an anticlimax. Then I'll talk to the new men.'

'The men seem happy enough. I thought we'd be digging in by now.'

'So did I.'

There was fresh meat and vegetables for dinner, and pudding.

After dinner I wrote to Kitty.

Three days later we marched out of the camp in single file along the side of the river. The road, more a track than a road, turned away from the river and took us up into higher ground. After two hours we halted and waited for George. He had gone ahead with Colonel Guy and the other company commanders to reconnoitre the ground and receive orders. We got orders to march on. The hills around us became larger and steeper.

'X Company?' asked a regimental policeman.

'Yes,' I said. I was at the front of my platoon, leading the company.

47

'That's your hill, Sir,' he said pointing upwards. 'You'll find Major Bulman at the top.'

We started the first of many almost vertical climbs, zig-zagging up the side of the hill. George was sitting on the top, looking north through his Zeiss field glasses. He had rescued them, he said, in Normandy from a panzer grenadier who had no further use for them. He also had a 9mm Luger automatic pistol from the same source. It was much handier than the .38 Smith and Wesson revolver officers were issued with, and much easier to get ammunition for. Serjeant-Major Budd now sported George's revolver as well as his own rifle. George carried a rifle, too, as I did.

'Have a nice stroll? Hard going country this,' said George. 'Take a shufti through your glasses. Can't spot a commo but you can see bits of our forward battalions, the gunners and brigade headquarters.'

Then he gave us our orders.

'Miles, you take the north-west, Burgo the north-east and Manky the south of the hill. I'll be behind the crest. All round defence. I'll take you round and show you.'

I surveyed my position with Big Steel. We set out the sections, sighted the fields of fire for the Bren light-machine-guns, chose a place for our platoon headquarters and mortar team, sited our latrines, took off our kit and started digging. We were past masters at it after Hong Kong. We dug quickly.

'What about wire?' asked Big Steel. He was showing his experience. A proper defensive position needed to be surrounded by barbed wire. We had done a lot of wiring in Hong Kong.

'The company commander didn't mention wire. I'll go and ask him. What I don't understand is there's no inter-locking fire between the platoons. It defies all the principles of war. We're on our own except for Z Company on the next hill and they're half a mile away.'

'Yes,' he said looking round. 'We are exposed, Sir.'

I found George lying with his head resting on his pack, flipping through the pages of a paperback.

'Colonel Guy said not to wire in this position,' he said. 'Besides, there isn't any wire. We're not to be here for long. We're in brigade reserve, remember? Tomorrow we'll be off. As to all round defence and interlocking fire, do what you can, Miles. We have to fit the tactics to the ground.

'Aren't you going to dig a command post?' I asked.

'Command post? This *is* my command post,' he said as he got up and surveyed the countryside. 'Look at it. Fine sunny position. Southern aspect. Commanding views. See for miles. This place would be worth a mint in the Home Counties. Not a Chinaman in sight. No, I don't think I'm going to dig a command post. I can't see hell's foundations quivering much here. Remember the old adage. Unless under fire, latrines first and then make yourself comfortable. Any fool can be uncomfortable. This will do me fine.'

He turned and raised his voice.

'Budd, where are those WVS paperbacks? This one's trash. You can't ask anyone to read such muck. I hope they're not all like this.'

Budd, who had been digging some yards away, raised his head and said, 'In the ammunition box beside you,' and went on digging.

'Stop being such a crusty-pot. It's your turn to dig,' replied George. Turning to me he said, 'I must get us sorted out here first. Then I'll come and see how you're getting on.'

As I walked back to my platoon I saw a section of the machine-gun platoon making its way up the hill, led by its commander Tony Strickland, who was carrying boxes of machine-gun ammunition. I waited for him.

'Where are you off to?' I asked.

'I've got to set up a section in your company area to lay a fixed line across Z Company's front. I've already sent a section across to them to lay one across yours. What a country. Where can I find George?'

'Keep going. He's just under the peak complaining his novel library is trash.'

'Some people,' he said and climbed on, his section following him with their guns, tripods, arcane paraphernalia and boxes of ammunition.

Much lower down the hill I could see a snake of bodies, climbing with agility and carrying huge bundles on their backs. Dermot was leading them. As they climbed nearer I could see they were Koreans with frames on their backs in the shape of an inverted 'A'. On these they were carrying bundles of wire, pickets, rations, water, ammunition and other warlike stores.

'These are our porters,' said Dermot as he came within earshot. 'I've got some goodies for you and some wire.'

'George has just told me we're not going to wire.'

'That's up to George. Take these porters. They've got your stuff. I'll take the others on. Where's George?'

'Just under the top, complaining his novel is trashy.'

'Budd will have to rectify that.'

'He's got an ammunition box full of paperbacks.'

'I wondered where it had got to.'

'Tony Strickland's up there, too.'

'Good, I've got some things for his people as well. On we go.'

I guided the porters round to my platoon position. Big Steel fell on the supplies and started organising and distributing them. I joined Maxwell, my soldier servant and platoon runner, who had been digging our trench.

'How are you doing, Maxwell?'

'Progress is being made, Sir.'

Maxwell was a National Serviceman. He was the son of a Birmingham jeweller and had worked in his father's shop before being called-up. He treated me as if he was behind the counter and I was a customer in his shop.

'Time to visit the sections,' I said.

'Very good, Sir.'

'Leave your kit. Just bring your rifle.'

'As you say, Sir.'

Our trench was in the middle of the platoon and the sections were about fifty yards apart at different levels on the hill. We were also on the forward slope of the hill looking out over Z Company that we could see digging in on the hill half a mile to the east. We could fire across their front but we could not see Burgo's platoon 200 yards to our left.

'Watch out for booby traps,' I warned Maxwell, 'though it doesn't look as if this hill has seen any fighting yet.'

'It's rather beautiful and peaceful up here, don't you think, Sir?'

We stopped and looked round. There were paddy fields on the flat ground below us, being worked by Koreans. Beyond were hills, seemingly untouched by war. We were out of sight of our platoon.

'Yes. It is very beautiful up in these hills.'

'I thought the way here was a little untidy.'

'Is that one of your understatements, Maxwell?'

'I suppose it is, Sir.'

We continued walking round the forward edge of the hill. There was a shout from behind us.

'Over here.'

We had walked too far down the hill and had to climb back.

'Come to get some tips on how to make yourself comfortable?' asked Burgo.

'We just wanted to know where you were,' I replied. 'Are you going to wire?'

'Not unless I'm told to. The rumour is that we are advancing tomorrow.'

'Who said that?'

'Dermot. Have you seen George?'

'When I last saw him he was complaining to the serjeant-major about his paperbacks and indulging his *spezzatura* to the full.'

'Good to hear he's settled in so quickly.'

'Come back with me and you can see where we are.'

We walked back, over the hill this time, to my platoon. Big Steel gave Burgo a smart salute. Burgo gave me a look.

'No need to salute in the front line,' I said. 'Better not let the enemy know who the officers are otherwise you'll be on your own.'

'Of course, Sir. I should have remembered,' said Big Steel.

'No, I should have remembered to say something. Let's make that a rule in the platoon. Will you tell everyone?' I said.

'Yes, Sir.'

When Colonel Guy had first arrived and guessed we might go to Korea he had made the officers wear berets and dress as similar to the soldiers as possible. 'You can wear what you like, within reason, in camp,' he had said, 'but when we're training or in the field I want you to look no different from the men. Every army has snipers. Don't risk unnecessary attention.'

A runner from company headquarters ran up, saw Burgo and me standing there and saluted.

'Serjeant-major's compliments, Sir, and the company commander has called an O group.'

'Don't salute in the front line, you nignog,' barked Big Steel.

'No, serjeant.'

'When?' I asked.

'Now, Sir.'

'We'd better go,' said Burgo.

We walked over to George's command post. There were some trenches there now and all the stores were arranged neatly. I could not see the ammunition box holding George's library. It was probably in his trench. We sat down round

52

him. Toby was there already with Dermot and Colour Crum. Budd joined us.

'I wanted to get you all together,' said George, 'while Captain Lisle and the colour serjeant were with us. Tomorrow the battalion is going to patrol to the north to find the enemy and establish his position and strength.'

He went on giving out his orders clearly. The axis of advance was to be the track on which we had approached. We would pass through the two battalions to our front. Y Company, on the hill behind us was to lead, to the left of the track. We were to follow them. W Company was to lead on the right of the track, followed by Z. We were to be supported by a troop of tanks, artillery and engineers. When we had made contact with the enemy and established where he was, we were to withdraw back to our present hill. George then covered the administrative arrangements, the orders for the night and asked for questions.

'What about saluting?' asked Burgo.

'What about it?'

'What are the orders about saluting in the front line?'

'We don't,' said George. 'Budd, ensure the platoon serjeants understand this. No saluting in the line. That doesn't mean discipline should in any way be relaxed. Living in close quarters can encourage this. The proper officer, NCO and man relationship must be maintained. You know the form. Good point, Burgo.'

'If we are to return here are we really going to keep our positions on the forward slope of this hill?' I asked.

'What do you suggest?'

'Pulling back on to the reverse slope and siting look-out posts on the forward slope. We'll be blown to pieces where we are.'

'They haven't got any artillery to speak of. Remember the Imjin. They'll swarm up the hill in their hundreds and thousands and try and overwhelm us by sheer force of numbers. We need good fields of fire. But they've shot their bolt. We don't need to worry about them for now. Our job is to go and find them. Miles, we've been landed with a machine-gun section to be positioned on our right flank. I've told them to site themselves next to you.'

He looked at each of us in turn. 'Is that all?' he said. 'Then let's synchronise our watches.'

We all looked at our watches while George called out the time. I had to move mine on a minute.

'Anyone want anything brought up next time I come?' asked Dermot. 'I won't see you again until tomorrow evening.'

'A little *patum peperium*?' said Burgo.

'No.'

'Any chance of having a little butter with my bread?' asked Toby.

'You've little chance of having any bread.'

'Well with my biscuits, then?'

'I'd tuck into these American C rations first. Then you'll see what you need. I could manage a little curry powder, I expect.'

'Curry powder for those as wants it, then,' said George. 'Time you bowled along to brief your men. I'll come round all your positions in half an hour, starting with you, Burgo.'

We dispersed.

'Have a lovely time,' said Dermot. As company second-in command he stayed out of the front line and lived at A Echelon a mile or two back with Colour Crum, where they looked after our administrative interests. Every day they were to bring up our rations, water, ammunition, mail and other supplies. If anything were to happen to George, then Dermot would come up as soon as he could and take over command of the company.

I returned to my platoon where I could see the machine-gun section digging in 50 yards to our right.

'I've looked at their fields of fire,' said Big Steel. 'We're all co-ordinated. It's good to have them with us.'

Big Steel and Little Steel had both been machine-gunners.

By the time George visited us the sun was much lower in the sky. I had been able to brief Big Steel and the section commanders, gone round the position again and ensured that everyone knew what we were going to do.

George arrived with Serjeant-Major Budd.

'Position's looking good, Miles,' he said. 'I know what you mean by it being exposed. These hills tax credulity. We've done the best we can. Have you ever seen such beautiful fields of fire? I can just see the commos coming at us and our knocking them over like shooting rabbits on a summer evening. And you've got the machine-guns. You're in clover.'

He kept talking while we walked round the position. His turn of phrase amused the men but I don't think he was aware of it.

'Now, Jones,' he said, turning to Butcher Jones, 'what are we going to do tomorrow?'

'We're going to find the fucking commos.'

'That's it, Jones. We may have to foot it a little to find the vulpine parasite but find him we will.'

George knew every man by name, and much more too. When I had first joined his company he had caught me out, knowing much less about my men than he did.

'Have you tried the American C rations, yet?'

'Just going to have our tea now,' said Jones.

'You'll love them. There's even chewing gum.'

'I don't like chewing gum.'

'Jones, you must learn to move with the times. Besides, they say gum cleans your teeth.'

He left us to go and talk to the machine-gunners.

'Here, Sir,' said Maxwell, giving me a mess tin of food and a cup of tea. 'I never fail to admire the major's sagacity, though I don't think you would want chewing gum. The

Yankee rations are different to ours. Not necessarily mellifluous but tasty, and certainly a novelty.'

I ate, sitting on the side of the trench. I had done this so often on exercise in England and Hong Kong. It was no different. Yet it was completely different. A sense of unreality, of being in an unknown country miles from home and not knowing where it would end made me acutely conscious of a new phase of life. I felt excitement and fear, the kind one feels when starting to do something challenging, the outcome of which you don't know. I sat gazing out at the Korean landscape and, for the first time, I felt alone. Nothing I had done so far in life had been like this. Nothing had had such intensity or unreality.

'Stand-to in half an hour, Sir,' said Maxwell, as he took my empty mess tin and mug away.

'Thank you, Maxwell. You are right. It is different.'

That night I slept on the ground beside the trench. I woke once, startled by dreams of Kitty. It was cold. I lay and gazed at the silence of the stars, wrapped my blanket round me more closely and fell asleep again.

## Chapter 4

## *Where is the enemy?*

'Sir, stand-to in ten minutes. Here's a mug of tea.'

Maxwell was shaking me.

It was dark and cold. I sat up, took the tea and sipped it. I put on all my clothes and equipment, sat on the edge of my trench and sipped more tea. I checked my rifle and sipped again. I looked around. The sky was still black.

I got up holding my rifle and walked over to Big Steel. He was sitting on the side of his trench drinking his tea. I sat down next to him.

'Sleep well?'

'Fine. And you, Sir?'

'Pretty good, despite the smell.'

'What is it?'

'Night soil. You know, human shit. The Koreans use it as fertiliser. It seems to be everywhere.'

'It's amazing how they're still tilling the paddy in the middle of the battlefield.'

'It's their land. They've nowhere else to go. Take that away and they've got nothing to eat or own.'

I looked at the luminous dial of my watch.

'Time to do the rounds.'

I set off round the sections and was challenged for the password. Then I slipped into a trench next to Corporal Foxton.

'All OK, Foxton?'

'Apart from the bloody stink, yes Sir.'

'You'll get used to that. Anything happen last night?'

'Nothing.'

Foxton was a solid NCO, very experienced and reliable though a little taciturn and short with words. The men called him Foxy behind his back.

'I'll go round the section,' I said.

They were all alert and in position, as I had expected.

I moved on to the next section and, after being challenged, I dropped into the Bren gun trench.

'Morning, Rothwell.'

'Morning to you, Sir, but I can't see it myself.'

Lance Corporal Rothwell was tall and a marksman. He was second in command, or 2i/c, of Corporal Wildman's section and led the Bren gun group. He was also a fine cricketer: a fast and accurate bowler.

'Don't think we're going to get much cricket in these hills,' I said. 'Have a good night?'

'Colder than I expected.'

'Colder than Hong Kong. I think we'll find the climate here more extreme. It'll get hot once the sun's up.'

I climbed out of his trench and moved to Corporal Wildman's.

'How's life, Wildman?'

'Never known better.'

Wildman was another experienced soldier. I was remarkably fortunate in my NCOs. Wildman and Foxton had fought in the Second World War against the Germans. I went on round Wildman's section which was all in place and looking steady. There were streaks of light in the eastern sky now.

I moved on to Corporal Whettingsteel's section, was challenged again and dropped into his trench. Little Steel, as he was known, was taller but thinner than his brother. There was five years' difference in their ages. Big Steel had served in the war and had a breastful of campaign medals. Little Steel had not been old enough to join until the war had ended. He was every bit as able as his brother.

'How goes it, corporal?' I asked.

'Everything's quiet,' he replied, looking to his front. 'Nothing happened during the night or I would have reported it. The section's fine.'

It was twilight now. I could almost see the paddy fields. The hills across the valley were much clearer. The stars had gone.

'Flint pissed in his trench, the bloody fool. Otherwise discipline is good.' I went on round the section. Everyone was in position, alert and in good humour.

Big Steel was waiting for me when I got back to platoon headquarters. 'All well?' he asked.

'All well,' I said. 'Except Flint has pissed in his trench.'

'Neolithic Flint's our weak link. I'll have to talk to my little brother about him.'

'If anyone is going to train him, it'll be your brother.'

'True enough.'

'How do you find the Duke's Own reinforcements are settling in?'

'They're in their element and our lads appreciate them. Their experience shows. They're a good bunch, especially Tidmarsh. Good idea of yours, Sir, to make him platoon mortar man. We'll learn something from him, too.'

'He said that's what he had done in the Duke's Own. We need a steady hand on the mortar. It's a useful weapon in good hands. We can see how good he is. When we have a casualty we can make him a section leader or 2i/c.'

Dawn had broken. The sun was still behind the hills but it was daylight. Time to stand down.

I stripped to the waist and washed and shaved in a mess tin

of warm water that Maxwell had produced. Not everyone was so fortunate. Maxwell had a knack of finding things.

'Breakfast, Sir,' he said.

'What on earth is it?' I asked.

'It's these American C rations. I chose you frankfurter chunks and beans. Not quite to the English taste but hot. Well, warm.'

'Thank you Maxwell. I hope you enjoy it, too.'

'I'll do my best. It's preferable to go to war on a full stomach.'

By the time I'd cleaned my rifle, been to the latrine behind the hill, checked my ammunition and grenades and packed up my kit it was time for the platoon to parade. We lugged our big packs to a point by company headquarters and set off down the hill in file, wearing our small packs in which we carried our day's rations and essential belongings. We were wearing the olive green uniform in which we had left Hong Kong, and which we were to go on wearing until well into winter, with ammunition pouches and small packs; and were carrying grenades, full water bottles, bayonets and entrenching tools. On our heads we wore our green berets. Our tin hats had been left with the quartermaster and we never wore them. We were dressed identically. As time passed people began to dress idiosyncratically. Many took to wearing the cap comforter, a hollow khaki woollen scarf that you could drape round your head in a number of shapes; we also dispensed with carrying a lot of kit, to move more easily. This first morning we still looked fit for the parade ground.

We fell in on the track, in front of the other two platoons.

'Glorious day,' said George. 'Miles, off you go. Keep a good four hundred yards behind Y Company.'

We marched north along the track until we came to the Han River. We could see the other two battalions of the brigade dug in on the hills to our left and right. Serjeant

Tom Body, the assault platoon commander, and his men were ferrying the companies across the river in assault boats. The crossing was uneventful. We climbed up the track on the other side. We marched on and up. The hills got larger. We watched Y Company scale a hill to our left. W Company was doing the same to our right. No enemy appeared. There was no firing. Then we were leading the way, leading the battalion. Now, I thought, we really are the front line.

'Clear that hill,' said George to me, pointing at an even higher one on our left.

Corporals Foxton and Wildman led their sections up, weaving between the bushes and the trees. Big Steel and I followed at a distance. Little Steel was close behind us with his section so that, if we came upon the enemy, I could get his section to outflank them. The sections ahead disappeared over the top of the hill. In a few minutes we came up to them and we could see more hills a mile or so ahead, the track weaving between them. In the paddies below us Koreans were working their rice fields.

I beckoned to the section commanders to join me.

'Seen anything?' I asked.

'No one's been on this hill,' said Foxton.

'Wildman?'

'Nothing, Sir.'

'See any movement on the hill in front?'

'No one on it, as far as I can see,' said Wildman.

I searched the hills through my field glasses, then handed the glasses to Big Steel.

'See anything? I can't.'

'Not a commo in sight, Sir.'

I reported back to George on our wireless. He told me to stay where I was while Y Company went through.

All morning the companies leapfrogged each other. At midday, while we watched Y Company ascend another hill,

61

we were able to stop and eat hurriedly. Burgo, Toby and I joined George.

'I told you there weren't any Chinks for miles,' said George.

'How could you tell?' asked Burgo.

'No signs of organised retreat. When an enemy is withdrawing he lays ambushes for you and booby-traps. He can give you a bloody nose. I don't see any sign of this, yet. They've abandoned this area. I doubt we'll catch up with them today. Don't be disappointed. Keep your eyes skinned all the same and look out for booby traps.'

'How much further are we going?' asked Toby. 'We must have done six miles.'

'Keen to get home to your feather bed, are you, Manky?' said George. 'We've one more hill to clear. Then we'll make for home.'

'Home?' said Burgo.

'Home is where you sleep. Miles, your turn to lead again. I want you ready to move. It looks as though Y Company has drawn another empty covert.'

A gunner officer with a wireless operator joined us. I had seen him with George before, in the morning.

'Sartorius,' said George, 'you don't know my subalterns.'

George introduced us to Captain David Sartorius, a forward observation officer, or FOO as we called him, of the New Zealand Artillery Battery that supported the battalion.

'Why don't you go with Miles?' said George. 'It's his turn to lead again. You won't see anything down here but you might higher up.'

David Sartorius and I walked back to my platoon. We got the signal to advance almost immediately. We crossed some paddy and went straight up the next hill, this time with Little Steel and Foxton's sections leading. The top was clear. We stood there scanning the hills in front of us.

'There's some movement over there,' said Big Steel.

'Where?' said David and I together.

'Track, left, ten o'clock, top of re-entrant under brow of hill, figures moving,' said Big Steel.

'So there are,' said David.

'Got 'em,' I said.

There were a dozen Chinese soldiers digging a position just under the top of a hill above the track about a mile away. They did not appear to have noticed us.

'Still everyone,' I said, and then turned to David and said, 'Well?'

'Well, indeed,' he said. He took the handset and microphone from his wireless operator and started talking, looking hard at his map.

Within a minute there was a whine above us, followed by the thump of an artillery piece behind us. A shot whistled over us and fell a little short of the Chinese soldiers.

'Up two hundred and fire for effect,' said David into his mike.

The Chinese looked startled, stopped digging, looked at the sky and started jabbering to each other. A salvo whistled over us and dropped among them. Some fell. Others ran. Then another salvo dropped on them. Then another. When the smoke cleared there was no sign of movement.

'Cease firing,' said David into his mike.

'That was accurate. Very impressive,' I said.

'Lucky,' said David, 'to get the first shot so close. Otherwise they would have dispersed before we could have got the range.'

'You've had a lot of practice,' I said.

'You could say that. We've been here six months.'

I reported to George over my wireless and was told to withdraw. We marched back to our hill beside the river.

'The colonel says that, so long as we leave piquets on the hill, we can swim in the river,' George told us.

63

Soon half the battalion was swimming and splashing in the river, naked. 'This is the life,' said Burgo.

Back in our position on the hill we had completed our weapon cleaning and inspections when Dermot and Colour Crum came up with the supplies.

'I hear we have your word that there's an enemy out there,' Dermot said to me. 'Did you make it up?'

'Ask David Sartorius. He's my evidence.'

'I'll have to believe you, then. Colour Crum has given the mail to Big Steel. Here's some for you.'

'Bloody hell,' I said, looking through it. 'Here I am on a hill in Korea and I get a letter from the bank, a bill from Jones, Chalk and Dawson and another from Thomas's. Ah, here's one from Hugh Jermy. And one from Kitty. Could you keep the others for me?'

'Don't you want to open them first?'

'Oh, all right.'

Dermot sat on the ground while I opened them.

'The bank sends its compliments etcetera, etcetera, and begs to inform me that it has received a credit from the Army Pay Office of twenty-six pounds, eight shillings and ten pence for my pay and that my credit balance now stands at thirty-seven pounds, twelve and a penny.'

'Not unhealthy. And you'll save money on this hill.'

'Jones, Chalk and Dawson's bill is now only fifteen guineas. I've been paying them off at five pounds a month for the last two years.'

'Don't worry about that.'

'Mr Thomas writes on his bill, "Dear Captain Player, I have heard you are going to Korea and I hope you will enjoy soldiering there as much as I did on the North-West Frontier of India between the wars. I am sure the Regiment will distinguish itself. We will be watching out for news of you. May I ask, when you have a moment, if you could see your way to settling this bill which has been outstanding for some time."'

'How much?'

'Three pounds, five shillings and nine pence.'

'How on earth do you run up a London barber's bill in Hong Kong?'

'He sends me hair lotion by sea mail. It takes a long time to get to me and the bill arrives first. So I take a long time to pay it. But I should, especially now I've got a penny or two in the bank.'

'Do it when the battalion comes into reserve.'

'Into reserve?'

'Yes. After a few days of this patrolling in force, we'll be pulled out of the line to rest and train.'

Dermot left. I opened the letter from Hugh.

Dear Miles (he wrote),

You are all missed here and Hong is quite empty without you. Even the Governor has said how different life is without your faces around, especially yours. Sonia says she is writing to you but asks me to send you her love.

I long for news of the battalion. Please write. The Governor says he will let me go as soon as I've done my stint with him. Secretly I think he'll let me go when he can find another ADC. You know he plans to have two now? I'm working on Sonia who understands and is sympathetic. The Governor says there are feelers being made through embassies about armistice talks. I can see that I will join you when it's all over but the Governor says that even if there are armistice talks the negotiations with the Chinese will be endless so it will be just my luck to arrive the day peace is declared, when you will all have won MCs.

Do write.

V. best wishes to you all.
Yours ever,
Hugh

P.S. Don't worry about Kitty. She's fine. She's riding a lot and mixing with the polo set.

I tore open the letter from Kitty. It covered several pages in a large hand, very loving, very personal, very lonely. Tear stains blotched some of the words.

I sat for a while with the letter in my hand, looking over the valley.

'The company commander has called an O group, Sir.'

Maxwell was standing over me.

'Now, Sir.'

I put the letter into my pocket and went to company headquarters.

'As you, Miles,' said George as he started his orders, 'spotted the enemy today, Colonel Guy has rewarded us by sending us out tomorrow while the rest of the battalion has a rest, or rather improves its position.'

'So I should expect,' said Burgo. 'Well done, Miles.'

'This time we're going with the Yanks. X Company is to support a company of the 77th US Medium Tank Battalion. We're going to probe further up that track, or should I call it road? We are to be mounted in Yankee armoured vehicles. Maybe we will meet a little opposition after today's encounter.'

He went on with his orders.

Dermot and Colour Crum had brought up some pup tents, small two-man tents. The Korean porters had carried them up the hill with the re-supply. There were plenty for all of us. I got one to myself. That night, we all slept snugly. I did not wake with the cold or with dreams.

In the morning Tom Body got us across the river in his assault boats. The squadron of Patton tanks and armoured vehicles were lined up on the other side of the river, nose to tail. The armoured vehicles looked like tanks but were open at the top. They could carry a dozen or so soldiers and were called half-tracks. The tanks and the half-tracks were wet and muddy having crossed the river by a deep ford.

'I don't like the look of this,' said George. 'We don't know them, we've never trained with them, we've no idea of their tactics and we speak a different language. Look at them, all lined up for a duck shoot. Ah, well. We'd better get on with it.'

We walked over to the tank company leader's tank. He jumped down and we shook hands.

'Hi, George,' he said. 'Nice to have you with us.'

George winced. He liked to take a little time to get on first name terms.

'You had any combat experience?'

'A bit,' said George.

'Well, you guys shouldn't need too much. We'll just run up this track. When we meet any Chinks we'll blow them to hell. If we get into trouble you can come and help us bug out.'

'We'll do our best,' said George.

'Just keep with us.'

George put me with the leading troop. The platoon mounted the first three half-tracks. We had no wireless contact with the tanks. The drivers said they had been told to follow the tanks in front. Directly behind us was the tank company commander in his tank.

The tanks rumbled off at about fifteen miles an hour in line ahead, yards apart. They did not appear to observe any tactical procedures, like two tanks going ahead while the other two covered them. They just kept going up the track. We passed the hills and the paddy fields we had advanced through before. Koreans were working in the paddies. They did not look up. Within half an hour we had advanced to the point my platoon had reached the previous day. On went the tanks, straight for the gap between the hills and under the point on which we had shelled the Chinese soldiers. I was standing up in the front of my half-track to get a better view, just as the tank commanders in front of me were standing up in their turrets, looking out through the open hatches.

The first tank entered the gap. There was an explosion. The second tank had run over a mine, its right-hand track blown off. There was another explosion. The third tank had hit a mine. The tank commanders' heads disappeared and the turrets clamped shut. The tanks started firing their machine guns but at what I could not see. The first tank started to reverse but the second and third tanks blocked the way. The fourth tank was, reversing fast towards us, firing its machine-guns. About 25 yards in front of us it halted. I ordered my platoon to disembark. We had stopped when we heard the first explosion.

'The major wants you, Sir,' said the wireless operator, as he handed me the headphones.

'What's happening?' asked George.

I did my best to explain what I had seen.

'You'd better go and help them,' he said.

I could now see a group of about twenty Chinese running at the two stranded tanks and the first tank, which had got locked in and could not move.

'Serjeant Whettingsteel!' I shouted, 'take Foxton's section and Tidmarsh with the mortar out to the right flank and give us covering fire. Wildman, you take the left of the track. Whettingsteel, take the right. Follow me. We've got to clear them away from the tanks.'

We spread out in a long line. Foxton and Little Steel had got their sections in the paddy. The paddy was dry. I was on the track with Maxwell and my wireless operator. We were rather conspicuous. We slipped down on to the paddy.

'Fix bayonets,' I ordered.

By now a group of Chinamen had climbed on to the first tank. One of them appeared to be attaching something to the tank. Big Steel's group started firing. A mortar bomb landed among the Chinese.

Now, I thought to myself, now we must go.

'Ready?' I shouted, looking to right and left. They couldn't hear me for the noise of the firing. I stood up and waved everyone forward.

'Charge!' I shouted as loud as I could and started to run forward. We had over a hundred yards to go. I looked to left and right. Everyone was running with me. We were keeping a good line.

There was another explosion. A Chinaman was blown off the first tank, which started to burn. We were getting nearer. The fourth tank had started up again and was moving back with us towards the Chinese, firing its gun and its machine-guns over our heads. More mortar bombs fell among the Chinese, some of whom were knocked over. They didn't react to us until we were thirty yards away, scrambling out of the paddy on to the level area in the gap. One or two fired at us. Then they ran.

'Stop!' I yelled at my platoon. 'Watch out for mines.'

I went forward gingerly with Little Steel. The first tank was a wreck. The remains of a Chinaman, torn limb from limb, lay beside it. There was no sound from inside the tank. I peered through the hole in its side. They were all dead. The men in the other two tanks started to climb out of them. One was an officer.

'Let's get the hell out of here,' he said.

They all climbed on the fourth tank, which moved back.

'Do you think we should get out of here, too?' said Little Steel.

'Yes, but first let me report to the company commander. I think it's just an ambush. Do we have any casualties?'

'No.

'A miracle.'

I talked to George on the wireless. He told me to get out.

'What about the Chinese?' asked Little Steel.

'Aren't they all dead?'

'That one's alive.'

'Let's take him with us. They'll come back for their dead later.'

We marched back to our armoured vehicles. While we had been attacking, the squadron commander and George had come up and positioned a second troop of tanks and Burgo's platoon across the road in a tight defence.

'Well done, Miles,' said George.

I gave a full report.

'Let's get that prisoner back to the medics,' he said.

'This, George, ain't tank country,' said the tank company commander. 'No, Sir. We'll have to come back to rescue those two tanks. Better get the bodies. Then it'll be time to turn for the base.'

We covered the American tank men while they recovered the bodies from the first tank that had been blown up. Then we motored back to the river and our position. Later we had a swim and heard that our prisoner had died. He was not that badly wounded. He was probably ashamed to have been captured and lost the will to live.

Sitting on the hill, Big Steel said, 'Those Chinks were crazy.'

'They were fanatical.'

'That Chinaman held the charge against the tank with his body. I was shooting at him. One second he was there. The next he was in pieces in the air.'

'They say the Chinese eat poppy seeds before they attack.'

'They were worse than the Hitler Youth in the war. Our lads did well, didn't they?'

'Very well. We must tell them.'

'I think they know but it would be good if you told them.'

'I'll do that. Wasn't it all so surprising and quick? I didn't have time to think about it.'

'Best that way.'

He was right. I just reacted. We all did. We did not have time to think or be afraid. Now, thinking about it, I was amazed it had happened so smoothly and we had had no casualties.

The next day we were out again. The battalion was to probe further still, but by itself, without tanks. A troop of engineers was to come with us to lift the mines. Once north of the river it began to rain. It bucketed down. Torrents of water turned the track into mud, the going got harder and the visibility closed in. Orders came to abandon the advance. As X Company had been the last to cross the river we were ordered to hold the hill just north of the river as a bridgehead while the other companies withdrew.

We took up an all round defensive position and started digging with our entrenching tools. As soon as we had dug a hole it filled with water. My platoon overlooked the river. I could see the water rising and the current increasing. Tom Body was having trouble controlling his assault boats. He had two in operation. For each he had rigged two ropes across the river by which his pioneers pulled the boats to and fro. They were having difficulty holding the boats on course. The river was in full flood, pushing the boats downstream. Y and Z Companies got across. W Company started to cross. As the last platoon was pulled across in the upstream boat, the boat's ropes gave way. It ran into the downstream boat whose ropes immediately broke. The two boats – one full, one empty except for its handlers – careered down the swirling river and disappeared out of sight.

We were cut off, marooned north of the river.

It rained for twenty-four hours.

We had our ponchos and our packs in which we had the rest of the day's rations. Water was not a problem. Food was. George called in all the tins and found there were few left. The men had either eaten them already or thrown away the tins they did not think they were going to need. We were hungry and, within an hour, we were all wet to the bone. We spent a miserable night huddling together to keep warm. We had to keep an eye open for the enemy, taking it in turns to stand guard. We couldn't see much in the dark and the rain. We sang. No one would have heard us. We told each other stories. George walked round getting us to do things.

'Keep moving,' he would say, 'or you'll stick to the ground and be pummelled into mud.'

The following morning we were so wet we did not notice, at first, that the rain had stopped. A helicopter arrived with rations, blankets, water, ammunition and rum. We didn't need the water or the ammunition. We lit fires, drank the rum and laid our cigarettes out to dry. It was another twenty-four hours before Tom Body was able to rig the boats across the river. The battalion cheered us in as we returned to our hill. We grinned.

For the next two days we sat on our hill, improving our position, digging and wiring. George still refused to build a command post. He said it would spoil his view and, if it rained, he did not want to drown in a half-built command post. He rigged an elaborate tent with drains. It did rain. We all got wet again but not as wet as before.

I wrote to Hugh telling him what we had been up to. I wrote to my mother to say that I was all right and asking her to pay Thomas's bill for me. I wrote to Kitty and Sonia.

Orders came for another battalion reconnaissance in force. We were to push further forward. Z Company and the engineers had cleared the mines and pinpointed the enemy position two miles beyond the scene of my platoon's action.

'We could end up assaulting their position,' said George. 'It's time we showed those fidgety forks our steel.'

We crossed the river and marched up the track, seasoned soldiers now. We passed the point of our engagement and marched on. Z Company was leading. Half an hour later we heard firing to our front and we were ordered to halt. We lay by the track at the foot of a hill unable to see anything. Burgo, Hugo and I were called to join George to await orders. There was more firing. Then the New Zealand battery started firing and we could hear the shells travelling over our heads. The three-inch mortars joined in, thumping away. W Company, immediately ahead of us, disappeared up the track. We moved up the track and still could not see anything. Half an hour inched by. George listened to the wireless following what was happening. There was a lot of firing.

'W and Y Companies are attacking the enemy position,' said George, putting the earphones down. 'We are to move up. As soon as they've taken it we are to continue the advance and follow up the enemy. He appears to be weak and moving out.'

The country opened out and flattened. On the low ground in front of us lay Chongbo, a village of thatched mud houses that straggled along the track. In the middle of the village the track branched. One arm led away to the west, the other continued to the north-east between hills that formed a formidable defensive position. We could see W and Y Companies moving fast up the hills, their leading elements at the top. The firing had stopped.

We marched through the village that Z Company had occupied. The villagers eyed us. We were not welcome: another army come to ravage their land and ruin their lives. We moved, as fast as we could, up the hill, through W and Y Companies and set out to chase the enemy. He had bolted.

We had lost contact. We returned and found ourselves on

an extremely well prepared defensive position, which we began to examine. Two-man foxholes commanded the avenues of approach. Behind them were communication trenches. As we investigated we found tunnels that we entered. They led into bunkers, an intricate warren of underground places, interconnected and proof against the heaviest bombardment.

While we were exploring Colonel Guy joined us.

'Have you seen anything like this, George?'

'Never, Colonel. Never so intricate and deep with all these tunnels.'

'They learned this from the Japs,' said Colonel Guy. 'I've never seen it but I've heard about it. Formidable. We wouldn't have winkled them out of here easily.'

'Yes, he'd have proved an ugly customer,' said George.

'The villagers say the Chinese have been moving out for two days. We only found a rear guard. They must have taken a lot of casualties in their last big push and outrun their supplies. I expect they're re-grouping. Make yourself comfortable here, George. Interesting there's no wire or mines, but watch out for booby traps. W and Y Companies have had more casualties that way than from enemy fire.'

We made ourselves comfortable and ate our midday meal. Orders came to withdraw to our hill. Some Yanks came and took over from us. The following day we were pulled back into Corps reserve. The enemy had pulled back too, according to air reconnaissance, to a line far to the north.

'So this is war?' said Burgo.

'Not yet,' said George.

## Chapter 5

## *The enemy find us*

'We're here for a week,' Dermot told us.

'We could be in Scotland,' said George.

We had arrived in a lovely spot, several miles up the River Han and far from Chongbo and the front line, which we had left two hours earlier. A tented camp was laid out for us. Dermot had gone ahead with the advance party and prepared everything.

'Smells like Scotland. Oh, the scent of pine,' said Burgo, breathing it in. 'We could be at home.'

'Can we swim in the river?' asked Toby.

'Get settled in first. There're showers and clean clothes for everyone,' said Dermot.

'Have we got a mess?'

'Yes. So have the serjeants and the corporals. There's a NAAFI and all sorts of un-rationed goodies.'

'It's not like home, then,' said Burgo.

We laughed.

'And the scoff?' asked Toby.

'Fresh food every day.'

'Time we had a blow out,' said George. 'Get the men settled in. Then we'll meet at the officers' mess and have a few sharpeners.'

I rejoined my platoon.

'What are we going to do here?' asked Big Steel, after I

had briefed them and they had settled into their quarters.

'Enjoy ourselves,' said I.

'You mean there are brothels, too?'

'I doubt Captain Lisle has gone to those lengths. Besides, Lady Mountbatten wouldn't approve.'

Lady Mountbatten was blamed, rightly or wrongly, for having the army's brothels closed wherever she went.

'Interfering bitch. We hear she takes her pleasure when she wants it.' The serjeants, as usual, knew a lot.

'Stop being contentious and run along to your mess. Start enjoying yourself,' I said.

'I am, Sir,' he said and saluted.

We were out of the line now.

They were lazy days. There was no standing to. No wiring. No digging. We played football and headquarter company won an inter-company competition. It generally did. We improvised a shooting range under a large hill where we zeroed our rifles and light machine-guns: that is we re-set the sights that had been knocked about since we arrived. Then we held a small arms competition which our Company won, and a boxing match that Y Company won. We swam and after dark we watched movies. We had an Officers' Day at which we shared what we had learned. We rid our bodies of grime and our faces of strain. Not that we had had that challenging a time, as George had pointed out.

Alongside us were camped the other two battalions in the brigade: a battalion of Highlanders and one from the Royal Australian Regiment. They were tough regiments, renowned as stubborn fighters. Both had been in Korea for months. We met in each other's messes and we competed on the sports field. We were delighted, and surprised, when we beat them both at boxing and football. The Australians smashed us at athletics.

I wrote to Kitty. There had been no more mail from her.

76

One evening Burgo and I were sitting outside the tent we shared with Toby. He was lying on his camp bed doing the crossword in a week old airmail copy of *The Times*.

'What do you make of this war?' asked Burgo.

'We've not seen much of it yet,' I replied.

'Surely enough to realise how odd it is? I thought we were here to defend the South Koreans and democracy. I've never seen anywhere look less like a democracy and the Koreans, apart from the porters we have, don't seem to have anything to do with the war.'

'It's a feudal society in transition. We've only seen the peasants in the countryside.'

'It's not that. It looks to me as if the Yanks are fighting the Chinese communists in someone else's country.'

'Does it worry you?'

'Puzzles me.'

'Are your men talking about it?'

'They just think it's all very foreign.'

'They're right there.'

'Don't you think about it?'

'I've got something else on my mind when I've got time to think.'

'Kitty?'

'Yes.'

'Heard from her?'

'Once. Hugh Jermy says she's fine.'

'What news from him?'

'Desperate to join us.'

'I wouldn't want to miss this. Poor Hugh. If any of us is going to be a general it'll be Hugh. And he's not here.'

'He'll get here and sooner rather than later. He'll see to that. I must write to him. He begged for news. I'd better do that now.'

Our days by the Han River were cut short. The US Eighth

Army had won a resounding victory across the central front. The Chinese were withdrawing along their whole line to the 38th Parallel. Our brigade received orders to move to the Western Front and regain the ground lost at the battle on the Imjin, the battle that we had heard about in Hong Kong when the other British brigade was driven back with great loss.

We climbed aboard the same two-and-a-half-ton trucks – the 'deuce and a halves' in American parlance – that had met us at Inchon. Back we went the way we had come, the road not so dusty since the rains. We were subjected to regular downpours, but nothing as violent as the rainstorm that had marooned us a few weeks earlier. We had learned to cope. When the rain stopped we dried quickly in the heat.

Through the ruins of Seoul we motored again. Then we turned north and after about thirty miles we dismounted and marched towards the Imjin River. All round us was the detritus of war. Weapons and equipment, British and Chinese, lay scattered beside the road left from the great battle some months ago now. Vehicles lay on their sides or overturned; or just sat unattended as if parked. We saw bodies, disfigured, bloated and rotting. There was a nauseating stink. We passed some abandoned carriers, similar to those our mortar platoon had, and a Sherman tank that looked intact.

'Serjeant Body said he'd like to find a tank,' said Big Steel. 'There's one for him.'

We laughed, but our laughter was strained. The scene was grim. 'Have you seen a battlefield like this before?' I asked.

'In Italy the Germans left a trail when they retreated. Not like this. This is the muck of two fucking armies.'

'I'm surprised at what the Chinese left. They must have been in a hurry not to have buried their dead.'

'Or they had so many fucking casualties they couldn't.'

'Their casualties were horrendous. They say the Chinese launched six divisions against our three battalions. Our gunners wrought havoc.'

'Our lads were fucking lucky to get away.'

'A lot didn't.'

We were directed to take up a position on hills south of the river, and overlooking it. The Australians were to our right and the Highlanders behind. Some of the ground had been occupied before. We dug and we wired. We plotted DFs, that is beaten zones of defensive fire to be covered by the artillery and our battalion's three-inch mortars and medium machine-guns. At night we put out standing patrols in front of our position to warn us of any enemy approach. The Korean porters carried up our hill all the stores we needed to fortify the position. George built himself a command post. We were in the front line. X Company was the forward left company. We saw no enemy.

The battalion was ordered to find them.

'Here we go again,' said Burgo, as George gave out his orders for the company to patrol across the river. 'Can I lead? Miles gets all the chances.'

'You'll get your opportunity to lead,' said George. 'Miles you go across the river first in the assault boats, hold the far bank and make it a firm base. You can have a section of mortars to support you. It can cover you easily from its present position. Then Burgo and Toby, you can take it in turns to leapfrog each other forward and I'll come with you. We'll have David Sartorius with us, as our FOO. We're the last company to patrol. None of the others has had any luck. Air reconnaissance says the enemy is definitely dug in on the main ridge about five miles back from the river. No one has been able to pinpoint any of his positions or been able to find anyone during a day patrol. This is our chance to show the other companies that they're a load of wankers.'

We went down to the river.

'Look, Sir,' said Big Steel. 'Serjeant Body's got a tank.'

At the place we were to cross, the assault pioneers had lined up their assault boats and equipment to take us across the river. Beside them Tom Body sat in the turret of a Sherman tank.

'Blister my kidneys!' said George. 'Body's excelled himself. I doubt he'll get away with it. That tank belongs to the Canadians. When they see it, they'll claim it.'

'Surely battlefield spoils?' I said.

'If he could hide it, yes. Have you ever heard of anyone hiding a Sherman tank? I bet it's not here when we come back.'

'A quid?'

'Taken.'

Body climbed down from his tank to supervise the crossing. His place was quickly taken by another of his platoon.

'Would you like to see over my tank, Sir?' he said to George.

'Nice dinky toy you've go there, Body. I didn't know you were a whizz at tanks, too. I'll have a look at it on my return if you've still got it. I'd try and hide it from the Canadians.'

'She'll make a very useful tractor and bulldozer for the battalion. I wouldn't part with her for all the tea in China.'

'I'd hide her, if I were you. Now let's get across this river.'

The pioneers paddled us across the river in their boats. I dashed ashore with my platoon. No one greeted us. I laid out the platoon position and signalled for the others to cross. My men were already digging in. Burgo led his platoon across first, then came George and David Sartorius with Serjeant Major Budd, and finally Toby Errington. They set off on patrol.

When I'd dug a trench I sat on the side and watched Tom

Body exercising his skills with his tank on the far bank. He was deft. Then he put a corporal in the turret and got him to command it. He was good at it too. They parked the Sherman. Then Body and his platoon rigged lines for their assault boats on pulleys so that they could manoeuvre the boats across the river swiftly.

A little after midday I saw some jeeps coming down the track. They stopped next to the tank. Out stepped Colonel Guy and David Sartorius's battery commander. There was a lot of laughter. Colonel Guy climbed into the tank with Tom Body. When they got out Tom Body was arguing with Colonel Guy. Colonel Guy laughed again. Tom Body looked as if he was beseeching him. Colonel Guy shook his head and got back into his jeep. Tom talked to one of his men, who climbed into the tank. The tank moved onto the track and motored away with a forlorn Body looking after it. Body crossed the river to check his boats. He came across to me and opened his heart. He was upset, frustrated and angry. The colonel had said he could keep the Sherman if he could get away with it but once the Canadians had heard that he had got it he would have to give it back.

'I found the fucker,' he said. 'I rescued the fucker and got the fucker going. Now I've got to give the fucker back to the Canadians, the fuckers.'

We were standing there talking when we heard firing. It was some way away but consistent for several minutes. Then the guns opened up. Two ranging shots first, then several salvos.

'They must have bumped the Chinks,' said Tom Body.

'How far away, do you think?'

'Some miles.'

I looked across the river. Colonel Guy was there listening on his earphones. I put mine on. They were out of range on my wireless net.

'I'll stay with you, Sir,' Body said. 'Best if I get 'em across the river from here.'

It was an hour before we saw Burgo's platoon come swinging down the track. Tom Body put them straight on the boats and sent them across. Then George and David Sartorius and their wireless operators came past, with Budd following. At that moment there was a crump followed by a whistle and a mortar bomb exploded next to them. George fell over. Another bomb exploded a hundred yards back up the track. There were screams. It had fallen among Toby's platoon.

Now bombs were falling among us. I was terrified. My first instinct was to dive to the ground and cover my head with my hands. I tried to but I could not move. I was like a rabbit caught in the headlights of a car. I stood paralysed with fear.

There were shouts for stretcher bearers.

More bombs fell. It was pandemonium. I heard someone shouting 'stretcher bearers this way!' Then I realised it was me and I was standing beside George with David Sartorius, who was untouched. One of Tom Body's corporals ran forward with a stretcher. David Sartorius, Budd and I got George onto it. George's right leg looked a mess. He was gasping with pain. They carried him down to the boats. Bombs were still falling around us.

I ran across to Big Steel, and lay down beside him.

'Can you see any enemy?' I asked him.

'No one for half a mile. They just seem to be mortaring us.'

'They must have been watching us all day.'

'What about putting some smoke down to hide us, Sir?'

I wished I had thought of that earlier.

'Bloody good idea,' I said.

I turned to my mortar fire controller, who had stayed by my side. 'Get some smoke down fast to cover us,' I said.

Toby came through us, the last of his platoon. He was holding his left arm. Some of his men were wounded. Others were carrying a body on a stretcher, made from rifle slings. Toby was keeping them going. They got on to the boats. Tom Body was working wonders to keep his ferry service going. Now and again a bomb fell. He went on loading the boats and pulling them across the river.

Our own mortars were now dropping smoke 150 yards in front of us. I did not know whether it would prevent the Chinese observers spotting us but I thought my men would feel a little protected. I did.

'Time we went,' I said to Big Steel. 'Take the two forward sections. I'll follow.'

They doubled down to the boats. A bomb fell. Corporal Foxton and two men tumbled over. Serjeant Body ran up with stretchers and carried them on to the boats.

Then, almost without thinking, I turned to Little Steel commanding the last section and said, 'Come with me.'

We ran up the track to the point where the second bomb had fallen on Toby's platoon.

'We must see that no one's been left behind,' I said.

We searched the area. I could not see anyone.

'Here's a sten gun,' shouted Little Steel.

'Take it. That all?'

'Yes.'

'Let's get back.'

The bombs had stopped falling. Foxton must have caught the last bomb. We gathered the last section and ran down to the river. Serjeant Body was standing there with one boat.

'We're the last, serjeant,' I said to Body as we scrambled on. He pulled us back across the river.

Colonel Guy was waiting for me as I landed.

'Are you the last, Miles?'

'I think so, colonel.'

'Don't think. You either know or you don't.'

'Yes, colonel. Corporal Whettingsteel and I checked. We are the last. No one's been left behind.'

'Good. Well done, Miles. Hand over your platoon to Sergeant Whettingsteel. I've sent orders for Dermot Lisle to come forward. Until he does you command the company.'

'Yes, colonel. Did we have many casualties?'

'Besides George and Toby we have six more wounded and three killed.'

'Serjeant Body was very brave.'

'I saw that.'

Tom Body lost his Sherman to the Canadians. But he was decorated for his bravery with the Military Medal. It was the first decoration the regiment won in Korea.

Dermot came up early. Colour Crum followed later with the Korean porters and the supplies.

'You take my place, Miles,' said Dermot. 'You're company second-in-command now. Tell me what happened. It sounds ugly.'

'We were the fourth company this week to patrol across the river using the same crossing point. We were sitting ducks. They must have positioned some mortars about a mile away and sat waiting for us. They couldn't have timed it better. They hit us when we were gathered together in the open. As soon as we got some smoke down they stopped firing. Either the smoke obscured their view or they'd spent their ammunition. They could have got more of us.'

'They got enough.'

'Dermot, I was terrified.'

'I'm not surprised. Being mortared is vile, especially in the open.'

'I'm rather ashamed.'

'Don't be. Colonel Guy says you managed it well. Now you know what it's like to be under fire.'

'How are the wounded? How's George?'

'You'll have to ask the doctor. I came up as soon as I was ordered. I didn't see them.'

'You'll find the men a bit shocked. It's not the wounded as much as the dead. I don't think any of the men have seen a friend dead before.'

'I'll go round and talk to everyone.'

'Big Steel and I have put Tidmarsh in charge of Corporal Foxton's section. He's short of two men. I've not made any other changes. Can I take Maxwell with me?'

'Of course. I doubt you'll be away for long. Just temporarily until Colonel Guy can appoint a permanent company 2i/c. I need you back here. He's said it's my company now.'

'I'm glad for you, Dermot. Congratulations.'

'Thanks,' he said, 'but not quite the way I would have liked it.'

'Will you write to the next of kin or shall I? George can't. Nor can Toby.'

'Why don't we both write? You can say what you saw. I can add to it. Letters help. Let's compare notes when you come up tomorrow. Best done immediately.'

'Budd's upset about George though he wouldn't admit it.'

'I'll go round and talk to everyone.'

As company second-in-command I was based at A Echelon, a mile and a half behind the front line. It was dug in but it was not a prime defensive position. There was a form of defence with trenches dug round its perimeter. Its purpose was supply, not fighting. There all the company second-in-commands and the colour serjeants were collected, their job being to receive supplies from the quartermaster, who lived at B Echelon even further behind the lines, and take them up to the companies. The company second-in-commands were there, not just to administer, but to be left out of battle in reserve, as Dermot Lisle had been, in case a company commander was killed or wounded. Each company had a truck. All the vehicles were dug into shallow trenches and camouflaged.

On my way back I had called on the doctor at the Regimental Aid Post, which we knew as the RAP. He looked tired.

'I've done my best for them,' he said, 'and sent them back. Most went by helicopter. George has been badly wounded in the leg. He could lose it. Toby got a piece of shrapnel in his left arm. I couldn't take it out. He'll be back with us in a month or two. So will Corporal Foxton who caught it in his side. They'll all live. Nasty business. What happened?'

I told him.

That evening I took the day's supplies up to the company with Colour Crum. They were subdued.

When I saw Burgo I said, 'You've got your war now.'

'You and I were damned lucky,' he replied. 'What happened to George was hateful. Just wait until I find a Chinaman.'

Life was different at A Echelon where I looked after the company's interests. Every evening I travelled up to the company with supplies, taking the truck to the bottom of the hill, then leading the Korean porters up the hill. Morning and night, of course, we stood to. It did not have the immediacy of the front line. It was more relaxed. I heard the gossip and rumours more quickly and thought I knew more of what was going on. But I don't think I did. There was always the apprehension of being suddenly called for. I found it an unsatisfactory job, and I was away from my men.

I wrote letters to Kitty and Hugh. There was more time to do so. I also wrote to George, telling him about Tom Body's Sherman, enclosing my cheque for a pound and telling him our news. Months later I got a long reply. He had had a series of operations that had saved his leg, and taken most of the pieces of mortar bomb out of other parts of his body. His wounded leg was now shorter than the other so he had had some special boots made, beautiful boots made in Jermyn

Street. He had learned to walk again and hoped to be ready for active service within the year. He spent a lot of time riding and, once in the saddle, he found this a great joy and was looking forward to hunting. Typically he sent pages of practical advice and said how he missed being with his girls.

Some weeks later I was at B Echelon collecting some supplies. Colour Crum had handed me a letter, which I saw was from Sonia, when RQMS Quartermain, the quartermaster's right-hand man, drew up in a jeep. Quartermain had been the company serjeant-major of X Company when I had first joined it. He was a cheerful and artful fellow and had been a great help to me. We were old friends.

'I didn't know the RQMS got his own jeep?' I said.

'He doesn't.'

'That isn't yours, then?'

'It is, Sir.'

'How come?'

'I bought it,' he said with a smile.

'Bought it?'

'Yes, I bought it from the Americans.'

'Won't you get into trouble?'

'Oh no, Sir. You can buy anything from the Americans. You see, the battalion is allowed so many bottles of whisky a week. If the messes don't take their full quota I take it up and sell it to the Americans. They're dry. I get $20 a bottle. I bought this jeep for a bottle of Dimple Haig. It cost me five shillings and nine pence. I've never seen so much kit as the Americans have, most of it going begging. Would you like a jeep, Sir?'

'I'd love one but I don't see what I'd do with it.'

'Going back to the front line, are you?'

'I hope so.'

'Captain Wildbore arrived here last night. He's gone up to

battalion headquarters to report to the colonel. You'll like him, I know. He joined us in the last months of the war in Italy. I expect he'll take over from you today.'

'It's always nice to know what's happening, RQMS.'

'Just you come and ask me if you need anything, Mr Player.'

Back at A Echelon I found Ben Wildbore waiting for me. We had never met as he had been on the staff when I joined. He had a quizzical look and a relaxed air. A cigarette drooped from the corner of his mouth. I had been told he was something of a playboy and that he liked his comforts. He turned out to be quietly very efficient and a past master at making himself and those around him comfortable. He was particularly good at blowing smoke rings.

'Colonel Guy has told me to take over from you immediately. They want you back with your platoon. I gather Dermot is short of officers. I brought Tim Seymour up with me. He's a new National Service officer. He's taking over Toby Errington's platoon. He went up to the company.'

'Did you bring any other reinforcements?'

'No'

'Let me show you round here. I'll take you up to meet Dermot this evening.'

When I had told Ben Wildbore all I knew I found a place to myself and opened my letter.

Darling Miles (Sonia wrote),

It was wonderful to have your letter and hear all your news and that you're all right. We miss you very much here. You are more a son to Ivan and me than a cousin. I've been meaning to write, I should have written before this, but I must write now and what I'm going to say is not going to be easy.

You know how Kitty and I used to go and watch the polo? I don't think you ever came but then you had your duties. Kitty is, as you well know, a superb horsewoman and fascinated by the polo ponies. Well, after you left Hong Kong she spent more time with the polo set by herself and she's got to know Horace Belcher well and they've been seeing a lot of each other. She says he amuses her, loves horses as much as she does and, of course, he's the finest horseman in the colony. He's rich, too. Well – and this is the difficult bit – Horace has asked Kitty to marry him and Kitty has said yes. She won't really talk to me about it. I know she likes him and, of course, in his way he is likeable, but I don't think she loves him and I have no influence with her – whoever did? – and you know how strong-headed she can be.

Oh, Miles. I'm so unhappy to bring you this news. I know you love her and I'm sure she loves you. She told me you had an understanding but now she says it was a very loose understanding, that she talked you into it and that you don't really love her. She's become implacably stubborn and there's nothing I can do. I really cannot understand her. She's got a bee in her bonnet about it all and she says she doesn't want to miss this opportunity after that unfortunate mess she got into in London, and you being in Korea and heaven only knows when you'll be back, and if you will.

Horace has finished his job looking after your regiment's interests here in charge of your rear party and goes to Singapore on the staff. So they're getting married in Hong Kong and going to Singapore together. Ivan says Kitty is old enough to make up her own mind.

Kitty said would I write and tell you as she didn't think she could.

How I hate this beastly war. I must now write to Kitty's father. Heaven knows what he will say. I feel terrible guilt and think I've let everyone down.

So much love, darling Miles,
     Sonia.

I re-read the letter twice. I just did not understand it. I sat frozen. How could she do it? Kitty, my Kitty. And with Horace? I tore the letter in little bits and threw them wildly away. Thank God, I thought, I'm going back into the front line.

That evening I took Ben Wildbore up to the company.

'Hello Ben,' Dermot greeted him. 'Very good to have you with us. I'm sure Miles has briefed you.'

'Yes. Very well. But he's being remarkably silent now. I think he rather liked being company 2i/c.'

'Miles, you've done a marvellous job. Thank you. Now go and see how your platoon are getting on. We'll have a chat later.'

The platoon was in fine spirits. Big Steel gave me a great welcome. Maxwell and I settled back in as if we had never been away.

'What's the matter, Miles?' Dermot said to me later. 'You look as though you've seen a ghost.'

'Kitty is marrying Horace Belcher.'

'Marrying? Horace Belcher?'

'Yes. Horace. The one George said Colonel Guy called a polo stick soaked in whisky. The one Colonel Guy left behind in Hong Kong as he didn't trust him in the field.'

'I don't believe it. How do you know?'

'Sonia Blessington has just written to tell me.'

'Oh, Miles.' He looked at me. 'You're going to be very lucky in war.'

'Am I?'

'Yes. And just forget about everything else.'
'It's a closed book.'
'Come into my command post and have a dram of whisky.'

## Chapter 6

# My parents, Kitty and Hugh

Kitty was not a closed book. She could not be. She had been my first real friend. We lived in India until I was eight, apart from a year in England when I was three. I have this memory of staying at a large house with a portico and Kitty. This may be prompted by a photograph of me, aged three, and Kitty, just two, standing hand in hand in front of Sherborne Court. This is one of the earliest photographs in the scrapbook my mother made for me. Just how much of these early years do I really remember, I wonder, and how much is prompted by the family photograph albums?

I was born in India, at Kamptee, in time for Christmas 1927. My early memories are happy ones with Nanny Meredith, my Anglo-Indian ayah; my mother, always smiling and laughing; the *syce* and my first pony; my father, who was there one moment and gone another. Throughout my early life my father was a jack-in-the-box.

'Where's daddy?' I would ask.

'Pigsticking,' mummy might answer.

'What's pigsticking?'

'Hunting wild pigs.'

'What a funny animal to hunt.'

I'd wait for daddy. As soon as he came in sight I would run to him. He always picked me up and kissed me. My mother rarely did.

'Where's daddy?'

'On manoeuvres.'

'What's manoeuvres?'

'Manoeuvres is the game soldiers play.'

'Can we play manoeuvres?'

'When you're a soldier, darling.'

When daddy came home that time he brought a box full of lead soldiers and we lay on a rug and played manoeuvres.

Sometimes when I asked where daddy was mummy would say he was marching. 'Oh good,' I would say and march round our bungalow. We had a beautiful bungalow, built on stilts, large and airy, with a verandah all round it.

One day daddy brought home a tiger skin and laid it on the floor.

'Did *you* shoot it, daddy?'

'You bet.'

'Where?'

'In the heart. That's the only place to shoot them.'

'Can I shoot a tiger?'

'When you're older we'll both go shooting tiger. Do you know this one, Miles?

> Would you like to sin
> With Elinor Glyn
> On a tiger skin?
> Or would you prefer
> To err
> With her
> On some other fur?'

I rolled on the tiger skin screaming with laughter and mummy said, 'Stop it, Fred,' and she laughed, too.

My father had lots of stories and limericks. One of our favourites was:

There was an old man of Madras
Whose balls were made of brass
In stormy weather
They clanged together
And sparks shot out of his *derrière.*

When he came to *derrière* I would shout it out too and we would both fall about laughing and mother would say 'Stop it, Fred,' but she laughed, too. Daddy liked the punch line or last word of his limericks to be in French or German, both of which he spoke well. Another of my favourites was:

There was a young lady of Nantes
Whose love life was terribly fraught
Her hole was so small
It was no good at all
Except for *la plume de ma tante.*

Again, I would shout the last words and rock with laughter, with no understanding of the meaning.

Then mummy stopped laughing. She had a baby, a sister for me she said, and the baby died. We were all sad. I was old enough to go riding. Daddy would take me out early in the morning with the *syce.* Soon we were laughing. Mummy never laughed as much again.

When I was nearly eight we came home to England. I had heard so much about England that, much as I did not want to leave my pony, or the *syce* or Nanny Meredith, I was too excited to think about anything except England and all the wonderful things that were going to happen to me there. I travelled home on a ship with my mother, my father having decided to travel overland with a brother officer. With no one to look after me I had the run of the ship and my first taste of freedom. We landed at Marseilles and took the train to Dieppe where we crossed to Newhaven, my first disappointment as I was expecting to see the white cliffs of Dover. We spent the first two nights in a hotel in London and shopped at the Army and Navy Stores in Victoria Street for winter clothes. Then we went to stay with General Fisher, who was an old friend of my father.

Kitty was standing at the door when we arrived.

'I'm Kitty Fisher,' she said in a very grown-up manner and offered me her hand. She was six.

'I'm to show you your room.'

She took me in hand, led me up the staircase, along a wide gallery and into a large room full of pictures and books and rugs with a single bed. Two windows overlooked a lake at the north of the house. Kitty sat on the bed and looked at me.

'You're not as brown as I thought you would be,' she said.

'Why should I be brown?'

'Aren't all Indians brown?'

'I'm not an Indian.'

'What are you then?'

'I'm an Englishman.'

'Oh, I am disappointed. I thought you would be an Indian and then we could play Cowboys and Indians.'

'Those Indians come from America. They're Red Indians.'

'I suppose,' she said, 'I suppose we could paint you red. Can you ride?'

'Yes.'

'I'll show you my pony.'

So began our friendship. We stayed with General Fisher for a month. He always seemed old to me. His wife, who had been much younger than him and a friend of my mother and of Sonia Blessington, had died when Kitty was born. I think General Fisher liked the idea of my mother being around as a sort of surrogate mother to Kitty. Kitty accepted her as my mother and as a sort of aunt but was far too independent to do more than that. In the end Kitty, with an intuitive sense of self-protection, became closer to Sonia Blessington than my mother. Kitty liked to be mother.

General Fisher always had a coloured handkerchief tucked up his left sleeve. He was very fond of my father and was our benefactor. He must have been about sixty. They were like father and son. The general found us a house in the next village, Sherborne St Mary. It was a red-brick Edwardian house, with large rooms, a long garden, stables and a cottage where the gardener lived with his family. It was not on the scale of Sherborne Court, much of which was old red brick, for Sherborne Court was originally a Tudor house. Its portico, of four columns and pediment, was added in the eighteenth century when the wings were built. It was a grand house, one of the greatest in the county, in which Fishers had lived for three centuries. I explored it with Kitty. There was always a new nook to find. When we moved into our house, we explored that together.

In India, my father had been commanding a company in the Second Battalion of the Prince Regent's Light Infantry. Now he was at the War Office in London, had received accelerated promotion and was a brevet lieutenant colonel. I saw less of him than in India as, during the week, he stayed in London, generally coming home on Saturday and returning on Monday morning. My mother hated this.

'We should have bought a house in London,' I heard her say.

'Terrible place for Miles to grow up,' my father replied. 'What's wrong with here?'

'I never see you.'

'You wouldn't see much of me in London.'

'Why not?'

'I've explained. I'm in the section of the War Office planning for war. We're overworked trying to catch up after all the years of neglect.'

'What do you do in the evenings?'

'When I've finished at the War House I go to the club for dinner, often with General Egerton. Sometimes we go back to the office. There's always something to read. You've no idea how much there is to do. Not like India at all.'

'I wish you didn't have that job.'

'I could hardly refuse it.'

'Then I'd better come to London. We'll sell the flat and buy a house so I can look after you.'

'What about Miles? There's going to be a war. You don't want to be in London if there's a war.'

'What about you?'

'It'll only be for two years.'

'What'll happen then?'

'If I'm lucky I'll get command of one of the battalions.'

'Back to India?'

'Maybe. Or Aldershot.'


I was sent to boarding school. I had never known such loneliness and I was backward. I remember my mother dropping me outside the school gates and my standing there, crying. It cannot have been like that but that is what I remember. I was placed in too high a form. Within a week I had been moved to the lowest form, where I was bottom of the class. All that week I cried myself to sleep. My bed in the dormitory was next to a boy with long, blond, curly hair who was in his second term. After the lights were put out he used to tell stories, mostly about Nelson: Nelson at the Nile; Nelson losing his right arm at Tenerife; Nelson's last words at Trafalgar. My favourite story was Nelson at Copenhagen. After I had been there a week I plucked up my courage.

'Tell us again the story about Nelson at Copenhagen,' I said.

'I told it last night.'

'Tell it again. Please.'

'Well, Nelson is fighting in his ship HMS *Elephant*, fighting the Danes and a shot hits his mainmast, knocking splinters all over him. "Warm work," he says, "this day may be the last of us." Then he says, "Mark you, I would not be elsewhere for thousands".'

'What does he mean by thousands?'

'Pounds.'

'Crikey.'

'Then his signal lieutenant reports to him that the commander-in-chief has signalled to leave off action. "Leave off action?" says Nelson, "damn me if I do." He puts his glass to his blind eye and says, "I do not see the signal".'

At which I closed one eye, put my imaginary telescope to it and say, 'I do not see the signal. Gosh, that's a topping story.'

'Are you going to be a sailor?' he asks.

'No, a soldier,' I say, and go to sleep with one blind eye.

A week or so later I was asked if I knew any stories.

'You must know some Indian stories,' he says.

'I know a limerick,' I reply.

'Tell us.'

I recited 'There was an old man of Bombay'. Everyone in the dormitory exploded with laughter and could not stop. The door flew open, the lights were turned on and Mr Beatty, the housemaster, was standing there.

'What's going on here?' he demanded.

No one said anything. Everyone was still sniggering.

'I'll stand here until I know,' he said.

After a little time someone in the corner I did not know said, 'We were laughing at a limerick, Sir.'

'Who told the limerick?'

Silence.

'I said, who told the limerick?'

Silence.

'I did, Sir,' I said.

'Come here, Player.'

I got out of bed very slowly and stood in front of him.

'You know there is to be no talking after lights out?'

'Yes, Sir.'

'So, you've disobeyed the rules?'

'Yes, Sir.'

'Hand me your slipper.'

I handed it to him.

'Bend over. This is what happens when you break the rules.'

Then the blond boy in the next bed to mine said, 'That's unfair, Sir. You can't beat Player. He's a new boy. What about new boy's benefit? You told us new boys are given a chance. I asked him to tell us a limerick. You'll have to beat me.'

'I'll beat the whole damn lot of you if I have to.'

By this time everyone was sitting up in bed glaring at Mr Beatty. He realised he had gone too far. He was a bully but there were ten of us in the dormitory.

'As this is the first time you've broken the rules this term I'll let you off with a warning. Next time it'll be six of the best for both of you.'

He turned the lights out and closed the door. The blond boy in the next bed was Hugh Jermy.


In the summer holidays I used to swim with Kitty in the lake. In the winter holidays we used to skate on it when it froze. All year round we rode together. In the winter we hunted with General Fisher and my father.

Kitty's nanny took us to the cinema in Basingstoke to see *Snow White and the Seven Dwarfs*. We went on the bus. It was a great treat.

'Nanny says the witch might be frightening,' Kitty said. 'If you find her so, you can hold my hand.'

When the witch appeared I didn't think her too frightening but I held Kitty's hand.

I thought how lucky I was to have Kitty as my friend in the holidays and Hugh in term time. They were glorious days for me. Not so for my mother.

'You never seem to be at the flat when I ring,' I overheard my mother say to my father.

'I've told you how busy we are. And we travel, visiting units all over the country.'

'You might tell me where you are.'

'I couldn't possibly tell you all my movements. I have to go wherever General Egerton goes and he often changes his mind at the last moment to keep everyone on his toes.'

'Where were you on Thursday night?'

'I can't remember.'

'I can tell you. You were at the Gargoyle with a woman I don't know.'

'I was at the Gargoyle with General Egerton. He said it was time we had some fun and he got a party together and insisted I went.'

'I think *you* suggested it. It was your party and you paid for it. You seem to be spending a lot of money.'

'We go there a bit. General Egerton likes it. Sometimes I pay, sometimes he does. We have to relax occasionally.'

'You could come home and relax with me.'

'Oh, Evelyn. You do go on. Are you hunting today?'

'No. We agreed we would spend the day here planning the garden.'

'We can do that tomorrow.'

'Tomorrow we're going to the Fishers.'

'I promised Miles we'd hunt today. I must go and find him.'

'You're just not interested in the garden or in me.'

At school Hugh Jermy and I had become firm friends. I had caught up and we were in the same form. I should never

100

have been bottom of the school, but I had come from India and had learned different things. I had also become popular by teaching many of my year my father's limericks. I discovered I was good at games, as was Hugh. Whenever we had time we would play in the slip machine by the cricket pavilion becoming more and more proficient at catching cricket balls. My father gave me a cricket ball on which the cricket master engraved my school number so I did not lose it.

'There's going to be a war,' said General Fisher. We were at Sherborne Court lunching with the general. I was old enough to be included for Sunday luncheon, as was Kitty.

'A certainty, sooner or later,' said my father.

'I thought Mr Chamberlain had stopped a war and promised peace in our time?' said my mother.

'For the moment,' said the general. 'Hitler will over reach himself one day and we'll have to fight.'

'Trouble is,' said my father, 'we're not ready. Chamberlain has given us time. We've no modem weapons to speak of. That ten-year rule wrecked the army.'

'What rule was that?' asked my mother.

'The rule,' said the general, 'formulated by the government in the 1920s that we should plan on the basis that there'd be no major war in Europe for ten years. It stopped development and modernisation. I warned them at the time and went on warning them until I was thrown out. That's why I was a major-general for fifteen years.'

'You should be CIGS,' said my father.

'Perhaps. I wouldn't mind working with Hore-Belisha as Minister for War.'

'He's got some good ideas but he doesn't see eye to eye with the CIGS. And he puts the generals' noses out of joint.'

'They're a lot of dead beats, out of date and probably trying to fight the last war again.'

101

'I wish they were. You and I know the British army by 1918 had become the finest army in the world. We beat the German army. The plans for 1919 were based on a mechanised tank army. We haven't got anything like that now.'

'By the end of the war we'd learned a lot and we had some good generals. How's your General Egerton?'

'He's asked me to stay on for one more year.'

'Oh no,' my mother said.

'Yes. I'm sorry, Evelyn. I was going to tell you. It only happened last week.'

'I can't stand another year like this.'

'Evelyn,' said General Fisher, 'there's going to be a war and we'll have to pay the price. Fred is doing a vital job. I'm glad they've recognised that.'

'Fred, you said that if you were lucky you'd get command and we might go back to India.'

'I *will* get command. I've been promised the second battalion. It's returning from India and I'm to command in a year's time.'

'Just in time,' said the general, 'to take the battalion to France.'

'We'll never,' my mother said, 'be together again.'


One holidays Hugh came and stayed with us. I took him to meet Kitty, who looked him over warily.

'You know I'm Miles's oldest friend, don't you?' she said.

'Yes, but you're a girl,' said Hugh.

'That doesn't make any difference. Can you ride?'

'Yes.'

'Let's see then.'

I was proficient on a pony and Kitty was outstanding. Hugh could ride but he was not in the same class. Kitty set him at some fences. He fell off. Then Kitty showed how it should be done. Hugh smarted. Every day we had to ride.

Hugh was determined to be as good as Kitty. He improved but he could not challenge her accomplishment.

I sensed a rivalry between Kitty and Hugh that was not just about riding. They were competing for my friendship.

One Christmas holidays, it must have been the last Christmas before the war, we went skiing at St Moritz. General Fisher organised it. Kitty came, as did my father and mother. Ivan and Sonia Blessington were there with Phyllida, who was three years old, and her nanny. There were some others. It was a large party. I remember the sting of the snowballs, falling over on the nursery slopes and losing my skis, rolling in the snow with Kitty, and my mother and father laughing together again and arm in arm. That's what the photographs say. When I went back to school and told Hugh he was envious, even angry he had not been there. I promised him we would take him the following year.

In the summer term, when Hugh and I were both eleven, we got into the first cricket eleven. Hugh was a batsman. I was a bowler. We were the youngest members of the team. We got in because we had also trained ourselves to be good fieldsmen and to hold our catches. My father came to play in the Fathers' Match. He hit my first ball for six. Next ball he was caught in the slips. He laughed. He had just left the War Office and taken command of the second battalion, which had returned from India and was stationed at Tidworth.

After the match I followed my parents as they walked to his car that was to take him back to his barracks. For a moment I don't think they remembered I was there.

'My father says you're still spending too much money,' I heard my mother say.

'London's expensive.'

'You're not in London now.'

'Tidworth shouldn't be so expensive.'

'I'm coming to live with you at Tidworth and I'm bringing Miles in the holidays. Neither of us sees enough of you.'

'It'll cost a bit setting up there. I don't suppose we'll be there for long.'

'What do you mean?'

'We'll be at war within a year.'

'Then I'm determined to be with you as long as I can be. Have you been gambling again?'

'Not really.'

'You've no right to gamble my money away.'

'When we got married we agreed to share. You know I lost mine in the Crash.'

'Only because you were gambling. My father said there was no need for you to have over extended yourself as you did.'

'I didn't. My brokers did.'

'You let them.'

'Do we have to go over all that again, Evelyn?'

'The money is as much Miles's as yours.'

'Your father will leave Miles money. He's no need to worry.'

'I do. What will happen to me when you've spent it all?'

'Your father has plenty.'

'How can you say that? I find that in the worst possible taste.'

'There's going to be a war, Evelyn. Face up to it. None of us may be here tomorrow. That's why I wanted you and Miles to live in the country.'

'I don't see that the possibility of war should be an excuse for bad behaviour.'

The last summer holidays before the war my mother took a house at Bembridge in the Isle of Wight, which we had done before. Kitty came, and Hugh came for the first time. We sailed scows, the small Bembridge dinghies. Hugh was better

104

than Kitty and me. That made Kitty and me closer, which Hugh did not like. In the evenings we played cards, rummy or *vingt-et-un*. When Kitty won, which she often did, that made Hugh and me closer.

Daddy came for a few days, smoked cigars and left in a hurry. Mummy left suddenly too, and we were left with Kitty's nanny. Then General Fisher arrived to take us home. He told us war had broken out and that daddy had taken his battalion to France.

I did not see much of daddy after that. Of course I saw Hugh at school and, for a time, saw as much of Kitty until she went away to school. Then we slowly began to grow apart, developing different interests and friends. We were thrown together again in Hong Kong. Maybe, I thought, I should have married Kitty before I left Hong Kong, as Kitty and Sonia had wanted. For Kitty to marry Horace Belcher I could not understand.

# Chapter 7

## *The Chinese are unenthusiastic*

'I hope you like your bunker, Sir?' asked Big Steel.

'You bet. What a piece of engineering,' I replied.

'The major said we were to make you one as you'd be coming back. So when the Americans came and helped us with their bulldozers we made it specially for you.'

It was morning, just after we had stood down. Maxwell had handed us mugs of tea. It was a good time to chat before the day got going, and we had a lot to catch up on. Big Steel and I were standing in the trench in front of our position that served as my observation post. From it we could see for miles across the Imjin to the north, as our platoon was the most forward one in the battalion on the left flank. To our left was the US Marine Corps, to our right Burgo's platoon. Some miles away we could see the line of mountains on which the Chinese had dug themselves in. There was not a Chinese soldier to be seen.

'You've done wonders building this position,' I said.

'We haven't had much else to do, only patrolling locally.'

'How did the men take to patrolling again after being mortared at the river crossing when we had those casualties?'

'They're over that, Sir. That's war. You have casualties. Some die. Some more will. You have to lump it. It's no good brooding on it. Digging this position has kept them all occupied and taken their minds off that. Everything's "All Sir Garnet".'

While I had been second-in-command of the company I had brought up tons of stores including wire, sandbags and wood. These had been carried to the top of the hill, on which the company sat, by the Korean porters on their A-frames. With these stores the company had turned the hill into a fortress. Behind a network of trenches, riveted and shored with sandbags and timber, were bunkers in which every man could shelter and sleep. The walls of the bunkers were made with sandbags. Across the top were laid green tree trunks, above them iron wiring pickets to give extra strength and on top at least two foot of sandbags. Around the whole position Big Steel had laid barbed wire, most of it at ankle height. Later we would learn to surround our positions with wire chest-high up to 25 yards deep. Below the wire the Americans had laid a minefield. Through the minefield and the wire there were gaps and lanes, well marked, to allow us entry and exit. We could cover these gaps and lanes from trenches that overlooked them. All the positions we held after this were dug and prepared in a similar fashion. When the Chinese next attacked we would be well prepared.

'Any sign of the Chinese?' I asked.

'Not on our patrols. They've withdrawn into those mountains and seem unenthusiastic about meeting us.'

'We're a long way away.'

'It's six miles to their forward positions.'

'Can't I see some people in that village?' I said, pointing to a group of thatched buildings across the river about three miles away. I was looking through my binoculars.

'We've cleared that village twice. We take a Korean interpreter with us. He explains they are in the middle of a battlefield and we move them out. The next day they're back.'

'They're working in the paddy fields, now?'

107

'The way they behave you wouldn't think there was a war.'

'It does seem to be rather peaceful here.'

Later in the morning the peace was broken when Dermot Lisle and David Sartorius, our New Zealand gunner, joined us on our position.

'Morning, Miles,' said Dermot. 'Time for our daily shoot.'

'Shoot?' I said. 'What can you shoot at this time of the year?'

'Plenty. Just watch.'

With their wireless operators they climbed down into one of the forward trenches that had been dug as observation posts, and started to scan the landscape through their binoculars.

'See anything?' asked Dermot.

I took up my glasses and started to scan the landscape, too.

'Take the village we call Chelsea,' said David. 'Go left eleven o'clock. There's some movement.'

'So there is,' said Dermot.

All the villages in the battle area had been given English names so that they could be easily identified. Most were called after areas of London.

'It's a possible target,' said David, ' but I can't quite make it out and it's near the limit of our range. Take Chelsea again. Six o'clock. In the paddy there's movement and it's much closer.'

'Aren't they Koreans working the paddy?' said Dermot.

'I thought we'd cleared that village two days ago.'

'We did but they're back. Surely the Chinese wouldn't be working in the paddy?'

'No. Then we can't fire at them.'

'If there are any Chinese watching us they'd be on the hill to the right. Let's stonk that.'

'Good idea. That's four miles.'

David started talking into his wireless set. A minute later a shot whistled over us. We saw it burst on the hill. David talked into his wireless set again. We heard the roar of the gun line and a salvo burst on the hill. There were two more salvos and then silence. The Koreans working in the paddy beside the hill took no notice. We waited for the debris to subside. There was no movement on the hill. Then we waited for the Chinese to retaliate with their artillery and fire on us. Nothing happened.

Dermot and David chose three other targets and stonked them. Nothing happened. At one point Dermot ordered the machine-gun section, which was positioned inside my platoon position, to fire on a target about four thousand yards away. They fired several hundred rounds. Still nothing happened.

'Let's call it a day,' said Dermot. 'I like the way you hit the first hill with your first shot, David.'

'I think I could do it with my eyes closed now.'

Turning to me Dermot said, 'Thanks for the loan of your hill, Miles.'

'Aren't we exposing ourselves a little,' I asked.

'Yes, but we have to in order to get them to expose themselves. They're a little shy at the moment but they'll come out one day soon.'

'Supposing they do retaliate?'

'You take shelter in your wonderful bunker. We've been doing this daily for three weeks but nothing happens. We also send out patrols but they find nothing. Your turn to take out a patrol tonight. Serjeant Whettingsteel has done it several times.'

'It seems very peaceful up here. More like training than war.'

'That's war for you. Long periods of inactivity and then all hell breaks loose.'

Dermot briefed me on my patrol. I was to take Corporal Whettingsteel and seven men and lie on our side of the river to ambush anyone coming across the ford.

That evening the enemy did retaliate. A solitary, ancient aeroplane chugged into view flying quite low.

'Air attack' cried Maxwell. 'Here comes Bed-Check Charlie.'

'Have a go, Bren gunners!' shouted Big Steel.

The aeroplane crept nearer and then was over us dropping grenades. All three of the platoon's Bren gunners were shooting at him. He had a charmed life and was never hit, or not enough to cripple him. He would fly over us several times a week. The grenades he threw landed wide, did little damage and never hurt anyone. We treated him like a shooting gallery at a fair ground: fun, harmless, but no prizes.

Little Steel and the seven men selected to lay the ambush had been on patrol at night before. I had not, not in Korea, or in the face of an enemy. This worried me. It is one thing to dash into action or be fired on and react instantly. It is another to lie out in the dark, hour after hour, waiting for something to happen, not knowing what or who it might be and trying to discipline your imagination.

I had briefed everyone before tea. We waited until after we had stood down and it was dark. We wore gym shoes, cap comforters and the minimum of equipment, having blackened our faces and hands. We carried only our weapons, ammunition and grenades. Apart from the Bren gunners everyone carried a Sten gun, the army's sub-machine-gun, unreliable and prone to jam. It was a Second World War weapon, as most of our weapons were. We had stripped ourselves of all our personal possessions, except watches. Our only means of identification were our identity discs, which we always wore on a string round our necks. There were two discs. If you were killed the person who found you was meant to take one of the discs with which to report your death. The other disc stayed on your body to identify it.

The moon was in its last quarter. When we started we could see fifty yards. We climbed down the hill at the back of our position, through the gaps in the wire, then the mine-field and walked slowly and silently down the track to the river. The ford was over a mile away and it took us forty minutes to reach. A hundred yards short of it I stopped to cover Little Steel as he went forward with one of the Bren groups. He settled on the bank on the right of the track. Then I moved up and settled on the bank on the left of the track with the other Bren group and my wireless operator. If we did run into the enemy, or they ran into us, I would be able to warn Dermot and he would be able to bring down artillery and mortar fire to protect us. The plan was to let the enemy get to our side of the river before opening fire. I would be the first to open fire. That way no one should fire prematurely and we hoped we would catch most of them in the water. We were not really strong enough to catch a prisoner, though this might be possible. It was eleven by the time we were in position. We waited.

It began to rain. We put on our groundsheets as capes. It sheeted down. My cap comforter was soaked. Water began to trickle down my face and neck and under my cape. It ran down inside my shirt. The rain falling on the surface of the river sent up a mist of water and created a constant, noisy patter. We lost sight of the far bank of the river and it became impossible to see or hear anything but the rain. We were all soaked to the skin. This is the time, I thought, for the enemy to cross the river. But nobody came. We were very wet but warm. I kept looking at my watch. The hands hardly seemed to move. The rain stopped as suddenly as it had started. The air cleared and silence returned.

Someone touched me and pointed. Sounds of splashing and grunts were coming from the far bank. I tautened. I could see some dark shapes slipping into the water and moving slowly across the river towards us. I heard the

Bren gunner cock his gun. I released the safety catch on my Sten gun. We watched and waited. They came nearer and nearer, and then emerged from the water. Three cows climbed up the bank and wandered slowly past us. I could sense the relaxation round me. This could be a trick, I thought. The Chinese could have driven the cows across to distract us. I peered as hard as I could at the river and the far bank. No one came. They were just three cows lost on a battlefield.

We lay there for another hour. Then it was time to return. As we walked back the motion and the warm air caught us so that we were almost dry by the time we had climbed to the top of our hill.

'I couldn't understand, Sir,' said Little Steel when we were back in our position and had been debriefed by Dermot, 'why you didn't fire. They were almost upon us and I was holding on to my Bren gunner to stop him firing. Then they turned out to be bloody cows. How did you know?'

'I couldn't tell. They seemed to be swimming at one point. I didn't think the Chinese could swim. It looked so odd.'

'I couldn't have faced my brother if we'd opened fire on some fuckin' cows.'

I settled into the routine of the line. Sleeping during the morning, main meal in the middle of the day, sheltering from the rain and repairing any damage caused by the rain, talking to everyone in the platoon to see he was all right and discussing administration with Big Steel. Then there were briefings for patrols and going on patrol. Whether I went on patrol or not I would be up some of the night, either taking my turn on duty or seeing everything was all right and encouraging my men. I did not have much time to myself. There was always something that had to be done and we were continually improving the position. Sleep was the main problem coupled by boredom with the rations, though these were American and generous and came with free cigarettes. I smoked, as did most of the platoon.

A short letter of commiseration about Kitty arrived from Hugh. Of course I thought about Kitty. But life on the hill was so different and intense that I found everything else unreal. Much as I longed for Kitty and life in Hong Kong, or anywhere else for that matter, it was difficult to believe that anything was real except my life with the platoon. I had always found the army gave me a great sense of comradeship. Now I found this at its greatest. The mutual experience and suffering, dangers encountered and hardships shared led to a cementing of brotherly love with the men of my platoon and with my brother officers. Dermot would gather his officers together to hear our thoughts and problems and to share his ideas. He was also very good with the men, knew everyone in the company and went out of his way to speak to every man individually and regularly. The men sometimes had problems at home. Dermot took a special interest in helping to sort them out.

'Come and visit the marines,' said Dermot one morning. 'Time we liaised with them again.'

He had been visiting my platoon, talking to the men and inspecting our improvements. Budd was with him, checking on our ammunition. Dermot was carrying his sniper's rifle, a Lee-Enfield with a telescopic sight. He had placed small targets – a boot, hat, water bottle – several hundred yards in front of the position and would lie for hours shooting at them, invariably hitting them. He had yet to have a Chinaman in his sights.

'Serjeant-Major,' he said, turning to Budd, 'you come, too.'

'Very good, Sir.'

Budd's job would be to see what he could scrounge. Like

113

most of the warrant officers and senior NCOs, Budd liked trading with the Americans.

'Put on your Sunday best, Miles, and meet me at the jeep head in fifteen minutes.'

The jeep head was at the bottom of the hill, behind the company position, where Dermot kept his jeep carefully camouflaged and out of sight. It was the point to which, when acting company 2i/c, I used to bring the company stores truck. It was the most forward point a vehicle could reach.

Ellis, Dermot's driver, was standing by the jeep when I reached it. He was polishing a new plate on the front of the vehicle. It carried a large regimental badge and the words 'OC X Coy 2 PRLI'. Underneath was the regimental motto *Cede Nullis.* This the regiment had adopted after capturing a French regimental eagle, on which it was emblazoned, at a critical moment in the battle of Waterloo.

I got into the back of the jeep as did the serjeant-major, who arrived a minute later with Dermot. Dermot was still carrying his sniper's rifle, the serjeant-major a Sten gun and I my rifle. Ellis started the jeep first time and we rattled down the track, sliding a little on the wet surface.

'Save your Brooklands stunts, Ellis,' said Dermot as we slid dangerously close to the edge of the track. 'We've got all morning.'

After George Bulman and Toby Errington had been wounded our next officer casualty had been the second-in-command of the battalion, who had been badly injured when his jeep, which he had been driving himself, careered off the road. He had been invalided out to Japan, never to return. He had been a puritan and an enemy of fun, drinking and gambling so most of the officers had been delighted, though not too openly.

We hit the main track, turned right and motored towards the river. Our hill stood high above us to our right.

114

'Have you seen the new badge on the front of my jeep, Miles?' Dermot said.

'Very pretty,' I said.

'The serjeant-major got Serjeant Body to run it up. You wait. All the other company commanders will want one when they see it.'

After a few hundred yards we came to a junction, marked by a few ruined houses. We turned left and motored west for nearly a mile when we were stopped by a group of US marines who stood up and waved us down. They were wearing helmets. They always did. We never did.

'Good morning,' said Dermot. 'I've come to see your company commander.'

'Jeez, officer,' said the marine serjeant. 'This is the front line. You just drove through our minefield.'

'You've mined the road?'

'Hell, yes. You's a lucky man.'

'I certainly am. Where can I find your commanding officer?'

'You limeys?'

'We are.'

'You all limeys?'

'We are.,

'What's your rank?'

'I am Major Lisle. I am the officer commanding X Company, Second Battalion The Prince Regent's Light Infantry. We are immediately to your right flank. With me are Lieutenant Player and Serjeant-Major Budd.'

'Well, major, I'll get one of my men to guide you. Hey, Lewitsky, guide these limeys up to the Captain.'

A marine separated himself from the group, spat on the ground and climbed onto the side of the jeep, holding on to the windscreen and the canopy bar.

'I'm Lewitsky. Let's go.'

We motored round a hill and found some jeeps and a truck parked behind it.

'You leave your jeep and driver here,' said Lewitsky, 'and follow me.'

We got out and followed Lewitsky who ambled up the hill, along a zigzag track which reached a promontory where there was a cluster of trenches and bunkers. There was no one in sight.

'Captain,' shouted Lewitsky into one of the bunkers, 'there's some limey officers to see you.'

'What the hell's that,' shouted a voice from inside the bunker.

'Limeys.'

'Who?'

'Limey officers. They want to see you.'

A big man with a crew cut and the butt of a cigar jutting from his mouth emerged.

'Whaddya say,' he said. 'It's the British army. Why fellers, that's real swell of you to come and see us.'

'They motored through our minefield.'

'You don't say.'

'We didn't know you'd laid a minefield,' said Dermot.

'Man, we're surrounded by minefields. I wanna sleep nights.'

More marines emerged from the bunkers. We were given beer to drink. The marines, unlike the US army, were not dry. The captain admired the sights of Dermot's sniper rifle. Dermot admired the captain's Colt .45 revolver, which he wore in a holster strapped to his right thigh, as if he were a gunslinger in a western. I fell into conversation with a lieutenant. Budd was taken off by a serjeant to look at some trenches and bunkers.

'Why the dark green beret?' asked the lieutenant.

'We're Light Infantry.'

'What's Light Infantry?'

'We were raised as skirmishers, covering the army. Now we function as infantry.' I laid it on a bit. 'We're elite troops.'

'Like the marines.'

'Yes, like the marines.'

'It's fine to know you're on our flank,' he said.

'That goes for us, too. You know we motored through your minefield? Don't you mark your minefields?'

'Sometimes. What's your cap badge mean?'

'It's a silver bugle surmounted by a crown. We used to play bugle calls to give out commands in the field. You know. Advance, withdraw, that sort of thing.'

I took my beret off and handed it to him so he could look at the badge more closely.

'Do you still? I haven't heard any bugle calls coming from your hill.'

'We only play them now out of the line and then just to mark the events of the day. Reveille, for example.'

'We do that, out of the line,' he said. 'So that's a crown. Whose is it?'

'It's the Prince Regent's crown. He was our colonel-in-chief.'

'Prince Regent?'

'King George IV before he was king.'

'You a royalist?'

'I suppose I am. I've never thought of it like that.'

'I'm a republican. What's that writing on the badge?'

'Those are the names of our two great battle honours. They're written on the strings of the bugle. I'm surprised you could see them. Waterloo and Washington.'

'Washington? *Washington?*'

'Yes, Washington. We beat you there in the War of 1812 and burnt the White House down. That's why it's called the White House. You had to paint it white to hide the damage.'

'Well I'll be darned. Hey, captain. These guys say they burnt the White House down in the War of 1812.'

The captain and Dermot had finished admiring each other's weapons and the position and were walking towards us.

117

'What's that, Loot?'

'These guys've got Washington written on their cap badge. They say they burnt the White House down in the war of 1812.'

'Time they did it again,' said the captain.

We all laughed. They produced more beer.

On the way back to the company position, we took a wide detour to avoid the minefield. Dermot reported he had persuaded the captain to mark the minefield and co-ordinate some interlocking fields of fire to protect each other.

'How did you get on, serjeant-major?'

'I got you a box of cigars, a pack of American capes, which are better than ours, for the lads going on patrol in the rain, and a Thompson sub-machine-gun for myself.'

'That's a good haul. What did you have to pay?'

'Not a cent. All scrounged.'

'Excellent. What about you, Ellis?'

'They gave me a beer or two.'

'Nothing pinched off my jeep?'

'Nothing, Sir.'

'And you, Miles?'

'I nearly lost my cap badge,' I said.

'They liked that story about the White House. It always raises a laugh.' When we reached our jeep head, Dermot walked round his jeep.

'Where's my brand new sign, Ellis?'

'On the front bumper, Sir.'

'No it isn't.'

'Oh, no.'

The badge had gone.

Dermot looked at Ellis. Ellis flinched.

'Oh, fuck,' he said.

'That's no way to speak to your company commander,' said Budd. 'I've put a man in the nick for less.' Then turning to Dermot he said, 'Don't worry, Sir. Tom Body will knock you up another. Cheap at the price, I'd say.'

As I followed Dermot up the hill I wondered if Budd hadn't traded it.

'What do you think of our American allies?' Dermot asked when we had settled in his bunker and were drinking tea.

'Very friendly.'

'Only when our interests are their interests too.'

'Are they rather simple?'

'Simplistic. They can be very single minded and sometimes quite naïve in the process.'

'I rather liked them.'

'They can be charming and ingratiating but I wonder how much they mean it. What do you think of them as soldiers?'

'I can't make them out. They seem to be all over the place, even the marines.'

'The marines are the best. America is an industrious and industrial nation. Americans like material. Whether it's Coca Cola or ammunition they need tons of it to move, and then they can move fast.'

'But they don't do the simplest things like marking their minefields.'

'They only know how to attack. Until Pearl Harbour they'd never been attacked. Why should they know anything about defence? Do you know that at West Point they don't study defence?'

'They know how to build defences.'

'That's engineering. They're great engineers.'

'I sometimes think they are as different from us as the French and the Germans.'

'They are. We think they're the same because we think they speak the same language. The words may be the same but the meaning can be different.'

'How do you know all this?'

'We saw them in Italy. Always remember they're out for

119

themselves, and they find it difficult to see any other point of view.'

A week or two later, at one of his regular sessions, Dermot told us that we were to be part of a Commonwealth division.

'You know,' he said, 'how our brigade has been working with American divisions commanded by American generals. Well, now we are to form part of the Commonwealth division made up of a Canadian brigade and two brigades of British and Australian troops. It's to be commanded by a Scotsman.'

We had heard of him. He was known as General Jim and was a very good soldier.

'This will also solve some of the problems of command. One of the reasons that the Gloucesters got into trouble is that the American general didn't understand their commanding officer's understatements. I think this is a good move and will please everyone.'

It pleased us.

'We're going into reserve. There is to be a parade to mark the formation of the division. And the band has arrived from Hong Kong to cheer us up.'

The Band played at the parade to mark the formation of the Commonwealth division. It was the only British military band in Korea at the time and it impressed and surprised everyone who heard it. We were proud that it was ours. Nightly it put on performances for us while we were in reserve. Then it left for a series of engagements with the US Eighth Army. The band and its music made us feel rather good, very 'All Sir Garnet'.

We were in reserve for only five days, enough to get clean and catch up on our sleep, when we received new orders.

'The Commonwealth division,' said Dermot, 'is to make a bridgehead across the Imjin, crossing from east to west about ten miles north of our last position. General Jim wants to get closer to the enemy. He says it doesn't make any sense our sitting behind the Imjin. We're not getting anywhere patrolling so far from the enemy and we're not putting any pressure on him. The Canadians are to capture the bridgehead. Then our brigade will take over from them and expand it. We hand over this position to the US marines. We move tomorrow.'

# Chapter 8

## *It happens in no man's land*

'I've no orders to hand over to anyone.'

The Canadian captain was truculent. He tried to stare Dermot down. 'No orders, at all,' he said again.

'I have clear orders to take over Hill 172 from D Company Thirty Third Royal Canadian Regiment,' said Dermot. 'This is Hill 172, isn't it? You are D Company Thirty-third RCR, aren't you?'

Dermot said it with a charming smile.

'Yes. Who are you?'

'X Company, Second Battalion PRLI. We have orders to take over from you immediately. Why don't you check with your headquarters?'

'I don't understand this,' said the Canadian captain and disappeared into a dugout.

Burgo, Tim, David Sartorius and I stood behind Dermot and waited. Earlier in the morning we had crossed the river and moved up to Hill 172 on which we now stood to relieve the Canadians, who had captured the bridgehead three days earlier with minimal resistance. Dermot had brought us up the hill. The rest of the company was sitting at the foot of the hill, waiting.

The Canadian captain returned.

'My CO and my adjutant are not available. I've been told I'm to stay put until I get orders.'

Dermot folded his arms across his chest and smiled. I could see he was irritated. There was a crump from behind us, followed by a high whistle over us and a bang out beyond the hill.

'What the hell is that?' said the Canadian captain. There was another crump followed by a bang.

'Sounds like someone ranging his mortars,' said Dermot.

'Who the hell's doing that?'

'I think it's our mortars who've taken over from yours.'

Dermot turned to his wireless operator.

'Are we in contact with Battalion headquarters?' he asked.

'We were a moment ago, Sir.'

'Good. Give me the headphones and mike.'

Dermot talked into the microphone for a little.

'I've just spoken to my commanding officer. He's with yours. You'll get your orders and he says we should go ahead with the handover.'

'I can't do anything until I get orders myself.'

'Quite right. Perhaps while we wait you would be so good as to brief us on your position.'

'I can't do that without orders.'

'Well then, we'll have a good look round ourselves. Come on you lot,' he said turning to us, 'follow me.'

'You can't do that.'

'I'm afraid we must.'

A Canadian soldier emerged from the bunker.

'Adjutant on the line,' he said.

At that moment there was another crump and bang. The Canadian captain scuttled into the bunker. Two minutes later he came out quite slowly, looking rather put out.

'My adjutant has now received orders for us to hand over to your battalion. I need ten minutes to brief my company. Then I'll brief you and take you round. We'll start the physical handover in thirty minutes.'

'I knew it would work out,' said Dermot.

123

Dermot, David Sartorius, Burgo, Tim Seymour, Serjeant-Major Budd and I were lying, about five yards apart, on the top of Hill 172. We were looking over a deep, undulating and wide valley covered by paddy fields and shrubs. Two miles across the valley was a range of hills. Behind that range was the main Chinese position, four to five miles away.

'How did it go?' asked Dermot.

Burgo was the first to speak.

'Rather well. Best position we've taken over, better than taking over from the Yanks. Considering they were only here for three days they've performed miracles.'

'I agree,' said Tim.

'You're being unusually quiet, Miles.'

'Burgo has said it all. They were very co-operative and professional once they'd decided to move.'

'Kind, too,' said Tim. 'They left lots of goodies.'

'What about you, David?' Dermot asked.

'There's a fine OP and everything's in order.'

'Serjeant-major?'

'I've taken over sufficient supplies of ammo and water. It's lucky they use the same ammo otherwise we'd be up Queer Street.'

'Dermot?' Burgo asked, 'Why wouldn't their company commander hand over?'

'He wasn't their company commander.'

'Eh?'

'He was the company 2i/c. The company commander was asleep, or should I say sleeping off the after effects of excess. He'd had the orders but he hadn't passed them on. That's why his 2i/c was so, shall I say, protective.'

'Dutch courage?'

'Not at all,' said Dermot. 'Last month he won the DSO. His men would follow him anywhere. He just likes his bottle. Now to business. We've obviously got to go on improving the position but our main task is to locate the enemy. On the hills in front of us you can see three prominent points of high ground. To the right is Hill 169, to the left of it and further away is Hill 272 and further to the left is Hill 211. Got them? Good. Air reconnaissance says they're all held but quite lightly. My guess is that there's not more than a platoon on each as a screen to protect their main position. We're going to have to identify their positions exactly. We might even be asked to get a prisoner. The point is that here, on this position, we can see the enemy positions, and we'll be in direct contact with him. He will be patrolling as well as us. We'll have to be very alert. We've had it cushy these last few weeks.'

I thought of the nights I had spent lying in ambush at the ford and wondered what Dermot meant.

Suddenly, to our right, there were shots, the hammering of short bursts of a Bren gun and the crack of the Lee-Enfield rifle followed by the rapid burp of Chinese sub-machine-guns.

'Well, well,' said Dermot, 'it's started already. Isn't that from your platoon position, Miles?'

There was more shooting.

'Yes. Big Steel was wiring when I left but he had a standing patrol covering him.'

'Dermot, I think I should go to my OP,' said David.

'Yes, David. See what you can do. There're no patrols out beyond our line, are there?'

'None,' we all said.

'Fire at will,' Dermot instructed David and then to me, 'Miles, perhaps you'd better go and see what's happening and report back here.'

I scrambled back behind the crest and made my way rapidly down and round the hill to my platoon. The firing had stopped. All the men were standing to in their trenches.

'Where's Serjeant Whettingsteel?' I asked.

'Down there, Sir,' said Maxwell pointing down the hill.

Big Steel was with his brother and some men.

'They've scarpered,' he said seeing me.

'Tell me.'

'They seemed as surprised to see us as we were to see them. We were here wiring, not making much noise, when suddenly they come out of that scrub fifty yards away. They saw us and we saw them. For a moment we just stared at each other. Then we both started firing, well Corporal Tidmarsh did – he did well – and they bolted but not before loosing off a few rounds. I think we winged one of them. We've just been searching the scrub. We found this, but nothing else.'

This was a Chinese cap with a red star in the peak. The top was torn by a bullet.

'Was anyone hurt?'

'No, no casualties.'

'Well done. Lucky we put Corporal Tidmarsh out to cover you.'

'Not lucky, Sir. Just routine.'

'Of course.'

'We'll just finish off this wiring. Then we'll come back.'

I returned to Dermot and reported.

'So,' said Dermot, 'Serjeant Whettingsteel thinks he was bumped accidentally?'

'I think the Chinese patrol might have got lost. The scrub there is dense. Once you're off the hill you might be anywhere.'

'What we have to learn from all this,' said Dermot, 'is that the Chinese have lost their shyness and are knocking on our door in broad daylight. It's we who must dominate no man's land. Not them.'

Burgo took out the first patrol, a day patrol as it was felt this was the best way to get to learn the lie of the land. He was to

126

reconnoitre Hill 169. He went out while it was still dark, found a well-hidden vantage point about half a mile from the hill, lay up and observed.

'On the hill,' he said at his debriefing, which Tim and I attended, 'we saw little movement but we got a good idea of their defences. I sketched them. It looks lightly defended, more like an outpost line than a proper position. Once we heard some Chinese moving near us but we never saw them. I decided we'd learned all we were going to and it was time to make our way back. The scrub is deceptive. Once you're in it you can't see much. I was taking a different route back for security and did not realise I had missed our way until we came upon a large open paddy. I thought we were close enough to our lines so I decided to cross it, keeping to one side. I should have stayed in the scrub. We'd gone about a hundred yards when they mortared us very accurately. Corporal Mortimer was killed and Cave was wounded. I got everyone back into the scrub instanter. We had to leave Mortimer's body. I debated whether I should wait till nightfall but then decided I should get Cave back as he was in great pain. We came back in the scrub on a compass bearing. I think we would be better off patrolling at night close to the open ground. The scrub is a bugger.'

'I'm sorry about Corporal Mortimer and Cave. You did what you could, Burgo, and brought back valuable information.'

'How's Cave?'

'On his way to the RAP.'

The RAP was the regimental aid post where the doctor practised his science. It was the first point in the line of medical evacuation.

'Tomorrow morning, Burgo, take a stretcher bearer party to collect Corporal Middleton's body. The Chinese won't interfere with you. They're probably there now searching the body.'

In the morning Burgo led a party to collect Corporal Middleton. He was lying near where he fell. He had been stripped of much of his clothing. The Chinese let Burgo carry him away without interference.

Tim Seymour took out the next patrol. He was to reconnoitre Hill 272. He took a corporal and his wireless operator, having decided to keep to a minimum number. He also chose to go out before dawn and return after dusk, lying up during the day. That way he hoped to avoid being seen by an enemy OP and mortared, as Burgo had been.

Burgo had not taken a wireless. Dermot now made it *de rigueur* that every patrol took a wireless. As voices carry, especially at night, he devised a series of codes that the wireless operator was to use by tapping his microphone. Dermot kept his wireless on all the time. When a patrol wanted to contact him it was to turn on its wireless and send its coded message by tapping the microphone in the agreed fashion.

Dermot and Tim planned the route out and the route back and two sets of codes: one to indicate where Tim was on the route; the other to indicate his situation. They spent time studying no man's land through their binoculars, discussing the route and hideaways. Dermot had told us that he had not coached Burgo enough, and had allowed him to go out insufficiently rehearsed. He did not want unnecessary casualties and he blamed himself for Corporal Mortimer's death.

Tim led his patrol out while all, except those on guard and the standing patrols outside our wire, were still asleep. Dermot saw him off. During the day we heard some machine-gun fire to the right of where Tim should have been. He sent no distress signals so we presumed him all right. When dusk fell he started to send regular signals. He was returning and making good progress. While he was doing this we learned that Andrew Chillingworth, of W

128

Company on our right, had taken out a large patrol that day and had been caught in the open by machine-gun fire. He had lost a man and had three casualties. It was ten o'clock when Tim regained our lines and brought his patrol to be debriefed by Dermot. Burgo and I were there, too.

Tim reported.

'We had no problems following the route out in the dark. We kept out of the scrub, as agreed, and stopped regularly to listen. We didn't find our hiding place until just before dawn as it took longer than anticipated to get there. Corporal Miner spotted a cave about one hundred yards to our left and above us and we moved there. It was ideal. We could see the reverse of Hill 169 and the front of 272. I then realised we probably wouldn't be able to send a wireless signal from inside the cave. As we'd only planned to send one if we got into trouble I didn't think that mattered. We took it in turns to watch and logged the activity on Hill 169. We counted five people come in and out of a bunker. The position seems more like an observation post than a strong defensive one. Hill 272, on the other hand, looked more heavily defended. Though we saw little activity the position looked stronger than the one Burgo sketched on the forward slope of Hill 169. I made a sketch of both positions.'

We studied the sketch, which Tim explained.

'Then we had a dodgy moment. A patrol of seven men came off the back of Hill 169 and approached us. It hadn't rained and we'd been careful to cover our footprints. But they found some and they started arguing about them. They looked up at our cave and two of them began to climb up to us. 'We'll send them to nirvana before they send us,' I said to myself, and woke the others. We got ready to make a suicidal stand. When they were only fifty yards away a Chinese machine-gun started stuttering away on the right flank. The Chinese all turned in that direction. There were some shouts and they all doubled off towards the sound of the firing.

129

Were we relieved? We had no more excitement. As soon as it was dark we made our way back, sending regular messages by wireless. It pissed like hell which slowed us down but the American capes were much more efficient than our ground-sheets in keeping us dry. I suppose it was a bit obvious to hide in the cave.'

'Very well done, Tim,' said Dermot and told him about Andrew Chillingworth's patrol coming under fire.

'When I next see Andrew,' Tim said, 'I must buy him a drink for saving our lives.'

Now it was my turn. I was ordered to reconnoitre Hill 211, the most southerly of the three hills facing us. I decided to take Little Steel and Jugg, my wireless operator. After Dermot had briefed me Little Steel and I spent a long time in the OP studying the ground. We decided to go at night, partly because that side of the valley was more open with less scrub and cover, partly because we wanted to get as close as possible which we would not be able to do during the day.

We worked out routes and codes with Dermot, then rested, had a meal and got ready emptying our pockets and blacking our faces. I kept my signet ring on, which my mother had given me on my twenty-first birthday. It had been my father's. I'm not superstitious but I'm happier with it on. We all carried Sten guns and grenades. I also carried my Smith and Wesson revolver in its holster on my belt. I thought it would be easier to shoot them or myself if one of us was mortally wounded and did not want to fall into the hands of the enemy. Perhaps I had seen too many heroic war films.

We left the hill by the back, walked round to the left and started to cross the valley, stopping every hundred yards to listen. We heard no one. It took us three hours to close with Hill 211. There was some visibility as, though dark, there was a clear sky. We started to climb the hill and found no wire to impede us. Suddenly we stumbled across a trench. We lay still for a while. Big Steel got up and followed it to the left and I followed it to the right. It was a communication trench. At the bottom we found a telephone cable. At one end, I thought, there must be an OP and another OP or bunker at the other end. Little Steel was carrying some wire cutters and I wondered if I should cut the cable. I thought better of it. Instead I got out my compass and took some bearings on all the hills I could see so we could identify the exact position of the communication trench on the map later. We retraced our steps to the bottom of the hill. We waited there for hours but saw or heard nothing. If we had waited longer, which I wanted to, we would have run out of time to return to our lines before dawn. Little Steel nudged me and pointed at my watch. I nodded. We turned on the wireless and tapped into the mike to indicate we were OK and returning.

We took longer to return. I was concerned about running into an ambush and rain slowed us down. When we were challenged, walking through the gaps of the wire in our position, we found the company was already standing to for the dawn. The serjeant-major relieved us of his valuable capes and Dermot gave us tea laced with rum. When the company had stood down and Burgo, Tim, David and the serjeant-major had joined us, Dermot debriefed us.

'You were right not to cut that telephone cable,' Dermot said. 'Let's work out exactly where that communication trench is.'

He placed a map on the table. I identified the hills and the bearings I had taken. Dermot drew them on the map and found they crossed neatly on the south east side of Hill 211.

'Do you think you could find that communication trench again on a dark night, Miles?'

'I don't see why not.'

'This is a wonderful opportunity to capture a prisoner and

this is how we might do it. For the next three nights, David, we'll shell all three hills sporadically between midnight and two. That'll get the Chinks used to it. On the fourth night you, Miles, will go out with a patrol and sit at the foot of Hill 211. We'll then shell all the hills again. As soon as we've stopped shelling Hill 211 you climb it hell for leather and cut the telephone cable. The Chinese will think the cable has been cut by artillery fire and will send a signalman to mend it. You will be waiting for them. You'll knock 'em on the head and carry them home.'

'What a wonderful plan,' said Burgo. 'Can't I do it?'

'No. Miles must do it. He's made the opportunity and he and Corporal Whettingsteel know the geography. It's a long shot. Well, Miles?'

'How many men do you think I should take?'

'At least a dozen to support you and help carry the prisoner back. You decide who they should be. Work out a plan and then let's discuss it. But now take your patrol back to your platoon and get some sleep. Well done, all of you.'

Later in the day Dermot made my platoon change position with Burgo's. Burgo had been in reserve on the back of the hill with Tim's and my platoons forward. Now I was put in the reserve position so I could concentrate on preparing for the patrol.

I kept my plan as simple as possible. I broke my patrol into two parties. Little Steel and I would form the snatch party to catch the prisoner. Big Steel would lead the support group. We would move as one body until we got to the final RV under Hill 211. Then Little Steel and I would climb up to the communication trench, cut the telephone cable and wait. We would each have a pick handle to use as a club. We would have to act quickly. Once the Chinese saw the cut in the cable they'd know it was a trap. The support group would have two back markers. If we were ambushed their orders were to get out fast, observe and take what action they thought fit on the outcome of the ambush. We had one wireless operator who would accompany Big Steel.

Dermot agreed the plan so we built a model of the ground from air photos and briefed everyone. There was a fight for places on the patrol and I had to disappoint some of my men who felt aggrieved they had not been chosen. Big Steel, Little Steel and Corporal Tidmarsh, who was to be in charge of the back markers, spent a lot of time studying the valley through binoculars. I wanted them to be as familiar with the ground as possible.

Another letter arrived from Hugh Jermy. He was impatient to be with us. He complained I was not telling him enough about what was going on. He thought he was missing the action, which he was. In reply I wrote that I thought there would still be lots of opportunities for him when he joined us and he'd be able to profit from our experience. Neither of us mentioned Kitty.

The day came for the patrol. I always get flies in my tummy before an exam, before a race or before a match starts. I was surprised they were not as bad as usual. Big Steel and Little Steel were so steady and the men so taut with excitement that I felt a little elated. Once we started what flies there were quickly disappeared. We went out down the back of the hill, round the bottom and out into the valley. We made our staging posts on time and arrived at the final RV at the time we had planned. We had allowed an hour before the guns started to be sure of getting there. So we waited.

Dead on H hour the guns shelled Hill 211, some of the shells landing only 200 yards in front of us. After ten minutes the guns stopped. I touched Little Steel and we raced up the hill to the communication trench, getting there in three minutes. Little Steel got into the trench, found the telephone cable and cut it. He climbed out and lay on the ground a yard from me. We waited. We had expected some-one would be along within an hour, if anyone were to come. An hour passed and no one came. Another hour went by. I was lying on my right side, with my pick handle in my right hand. Across my chest I had my left arm so I could peer down and look at my watch. My right ear was nearly on the ground, listening. It was not a comfortable position. Little Steel was within touching distance. Anyone seeing us would have thought we were dead. I wondered if anyone would come. I also wondered what Big Steel would be thinking. Our orders were to abort the patrol if no one came within three hours. I could not believe that no one would come. Then I worried if I could stay awake and kept wriggling my toes to keep them alive.

I felt a touch on my leg. I could hear nothing so I looked at my watch. We had been there nearly three hours. I thought Little Steel was touching me to remind me. Perhaps not, for wasn't there a noise along the trench? Yes. I could hear some chattering. It sounded like two men talking to each other as they slowly came along the trench from behind me. I touched Little Steel. They came closer and closer. A yard short of me they stopped and started jabbering. Now, I thought. I rose to my feet, tried to lift my arm, dropped the pick handle and fell into the trench on top of them. My right arm and hand were numb. I grabbed one of the Chinamen with my left hand. I was lying on top of both of them. The Chinaman I was not holding pulled himself free and began to crawl away. Little Steel jumped into the trench and swung his pick handle at him. He missed. The Chinaman dropped his signalling equipment and fled. Little Steel ran after him, tripped on the signalling equipment and fell headlong.

'Corporal, here!' I shouted. I was losing my grip on the Chinaman I was holding, and my right arm and hand were still numb. The Chinaman jabbed me in the balls. I cried out and let go. He got up, started to run down the trench and ran, head down, into Little Steel. He winded Little Steel but the blow on the head floored him. Little Steel recovered and got him in a half-Nelson.

'Got him,' he said.

The Chinaman screamed.

I was feeling better and the blood was coming back into my right arm. 'I'll get out of the trench,' I said. 'Hand him up to me.'

We had not practised this.

I climbed out of the trench and knelt on its side.

'Now.'

Little Steel stood up and pushed the Chinaman up to me, head first. I gabbed him under the arms. He spat at me. I fell over backwards with him on top of me. He kneed me in the balls again and I released my grip. He struggled free, kicked Little Steel on the head, jumped into the trench and ran. Little Steel sat in the trench, stunned.

'Bugger, bugger, bugger,' I said.

'Crafty little fucker, wasn't he?' said Little Steel.

'Let's get out of here.'

Big Steel was waiting for us at the foot of the hill.

'They escaped,' I said.

'We heard,' he said.

'We'd better get going.'

We moved fast. We had anticipated retaliation and moved directly to the south along the foot of the hill and away from the obvious route back to our lines. Sure enough, within five minutes the Chinese were mortaring that route but we were safe, five hundred yards from where the bombs were falling.

When Dermot debriefed us I was ashamed and unhappy. The patrol had gone like clockwork except the key action, which had been entirely my responsibility and had been farcical.

'Don't be disappointed,' Dermot said. 'You did very well. Capturing a prisoner is an extremely difficult thing to do. All

135

right, it didn't come off. The odds were against you. But you will have given the Chinese a terrible shock. Imagine what you did happening in our own lines. We'd be quivering in our bunkers wondering what was going to happen next. If you had pulled it off you'd both have been decorated.'

That made me unhappier.

## Chapter 9

## *Is it all over?*

Far from our names being mud, Little Steel and I had gained kudos and a certain notoriety. We had surprised the enemy in his own lines, outwitted him to avoid his retaliatory mortar bombardment and returned safely without a casualty. Our failure to capture a prisoner was considered unlucky. Our stock had gone up. Colonel Guy regarded it as the turning point in the battalion gaining the initiative in no man's land and the battalion took heart from it.

'There,' said Dermot, several days later, 'I told you so. You did well. Next time you must have a larger snatch party. I should have seen you did.'

I did not get a next time. The following day Colonel Guy sent for me.

'What can he want?' I asked Dermot.

'Better he tells you himself,' he said. 'Ellis will take you in my jeep.'

The jeep, I noticed, was once more adorned with Dermot's personal badge, a replacement run up by Tom Body.

Battalion headquarters was about a thousand yards behind X Company's position, dug in on the reverse slope of another hill, and protected by the bugle platoon, now forty strong and the largest platoon in the battalion. This made battalion headquarters as much a strongpoint as a head-

137

quarters. We took the main track back that was mostly out of sight of the enemy though he did toss a few mortar bombs at it occasionally. Ellis parked the jeep in the jeep head behind the hill and I climbed up to the dugouts. You could tell it was a headquarters from all the wireless aerials branching out of the bunkers.

Colonel Guy was sitting in a camp chair in the sun outside his bunker. He was dressed, as everyone was, in olive green and distinguished only by his air of authority. I saluted him.

'Miles. Come and sit down.'

I took off my beret and sat down in one of the other camp chairs.

'I'm making some changes. Pat Bussell is leaving us for the staff. I want you to take over from him as my intelligence officer. Fancy it?'

'Yes, Colonel. Thank you, Colonel.'

'Don't thank me. You've done well here. I think you've the experience to do it. So does Dermot, though he's sorry to lose you.'

'I shall be sorry to leave Dermot and my platoon.'

'Of course. So you should, but I need you here. You'll find Serjeant Savage perfectly competent to run the intelligence section though you, of course, will be responsible for its actions. I regard you as my personal staff officer and battle adjutant. Percy Smythe is responsible for battalion head-quarters and he spends a bit of time at A and B Echelons. When the battle becomes fluid he stays here and you come with me. I also want you to be responsible for co-ordinating all patrolling. I'm not sure we are as co-ordinated as we should be. We need to assemble and share our experience and knowledge more than we're doing. I'd like you to work with the company commanders on that. Come and join us tomorrow and take over from Pat as soon as possible. He'll show you the ropes.'

I was elated and sad. Elated because this was a promotion,

a step up the ladder. I admired Colonel Guy, we all did, and the opportunity of working with him was God sent. Sad because I would miss Big Steel and the platoon for we had become very close and, in a way, I loved them.

'Well,' said Dermot when I returned to the company position, 'are you happier?'

'Stunned.'

He laughed.

'I said you were going to be lucky.'

'What will happen to the platoon?' I asked.

'We've two new officers, Chris Worthington and Robin Brett. One of them will take over.'

'I meant the Whettingsteels and Tidmarsh, Wildman, Rothwell and the rest of them?'

'Big Steel is to be promoted colour serjeant. He's to take over from the CQMS of Support Company who lost a leg when his truck ran off the road. Foxton is due back with us any day now from his convalescence. He'll take over from Big Steel as platoon serjeant. Little Steel is to be promoted serjeant and will join the machine-gun platoon as a section commander.'

'Do they know?'

'Not yet. Don't tell them.'

'I'm glad for them. Can I take Maxwell with me?'

'Can he drive? Won't you need a driver?'

'I'll have to find out.'

'I'm sorry to lose you, Miles.'

'I'll miss you, Dermot. Thank you for all you've done for me.'

'Don't be silly. Now go and find out if Maxwell can drive.'

I walked back to my platoon, my mind buzzing.

'Congratulations, Sir,' said Big Steel. 'That's a good job. You'll enjoy working with Monty Savage. They call him Monty because he's always saying, "Well, I don't know what the colonel's going to do but Monty would knock 'em for six." Are you going to take Maxwell? He'll be hurt if you don't.'

'Do you know if he can drive? The company commander seems to think he may have to drive me.'

'Knowing Maxwell he probably can.'

He shouted for Maxwell who popped up out of my bunker. He liked lying on my bunk when I was away.

'Yes, serjeant.'

'Can you drive?'

'Drive, serjeant? Are we being motorised?'

'You are if you can drive.'

'It is a competence I have acquired. I don't have my licence with me as I did not think it would be needed in Korea.'

'If you can drive,' I said, 'how is it that you weren't snapped up by the motor transport platoon when you first arrived?'

'I didn't pass the football test.'

'The football test?'

'You have to be good at football to get into the MT platoon.'

'Did you know that?' I asked Big Steel.

'That's why they always win the football,' said Big Steel. 'They cream off the best footballers for headquarter company and the MT platoon when the new drafts arrive, whether they can drive or not. The orderly room serjeant fixes it.'

'Chess is my game, as you know, Sir,' said Maxwell.

'You'll have plenty of time for chess. You're coming with me to the intelligence section. I'm to be IO. You may have to drive me as well as look after me. Think you can manage?'

'I shall look forward to that, Sir.'

I now moved into a new life. At battalion headquarters we still stood to at dawn and dusk and took turns to stand our

140

watches at night. We were also shelled and mortared, especially later in the war. The officers had a mess of sorts, as did the serjeants. That is we had a bunker where we could congregate, have a drink and entertain visitors. Colonel Guy also used it for his orders groups. It was a meeting place more than a mess. We still ate by platoon and section and, in every other way, led the same life as the soldiers.

'Serjeant Savage knows what to do,' said Pat Bussell from whom I was taking over. We were standing in the open outside the intelligence section bunker. Hugh Jermy and I had always found Pat superior and offhand. He was tall with a pasty face, long greasy hair and an affected air. Attached to us from another regiment he would talk about it in a way that implied it was superior to ours. We often wondered why he was with us, and why Colonel Guy tolerated him.

'Ask Savage,' he went on. 'Basically you're responsible for maps and gen.'

'Gin?' I asked.

'Gin, too. Colonel Guy likes his gin. No, gen. You know, information of any sort. You collect it and disseminate it. Backwards and forwards. We'll go to brigade and I'll introduce you to the chaps there.'

'Thanks.'

'You're responsible for prisoners, too, that's if anyone ever catches one. You didn't have much luck, did you?'

I began to dislike him.

'Mostly, though, you need to look after Colonel Guy. He likes pink gin before lunch and whisky and soda before dinner. No ice. Not that there is any.'

'I see'

'By the way, I'm taking my soldier servant with me.'

'I've brought mine with me.'

'I hope he fits in. They're a tight lot, the intelligence section.'

'He's very adaptable.'

141

'Hmm. Well that's all you need to know from me. Let's go and visit brigade.'

'I think I should go and see the adjutant first. I haven't said hello to him.'

'You won't find him much help. Far better to go to brigade.'

'And I'd like to ask Serjeant Savage to brief me first, so that I know something before I go to brigade.'

'I've always thought you a headstrong fart,' he said and he disappeared into the intelligence bunker.

I found Percy Smythe in the operations bunker, shuffling through some papers.

'Miles, welcome. Come in and sit down if you can find a pew. Why is it one can never find something when one wants it? I'm very glad to have you with us at battalion head-quarters. Have you brought your soldier servant with you?'

'I've brought Maxwell. He is a jeweller from Birmingham.'

'Don't think we can find him any work in that line here but he'll be a useful addition to our numbers. You know I commute between here and the echelons?'

'Dermot thought that Maxwell might have to drive me. He can drive.'

'Oh no, I wouldn't do that. He'll have his time cut out looking after you. The intelligence section has a driver, a good driver. Doughty's the name. And don't go telling any-one that your Maxwell can drive. I'll have the MTO bullying me for him. Mum's the word.'

'Of course, Percy.'

'Anything you want to know ask me. What are you going to do now?'

'I'm going to ask Serjeant Savage to brief me. Then Pat Bussell is going to take me to brigade.'

'When you've done that, come back and I'll show you what's going on here.'

I found Serjeant Savage in the intelligence section bunker with two others NCOs. They all stood up. They knew who I was. The bunker was large enough for all the section to work in. Off it, separated by a blanket, was a smaller bunker, which was mine. The blanket was drawn back and I could see Maxwell moving about in it, arranging my kit. In the large bunker were desks made out of old ammunition boxes and planks of wood. Ammunition boxes also served as chairs.

'Which is my box?' I asked. They pointed to one in the corner, set apart from the others. I sat down. They were all civil enough but I sensed some hostility.

'Would you brief me, serjeant?' I asked.

On one wall of the bunker was a map covered in talc, a transparent overlay on which military symbols were super-imposed in coloured pencil. It showed the disposition of all the units on the front and Serjeant Savage explained it in detail.

'Where,' I asked, 'do we get all the information?'

'It comes from the companies and from brigade. It's Corporal Low's duty to keep the map up to date and to ensure all the company commanders and the battery commander have a copy.'

Corporal Low nodded. He was dark and short. I learned later that the others called him Lofty behind his back. A serjeant during the war, he had left the army and had only recently rejoined to get away, the others said, from woman trouble.

'And the other members of the section?' I asked.

'Lance Corporal Witney is my No 3,' said Savage, indicating the other NCO in the bunker. 'He's a draughts-man and is responsible for the maps.'

Witney, I quickly found out, was a pessimist. The others called him Corporal Blanket, partly because of his epony-mous town, partly because they found him wet. He was a fine draughtsman.

'Then there's Snowball and Rumble. They're out with the RSM at the moment helping to strengthen the position.'

143

'And Doughty?'

'He's taken Captain Bussell to brigade.'

'Taken?'

'Captain Bussell said he realised you had better things to do so he went to Brigade to say goodbye.'

'Did he now? Thank you for the briefing, Serjeant Savage. I need to have a word with Maxwell.'

Maxwell followed me out of the bunker.

'It appears the intelligence section has a driver,' I said.

'So I understand, Sir. He's called Doughty.'

'The adjutant says there'll be plenty for you to do here just looking after me.'

'I'm perfectly happy with that, Sir.'

'The adjutant also says not to tell anyone you can drive. If the MTO finds out he'll try and claim you.'

'What – and get me to join those footballing hooligans? No, Sir. Mum's the word.'

Later in the day Colonel Guy called a conference to discuss patrolling. All the rifle company commanders attended, as did Percy Smythe and I.

'Gentlemen,' he started, 'patrol we must. I'm sure you're as pleased as I am that we're winning in no man's land but we must maintain the pressure. I recognise that asking the forward companies to patrol constantly is putting them under considerable strain. I want to discuss how we can share the burden.'

Colonel Guy could be decisive when it was necessary but I found he liked to involve his officers in the broader decisions so that they felt they were working out the plan themselves and became committed to it. His company commanders were all very experienced.

'I also think,' he went on, 'that we need to co-ordinate our patrolling activity more than we have. We've avoided any major accidents by fortune rather than judgement. I welcome your views.'

144

'Perhaps,' said Arthur Hickey, who commanded W Company and had done most patrolling, 'we might distinguish between offensive patrols and defensive patrols.'

'In what way, Hadji?' asked Colonel Guy.

Arthur Hickey, who had transferred to us from the Indian Army after the partition of India, explained. Whether he'd been to Mecca or not he had gained the sobriquet 'Hadji'. He'd spent much of his youth in Persia where his father had been a diplomat. His dark colour and sharp features suggested some Arab blood though I knew his mother had been French. During the war he had fought in the Western Desert and Italy with an Indian division. Hadji liked to sprinkle his speech with a few Anglo-Indian words and phrases. It was not too difficult to understand what he meant.

Dermot, and then Rex Topham, who commanded Z Company, took up the argument. Rex could be fiery. I thought that he might even try and lead a patrol himself, which was not his job. In the war he had commanded a battalion of another regiment in Burma and was much decorated.

'Points well made,' said Colonel Guy. 'Now, do you all know enough about what the other companies are doing and what the flank battalions are up to?'

'I've no idea,' said Tom Warburton, who had taken over Y Company from Horace Belcher when we left Hong Kong, 'what the Highlanders are up to. Could we be told when they're out? The other night one of their fighting patrols came in through our lines and we only knew who they were when we heard the Jocks swearing.'

Tom's grandfather and father had served in the regiment. He was a gentle soul and had fought in north-west Europe during the war.

'The Aussies are the same,' said Dermot, 'though we can generally tell they're not Chinese from their swearing, too.'

The discussion continued.

'What I think we'll do is this,' said Colonel Guy. He proceeded to sum up the discussion clearly and concisely. Then he turned to me.

'Miles, I want you to work up a way to keep all company commanders informed of the night's patrols, both ours and the battalions on our flanks, and to be sure the other battalions know about ours. We can't afford any accidents. Is everyone happy with this? Good. Remember we have to keep up the pressure and there's a divisional order to capture prisoners. I'd like to have your ideas on that. We don't have enough information about the enemy to our front yet.'

Colonel Guy, I knew, had worked out what he wanted to do before the meeting started but the way he got the company commanders to think they had worked it out was masterly. We broke up, all very cheerful, and Colonel Guy's soldier servant, Roberts, and Maxwell handed out drinks.

'Pleased with your new job, Miles?' Tom Warburton asked me.

'I'm very lucky,' I said.

'We all need luck. It's when she turns against you that you need to look out. You know, you look just like your father. I was a second lieutenant at Dunkirk when he brought us out. Seeing you now reminds me vividly of those days. Tragic he was killed in that plane crash. He was going straight to the top. Remarkable man.'

'Would you tell me more about him? He was away so much when I was young I can hardly remember him.'

'Come and see me soon. We can have a long chat.'

'Miles, when are you going to come and tiff with me?' asked Hadji. 'My men will want to see the new intelligence Bahadur. I've the finest OP in the battalion and the best bobachee in the line. Why, we have kedgeree, congee and mulligatawny on tap.'

146

'Bobachee?'

'Cook. I've trained up a Korean porter and taught him a thing or two.'

'Hadji, does this war bear any relation to the last one?'

'Bobbety Bob, no. This is only a skirmish. An ugly one but no more than a skirmish. Is that your man with the drinks? Yes? He'll be useful here.'

He went after Maxwell.

'How are you settling in?' asked Dermot.

'No thanks to Pat Bussell, all right so far.'

'He's an odd one.'

'How did he get a staff job?'

'Colonel Guy engineered it.'

'You mean—?'

'Yes, he was moved on. He'll pop up somewhere one day and no one will be the wiser for it. Best that way, seeing he's not one of us. Colonel Guy's been trying to move him for some time, I know. His regiment will have to deal with him in the end.'

'The intelligence section isn't very friendly.'

'They will be. Pat was an idle bully so they kept their distance. Once they get to know you they'll be different.'

'I'm glad to hear that.'

'What are you glad to hear, Miles?' asked Rex Topham.

'That the intelligence section will relax when they get to know me.'

'I can't think why Colonel Guy tolerated that sod Bussell for so long. Good riddance. We're looking for great things from you, Miles. I wouldn't visit Hadji if I were you. He'll poison you with all that Indian muck. Come and visit me and I'll give you some tips. Hello? Why's Percy left us? Message from brigade, do you think? Things about to look up? You may think this patrolling is fearsome, and of course it is for those that do it, but you wait until the real war starts. Then we'll have some fun.'

147

I wondered if Rex just talked tough or whether he was really fiery. Surely it had to be put on?

Percy re-entered the bunker and handed a message to Colonel Guy. Everyone watched Colonel Guy, who raised his eyebrows as he read it.

'Here's some news,' he said. 'I won't read you the whole message but the nub is peace talks have started.'

'Peace talks?' we said in unison.

'Yes. United Nations representatives have met with representatives of the Chinese Volunteers Army and the Peoples' Republic of Korea at Kaesong and are drawing up an agenda to discuss an armistice.'

There was silence.

'Is it all over, then?' asked Rex.

'Far from it, I'd say. Have you ever tried to negotiate with a Chinaman *and* a Korean at the same time?'

# Chapter 10

## *We attack*

I remember the battle vividly. I was at the centre of operations with Colonel Guy at his tactical headquarters, so I had an overall view of how the battle progressed. We could not see the closely fought actions but we were able to observe most of them from a distance and we learned what was happening, minute by minute, from the wireless traffic.

In fact there were two battles: 'Mansok-San' and 'Hill 220'. Both are regimental battle honours. The first we share with other regiments, notably the Highlanders, the Royal Australian Regiment, the New Zealand Artillery and the Hussars. The second battle honour 'Hill 220' was awarded only to the regiment.

The peace talks made little difference to the war. We went on fighting. After six weeks in the line we moved back behind the Imjin into a tented camp and engaged in some serious training. The RSM built a drill square and got the battalion 'square bashing'; he also ran an NCOs' cadre. Afternoons were devoted to sport. Once again headquarter company won the inter-company football, the Australians beat the battalion at athletics, and we trounced both the Australians and the Highlanders at boxing, and then football.

'Have you noticed,' Colonel Guy said to me one morning, 'that the place is crawling with pheasants?'

'Yes, colonel.'

'And pheasant shooting starts on the first of October?'

'In England, colonel.'

'I don't see why it shouldn't here. You brought your gun, didn't you?'

'Percy Smythe told me to. It's with the RQMS.'

'Good. Miles, organise a shoot, would you? Find out who did bring guns and invite them. Recce the area round here. You'd better warn the neighbours. The bugle major can provide beaters and don't forget to tell the RSM. He does like to know what's going on. We'll have some fun.'

'Yes, colonel.'

'And Miles, when the pheasants are properly hung, we'll have a dinner night.'

'What would you like to drink?'

'What shall we drink? Claret? Do you think you could lay your hands on some claret?'

'I can try.'

'Good man.'

I returned to the intelligence tent where I found Serjeant Savage alone.

'Where're the others?' I asked.

'The RSM has them on the square.'

'Poor buggers. The colonel wants me to organise a pheasant shoot. Let's have a look at the map. Then I'll want Doughty to take me on a recce. Do you want to come?'

'Make an outing, Sir.'

My relations with the section were beginning to build.

We took the bugle major, as the colonel had suggested, recced the area and agreed on the areas we would shoot and the drives. Then I went to find RQMS Quartermain to ask who had left shotguns with him.

'I've yours, Sir, and the colonel's. But most of the officers told me to leave theirs in Hong Kong.'

'Whose did you bring?'

150

'About five in all. I'll check. They're at B Echelon.'

'Have them brought up. We'll need ammunition. No. 6 shot.'

'That shouldn't be too difficult. I can get that from Japan.'

'One more request. Could you get some claret?'

'Claret, Sir?'

'You know, red wine from Bordeaux.'

'Oh, claret, Sir. That's a tricky one. I've not been asked for that before.'

'The colonel said he specifically wanted to drink claret with his pheasant.'

'I suppose he wants silver goblets, too?'

'Now RQ.'

'Silver goblets would be easier than claret, for fuck's sake. What will he ask for next?'

He went off mumbling, 'Fucking hell, now it's fucking claret.'

Later the RQMS reported that Dermot Lisle, Percy Smythe and Tom Warburton had also brought their guns to Korea. I told Colonel Guy.

'Only five of us? Well that'll make it easier to organise. I've a pair in my case. What about you?'

'I've a pair, too,' I said. 'They were my father's. So has Tom Warburton.'

'That makes eight guns. Ask the other company commanders. Any luck with the claret?'

'Not yet, colonel.'

'Keep trying. By the way, I've been asked to brigade for a preliminary briefing. I smell something big in the air. You'd better come along, too. Follow me in your jeep.'

Colonel Guy and I went to brigade headquarters. I was not allowed to attend the brigadier's briefing so I went looking for the brigade intelligence officer to find out what was happening. I ran into Captain Kim, the interpreter. Most Koreans who spoke English, and very few did, spoke with a marked American accent. Not so Kim In Sup, a scholar of Seoul University, who spoke good and accurate English with an eclectic vocabulary, and the occasional American wise-crack. He was short and stocky, with a wide face and merry, sparkling eyes. He spoke Mandarin Chinese and Japanese, too. He wore the uniform of the Republic of Korea Army, or the ROKs as we called them. He was great fun, and always had a fund of stories and a joke. I liked him instantly and made a friend of him.

'Captain Kim,' I said, 'just the man I want to see. I need your help to organise a pheasant shoot.'

'You English do have lovely surprises. A pheasant shoot?'

I explained what we wanted to do and where we wanted to shoot.

'I don't think the villages will object. The pheasants are copious. But I'd better have a word with them. Leave it to me.'

'Thank you so much. Captain Kim, you know everything. My colonel wants claret to drink with his pheasant.'

'Claret and pheasant? Are these code words?'

'No. He wants to drink the red wine that comes from Bordeaux in France when he eats his pheasant.'

'Where's he going to get that?'

'That's what I want to ask you.'

'Have you tried your NAAFI?'

'Yes the RQMS has and reports they laughed.'

'What about in Japan?'

'How am I going to get something like that from Japan?'

'Quite easy. You get someone to bring it. You must have someone coming through.'

'Yes, but I doubt the NAAFI there will have any.'

'No, I can see that. Look, there is an old hotel in Tokyo, called the Imperial, that was favoured by men from your embassy before the war. I've been there. It's old fashioned and never changed hands. If anyone has claret in Tokyo they will. Get your contacts in Tokyo to go there and ask.'

152

'You are clever, Captain Kim. I'll do that. Now, have you seen the brigade IO?'

'He was off to the bog when I last saw him. I'd attend in his tent.'

I found him in his tent.

'Miles,' he said, 'just the person I want to see. Your antennae are working well. Let's go outside.'

We walked out into the open, out of earshot of his section.

'I shouldn't tell you this but you'll learn sooner or later. The American army commander has decided to rattle the Chinese to move things along at the peace talks. He wants to give them a bloody nose and drive them back further beyond the Imjin. He's ordered General Jim to do it. "Jeez Jim," he's reported to have said, "I'm giving you the chance to make your division famous." I'm not sure General Jim thinks it's that marvellous an idea but he's accepted it. He's given our brigade the toughest task. To capture the mountain Mansok-San that dominates our line. I've got some maps and air photos for you. You may as well have them now. Can you read an air photo?'

'I'm no expert but Serjeant Savage and Corporal Low can.'

'They'll need to be expert. This country is hellish difficult to read. Don't worry. I've included a trace with all the enemy information but you'll find the air photos invaluable to study the ground. By the way, it's to be called "Operation Hammer".'

When I got back to battalion headquarters I gave the maps and photos to Serjeant Savage and then sent a message, marked 'priority', to Toby Errington, who had been convalescing in Tokyo and was due to return to the battalion any day, to go to the Imperial Hotel. It was a long shot.

Later in the day Colonel Guy asked me to join him again when he had his first briefing with the New Zealand battery commander and the hussar squadron leader. The latter, I learned, was under Colonel Guy's command for the operation. Colonel Guy had already studied the map and the air photos of the area with me. He laid the map and the trace, with all the enemy positions, on a table.

'Here is Mansok-San, looking like the Rock of Gibraltar,' he said, indicating it with his hand. 'And here, below it, is the track running west that is our axis of advance. And below that is the ridge we have to take. The enemy appear to be here, here, here, and here on all the high ground along the top of the ridge. Look, it's a series of hills, each slightly higher than the last. Then, across the valley, our final objective, Hill 220.' He moved his hand along the map. 'It's a steeplechase with five fences. Looks simple enough.'

He looked at the hussars' squadron leader, Henry Hammersley. Henry was tall. I often wondered how he fitted into his tank. Like all his officers he was dressed differently to us. His shirt was a lighter shade of khaki and he carried far less equipment. What distinguished him most was his headgear, a fore-and-aft cap taller than the rifle-green one we used to wear in Hong Kong and made of blue and red doeskin trimmed with gold lace. Henry and all his officers wore these throughout the campaign.

Colonel Guy looked at Henry and said, 'Your chaps have done some steeplechasing, haven't they, Henry?'

'Not over country like this,' said Henry. 'It's not exactly tank country.'

'No, I didn't think it was, but I'd like you to lead. The Chinese haven't any anti-tank guns. You can motor up on to the objectives and my chaps can mop up after you.'

'We'll do it if we can but the ground looks very soft going and what doesn't is covered with trees.'

'I'm going to send my company commanders up in the air to have a look. You might like to go too?'

'Anything to have a closer look.'

'We can also look at it together from the ground.'

'I'm game, colonel.'

'What about you, Desmond?' he said to the battery commander. 'Can you cover us all the way along the ridge without having to reposition your battery? I need the whole battery on call all the time.'

Desmond Dennis had been in Korea the longest of the three of them. He was tall, lean and a most professional gunner.

'Yes, Sir. I'll find a place where we can do that. You know you'll have the regiment's support too, in fact, the whole divisional artillery if you want it?'

'Either of you see any problems?'

'What are the plans to take the Rock?' asked Henry.

'The Highlanders are taking that. Our job is to protect their left flank.'

'Doesn't our advance depend on them? We can hardly chase along this ridge with the Chinese looking down on us from the Rock.'

'You're right. We can only go as fast as the Highlanders. We'll have to take it in turns, as we'll both want all the artillery support we can get. All the more reason for your tanks to show us the way.'

'Have we got air support?'

'Yes.'

'Do you intend to use it?'

'No.'

There was a long silence while we all looked at Colonel Guy.

'Only *in extremis*,' he said. 'These pilots are as likely to shoot us as they are the enemy. We're going to do it without them. We'll have enough casualties without their adding to them.'

There was another silence.

'Either of you bring a gun to Korea?'

155

'A gun, Sir?'

'Yes, a shotgun. Miles is organising a pheasant shoot to open the season. You're both welcome.'

'I have, colonel,' said Henry.

'You will join us Desmond?'

'I've guns all right but not that sort,' said Desmond, laughing.

'We'll keep a brace of birds for you,' said Colonel Guy.

The bugle major had called for volunteers to beat from the bugle platoon and all had stepped forward. Then Tom Body, a great friend and rival of the bugle major, had shown interest and gathered a group of Korean porters together to beat too, protesting that local knowledge and country skills were more important than favouring the bugles. He also said his porters would pluck the birds. In the end they agreed to share the day, the bugle major choosing about every third man in his platoon on the basis of their countryside knowledge. I gave them different areas to beat and they took bets on the bags we would get from each drive.

We had done the air reconnaissance. I thought it had not helped much. It did not clarify the difficulties of the country we were to attack over and made the ground look easier and flatter than it was, probably because, from the air, the dominance and importance of the Rock, as we now called Mansok-San, was less obvious. The hills were so wooded that it was difficult to get an idea of the extent of the enemy positions. The air photos showed us much more. The following day we were to view the ground from the front line. Today we were to have fun.

Percy Smythe had opted out on the pressure of work, as had all the company commanders except Tom Warburton and Dermot. With the colonel and Henry Hammersley we were only five guns. Captain Kim had agreed to come in case we ran into difficulties with the local population. We were shooting over land not far from the front line that was still being worked. Kim In Sup also wanted to see the shoot, the idea of which amused him. We had visited the villages together and talked to the headmen who had shrugged their shoulders at one more imposition of war.

We started at ten o'clock. I had briefed Colonel Guy on my arrangements and he took charge, putting Henry Hammersley and Dermot on his right and Tom Warburton and me on his left, and declaring no ground game. We walked up the first paddy and then the beaters drove the scrub at the top. Pheasants were everywhere, springing up, fluttering out of the scrub, rising out of the occasional tree. By lunchtime we had over forty brace and Colonel Guy called it a day.

It had been an exhilarating morning, cool, and with more than a hint of autumn. We had not had such an enjoyable few hours since we had arrived in Korea. We felt relaxed and fulfilled, and that included the beaters. For a whole morning no one had thought about the war.

'You're dead-eye-dicks,' said Captain Kim. 'I wouldn't want to be a Chinaman caught in your sights. What a sport.'

'Have some beer?' I said.

'Yes, Sir.'

'Any trouble with the villages?'

'It would be a kind idea to give them some birds, especially if you want to repeat today.'

'We'll do that. I'll come with you. But first let's have lunch.'

Maxwell had produced a shooting lunch: sandwiches (corned beef, of course, but with chutney) and some hard-boiled eggs (heaven knows where from). There was even a bottle of port, which the RQMS had produced. We drank it in tin mugs. There was still no sign of claret on the horizon.

I sat down next to Tom Warburton.

'Did you ever shoot with my father?' I asked him.

'No. I joined the battalion in Aldershot just before we went to France in September 1939 so I missed the shooting season in England, not even a partridge. In France I seem to remember your father shot with the Frogs but I wasn't asked. In fact the shooting near Lille, where we were most of the time, wasn't up to much.'

'You were going to tell me about my father at Dunkirk.'

'It was wonderful being with him. He was the only officer who had been in action before, so every man in the battalion felt himself in good hands. Your father was very steady and composed. Nothing rattled him.'

'That's not how I remember him and my mother.'

'I wouldn't know about that.'

'Rows. Endless rows.'

'Rows? I find that hard to believe. What about?'

'My father's drinking, not coming home when expected, and money.'

'Money? But your father had bags of that.'

'It was my mother's money and she was always complaining he was spending too much.'

'He did spend a lot and he was generous. Do you know on my twenty-first birthday he took me out to lunch? It was the twenty-sixth of April 1940. I was intelligence officer by then. We were in a tiny village on the French and Belgian border, waiting for Hitler to invade Belgium, which we knew he would. Your father discovered it was my birthday. "This calls for a beano," he said. He took me and the adjutant down to the *estaminet*, there was only one in the village, and we each had a six-egg omelette, washed down by a bottle a head of champagne, Pol Roger as I remember, followed by cheese, coffee and kirsch from Alsace. Then your father brought out his cigar case and we all puffed away on Romeo and Juliets, the brand he always smoked. He was something of a romantic, your father. It was one of the best luncheons I'd ever had and I said so. "We had to live on champagne and eggs when we were out of the trenches in the Great War," he said. "I thought it was rougher than that," I replied. "It was in the trenches and when we attacked," he said. "But we never spent long in the trenches at a stretch and we attacked rarely, until the last few months. Much of the time we spent behind the lines, reforming, training and living in the *estaminets*."'

'Tell me about Dunkirk.'

'When Hitler attacked we advanced into Belgium to stop him. It was a rotten plan, or rather the Germans had a better one. They broke through in the Ardennes, split the Allied Front and motored for the channel ports. Every day we retreated and couldn't understand why until we realised we'd been cut off. In the retreat we lost detachments and suffered casualties, as we were fighting the Germans most of the way. Your father kept our morale up and our discipline. He was amazing. We were one of the last to be evacuated. The battalion was under four hundred strong when we marched to the pier at Dunkirk but we marched to attention, and in step. Then we got broken up to get on the boats and it was chaos. Your father left us when we got to England. He was immediately given a brigade.'

'Time,' said Colonel Guy, who had walked over to us, 'to divide the spoils.'

The beaters had laid out the birds in a long line.

'Forty-two brace,' said the bugle major.

'Who won the bet?' asked the colonel.

'Serjeant Body, Sir, but it was a close thing.'

'Then you must share half the bag. Can you manage that?'

'We can, Sir. Thank you, Sir.'

'Thank you for beating. We had some fun, didn't we?'

'Do it again any morning, Sir.'

'Grand. Now we should keep a brace for our brave New Zealand gunners and a brace for the bold hussars, Henry. Then a brace for each company, and we mustn't forget the RSM. If you, Miles, take two for the officers' mess at battalion headquarters, who have I forgotten?'

'I'd like a brace for the RQMS, Colonel, and then, if there are no further claims Captain Kim and I will take the rest to the villages over whose land we shot.'

'Maybe a brace for the brigadier?' said Kim.

'Good heavens, yes. And two for the staff, Captain Kim.'

'That leaves six brace for the villages. Is that all right?'

'More than sufficient,' said Kim.

'That's all settled then. We must do this again.'

But we never had another opportunity to do it again in quite the same way.

The date for the attack was advanced again and again. General Jim was concerned that we kept surprise. With all the preparations and reconnaissance activity he could not be sure that the enemy would not sense we were about to attack. Colonel Guy called his O group to give out his final orders.

'You all know,' he started, 'what we have to do. Now we have to decide how we do it. We are agreed, Henry and I, that the hussars will lead us on to every objective, but they might find the going too difficult in places, so we must prepare each attack with a thorough artillery bombardment. Now who would like to go first?'

'I'd like to lead,' said Rex Topham, commanding Z Company, 'whether the tanks are with me or not.'

'No, Rex. I want to keep you in hand in case we run into unseen trouble.'

'But, Colonel ...'

'No buts, Rex. In this attack you will be the Old Guard and you should be well pleased with that.'

'Could I be the Young Guard and lead, colonel?' said Dermot. 'I am the newest and youngest of the company commanders.'

'Very good, Dermot. You take the first objective and then

160

Tom can take the second and Hadji the third. Everyone happy with that?'

Everyone concurred.

'Right, let's get down to the detail. Miles, start by going over the situation so everyone is completely clear.'

The O group took time. Colonel Guy kept on checking that everyone understood what he was to do. He asked and took questions as he went along. This was not what the Army taught at the time but Colonel Guy liked everyone to be involved in making the plan, so that every participant felt that he owned it. He used to tell me that more cock-ups occurred from orders being given out rigidly than from anything else. Orders had to allow for things going wrong. They had to be flexible. So long as his company commanders understood his purpose then it was up to them to carry it out in their own way.

Finally there was more discussion about Mansok-San, the Rock, overlooking our axis of advance.

'The enemy on Mansok-San will be able to see our every move, colonel,' said Rex.

'They'll be fully occupied fighting off the Highlanders, Rex.'

'Even the Highlanders won't be able to occupy their attention all the time.'

'This is a three-pronged attack. Each of us has to support the others. The Aussies on the right, the Highlanders in the centre and us on the left. Our tanks and artillery give us overwhelming firepower.'

'What about air support?'

'They'll be hammering the Rock in support of the Highlanders.'

'What about supporting us?'

'You know my feelings about air support.'

That evening we were to have our pheasant dinner. The pheasants had hung for a week and this would be our last

161

opportunity to eat them in any comfort. Toby Errington had arrived back and returned to X Company, but not before leaving me a beautifully packed parcel of bottles.

'I could only carry six bottles. I hope that's enough,' he said.

'Toby, how wonderful. Just one bottle would have been something.'

'I was rather pleased to find them. I think you'll like them. They're rather special. The hotel packed half a dozen wine glasses, too.'

'How clever. How much do I owe you?'

'Not that much. They assured me they were pre-war prices. With the advantage of the exchange rate they work out at ten and six a bottle, so you owe me three guineas.'

'Sounds a bargain. I'll write you a cheque. Did you have a good time in Tokyo?'

'Tremendous, but I'm rather glad to be back.'

'I'm glad that you are, Manky.'

'No one's called me that for some time.'

Maxwell and Roberts had told me that I would have to bribe the cooks to prepare our pheasant dinner, but they were delighted to have something else to cook. Being in reserve, we were living on fresh rations so we had roast potatoes, peas and bread sauce with the pheasant which the cooks had roasted. The only thing the cooks funked was game chips.

Colonel Guy had asked the New Zealand battery commander, Desmond Dennis, and Henry Hammersley, the hussar squadron leader, to join us. With Percy Smythe and the padre we were six. There were six glasses and six bottles. Maxwell and I had unpacked the bottles, each bottle lovingly wrapped in straw, and I was amazed at what we uncovered. There were six bottles of Château-Haut Brion, 1932.

'Was that a good vintage, Sir?' asked Maxwell.

'I can't remember but Haut Brion makes good wine in a

162

bad vintage. Nineteen years old. They'll be wonderful. It's a miracle, Maxwell.'

'I'll take your word for it. Are you going to decant them, Sir?'

'We'd better do that. What into, do you think?'

'Water bottles, perhaps?'

'That's an idea. See the bottles are really clean.'

'Of course, Sir. Shall I do it or would you prefer to.'

'I've got rather a lot to do. Could you? You know how to do it?'

'Sir, I've decanted claret before. It would be a pleasure.'

'Oh, thank you, Maxwell.'

We gathered in the officers' mess tent where Maxwell and Roberts had organised everything well. The six glasses and the six aluminium water bottles were on the table with six military-issue knives, forks and spoons.

'Padre,' said Colonel Guy, 'would you say grace.'

'Let us thank the Lord,' said the padre, 'for the comradeship of drinking and eating together the fruits of the vine and the birds of the air. Praise him.'

We sat down and the food was brought in.

'Are we drinking water, then? The padre mentioned the fruits of the vine,' asked Colonel Guy.

'No Sir,' said Maxwell, who had adopted the role of wine waiter, 'claret.'

'Claret! Miles, you got some claret? You'll be mentioned in despatches.'

'Toby Errington brought some from Japan. There's a bottle each.'

'Great heavens, what is it?'

'Haut Brion, 1932.'

'I don't believe it. Where did you say you got them?'

'From a hotel in Tokyo patronised by our embassy there before the war.'

'I hope we'll be as lucky in battle.'

Maxwell poured the wine.

'Modest colour, rather light for Haut Brion,' said Colonel Guy. Then he sniffed it. 'Oh dear, this one's corked. I suppose if it's been in Tokyo for so long one must expect some of them to be off. Lucky we've six bottles.'

Maxwell poured each decanter out in turn. Every one of them was corked or wrong.

'I'm terribly sorry, Colonel,' I said.

'Don't be,' he replied. 'I'm amazed you found any claret at all. Why should these bottles have survived in a Tokyo hotel all these years? The point is, you tried. One should always try. That doesn't mean you must always win. Henry, would you like a glass of beer to go with this delicious pheasant?'

The companies moved into the assembly area the following day, crossing the Imjin and going forward by foot. Battalion tactical headquarters – being the colonel, Desmond Dennis the battery commander and me, with our jeeps, drivers, wireless operators and soldier servants – crossed late in the afternoon, and set up camp next to the mortar platoon. Roberts and Maxwell produced curried pheasant for dinner. Night fell. You could feel the cold now. We were still wearing the olive green uniforms we had worn in Hong Kong. I wrapped a blanket round me and slept fitfully. We were up early well before dawn.

The artillery bombardment on the first objective started at 0500 hours, when Dermot's X Company crossed the start line. It was still dark. We had moved Tac HQ up there to be with them when they started. They went off at a fast pace straight for their objective, the first hill, looking determined. The noise of the guns must have given them comfort. It did me. We could see the shells exploding on the hill. The shelling stopped. There was some small-arms fire. We waited. Then, about 0600 hours, as dawn started to break, Dermot came on the air and reported the hill secure. He said there had been little opposition. The hill, though extensively dug, had only been held by an outpost and most of the enemy had withdrawn when the shelling stopped. He had had no casualties.

We moved Tac HQ up 1000 yards.

'Miles, find out where the Hussars have got to. I don't want Tom Warburton to carry on the attack without them,' Colonel Guy said.

Tom Warburton and Y Company had followed close behind X Company and were waiting at the bottom of the hill for the tanks.

I got Henry Hammersley on the wireless.

'Where are your tracks?' I asked.

'We're across Rainbow' (code name for the Imjin) 'but the going's terrible. Some of my tracks are bogged down already.'

'We've completed phase one. When can you get here for phase two?'

'I can't predict but I know I can't stick to your timetable.' I told Colonel Guy.

'To be expected,' he said.

He turned to Desmond Dennis. 'Can I have the battery, or the whole regiment if possible, fire on the next hill for fifteen minutes?'

'I'll see,' said Desmond, and picked up his mike.

There was a hell of a bombardment going on behind us and we could see the shells exploding on the lower slopes of the Rock to our right.

'The divisional artillery is fully engaged on the Rock,' Desmond reported. 'They've met a lot of resistance. My commanding officer has discussed it with the brigadier. We can't have any artillery support until they've taken their first objective. The brigadier says he'll lay on air support for you.'

'No he won't. Who's commanding this battalion? Tell him we don't need it. We'll manage without.'

'What about our mortars?' I asked.

'Not really enough, but get them to range on the hill now and wait for further orders.'

The mortar platoon commander had joined us. I passed on the colonel's orders, while he talked to Tom Warburton on the wireless.

'Tom's going ahead,' said Colonel Guy. 'I don't really like it but I don't want to lose momentum and Tom's keen to try. Besides, we won't get any trouble from the Rock while it's being attacked so heavily.'

It was full daylight now. We watched Tom's Y Company move up through Dermot's and then advance out of sight.

The mortars started bombarding the hill but we couldn't see what was happening. We waited. After fifteen minutes the mortars stopped. There was silence. Then we heard small-arms firing and grenades bursting, both quite heavy. Then silence.

Colonel Guy looked impassive. We waited. Tom came on the air. They had got close to the hill but had been met by a hail of grenades and machine-gun fire. The leading platoon had had several casualties, including the platoon commander. The mortar bombardment had not been able to make sufficient impression on the heavily wooded position. He had decided not to press the attack and was withdrawing.

'Quite right,' said Colonel Guy. 'We'll have to wait for the tanks or the artillery, preferably both. Miles, ask the hussars how they're doing.'

Henry Hammersley reported they were making slow progress. We waited. We could still see and hear the battle raging on the Rock. Roberts and Maxwell produced breakfast.

'Why don't you want the American Air Force to give us support, Colonel?'

'It's not just the American Air Force, it's any air force in this kind of battle. You have to be precise about indicating your target. This is very imprecise country. The pilots would

166

be very unlikely to identify the target correctly. So they'll fire at whoever they do identify. In my experience they fire at you. If we had our own air liaison officer with whom we'd trained and I trusted him, I'd try it. Remember what happened to the company of Highlanders that was the first to come to Korea?'

'No, colonel.'

'They were sitting on a hill waiting for their air support to arrive before attacking their next objective. The fighter bombers appeared, dived straight at them and dropped their bombs on them. They had terrible casualties. No, it's asking for trouble and I'm not prepared to run the risk of those sort of casualties.'

Desmond Dennis came over.

'We can have the regiment's guns at 1100 hours.'

'What's the time now? Nine o'clock? Fine. What about the tanks, Miles? Any progress?'

I got on to Henry Hammersley on the wireless. He told me to stop bothering him. He would contact us once he knew when he could get some tanks up to us. He was abrupt and sounded exasperated.

'No progress to report from Henry,' I said to Colonel Guy.

'Then we'll have a thorough artillery preparation before Tom attacks again,' he said.

Tom decided that it would be better to attack from the left flank in his second attempt. That would allow X Company to give him covering fire. Colonel Guy ordered the machine-gun platoon up to give support. The mortars made a second bombardment.

Tom's Y Company attacked at 1130, with massive support. Dermot later told me that he watched the hill slowly disintegrate under the bombardment, trees falling this way and that, the hill seeming to move with the explosions. As Y Company swept over the hill and into the trenches he could see the flash of bayonets and the enemy running for their lives.

167

Tom reported the hill taken with no casualties and that he had captured an army's supply of grenades; but he had come under heavy fire from a hill a few hundred yards to his right front.

'Have we still got the guns in support?' Colonel Guy asked Desmond.

'Yes.'

'Let's use them, then. Train them on that hill and smash it.'

Then he talked to Hadji and ordered him to take the hill with W Company and with covering fire from everyone. Hadji moved fast. Within thirty minutes he reported the hill taken. He had had some casualties but he had captured many prisoners and a lot of equipment. In clearing the hill he said his men had to fight with the bayonet and had killed over a dozen enemy.

'What news from the hussars?'

'None, colonel,' I said.

'Then I think I'll call it a day. If we go any further we'll over-expose ourselves. I see there's some progress on the Rock, but not enough.'

We could see and hear another battle going on there.

'Let's consolidate on these positions,' Colonel Guy went on. 'Bring Z Company up on the left flank. Tac HQ will make a position with the mortars. Tell battalion HQ to remain where it is and to get working on re-supply. And tell them we need the RSM up now with the ammo.'

I moved Tac HQ alongside the Mortars while Colonel Guy went up the hill to take a look at the lie of the land and talk to Dermot. The enemy started to mortar our positions, not heavily but enough to annoy and cause a casualty or two. He did not touch us. He probably could not see us. Later in the afternoon a troop of three tanks arrived. I walked over to them.

'Advance party?' I asked.

'I'm afraid the only party,' Roddy Kington, the troop commander, replied. 'This country's impossible. All the others are bogged down, including Henry. They'll pull themselves out eventually but not today. What do you want us to do? You seem to have done rather well without us. I've a composite troop, all tanks commanded by officers.'

I looked at the other two tanks. Officers, wearing their tall red and blue fore-and-aft hats trimmed with gold lace, were looking out of the turrets.

Colonel Guy came across.

'Well done, Roddy,' he said.

Roddy Kington jumped down from his tank and saluted.

'I know we're late, colonel,' he said, 'but I'm surprised we got here at all. We've supplies we could take up to the companies. The going is better the higher we get. It was the swampy paddy that did for us.'

'Show me your map,' said Colonel Guy.

Roddy produced his map and Colonel Guy instructed him on the company positions and what he was to do.

'When you've done that, laager back here with X Company for the night. I'll want you to go with them tomorrow.'

That evening Colonel Guy ordered Dermot to capture the last hill on the ridge by 0900 hours the next day with the troop of tanks under his command.

Maxwell and Roberts served curried pheasant again for our dinner.

'So far, so good, colonel?' I asked.

'We've got off lightly so far, Miles. I'll be a much happier commanding officer when the Highlanders have taken that rock,' he said. 'I'll be happier, too, when Roberts and Maxwell run out of curried pheasant. Have we any whisky to take away the taste?'

## Chapter 11

# ... and attack again

It was a long night but there was no trouble from the enemy. We were up before five, had a quick breakfast of tinned frankfurters and beans and then moved Tac HQ up to the top of the hill, so we would be able to watch the attack and get a better idea of what might be happening. We left the jeeps where they were. The wireless operators put their sets on their backs. We were on foot now, like the rifle companies.

Colonel Guy chatted to Dermot. I talked to Robin Brett, Serjeant Foxton and my old platoon, wishing them luck. Then I found Burgo and his platoon.

'I wish I were going with you,' I said.

'Don't be a damn fool, but I wish you were,' he replied.

I couldn't think of anything else to say.

'Where's Manky?' I asked.

'Forward. He's leading.'

I walked forward fifty yards and found Toby Errington.

'How was the claret?' Toby asked.

'I'm sorry to say that it did not quite live up to its promise.'

'But it was drinkable? You enjoyed it?'

'Undrinkable and unenjoyable. All corked or over the top.'

'Oh dear. But you might say that over the top is the order of the day.'

'Where did you find it? I never asked.'

'In the corner of an old store room in the Imperial Hotel, as you suggested. There was an open case, half full. It looked as though it had been sitting there since 1941. I did rather wonder about the condition.'

'Funny how wine doesn't mind the cold but hates heat. It was rather too well cooked.'

'My guess is that it belonged to somebody at the embassy who had to skip off in a hurry after Pearl Harbour. Oh dear, all that trouble for nothing. What did you do?'

'We drank beer.'

'What did Colonel Guy say?'

'He was rather decent about it. He said that when we came out of Korea we wouldn't have you on the mess committee as the wine member.'

'Thank God. I suppose you want your cheque back?'

'Only if you did it deliberately. Did you?'

'There was no choice. At least the bottles looked pretty. Admit that. How awful. Now leave me to ginger up my lads.'

I rejoined Colonel Guy. It was 0630 and light enough for the tanks to see their way. The artillery bombardment started. Dermot and X Company moved off, with the three tanks moving in bounds, the platoons spread out in open order. They had a mile and a half to go, covered by our artillery bombardment all the way. It was a heavy preparation. We watched them disappear over the hills and picked them up again as they climbed the next incline. They were moving with the rising sun behind them into what was still a dark sky in the west. If the enemy was watching he would be able to see them silhouetted from time to time. But, in the weight of the bombardment going down on his position, any enemy not deep in his bunker was risking certain death. The hill was exploding, trees being thrown bodily out of the ground. When the bombardment stopped less than half the trees were still standing and none was untouched.

Colonel Guy decided to move Tac HQ further forward so

that we could get closer to the action. He told Tom Warburton and Rex Topham to join us. He had already ordered Rex to move his company on to the hill Dermot's company had just left.

'When did you last watch a battle like this?' asked Colonel Guy.

'In the desert there were vantage points,' said Hadji, 'but you often couldn't tell which side was which, the battles were so fluid, and whether what was coming at you was a line of garries or the real cheese. Later, in Italy, one could sometimes watch a pukka battle like this, but the Krauts would generally be shelling one. Why aren't the Chinese shelling us?'

'It looks as though we've caught them by surprise and they're not prepared.'

'I still don't understand why we're not being shelled. No more than a little cutcha mortaring and shelling last night, nothing first-chop, and now X Company is advancing across open ground and getting off buckshee.'

'They've always been short of artillery,' said Rex. 'I wonder if they've any anti-tank guns?'

'There wasn't a sign of one on the air photos,' I said.

'Yes, Miles, but you can hide one in an emplacement and push it out at the last moment.'

I refrained from saying we had not identified any emplacements either. Rex was not a man to cross swords with.

'At least they won't have those 88mm anti-tank guns the Germans had,' said Tom Warburton. 'What was so unfair about fighting the Germans was that their anti-tank guns outranged our tanks and their tanks outranged our anti-tank guns.'

'You're right,' said Hadji. 'Most of their weapons were better than ours. It's a wonder we won. Now we've finally got a pukka tank in the Centurion and it's a bandicoot in this country.'

'They should have given Sherman tanks to the hussars like

172

the Canadian cavalry have. Far more manoeuvrable on this sort of ground.'

'What happened to Tom Body's Sherman? It would have been useful today.'

'I made him give it back to the Canadians,' said Colonel Guy.

'Unlike you, colonel.'

'Better he gave it back than have a row with the Canadians. The brigadier would have taken their side. Besides it was deflecting Tom from his proper duties.'

'It was like confiscating a schoolboy's meccano set.'

'Let's see if Dermot can confiscate that hill from the Chinese.'

The bombardment had now stopped and, through my field glasses, I could see the tanks mounting the hill, firing at point blank range into the defences. Men were scurrying on to the hill and into the trees in small groups. The sound of firing increased, especially the rattle of machine-guns and the crack of grenades. The tanks rolled over the hill out of sight. Now and again we could see groups darting about the position, accompanied by bursts of fire. We waited. The activity flared up again. One of the tanks returned and there was a lot of action on the right of the hill. Then it died down. We waited. There was no more firing. Sometime later a group of Chinese, hands above their heads, wound its way down the hill under escort. Well before nine o'clock Dermot reported the hill taken and secure.

As soon as the action on the hill died the noise of battle started up to our right on the Rock. The top of the Rock was under heavy bombardment and we saw groups manoeuvring on the lower slopes.

'They're having a much tougher fight over there, colonel,' said Rex.

'We don't yet know how tough a fight Dermot has had,' Colonel Guy replied.

'Shall I ask for a full report, colonel?' I asked.

'No. Dermot will tell us when he's ready. We can't do anything more until the Rock is taken. I hope they manage that soon.'

'We're even more exposed now than we were yesterday,' said Rex.

'Exactly, Rex,' commented Colonel Guy.

Dermot came up on the wireless. He reported over forty enemy had been killed, and not just by the bombardment. There had been some hand-to-hand fighting. They had captured fifteen prisoners and much equipment, including a machine-gun, some light-machine-guns, a bazooka and two mortars. The rest of the enemy had withdrawn, though the tanks had pursued them and caused more casualties. He had had one man killed and six wounded, including Burgo Howard.

'Report this to brigade, Miles,' said Colonel Guy. 'Ask them if they found out anything from the prisoners we sent back yesterday. No, better, ask them if Captain Kim can come up and interrogate the prisoners we've just caught. I want to know what they can tell us and get any information they might have about Hill 220, our final objective. We can't have a go at that until the Highlanders have captured the Rock, but we can make use of the time meanwhile. Rex, you'd better be at fifteen minutes notice to move.'

'A job for the Old Guard at last, colonel?'

'Maybe.'

I made my report to brigade.

'I still can't understand,' said Hadji, 'why we're not being shelled.'

'They're too occupied with defending the Rock,' said Colonel Guy.

The Rock was shaking with another bombardment. I could not see a tank anywhere on that hill. The Highlanders were having to take it with artillery support only.

Prisoners were one of my responsibilities. Normally I would send them back to battalion main headquarters, where Serjeant Savage would send them on to brigade. When those Dermot had just captured arrived at Tac HQ I kept them to wait for Captain Kim. Maxwell and Roberts guarded them, which made a change from making curried pheasant. The prisoners were a sad bunch and they looked terrified. We kept them downwind. They smelled vile.

We watched the Highlanders assault and take a kidney-shaped ridge half-way up the Rock but, it seemed to us, not without casualties. Nor could we see any Chinese withdrawing. The bombardment on the top of the Rock continued.

'How many guns would you say are bombarding the Rock now, Desmond?' asked Tom Warburton.

'More than just our brigade's. I would say probably all the division's guns,' said Desmond Dennis, our New Zealand gunner. 'Once in Italy I had to call the corps artillery, and that was three divisions, to break up a German attack. We broke the attack but I couldn't hear for a day.'

'It sounds as if the bombardment is getting heavier,' said Hadji.

'There're some heavier guns firing now,' said Desmond, 'the ones the Yanks call Persuaders. They make a lower pitched sound when fired and you can see a larger explosion where they land. Look now.'

'The Persuaders are corps artillery,' said Colonel Guy. 'It looks as though they may be in the final furlong and they're giving it everything they've got.'

We watched the battle on the Rock and listened to the fury of the guns. It was a long final furlong.

Maxwell tugged my arm.

'Sir, that ROK officer friend of yours is here,' he said.

Captain Kim had arrived and was talking to the prisoners. I walked over. The prisoners were talking freely and angrily. No 'name, rank and number only' for them. There was a stream of chatter, and probably abuse, the way they were talking, and Captain Kim was listening carefully, asking questions only occasionally. After fifteen minutes he stopped and beckoned me over. The stink was overpowering.

'I've got as much as I'll get for the moment,' he said. 'I'll take them back, but let me tell you what they've said.'

'Let's get away from this stink. Come and tell the colonel direct,' I said. I edged away from the prisoners and we joined Colonel Guy and his group.

'Morning, Captain Kim,' said Colonel Guy, 'Have you learned anything useful?'

'Yes, Sir. It's fairly straightforward what this group is saying and what the prisoners you sent back yesterday said. They were not expecting an attack and were completely surprised. They certainly were not expecting such a bombardment. Most of all they were amazed by the appearance of tanks. They did not believe tanks could operate in this country and they had no anti-tank guns. They were terrified by the bombardment but they were even more terrified by the tanks, which apparently shot into their bunkers and trenches at point-blank range and there was nothing they could do about it.'

'Why haven't there been any counter attacks or shelling?'

'They say their division, it's the 177th Infantry Division, has little artillery. They are from a battalion of the 365th Infantry Regiment and they only have mortars and limited ammunition.'

'What do they say about the Rock?'

'They're thankful they're not on it. The bombardment they suffered was bad enough. The Rock is held by another battalion of the 365th Infantry Regiment. They don't hold out much hope for them.'

'And Hill 220? Do they say anything about that?'

176

'They've no personal knowledge of it, but they think it's strongly held.'

'Thank you so much, Captain Kim. If you find out anything else you think would be useful to us you'll let us know, won't you?'

'Most certainly, Sir. It's a great pleasure for me to be able to assist you. May I thank you for what you are doing to help my country.'

Captain Kim saluted and left with the prisoners.

'I'm not at all sure what we are doing to help his country,' said Colonel Guy. 'Look at it. Shattered wherever we go. Hundreds of thousands killed. Maybe millions. I'm glad he thinks we're helping him.'

We turned our attention back to the Rock.

'Rex,' said Colonel Guy, 'if the Rock is captured by midday it'll be time for your Old Guard. I'll want you to take your company through Dermot's and capture Hill 220. We can't do it until the Highlanders have taken the Rock. I'm going to move my Tac HQ up to Dermot's hill. You come with me and we'll look at Hill 220 from there, but you are not to move your company until the Rock is taken. We're taking a bit of a risk moving forward, but what's life without risks?'

The wireless operators put their sets on their backs and Colonel Guy, Desmond Dennis and I trudged in the footsteps of Dermot and X Company, with Rex and the other company commanders. As we came closer to the hill we could see the devastation of the position and could smell the reek of cordite. We had a great welcome from the soldiers who were digging in, grinning through the grime and sweat on their faces. They directed us to Dermot. He had set up an OP on the far side of the hill. We had to find our way through the devastated wood but a path had already been hacked out. As we came over the top of the hill we saw the three tanks about 200 yards down the hill and a hundred yards apart, their guns trained across the valley. All the time I had been looking out for Burgo, wondering how badly wounded he was and where he could be.

'Well done, Dermot,' said Colonel Guy.

'Thank you, colonel.'

They looked at each other kindly: the one in gratitude for a job well done, the other in gratitude for recognition.

'Show us the ground,' Colonel Guy asked. Dermot put us into some Chinese trenches he had made into his observation post.

'There's Hill 220,' he said, pointing at a wooded prominence across the valley on the western end of the Rock. 'We haven't had any interference from it but we've seen movement. My guess is it's well held.'

Along the bottom of the valley ran the track that was our axis of advance. Beside it ran a stream.

'Well, Rex?'

'I'd like the three tanks to lead me on to the hill as they did for Dermot and I'd like the longest possible artillery preparation.'

'You can have the artillery preparation when we get the guns. We'll have to ask the troop leader if he thinks he can get his tanks across that stream and paddy. Miles, would you ask him?'

I spoke to the troop commander on the wireless and reported back.

'He says he couldn't cross the stream without a reconnaissance on foot. If you want to attack now he proposes he sits on the hill and shoots Rex in from here. It's under a mile, well within range. He's already had a good look and he can see the enemy positions.'

'That troop commander is a very able young officer,' said Colonel Guy. 'I think you should accept that, Rex. It won't have quite the same element of terror for the Chinese but you'll have pinpoint direct fire. Take your time to think this through. Discuss it with the troop leader yourself.'

Desmond Dennis was called by his wireless operator. He returned to say that the Rock had been captured and we could have the division's guns when we wanted.

'There you are, Rex. What's the time now? Ten minutes to midday. Capture Hill 220 by 1600. You may bring your company up immediately.'

Rex started to talk on his wireless set, giving orders to his company.

'Where's Burgo?' asked Colonel Guy. 'Is he badly hurt?'

'He caught a bullet in his left arm. He was clearing some trenches that suddenly sprang alive. He refused to go back and stayed with his platoon until the position was cleared. They did well, especially Burgo. They wrapped him up and put his arm in a sling. I had to order him back a few minutes ago. You must have just missed him.'

'I'm glad it's not too serious. Who was killed?'

'Flint, colonel.'

'Flint? A regular wasn't he? I don't think I knew him that well.'

I knew Neolithic Flint, as they called him. He had been in Little Steel's section in my platoon. Big Steel had named him the weak link. He was always getting into trouble or doing something silly like pissing in his trench. Little Steel had gone to great pains with him but he never changed.

'Poor Flint,' I said. 'He was in my platoon, colonel.'

'I expect you'll want to write to his parents, too.'

'That would help,' said Dermot.

'Of course,' I said.

'Miles,' said the Colonel, 'it's time Tac HQ ate. Let's get behind the hill.'

'Follow me, colonel,' said Dermot.

He led the way back to a Chinese bunker he had appropriated. We sat outside it on the ground in the sun. Roberts and Maxwell brewed some tea and produced some cheese and biscuits. We had not had anything to eat since five o'clock that morning.

179

'What did you do with our shotguns?' Colonel Guy asked.

'I sent them back to the RQMS at B Echelon.'

'Have you noticed the pheasants?'

'They're almost tame.'

'When this battle is settled we must get the guns back.'

When we'd finished eating the colonel lay on his back and closed his eyes. Dermot and I moved away a little.

'How was Flint killed?' I asked Dermot.

'It was an accident. I'm glad you didn't ask earlier. He'd got separated from his section. Then he spotted them the other side of a tank and ran across behind the tank to join them. As he passed the tank it reversed. He ran into it, fell under the tracks and was killed. It wasn't the tank's fault.'

'He was fated to meet a tragic end.'

'Will you write to his parents? You knew him best of us.'

'Flint was an orphan. He was brought up in institutions. He joined the army as a boy. He only survived because everyone protected him. The men had a soft spot for him. He was a cross between the platoon's mascot and scapegoat.'

'Serjeant Foxton was upset and he's tough.'

'I wish I'd seen Burgo.'

'Burgo was brave. He went on far longer than he should. I had to order him to leave.'

'And Manky and Robin Brett?'

'They did well, too. Everyone did well. Burgo was exceptional, as was Corporal Wildman. Together they captured most of the prisoners. The Hussar troop commander was exceptional, too.'

'Did the tanks get away unharmed?'

'The Chinks had a bazooka and hit one of the tanks. I asked the tank commander if he'd suffered any damage. He laughed and said it had cleared some of the mud off his tank and if he had been hit more often he'd have had a cleaner tank.'

'This hill's a mess. The colonel will want to have his Tac HQ here for Rex's attack. Can you suggest a good place?'

'It's a big position. There're plenty of places overlooking Hill 220. Let's go and find one. You can see how intricate the defences are.'

I could.

Rex attacked with Z Company at half past two. A heavy artillery preparation covered his approach and slowly demolished Hill 220. The tanks fired over his head and kept firing until he was right on the position. The men doubled up the hill in waves and disappeared into the trees and scrub. The firing went on for a long time. When, just before four o'clock, Rex reported the hill taken we could still hear firing.

The tanks advanced into the valley. We watched the tank commanders climb down from their vehicles and reconnoitre the paddy and the stream on foot. After a little they returned to their tanks and, one after the other, they crossed the stream at the same point and motored up on to Hill 220 and over its western side.

Colonel Guy ordered Dermot to stay on his hill and the other companies to form a tight defensive position behind Hill 220. He moved Tac HQ across the valley on to a spur beside the mortars, where our jeeps caught up with us. So did Henry Hammersley, motoring up with three more tanks behind him.

'In the nick of time,' said Colonel Guy. 'The Chinese will counter-attack any moment now.'

Some shells fell on the track where the porters were lugging up our supplies on their A-frames. The porters scattered. No shell fell near us. No one was hurt, and the shelling stopped. The porters re-assembled. We could still hear firing from Hill 220. We waited, but there was no counter-attack.

181

'What delicacy are we eating tonight, Roberts?' I heard Colonel Guy ask.

'No curried pheasant today. You've eaten it all.'

'What a shame.'

'I know how much you like your curried pheasant. Well, you'll have to make do with C rations until you go shooting again. It's ham and lima beans tonight.'

'I quite like that.'

'I know you'd prefer curried pheasant. I made the pheasants go as far as I could. I even got some off the bugles. You shouldn't have given so many birds to the bugles. We'd have had pheasant again tonight if you hadn't.'

'I'll try and keep more back next time.'

'You do that, Sir.'

'Just as you say, Roberts.'

Dusk fell. The firing on Hill 220 stopped.

'Another successful day, colonel?' I asked.

'I'm relieved the Highlanders took the Rock when they did. I never liked the plan. Rex was right about our being over-exposed. If the Chinks had been more awake they could have given us a bloody nose. As it's turned out, Miles, you can say we've had a bloody good run with not too many casualties. And I'm glad we're out of curried pheasant. I don't think I could have borne another meal of that.'

# Chapter 12

# *Attacked*

For the next three days a furious battle raged to the north of us. The Australians and the Highlanders pressed forward and took all their objectives. The Chinese concentrated on trying to beat them off and left us alone. Occasionally they shelled the track that had been our axis of advance and was now our main supply route. We called it the 'Mad Mile' as any movement along it in daylight generally drew enemy fire. We had sited battalion headquarters next to the track and the shells fell uncomfortably close, so we moved ourselves further up a spur below the Rock.

'Let's go and see how Rex is managing on Hill 220,' Colonel Guy said to me.

We walked up, over the hills and away from the track to find Rex and his men working hard at wiring. The top of Hill 220 was no larger than the size of two tennis courts. The Chinese had built a trench ringing the hill, about ten yards below the crest. Behind the trench were bunkers large enough to take three or four men. Communication trenches connected the bunkers to the main trench and other bunkers. The hill had once been heavily wooded. Now many of the trees had gone, blasted by our artillery bombardment and the tanks when we had attacked it. Rex and his company were surrounding the hill below the trench with barbed-wire entanglements, the wire humped on to the position by the Korean porters.

'Not an ideal company layout, colonel,' said Rex, 'but I can't see any other way to defend it.'

'Nor can I.'

'I could only fit two platoons on the top. My third platoon is on the little knoll behind. They're digging in on the reverse slope.'

'Where is your company headquarters?'

'Between the knoll and the top of the hill.'

'The whole position is quite commanding.'

'Exposed, I'd say.'

To the north you could see the prominent hills held by the Highlanders and Australians and to the south the Canadians. To the front the hill fell away a thousand yards to a valley beyond which were hills, some empty, some occupied by Chinese. Hill 220 was the most advanced position the division held.

'They have to counter-attack,' said Rex.

'The question is when. Dig deep, Rex. I can't believe they haven't got much artillery. Let's have a look at your bunkers.'

We had been standing in the trench on the forward slope. We followed Rex into a communication trench and then into a bunker.

'Big bunker. Strengthen it, Rex. Strengthen all your bunkers.'

We moved back into the trench and looked at the wire in front of it.

'How far down do you propose to wire?'

'We've laid about five yards of wire so far.'

'Double it. Quadruple it. At least the length of a cricket pitch. More if you can. I'll send you up all the wire you can use. Make yourself impregnable, Rex.'

'We'd thought we'd make some fougasse.'

'Fougasse?'

'Yes. We'll dig pits in the wire and fill them with jerricans of napalm. We'll detonate them by cable from the trench.'

'Splendid idea. Fougasse, eh? I'd forgotten about them. I hope you can make them work.'

Rex had scored a point.

'Now show me where you're patrolling.'

Rex talked us over the ground in front of his position, concentrating on two particular areas.

'That hill to our right front is the dominating feature. It's Hill 159. It's clear of the enemy at the moment. If he's going to attack us he'll have to hold that hill. I've a standing patrol on it now. The other obvious point is down in the valley to our left front, where all those tracks meet going in every direction, the one we call Piccadilly Circus. That's clear of the enemy too, at present.'

'I'll get the other companies to make regular sweeps so you can concentrate on building your defences here by night. You're too exposed to do it by day. Miles, let's discuss this when we get back. Rex, are you happy with your DFs?'

DF is the military abbreviation for defensive fire, those areas round a position on which the artillery, mortars and machine-guns range on and record as targets, which can be fired immediately when called for.

'As happy as I can be. We're covered to break up an attack from any direction.'

'I'll ask the RSM to bring you up more ammunition and grenades. You might find some extra Bren guns useful, too. Stockpile, Rex. You're going to need it.'

We moved round to the back of the position. The Colonel spoke to all the platoons. They were cheerful enough.

On the way back to battalion headquarters we called on the machine-gun platoon. All six guns were dug in on a spur behind Z Company.

'Hello Sir,' said Little Steel, beaming.

'You look cosy here, Whettingsteel,' said Colonel Guy.

'We are, Sir. Just waiting for the hordes to walk into our sights.'

'I hope you're prepared to be shelled. Dig deep, Serjeant. Put out more wire. They have to counter-attack. I can't tell you when but counter-attack they will.'

Colonel Guy went on to talk to Tony Strickland, the platoon commander. I stayed and talked to Little Steel.

'Wonderful fields of fire here, Sir,' he said.

'Nice position,' I replied. 'I'm afraid Flint was killed.'

'Yes, I heard that. We can fire down both sides of Z Company.'

'It was an accident.'

'He was always going to have a fatal accident. You see the Highlanders to the north. We can fire right across their position.'

'You did your best for him.'

'It wouldn't have made any difference my being there. He had to learn to look after himself. We can turn the guns almost 180 degrees and cover the Canadians to the south.'

'Serjeant Foxton was quite cut up.'

'Foxton's a tough bastard. He'll do well. Then we can turn the guns back and cover the north of the Rock behind us.'

'The company did well.'

'I hear Wildman lived up to his name. You see the hill in front of Z Company on the Chinese side? They call it Hill 159.'

'They say he was very brave.'

'I heard that. We can harass that fair and square and drop bullets into the valley behind it. Sorry to hear about Mr Howard. They say he did well too.'

'He'll be all right.'

'I hope so. It's a fucking good position, isn't it, Sir?'

'It certainly is. I'm glad you've settled down so well with the machine-guns.'

'They're a fucking good mob. Different from what ours was, but fucking good, too.'

The colonel beckoned me and we went on our way back to

battalion headquarters. Around us were signallers laying telephone lines to connect all the companies with headquarters. We always laid telephone lines in a defensive position.

'Z Company seems rather exposed, colonel?'

'They are, Miles. They are. I don't like that position at all, but it's better we hold it than the Chinese.'

For some days the Chinese did nothing beyond sending over the occasional shell. One morning I was sitting outside my bunker when an American officer motored up the track in a jeep followed by a 155mm self-propelled gun, the one known as the 'persuader'. I waved at them but they drove serenely on up the track towards the enemy.

'Where on earth could they be going?' I asked.

'Peking?' said Serjeant Savage.

'Take the jeep and stop them,' I said.

Serjeant Savage picked up his Sten gun, shouted for my driver Doughty and ran down the hill to our jeep head. By this time the American officer had travelled a few hundred yards. The self-propelled gun was finding it hard going and had dropped behind. Savage, with Doughty at the wheel, chased the gun, caught up with it and started hooting his horn, shouting and waving. The gun motored on. Then it stopped suddenly and Doughty had difficulty braking quickly enough. He only avoided running into the gun by veering off the track. Savage got out of the jeep and shouted at the gun's crew. By now the American officer in his jeep was far ahead, motoring into no man's land. We watched him motor on and turn behind a knoll beyond the end of the 'Mad Mile', towards Piccadilly Circus. Then we lost sight of him. The 'Persuader' turned round and made its way back. The Chinese must have observed all this but they never fired a shot.

'What do you make of that, Sir?' asked Serjeant Savage when he returned to an admiring group of spectators.

'The Americans will give you a Purple Heart for saving that gun,' I said.

'Do you think so, Sir?'

'No, but you did well. Where did the Persuader's crew say they were going?'

'Their officer had told them to follow him.'

'Had they no idea where they were going?' I asked.

'They had a map reference.'

'Did you get it?'

'Yes.'

We got a map out and found the map reference. It was deep in the Chinese lines. We looked at each other, greatly puzzled.

'Why, he must have mixed up his map references,' said Corporal Low, 'and mistaken his target for his gun position.'

As the meaning sunk in we all fell about laughing. The American officer was never seen or heard of again.

In my mail was a letter from Hugh Jermy. He had heard about the battle and was terribly disappointed he had not been with us. He would do anything to join us. Ivan Blessington had said he could go soon but Hugh knew it would all be over by the time he arrived. There was also a letter from Sonia. Kitty had had a miscarriage in Singapore and had been very ill. Sonia hated having to tell me but she thought I would want to know. She was not sure whether Kitty would be able to have children now. In the last paragraph she wrote, 'Do please write to Hugh and tell him to stop worrying about joining you. Ivan has agreed it with your colonel and it's now up to your colonel to send someone to replace Hugh. Ivan says the peace talks will drag on and on and Hugh will see plenty of action. Hugh frets about it and is becoming melancholy, so unlike him. I worry about him. He was unplaced in the racing last weekend, just unbelievable.'

Ten days later the Chinese counter-attacked. Battalion headquarters was tucked in behind a hill so we could not see what was happening but we could hear. As night fell the Chinese artillery opened up, growing in intensity. It was the heaviest bombardment we had seen, all concentrated on Rex and Z Company on Hill 220. About 2300 it stopped. Immediately Rex called for his DFs and our artillery and mortars started a furious bombardment to defend Hill 220, laying a curtain of fire around its front. Underneath the roar of the artillery and the crump of the mortars we could hear the rat-tat-tat of the six guns of the machine-gun platoon firing almost continuously.

Colonel Guy, Percy Smythe, Desmond Dennis and I were in the battalion headquarters bunker. We listened and we waited. The telephone lines went dead. The Chinese bombardment had cut them. Later we heard that it had also cut the wires to detonate the fougasse, so they could not be exploded. Rex contacted us on the wireless and called for more fire. Then he switched it from his front to his right flank and called for more. He said he was being attacked continually. Small groups of Chinese were rushing his trenches through gaps in the wire, which had been destroyed by the Chinese bombardment. About 2 a.m. Rex reported that the attack had petered out.

At dawn Rex sent out patrols. In the remains of his wire and on the ground below he found thirty to forty Chinese dead. One Chinaman was discovered to be alive, was sent back to us and then on to Captain Kim. The prisoner said it had been a battalion attack. As the Chinese always recovered their dead and wounded they must have suffered far greater casualties than those Rex found.

Colonel Guy took me up to Hill 220 to have a look.

The hill was a shambles: not a tree left, the earth churned horribly, much of the wire and the trenches a wreck. Most of the bunkers had stood up well but Rex had lost one killed and three wounded. The platoon on the reverse slope had been relatively untouched and the men still looked cheerful. The two platoons on the top of the hill had taken the punishment. The men looked strained and tired.

'We've got to hold this hill, Rex. You can, can't you?'

'It depends on how many casualties the Chinese are prepared to take. I've seen off a battalion attack. Could I see off a brigade?'

'If anyone can, you can, Rex.'

'Don't leave us here too long. The lads are getting jumpy.'

The Chinese did not renew the attack. They let us be. Rex began to repair his position, rewire it and dig deeper and stronger.

The Brigadier called an O group. The Australians and the Highlanders had been attacked heavily too. I went with Colonel Guy. Waiting for him while he took fresh orders I found Captain Kim.

'What are the prisoners saying?'

'The Chinese High Command is angry.'

'So?'

'They are angry we have won the commanding heights, especially the Rock. Heads have rolled.'

'Do you mean literally?'

'Yes.'

'Literally?'

'Well, firing squads.'

'The brigadier,' Colonel Guy reported to me, 'said all the signs are that the Chinese are preparing to attack in great force. They're bringing up a lot of artillery. I persuaded him to let us take over the Rock so that we have the whole feature to defend. We'll be able to make it into a much stronger position.'

'Do we have the troops to do it, colonel?'

'We're too concentrated, Miles. The companies are too close and battalion HQ too far forward. If Z Company were overrun we'd be in the front line.'

'Are you going to leave Z Company on Hill 220?'

'No. Dermot's X Company can relieve them. Z can hold the Rock. Rex will like it up there. He may have a fierce fight again but he likes that. He needs a change.'

'What about battalion HQ? Should we be by ourselves?'

'No, we shouldn't. I'll pull Hadji back to the promiment hill we took at the beginning of our attack and we'll go in with him. Hadji will be our reserve ready to counter-attack.'

'And Tom's Y Company and the machine-guns?'

'They can stay where they are. His is the only position I like.'

'Won't we be rather spread out, colonel?'

'You can be too close, Miles. We were. We'll be stronger now. The weak spot is Hill 220. I hope Dermot can hold it, though I wouldn't say that to Dermot. If you want someone to be confident you have to show you have confidence in him. I have in Dermot but it's a bugger of a hill.'

There was some jeering in the companies when battalion HQ moved back 1,500 yards and slipped inside Hadji's company position. The intelligence section were embarrassed but they felt safer, as I did. We dug a new headquarters, deeper and stronger. The signallers were busy relaying telephone lines. Everyone was busy getting ready for the next attack. Dermot sent out a patrol to Hill 159 and found it strongly held by the enemy. Any day now, I thought. But still no attack came.

So Kitty has had a miscarriage, I thought. Poor Kitty. From time to time I thought about Kitty. Not all the time. Only during the long periods of inactivity when I couldn't help but think about her. I'd got used to the idea that she was no longer mine, that I'd lost her. I didn't like it. I'm not sure I

191

accepted it. I just recognised that it had happened. Her miscarriage made it more real.

What I still failed to understand was how Kitty had fallen for Horace. I supposed it must have been the horsiness. I liked horses and I enjoyed riding. That was different from being horsy. Horace was a horse. Kitty was far from being a horse but she was a little horsy and that must have been the attraction. As much as I debated this in my mind I couldn't quite come to believe it. Why, oh why? I had asked Sonia but, in her letters, she had said no more than she had before. I was, I thought, lucky to be in Korea. At least there were distractions. What would life be like if we both were still in Hong Kong? But if we had been it would not have happened. It only happened because of Korea.

Round and round my thoughts travelled, images of Kitty revolving in front of my misty eyes. Horsy, headstrong, heartless and Horace's, I thought, and I still love her.

Three weeks after the first Chinese counter-attack they attacked again. One morning they started shooting on to Hill 220. Not a bombardment, just a steady stream of shells falling, one at a time, all over the hill. It went on all morning and afternoon. Dermot and his men stayed in their bunkers.

'They're ranging their guns,' said Desmond Dennis, 'one at a time.'

'If it's one at a time they must have a lot,' I said.

'They have to range them individually. We only have to range one gun and the rest of our guns can get the range. The Chinese don't know how to do that. The Russians do. I'm surprised they haven't taught them.'

'They will,' said Colonel Guy. 'How many guns do you think they're ranging?'

'More than we've seen before. And now they've begun to range on the Rock.'

The bombardment started at five o'clock. It was heavier

than anything we had experienced, like a thunderstorm circling, circling and never going away, hurling a deluge of destruction down on the hill. Then it stopped and our own DFs started. The Chinese attacked in overwhelming numbers, seemingly oblivious to our fire. After an hour they overran the top of the hill. Dermot withdrew to his reserve platoon. He was in touch with us by wireless, all the telephone lines being cut. He called for the DFs to be directed on to his position. Later he tried to counter-attack but withdrew again.

The Chinese attack on the Rock was not pursued half as vigorously. Rex and his Z Company fought it off easily.

A little after dawn, with heavy artillery preparation and supported by three tanks, Hadji's company attacked and re-occupied Hill 220. The enemy had withdrawn. Hadji spent the day clearing the position, finding men buried or lying up in their bunkers, hiding. He patrolled forward and found enemy dead everywhere. He fortified the hill as best he could and waited.

Dermot retired with the remnants of his company.

'We held on as long as we could but they just came on coming at us,' he said.

'You held on longer than we thought possible,' said Colonel Guy, 'and you counter-attacked. How did you do it?'

'I've never known a bombardment like it. Far worse than anything we suffered in North Africa or Italy. It was terrifying. The bunkers were deep but most of them were knocked about, the wire destroyed, the trenches a mess. My bunker was destroyed and I was buried in it. Budd pulled me out. He was as brave as a lion. We went forward and joined one of the platoons. We got into the trenches as best we could. The Chinks attacked in groups with lots of bugle calls. They seem to control their men by bugle calls. As soon as we'd knocked one group down, another came in. Then they wheeled up a machine-gun protected by armour plate. It kept our heads down until Serjeant Foxton got his bazooka and knocked it out. It blew up. That cheered us.'

'Remind me about that,' Colonel Guy said.

'But they came on coming, bugling furiously. The men said there was a woman in black urging the Chinks on. I never saw her myself but I can believe it, a female commissar driven mad by poppy seeds. I've never seen men attacking like the Chinese were. Budd stood there firing the Thompson sub-machine-gun he'd got from the marines. When he ran out of magazines he clubbed a Chink with it. Then he picked up a Bren gun and fired it from the hip. Still they came on. Finally they were in our trenches. There were too many. There was no stopping them. Budd and I managed to pull some of the men back to the reserve platoon. That's when I asked you to bring fire down on the top of the hill. After a bit we got the reserve platoon out of their trenches and we tried to rush the top of the hill. The Chinks saw us off. There were just too many of them. We retired back to the platoon position and I asked you to bring more fire down on the top of the hill. That probably stopped them attacking us any further.'

'You did more than I could have asked you to,' said Colonel Guy.

'I don't think anyone can hold that hill, Colonel. It's been too knocked to pieces.'

'I cannot believe that even the Chinese can go on losing men at this rate.'

'No,' we all said.

At last light the Chinese attacked again after another terrific but short bombardment, followed by massive DFs being fired by our own guns. Our mortars had fired 7,000 rounds the previous night. Now they fired another 4,000. Finally the Chinese swarmed over the hill, which no longer had any real defences. As the fighting became hand-to-hand, Hadji asked to withdraw. He was given immediate permission. Even so he did not manage to get all his men off the position

194

with him. The enemy then started to fire tracer at the Rock. This was his usual signal for the next objective. We waited. No attack materialised.

At dawn a patrol discovered the enemy had abandoned Hill 220. The patrol probed forward and found hundreds of Chinese dead in the forming-up places on the side of the hill where the DFs had fallen.

The hill was so blasted that we made no attempt to hold it again. Nor did the Chinese. We kept an observation post on it during the day. The Chinese came at night to remove their dead but they did not come near it again.

So the battle ended. Rex's company had fought off a battalion attack. Then Dermot's had halted a brigade attack. Then Hadji's had brought to a halt another brigade attack. The Chinese had thrown a division at us.

Two days later we were relieved by American troops, carrying turkeys. It was Thanksgiving Day. We withdrew to a reserve position and rest area by the Imjin. First it rained. Then it snowed. Then it froze.

# Chapter 13

## Winter attacks

We had lost twenty-three men killed. Seven were missing and three officers and sixty-three men had been wounded. Ninety-six in all, almost a whole company. X Company had had most casualties and was reduced to two platoons. Every company had suffered and there was not a platoon up to strength. We now had a turnover of National Servicemen. Many were leaving at the end of their time to be replaced by a fresh intake, who had to be trained. We were never fully reinforced and, for the rest of our time in Korea, we were under strength. A certain sadness overcame everyone. This was soon dispelled by the need to keep warm, which became a full-time occupation. It was very cold.

We dug new bunkers, which some called hoochies and others bashas, and we learned to heat them with chuffers. These were stoves made out of old ammunition boxes into which petrol dripped from a copper tube, fed from a can fixed high on the outside. We made chimneys from old shell cases. There were plenty of those around, and empty ammo boxes. We were meant to use diesel but it flowed too slowly to get a good burn. Diesel would have been safer.

Ten trucks of winter clothing arrived. We were all given string vests, long johns, under trousers, trousers, thick rubber-soled boots, a heavy pullover and a parka. The last was a wonderful fur lined coat with a wired hood you could close round your face and a flap at the back that you pulled between your legs and buttoned up in front. I still have mine. We were given sleeping bags, too.

'Did you hear how Mr Errington escaped, Sir?'

Serjeant Savage and I were sitting in the intelligence section's tent, for we had some tents in reserve, warmed by a chuffer.

'He never told me the details,' I replied.

Toby Errington, as a National Service officer, was due to return to England to be demobbed. He had just been to say goodbye to me.

'Manky,' I had said, 'I thought we'd lost you.'

'It looked like it but I remembered I'd got a place at Oxford and I couldn't let the Chinks keep me from that.'

He had grinned and we shook hands.

'Well,' said Serjeant Savage, 'he and the FOO, that New Zealand captain. What was his name?'

'Captain Sartorius.'

'Yes, Captain Sartorius, Sir, and half a dozen of them had been captured and they were being escorted off the hill towards the Chinese lines by a couple of Chinks with burp guns. Mr Errington said it was very dark but you could see quite a bit some of the time because of the exploding shells from the DFs we were firing and he didn't think the escorts looked at all friendly. Then when they got near Piccadilly Circus, you know, those crossroads in the valley, he heard the click of a burp gun being cocked and he knew they were all for it and were going to be massacred. So he shouted 'Run' and they all ran for it. The escorts fired their burp guns, but you know what firing at night is like, Sir, and our lads got away without another scratch. Two of them were already lightly wounded from the bombardment. They ran along the valley, lay up until dawn was breaking and made their way up into the Canadian position. One of the lads told me all this.

197

Bloody lucky, if you ask me. But brave of Mr Errington to do it.'

'No,' I said, 'he never told me.'

Manky had just grinned. Despite his chaotic appearance he had been an excellent officer much loved by his men.

In the chaos of battle a number of men had escaped from Hill 220. A few had withdrawn when they were overrun and saw the battle was hopeless. They made their way to the machine-gun platoon and Tom Warburton's Y Company. Others had walked across to the Canadians. They all carried their weapons and had little ammunition left. Quite a few just got buried in their bunkers and were dug out the following day not knowing who was digging them out. One or two of these had been seriously wounded, though most of the wounded had been evacuated off the hill during the battle.

Two of the wounded had been captured, taken prisoner and later released by the Chinese. One was allowed to walk back. The other was carried on a stretcher to within a hundred yards of the Canadian position at night. He was left with a large notice and plenty of propaganda material. In the morning the Canadians heard him and brought him in. Both had had their wounds simply dressed and reported they had been well treated. They had been subjected to some political interrogation and had been told that, as wounded, they would be better off being looked after by their own people. This was in marked contrast to the way Toby Errington found he was about to be shot. As with every army, it depends into whose hands you fall.

'There're some decorations and awards announced in Part One Orders,' said Corporal Low as he came into the tent, where Serjeant Savage and I were discussing maps, with the day's orders sheet.

'Read them out,' I said.

Dermot had been awarded the Distinguished Service Order and Colonel Guy had been given a bar to his. Hadji and Rex had been mentioned in despatches, as had five others. Three officers had been given Military Crosses, including Burgo. There were five Military Medals, among them Foxton and Wildman. And Serjeant-Major Budd was awarded a bar to his Distinguished Conduct Medal. Later we heard that David Sartorius, the FOO, and Roddy Kington, the Hussar troop commander, had also won MCs.

'All very fair, if you ask me,' said Serjeant Savage. 'What do you think, Sir?'

'All hard earned and well deserved,' I said.

But how did I know? I thought Colonel Guy's and Dermot's DSOs well deserved. Hadji had done well too so why hadn't he been given a DSO? Burgo deserved his MC, as I knew Foxton and Wildman deserved their MMs. And Budd I knew to be the bravest man. But I did not know the circumstances of the other awards. It depended how someone had behaved, given the opportunity to display exemplary courage. Had he saved the day? Above all, who had seen him and what had been reported? Awards could never be completely fair. What is in life? These seemed even-handed enough, though I thought there might have been more. Months later I discussed this with Colonel Guy. He said recommending honours and awards was the hardest thing he had to do and he regretted not having made more recommendations. It was not, he said, the regiment's way to go overboard on decorations. Everyone was expected to be courageous and only exceptional actions were recognised.

'What do you think of this war, Sir?' asked Serjeant Savage.

'What do you mean?'

'Well, Sir, is it a just war? Is it a good war? How can we justify all these casualties? And while peace talks are going on?'

I reached for a tin of cigarettes, chose one carefully and took my time lighting it. I had been taught that, when asked a difficult question, lighting a cigarette gives you time to think.

'Is it a just war? Yes, it's justified. If we hadn't stopped the communists here, where would we? Stalin could walk in anywhere. Is it right to fight when the peace talks go on? What else can we do? We have to show the Chinese we mean business. They want to wear us out so that we get fed up and settle on their terms, or worse, just pull out. We can't sit in our trenches and do nothing. We must show them we mean business.'

'It seems a lot of casualties for a few hills and paddies.'

'You can't measure success by the four miles we've taken. You measure success by the effect on the enemy's mind.'

'And what is that, Sir?'

'Captain Kim says they're rattled by our success.'

'Why,' said Lofty Low, 'don't we do an all-out attack and chase them out of Korea? We could.'

'What do you think about that, Serjeant Savage?'

'No one would let us. The American public wouldn't accept the casualties, nor would the British.'

'How do you know?'

'Witney had a letter from his mum this morning asking him what he was doing here. She said none of the neighbours know there's a war on and she doesn't know why there's a war. As far as they're concerned we don't exist. There's no stomach for a war in England.'

'We *are* fighting in a forgotten war. But there're still a lot of post-war problems at home. Rationing, housing, coal and other shortages. You can't expect people to think about us much. We have to go on and do our duty.'

They listened in silence.

'Are the men talking about it?' I asked.

'No, Sir,' said Serjeant Savage. 'Occasionally they wonder. Mostly the National Servicemen. But it does upset them when, like Witney, they get a letter saying they're forgotten.'

'I can see that. It's quite difficult to explain.'

'You've explained it very well, Sir,' said Corporal Low. 'It's just not that easy to put into a letter.'

Maxwell entered the tent.

'Sir, Roberts says the colonel wants to go shooting and have you asked the RQMS to send up your guns?'

'No. I'd better do that now. Corporal, would you get the RQMS on the telephone for me?'

The signallers had once again laid telephone lines connecting everyone. It was a luxury to sit in a tent, even if on an ammunition box, and talk on the telephone without a bombardment all around one.

'*All* the guns, Sir?' asked the RQMS when I got him.

'Just the colonel's and mine. You'd better ask the others if they want them.'

'And ammo, Sir?'

'Yes.'

'And silver goblets and claret?'

'If you have them.'

'Fucking hell, Sir. Where do you think we are?'

I put the telephone down, hoping the others had not overheard. They had. They were grinning from ear to ear.

'What I'd like to know,' said Corporal Low, 'is what's happened to the British Empire?'

Time, I thought, for a cigarette.

'Well, Sir?'

'What do you think?'

'I don't understand it,' said Low. 'I was brought up to think we were top nation with an empire on which the sun never sets and that we won the last war. You tell that to the Yanks and they laugh at you.'

'Have you?'

'It was humiliating, Sir. When I was at division on the intelligence course there was an American officer there among the instructors. He asked me how many divisions we

201

had in Korea and I said one. He said he'd heard that most of our division were Canadians and Australians and New Zealanders and there were seven American divisions in Korea and Britain hadn't really got *one.*'

'America is a bigger country.'

'Only four times our size, not seven, Sir. Perhaps we're not top nation.'

'Empires rise and fall. The Americans are on the rise and we are on the fall.'

'Why's that, Sir?'

'Two world wars have drained our resources.'

'The United States has grown from them.'

'There's still an empire, Corporal Low. We may have given India her independence but there's half Africa—'

Maxwell had stepped into the tent again.

'Roberts says the colonel's asking for his gun. When do you expect it to arrive, Sir?'

'I think, Maxwell, it would be a good idea to go and get the guns if the colonel is becoming impatient for his. You'd better find Doughty.' I turned to the others. 'I'll have to go,' I said, and followed Maxwell out of the tent. Of course, I could have sent Maxwell and Doughty to get them, and I did not really want to go out into the freezing cold, but Corporal Low's questions were beginning to rankle. He was asking questions that I had been asking myself and could not really answer. Nor had I got used to the idea of not being top nation any more.

I delivered Colonel Guy his guns into his own hands.

'Miles, how clever. I was going to ask you. Let's go shooting tomorrow morning. Just you and me. There're pheasants everywhere. Roberts has been nagging me about getting our guns. I suppose he wants to curry some pheasant again, God forbid.'

I should have guessed it was Roberts, not the Colonel, asking for the guns but it was good we had them.

'I'd like that, colonel. When Toby Errington left we should have asked him to send us some claret.'

He laughed.

'Now, there's an idea,' he said. 'Hugh Jermy's joining us soon. He could bring some from Hong Kong.'

This was news to me.

'When's he coming?'

'He's been nagging everyone for months now, which was disagreeable of him. I'd arranged everything with your cousin before we left Hong Kong. Hugh had to do his year. Burgo's in need of a good convalescence so when he's well enough he'll go to Hong Kong and take over from Hugh. I've agreed for Burgo to stay until the battalion returns to England, whenever that is. Then it'll be someone else's turn. Your cousin is keen on the regiment. It's good to be able to dispense such a sinecure.'

'Will Burgo return to us first?'

'He'll be here for Christmas. So will Hugh. Quite soon now. The Blessingtons are going to England for a few weeks in December so Hugh will join us as soon as they've left. He can brief Burgo here. Don't forget to ask him to bring some claret with him.'


Colonel Guy and I went shooting, accompanied by Roberts, Maxwell and our drivers. We motored towards the Imjin and then walked up five paddies and two spinneys. Within a short time we had five brace of pheasant and a brace of duck.

'We'll keep the duck,' Colonel Guy said to Roberts, 'but give a brace of pheasants to the RSM.'

'Could we give a brace to the RQMS?' I asked.

'Of course. Anyone else?'

'You'll be spoiling everyone again,' said Roberts. 'You'll be out of pheasants in no time and complaining there's none.'

'We can shoot more when we need them.'

'You're not stopping now, are you?' said Roberts.

'Yes, it's bloody cold.'

Roberts carried the pheasants to the colonel's jeep, grumbling away to Maxwell. I supposed he had wanted to give some to his mates and would not be able to. Out of the line we were living on fresh rations provided by the Americans and cooked by the company cooks on huge petrol burners. The men found the food too rich, especially turkey that arrived regularly. They were not used to the luxury and preferred simpler, English food. Not many liked pheasant either. None of the intelligence section would eat it. Roberts wanted to show off his position as the colonel's soldier servant. He could be a pain in the neck despite looking after Colonel Guy admirably.

One of those that did appreciate his pheasant was our Church of England padre, Captain Frank Parsonson, who visited the intelligence section's tent one afternoon.

'I'm looking,' he said, 'for volunteers.'

Everyone laughed.

'To do what, padre?' asked Serjeant Savage.

'Build a regimental chapel. It's time we had a chapel in the field where I can base myself and you can come and sit and get away from the trials and tribulations of this war.'

'What are you going to call it, padre?'

'Saint Birinus. He's a saint who's always appealed to me. Sent by Rome to England to convert the heathen English west of the Thames he never got further then Dorchester-on-Thames. He's the source of many interesting stories.'

'What kind of stories?'

'Well, how he persuaded some reluctant soldiers to save their souls by helping him to build a church. Serjeant Body has promised to help me.'

'His soul needs saving,' said Serjeant Savage.

'Mine too,' said Lance Corporal Witney.

'Oh, Blanket,' groaned Corporal Low.

'Thank you, Corporal Witney. One volunteer is enough

from the intelligence section but I'll take another if there's willing flesh.'

'Count me in,' said Maxwell. 'I've built plenty of bunkers but never a church.'

'This will be a church in a bunker, Maxwell.'

Whether Witney and Maxwell had been attending Frank Parsonson's services or not, I did not know. Frank had got to know almost every man in the battalion. He had an admiring following as a man, I thought, rather than a churchman.

Before St Birinus's Chapel was finished the battalion was called out to hunt guerrillas.

'Guerrillas, colonel?' said Rex Topham at the briefing Colonel Guy was giving us. 'How will we recognise them?'

'They'll be North Koreans who've either infiltrated our lines or were left behind in their last retreat. Anyone living outside the villages in this weather will be a guerrilla. The most important thing about this operation will be to keep warm and see no one gets frostbite.'

'Isn't it going to interfere with our finishing this reserve position and our training programme?'

'Yes, Rex, I know. Brigade says there are a mounting number of incidents in rear areas which can only be due to guerrillas: trucks being sabotaged, men disappearing. They and division are more interested in our putting an end to this than in anything else we are doing.'

'They're windy, colonel.'

'You could say that.'

'How long will it take?'

'A few days. We'll return here every night.'

For the next few days lorries arrived early to transport us along the frozen tracks and roads, back across the Imjin to areas behind the lines where the echelons and rear parties were sited. Split up into search parties, the companies combed the paddies and hills. Sometimes it snowed. Every night it froze. Nobody saw a guerrilla. But the operation took its toll.

One evening, when dusk had fallen, a lorry returning to our position skidded on an icy bend and ran into the back of Tom Warburton's jeep, which was stationary, and crushed it. Sitting in the back of the jeep Tom's wireless operator was killed immediately. Tom and his driver were trapped in the wreckage. When finally released the driver was found to have smashed his legs and Tom his right arm. They were evacuated as fast as possible to the field hospital where Tom had his right arm cut off at the shoulder and the driver his right leg at the knee. Someone said they were lucky to get away with their lives. How incongruous, I thought, that after all they had been through in the recent battles they had been levelled by a traffic accident, not the hazard of war. Tom had been a friend. He had also been due to return to England as he had been in the East for four years. When we travelled out the next morning the wrecked jeep was still standing by the track. An angry Colonel Guy ordered it to be removed immediately.

Ben Wildbore, who had been Dermot's 2i/c in X Company, took over Tom's company, being the senior captain in the battalion. He was promoted major.

A day later the operation was called off. We never found a guerrilla. We returned to our picks and shovels, wiring parties, training programmes and, for some, the building of the Chapel of St Birinus.

I was lying on my bed in my hoochie, trying to keep warm, when a familiar voice said 'Miles? Miles, are you there?'

'Hugh? Is it you?' I said. 'When did you get here?'

He took off his new parka, sat on an ammunition box I used as a chair and offered me an Egyptian cigarette. Yes, it was Hugh with his blond, curly hair, blue eyes and irresistible smile.

'I nearly got stuck in Pusan. They said I had to wait to bring up a body of National Servicemen that was expected from England. That was the last thing I was going to do, linger at base. I hitched a lift on a three-tonner from divisional headquarters and it dropped me at B Echelon. Damned uncomfortable and bloody cold. You might have warned me about the cold.'

'It's only got cold in the last three weeks. Did you bring some claret?'

'I left it with the RQMS. As soon as he saw it he said he'd look after it. Why the hell claret?'

'To eat with pheasant.'

'Pheasant?'

'The place is crawling with them. It's our staple food.'

'I never brought my gun.'

'Silly you. I told you to.'

'That ass Horace Belcher had all the guns left behind in Hong Kong packed up, crated and marked "Return to UK". No one could identify the crate with my gun in it. It's probably already in England.'

'Why did Kitty marry Horace?' I asked.

'Beats me. When you left she was unhappy, the unhappiness of separation. We used to talk about you a lot: how long you might be away, the chances of your being wounded or worse and when she might see you again. Then, almost overnight, she changed and never spoke about you again. She set her cap at Horace and that was it.'

'She didn't have to marry him.'

'It appeared there was nothing she wanted more. You know Kitty. If she wants something she gets it. Horace fell immediately.'

'I can't understand it.'

'Sonia said it must have been because she felt insecure, her first engagement going wrong and then you leaving for Korea. She had to get married. That's what Kitty said, "I've got to get married and I'm going to marry Horace".'

'I suppose I'll never understand.'

'Sonia send lots of love.'

'How is Sonia?'

'They've gone to London. Ivan had meetings to attend. They'll be there for Christmas. That's why I was able to come here. Sonia was very good to me. I love Sonia.'

'Everyone gets to love Sonia,' I said, but I wondered quite what he meant.

'I'm in Dermot's company.'

'He's the best of the company commanders. In fact, he's the best soldier in the battalion after Colonel Guy. You know he won a DSO?'

'I hope he'll help me win the MC.'

'Oh, Hugh. The men don't like officers who are bent on winning medals. They're too dangerous. If you get an opportunity, well and good. Don't go out to win at any cost.'

'Burgo's got one. I must have one. You know Burgo's going to Hong Kong to take my job?'

'I've heard. Have you got any more of those Egyptian cigarettes?'

'Have the packet. Unless there's another big battle I won't get a chance. Ivan said there wouldn't be another big attack. We can't afford the casualties. I can't tell you how galling it is to have missed it. Well, I'd better cut along now.'

Ten days before Christmas, Percy Smyth put his head through the flap of my tent, then walked in quickly and stood in front of my chuffer.

'Wonderful news, Miles,' he said. 'We're going back into the line. We've got to take over from some rumbling redcoats who are being pulled out for some intensive training. We're the only battalion that can be trusted to hold the line.'

'Sometimes, Percy, I don't believe a word you say.'

'Mostly true. We are going back, just for seven days. The brigadier has promised us we'll be back for Christmas in this idyllic place. When did you last have a freezing white Christmas?'

'He can't do that. Send us back for seven days, I mean.'

'He can and he is.'

'It will be unpopular, very unpopular.'

'We all know that.'

We looked at each other.

'I know one person it will please,' I said.

'Who on earth? Oh, yes. Hugh. He's going round like a dog with a cockstand. It might cool him down. I hope he lasts. Maybe he's lucky.'

'He thinks he's missed out.'

'No chance of that. The War Office has forgotten we're here. They probably won't relieve us until the year after next.'

'As soon as that?'

'Except there won't be anyone left in the battalion by that time.'

'Tell me. Where in the line are we going?'

'The Samichon Riviera.'

'At least that's a quiet stretch of the line.'

'It was.'

'I'd better go to brigade and get briefed and fetch the maps.'

'Ah, you've twigged this isn't a courtesy call. That's the message.'

There was a commotion outside the tent. Then followed a shout of 'Fire!', which was repeated by several other voices in the distance.

'Oh no,' said Percy. 'Not another. That's the third this week.'

He walked out of the tent. I followed him when I had put on my parka.

'Bloody Z Company again,' he said. 'Rex is over-playing his hand.'

The Samichon River rose somewhere behind the Chinese lines and flowed down into the Imjin in our lines, to the south of the site of the October and November battles. It was an area new to us. The hills were lower and had not been fought over. We took over a position, quite well laid out and prepared, from what Percy had, unkindly, called rumbling redcoats and Colonel Guy, accurately, referred to as a compass regiment, one of those regiments whose county name was prefixed with north, south, east or west. This was part of the competitive badinage between regiments. Heaven knows what they called us.

'Are we really going to send patrols out in this weather, colonel?' I asked.

'Have to. Must patrol. The Samichon River must be a frozen trickle at this time of year. It's a likely place for ambushes. The forward companies must have standing patrols out too. They don't want to be surprised, though I doubt even the Chinese would attack in this weather. Make plans, Miles. We're only here for a week.'

I made a plan to lay an ambush on the Samichon River and Colonel Guy told me to take it to Dermot as X Company, being the weakest, was in reserve and, as reserve, was to provide the patrol.

'Here's a chance for Hugh to acclimatise,' said Dermot. 'He needs to let off steam or he'll explode.'

We briefed Hugh, who asked all the right questions, and set off with his patrol. Dermot had sent him out with Serjeant Foxton. They sat it out until 2 a.m. when they reported they were freezing and asked to come in. Dermot gave permission and told them to report back to him personally. He wanted to see how cold they really were as well as debrief them. I had stayed with Dermot, for his was the only fighting patrol out that night, so we could control it together. At one stage we heard shots. They could have come from anywhere on our front. There was no report on the radio. Finally the patrol came in and, one by one, entered the bunker, snow on their boots, grass frozen on their parkas and frost on their eyebrows. We gave them hot drinks laced with rum and let them thaw out a little.

'We bumped,' said Hugh.

'We wondered. What happened?'

'It was so cold I thought we'd freeze to the ground if we stayed any longer. Serjeant Foxton and I discussed it and we decided it was time to come in. It was better when we started moving. I didn't think anyone else could be out. We saw them when they saw us. We were thirty to forty yards apart. They were coming back from our lines. They must have thought we were Chinese too as they stopped and did nothing. Serjeant Foxton said, 'Chinks' so I said 'Fire!' Most of the Sten guns jammed. Corporal James got off a burst with his Bren gun. They fired a shot or two back, quite wild. Then Serjeant Foxton threw a grenade and they scarpered, just disappeared into the night. There can't have been more than five of them. We followed up to where they'd been but there was no one there, no bodies or anything. With the Stens jammed and the cold I thought it best to get back as fast as possible. We followed the route between the forward companies and here we are.'

I watched Serjeant Foxton. He was looking at Hugh with approval. I thought they would make a formidable team. There was no sign that the night had tempered Hugh's ardour.

## Chapter 14

# Growing up with Hugh

'Marbles or conkers?' I asked.

'Conkers,' said Hugh. 'I've won most of your marbles off you.'

'I want to win them back.'

'You'll only lose more, Miles.'

We were standing in the playground outside the Old Hall, at our private school. It was Michaelmas term 1940.

'All right then. Mine's a sixer. What's yours?'

'A fourer.'

'I go first.'

Hugh held up his conker and I swiped at it with mine and missed. Then I held up my conker; Hugh swiped at it and grazed it. He held his conker up again; I took aim and hit it well and true. We examined the conkers. There were a few fissures but nothing that looked fatal in either, so I held up my conker again and Hugh brought his conker down on mine, fair and square. It flew into pieces and I was left holding an empty string.

'Hard luck,' said Hugh. 'Now mine's a tenner.'

'Let's play marbles. I want to win the sixpenny marble back.'

'You'll only lose another but all right.'

Another boy came up to us.

'Player?' he asked.

'Yes.'

'The headmaster wants to see you.'

'Now?'

'Yes.'

'What have you done?' asked Hugh.

'I've no idea,' I said, wondering what the headmaster could want me for and stuffing my last few marbles back in their bag and into my pocket. I ran through the playground, past the covered rink, between the masters' lodge and the playing fields, across the road and into School House, my heart pounding away and my head full of foreboding. Was he going to beat me again for my Latin prose? I could think of nothing else I might have done wrong. He must be going to beat me for something. I walked along the passageway to his study, stood for a moment outside his door and knocked.

'Come in,' he shouted.

I opened the door and walked bravely in.

'Oh, Miles. Your father's just rung. He's going to come and watch the match this afternoon. A nice surprise.'

'Oh, Sir. Yes, Sir.'

'He's bringing Mrs Knox with him. Will you find Jasper Knox and tell him?'

'Yes, Sir. Is that all, Sir?'

'Yes, Miles.'

'Thank you, Sir.'

Jasper Knox was four years younger than me and in his second year at the school. I was in my last year and a prefect, as was Hugh Jermy. Jasper's father had been in the regiment with my father and had been killed at Dunkirk a few months before. Jasper was a game little chap and I felt sad for him. I ran back to the playground to find him. The bell was going for the next lesson so I went into Old Hall and found him going into a classroom.

'Knox,' I said.

'Yes, Player?'

213

'The headmaster has asked me to tell you that my father is bringing your mother to see you this afternoon. They're coming to watch the match.'

'Really, Player?' he said, brightening.

'Yes. I'm playing so you'd better meet them outside School House. If anyone asks why you're there say I gave you permission.'

'Gosh Player. Thanks, Player.'

By the time I had reached my classroom the lesson had started.

'You're late,' said Mr J.J.B. Barley, our English master, as I slid into my place. He was a large man with long flowing hair, dressed in old tweeds. He had a multi-coloured scarf round his neck and wore three waistcoats, one upon the other, all different and none too clean. It was not that cold a day. The waistcoats were one of his eccentricities.

'The headmaster sent for me, Sir.'

'Well, let's see if you can remember your prep. What was it I set you?'

'Othello's last speech.'

'Let's hear you recite it.'

He dug his hands into the pockets of his largest waistcoat while I stood up and recited. I was good at recitation and liked doing it.

'Well delivered. Full marks,' he said. 'A wonderful speech, alive with meaning. What's Shakespeare got? Why's he so good? Anyone?'

'The stories, Sir?' said someone in the front row.

'No, no, no. Not the stories. If you want to read the stories you can read them in *Lamb's Tales from Shakespeare*. He pinched most of the stories from Plutarch. No, no, not the stories. Anyone?'

'The words, Sir,' said Hugh, 'and the way he tells the story. He puts the words together and plays with them so they become music.'

'Exactly, Jermy. Let's listen to them again.'

That's what I thought, I said to myself. Why didn't I say that? Hugh was always first to express the thought, the first past the post. No wonder he's top of the form. I looked at him, with his blond curly hair falling over his eyes and his engaging smile as he listened to Mr Barley and I thought how lucky I was that he was my friend.

That afternoon we were playing rugger against our deadly rivals Beauchamp Hill. After lunch the team changed into its rugger gear and ran out on to the 1st XV pitch to practise passing and kick balls around, waiting for the Beauchamp Hill XV to arrive. They ran on to the pitch wearing white tops and shorts and white and red stockings, all very smart and clean. Our team was in blue and our kit was mud-stained. Our boots were rather dirty, too. On turnout Beauchamp Hill won the day but we thought them rather sissy.

The game started. It was fast and we scored a try quickly. Hugh converted the try. He was playing at fly-half. I was full-back. Then their forwards rushed us and scored. They converted too. The score was five all. There was a long period without any scoring when, suddenly, one of their quarter-backs broke through and ran straight for the corner. I raced across the field, threw myself at his knees and brought him down into touch.

'Well tackled, Player.'

I looked up and there was my daddy in uniform with a beautiful woman wrapped in furs and Jasper Knox. I glowed.

At half-time the score was still equal. Then we began to get the better of them. We scored another try, unconverted, and shortly afterwards I joined in an attacking movement. Hugh broke through and was running with the ball as two Beauchamp Hill players closed in on him.

'Pass, Hugh, pass,' I cried as I ran outside him, unmarked. Hugh ran on, heedless and determined. They pulled him down too late. He was over the line and had scored. Then he converted. We won 13–5. I ran off the field to my father, who kissed me on both cheeks.

'You'll play for the army if you go on like that,' he said. 'How are you, Miles?'

'All Sir Garnet, Sir.'

'That's the stuff. You know Jasper's mother, don't you?'

'Hello, Miles. It's lovely to see you. Jasper says you are one of the top boys and you've been kind to him.'

'I'm glad Knox is here with us, Mrs Knox. We have five boys from the regiment here.'

'As many as that?'

I looked my daddy up and down. He was in service dress, made of a heavy material. His trousers had turn ups, and he wore red tabs on his lapels and a badge on his hat I did not recognise.

'Daddy, what's that cap badge you're wearing?'

'I wear it because I'm a brigadier, now.'

'I know. Where's mummy?'

'Mummy's got a cold and is not feeling well. So I brought Mrs Knox to see Jasper.'

'That's very nice of you. I think I prefer the bugle badge.'

'So do I, but I can't wear it any more now I'm a brigadier. We're going to take you and Jasper off to tea.'

'I can't do that,' I said. 'I have to have tea with the visiting side.'

'The headmaster has said you can come out.'

'Oh, has he? Then could I bring my friend Jermy?'

'I'm sure you could. The motor's outside School House. Meet us there.'

I changed as fast as I could, collected Hugh and we ran to the car. It was the large family Wolseley, driven by a corporal with a bugle badge. I felt at home. Jasper sat between his mother and my father on the back seat. Hugh and I sat in the jump seats.

'I should have passed you the ball,' Hugh said to me.

'You scored.'

'Yes, but I should have passed the ball. It was selfish, Miles. It was bad play and I was lucky to get away with it.'

That's what made me like Hugh so much. He was impetuous and determined but he was kind and thoughtful, too.

We sped into the town and stopped outside a hotel in the High Street. We had scones and jam and cream and lemonade. Mrs Knox drank tea. My father called for a soda siphon. When it came he took a flask from an inner pocket and poured himself a whisky. Then he lit a cigar.

'Will the war go on long enough for us to fight?' Hugh asked.

'It'll be a long war but I hope not that long,' my father replied. 'Are you still going to join the regiment one day, Miles?'

'You bet.'

'What about you, Jasper?'

'Of course,' said Jasper.

'And you, Hugh. What are you going to do?'

'I'd like to be with Miles,' said Hugh.

'Then you must join the regiment, too. I'll write to the colonel of the regiment and put your name down. Would you like that?'

'Oh, please, Sir.'

'Will your father approve?'

'My father's a businessman and he doesn't know anything about the army. He wasn't old enough to fight in the Great War.'

'That's settled then. We'd better get these boys back to their school, Verity, or we'll be late for the theatre in London.'

Shortly after this visit my father went to North Africa. He wrote to me rarely. Occasionally I read about him in the

217

newspapers; sometimes there was a picture of him in the desert; once I saw him in a newsreel. He was a general now, commanding a division. In 1943 he came home and made a sudden visit to me at my next school, without warning.

It was July and I was playing in a cricket match, the last of the term. Our side, the Under-16s, was batting. I was sitting outside the pavilion in the sun, fully padded and ready to go in, watching Hugh at the crease when a voice said, 'Hello, Miles.'

'Daddy' I cried.

I jumped up and we kissed each other on both cheeks. He was sunburnt and looked older and tired. He was wearing a grey flannel suit, had a felt hat and was smoking a cigar.

'You're almost as tall as me,' said daddy.

'When did you get home?' I asked.

'Two days ago.'

'For good?'

'For a bit. I'll be able to see more of you.'

'Where's mummy?'

'Mummy's got a headache and is resting. I brought Mrs Knox, as she's keen for Jasper to come on here and join you and she wanted to have a look at the school. We've just seen the headmaster and he told us you'd be here. Verity, you remember Miles?'

Mrs Knox was as beautiful as I remembered, possibly more beautiful. She was wearing a silk, polka-dot dress, hat and gloves and shimmered before me.

'Hello, Miles,' she said and kissed me on the cheek. I fell for her immediately.

'How's Jasper, Mrs Knox?'

'He's fine. He's become very keen on riding and is quite the little horseman.'

'Has he a pony?'

'Yes, he keeps it with my brother and spends most of his holidays there.'

'I've a pony too though I'm really too big for him. Daddy, General Fisher lets me ride his horses.'

'That's very civil of him. Who's that who just hit that four?'

'That's Hugh Jermy. You remember him.'

'Didn't he say he wanted to join the regiment? Why he's hit another four. Elegant cut, that. Can he ride?'

'Yes.'

'He'll be an asset.'

'He's got forty runs, so far. He's our captain. In the last match he got sixty-seven.'

'He looks set for fifty again. I must tell the colonel of the regiment about him.'

'General Flaxman was here earlier in the term and met Hugh.'

'Well done. He's just the sort of chap we want. Have you made many runs?'

'Not as many as Hugh but I've taken some wickets.'

'You'll make a handy pair. The headman told me you've just taken your School Certificate.'

'We won't hear the results until the holidays.'

'So you'll be in the Sixth Form next term?'

'I hope so.'

'What are you going to do?'

'I'd like to do history and French but my house beak says I should stick with the classics.'

'Do you enjoy classics?'

'Not as much as history.'

'You can speak French?'

'Not really.'

'Everyone should speak French. You can go to France when we've re-taken the country and learn the language there. You can read history at any time. Your house beak is probably wise to say stick with classics.'

'You think so?'

'It's a better mental discipline. Miles, I'm afraid we're going to have to go.'

'Can't you wait and see me bat and bowl?'

'Sorry, old boy. I must take Mrs Knox home. Look, your friend has hit his fifty.'

We clapped.

'I think he's declared. Verity, we must stay a moment so I can congratulate him.'

He pressed a five-pound note into my hand and went to meet Hugh who was striding towards the pavilion with his fellow batsman.

'I'm sorry we have to go so soon, Miles,' said Mrs Knox. 'You know your father's been made a lieutenant general and he's going to command a corps? Isn't that exciting?'

'I wish he wasn't quite so busy. I hardly know him.'

'Now he's back in England you'll see lots more of him.'

I did not see him again. Three weeks later he was killed in an air crash.

Hugh and I were commissioned into the Prince Regent's Light Infantry early in 1948. He passed out above me, had been a senior under officer and could have chosen any regiment in the army. Many wooed him. He was adamant about joining the Prince Regent's Light Infantry with me.

'Come and spend a week in London with my parents,' he said. 'We can have some fun.'

He had a car, a 1930s MG open tourer, painted racing green. We piled our kit into it and motored off up the A30.

'My parents are out tonight so we'll go out to dinner,' said Hugh. 'How much money have you got?'

'My mother has given me twenty-five pounds as a commissioning present and I've got my pay and my uniform allowance.'

'You should be able to have a good week on that.'

'I don't want to spend it all and I must go to the regimental tailor to try on my uniforms.'

'You're not going to pay him, are you?'

220

'Why not?'

'He'll give you credit. You can pay him by bankers order so much a month. Then you can use your uniform allowance on anything else you need.'

'You mean like theatres and night clubs?'

'Exactly.'

I had not thought of that. As we motored through Bagshot I felt I was going to enjoy the week.

'Your mother gives you an allowance, doesn't she?'

'She gives me money from time to time, not an allowance.'

'You should try and get her to give you an allowance. My father gives me £250 a year.'

'Your father's got money.'

'Surely your mother has?'

'Not as much as she had, she says.'

'That's a pity.'

'She says my father spent it.'

'I liked your father. He was fun. He gave me a fiver once for making fifty runs.'

'I remember.'

He had given me a fiver that day, too. Motoring on through Sunningdale, Egham and Staines I wondered how many fivers he used to carry to give them away so readily.

'Do you think we should call on General Flaxman?' Hugh asked.

'Not until we receive a letter from him welcoming us into the regiment. General Fisher told me that.'

'I like General Fisher,' said Hugh.

'He's been very good to me.'

'Have you seen Kitty recently?'

'We seem to have rather lost touch.'

Hounslow and Osterley, Brentwood and Chiswick passed by as I wondered if my friendship with Kitty had merely been a childhood one and we would now go our separate ways.

'Nearly there,' said Hugh as we came into Hammersmith

and along the Cromwell Road. In a few minutes we were stopping outside a tall, stuccoed house in Wilton Crescent.

That evening we dined in Jermyn Street, and went on to a nightclub in Piccadilly. When we left it in the early hours of the morning there was not much left of my twenty-five pounds.

'Do you do this every night in London?' I asked, as I threw my cigar into the gutter at Hyde Park Corner on our walk home.

'Never done it before,' he said, and we laughed the rest of the way to Wilton Crescent.

'What time did you get home?' asked Mrs Jermy at breakfast. She was the most sophisticated woman I knew.

'About two,' said Hugh.

'As early as that?'

'We were running out of money,' I said.

Hugh's father laughed. He was a distinguished looking man, wearing a suit of Prince of Wales check. He had half-moon spectacles on the end of his nose and looked at us over them. Then he looked through them at the copy of the *Financial Times*, whose pages he was turning and scanning.

'If you must go to such expensive places I'm not surprised,' he said.

'They were celebrating,' Mrs Jermy said. 'You should offer to pay for their dinner, Jeremy.'

Turning to Hugh and me she said, 'What are you thinking of doing today? Last night we saw Noel Coward in *Present Laughter*. You might enjoy that.'

'I rather fancy a musical, mummy,' Hugh said, as he looked through the theatre column of the newspaper he was holding.

'There's *Bless the Bride*, *Oklahoma* and *Annie Get your Gun*,' she replied, 'but haven't you seen them?'

'Not *Oklahoma*.'

'What does Miles want to see?' asked Hugh's father. 'You

be careful, Miles, or you'll spend your week doing things that Hugh wants, whatever you say.'

'Hugh and I generally enjoy the same things,' I said. 'I haven't seen *Oklahoma* either but I'd rather like to go to the opera while I'm in London.'

'Excellent idea,' said Mrs Jermy. 'Schwarzkopf is singing in *Traviata* at the Garden.'

'The boys are low on funds, darling. The only tickets left will be expensive.'

'Then I'll take them, if you won't. I want to hear her. What else, Miles?'

'Are there any exhibitions?'

'There's Paul Nash at the Tate and the Redfern have some rather good Sickert drawings.'

'I'd like to see those,' I said. 'What about you, Hugh?'

'Rather, and I'd like to see the Nash. He's good at battle-fields. But why don't we go to the movies today? Who'd like to see *The Road to Rio* at the Plaza?'

'I'd like to see that,' said Mr Jermy.

'You're both barbarians,' said Mrs Jermy. 'Miles, I live among the uneducated. I am trying to bring a little knowledge and elegance into their lives and all they want to do is see Bob Hope and Bing Crosby.'

'No, mummy. We want Dorothy Lamour, too,' said Hugh.

'I refuse to be teased any more,' said Mrs Jermy with a smile and got up. At the door she turned and said, 'Let me know if you'll be in for dinner, won't you?' She left the room.

'She's not seriously upset,' said Mr Jermy. 'It's a game we play. She likes to tease Hugh and me. She rather disapproves of Hugh becoming a regular soldier. She thinks it will make him into a barbarian. That's because she doesn't understand Hugh's athleticism or the army. So she pretends we're both barbarians. I think the army is a good idea. The war's over so it's pretty safe and a wonderful life for a young man. You'll learn a lot about life, Hugh. When you're bored with it you

223

can come and join the business as a mature man. Anyhow, Miles, he's made up his own mind. He's very determined. I'm sure my wife will get tickets for the opera but we'll both have to go with Hugh today to see *The Road to Rio.*'

# Chapter 15

# *Christmas fireworks*

Christmas Eve is my birthday. This was a birthday to remember.

'RQMS on the telephone for you, Sir,' said Corporal Low.

I lit a cigarette and took the telephone.

'Happy birthday, Mr Player,' said the RQMS.

'Thank you, RQ. Fancy you remembering.'

'Oh, I remember our first Christmas in Hong Kong well, though you might wish to forget it.'

The RQMS, then the company serjeant-major of X Company in which I was a platoon commander at the time, had got me helplessly drunk in the serjeant's mess on Boxing Day, feeding me drinks continuously on the pretext that he had failed to have a drink with me on my twenty-first birthday.

'I *am* trying to forget it. Happy Christmas to you.'

'We'll have a happy Christmas at B Echelon, you can be sure of that. You should see what I've got off the Yanks. Happy Christmas to you, Sir, and I've a case of claret for you. A whole case. I got it from Hong Kong.'

'Is that the case you took off Mr Jermy?'

'Mr Jermy, Sir? How did you know about that?'

'I asked Mr Jermy to bring it.'

'Yes, but you see I've been keeping it safely for you here, Sir.'

'At a properly regulated temperature, I trust?'

'Now come on, Sir. I'm sending it up today with some champagne for your birthday. You didn't know about that, did you, Sir?'

'Where did you get *that* from?'

'That's my secret, Sir.'

'What about the silver goblets?'

'Fucking hell, Sir. Isn't champagne enough?'

I put the telephone down.

'Happy birthday, Sir,' said Corporal Low. 'I've been keeping these for you.'

He handed me some letters and parcels all marked that they were not to be opened until 24 December. Sonia had sent me a copy of Tolstoy's *Tales from the Outposts* in the small World's Classics edition, writing 'Is your war anything like this? I hope not'. George Bulman had sent an Everyman Surtees titled *Jorrocks' Jaunts and Jollities,* writing 'to brighten up your birthday and Christmas and for sending me all the news'. I had been writing to him regularly. Colonel Guy borrowed the book as soon as he saw it. My mother wrote that she was very sad to think I would be spending my birthday in a trench dining out of tins. Little did she know I was going to sit down to dinner with pheasant, champagne and claret. She sent some gloves she had knitted specially, which were not warm enough for the Korean winter, and a heavy woollen scarf knitted in the regimental colours of blue, green and red, which was much admired and proved most useful. Finally there was a tin of Turkish cigarettes from my men 'to celebrate the new aroma you've brought to the intelligence section'.

'Where on earth did you find these, Corporal Low?' I asked.

'The Turkish brigade. They're in reserve at the moment, not far from here. Did you know they are commanded by a general who boasts he fought General Allenby in Palestine in the Great War?'

'Perfectly possible. They're a tough lot.'

'They are, Sir. I asked the Turkish chappie I got these from if they were enjoying the war. "Not enough fighting," he said. "Last week we attack hill with bayonets. Chinese run away. We put bayonets in scabbards without blood. Not good war." It wasn't a joke. He really meant it.'

Christmas Eve was to be like any other day except that the colonel had arranged for a battalion concert to tour the companies over Christmas. The first performance was to be in front of battalion headquarters, the Bugles and the Mortar platoon in the afternoon. The RQMS had found a piano. Tom Body had built a stage that could be easily collapsed to take round the companies. There were to be the usual satirical skits that dominated such concerts. Tom Body was the main producer and he had concocted the *tour de force*, which I'd seen him practising. He had selected the twelve Korean porters with the most effeminate figures and looks and trained them to dance the can-can. Many male Koreans are slightly built. Made-up as women and dressed in bodices and skirts they formed a glamorous eastern dancing troupe.

As it was my birthday we had a few drinks before lunch. Burgo had returned to us that morning having been repaired in Japan. He had complete use of his arm. He was thinner. Otherwise he was the same old Burgo. With him had come Major Jack Trench, a tall, thin, ascetic-looking man who was joining us as a company commander. Colonel Guy had explained to me that he needed new officers of every rank so that he could move officers around to give them a change and keep them fresh. Commanding a company continuously on active service was taxing. By the time we left Korea none of the companies would be commanded by the officers who had brought them to the war. Where this was not due to casualties – we had already lost George Bulman and Tom Warburton – it was by design.

Colonel Guy also explained that he believed that one had a bank of courage. If one drew on it continuously, or too often, one could overdraw it. All the more reason, he said, to relieve officers and move them around, warrant officers and NCOs, too. He thought the bravest men in the battalion were the junior NCOs as they had to lead the men in their sections, which was the hardest job of all. The company commanders had the greatest responsibility and the greatest strain.

'Welcome, Trench,' Colonel Guy said. 'We're going to keep you at battalion headquarters for a day or two so you can get the feel of things.'

'What about taking over my company, Sir?'

'Plenty of time for that after Christmas. There's a lot I'd like to talk to you about. It's Miles' birthday. We're going to celebrate that and Burgo's return tonight. And this afternoon we've a concert. You'll be able to see the style we live in.'

He laughed but Jack Trench looked stony-faced.

At the concert the officers sat in the front row. The total audience was about seventy. The concert started well. A series of turns, some polished, some earthy, most of them *risqué* and based on our experiences in Korea, got everyone laughing. What Jack Trench did appear to understand – I was sitting between him and Burgo – he seemed to disapprove. Everyone was in a lively mood when Serjeant Body's *corps de ballet* danced on to the stage as the finale. They were greeted with shouts and whistles and a few catcalls. The pianist hammered out Offenbach and the troupe started dancing the can-can. They were incredibly realistic and a good deal more elegant than some can-can dancers I had seen. The audience started clapping and cheering long before the dancers had finished. When they did there was pandemonium, men stamping their feet, shouting, whistling and demanding an encore. Jack Trench whispered in the colonel's ear but Colonel Guy was clapping away and seemed unfussed by the performance. Then the

228

RSM signalled to Tom Body. Tom quietened everyone down. He said we had been a wonderful audience, that they now had to go and repeat the performance for Z Company and asked us to stand up and sing 'God Save the King'. We sang loudly.

The audience broke up, excited and a little wild-eyed. The colonel walked up to the stage to talk to Tom Body and congratulate him. Jack Trench found the RSM. I watched them. They clearly exchanged disapproving words.

'That Major Trench,' said Burgo, 'is not quite the thing. He made a damn nuisance of himself on the way up, finding fault in everything. You'd best keep a distance from him. I'm glad I'm off to Hong Kong. I'd hate to be in his company.'

'Where's he popped up from?' I asked.

'He's been with the paras.'

'He'll be very heavy then, demanding to be called "Sir".'

'Too right. I called him Trench, as the Colonel did just now, and we always do with newcomers until we get to know them. He said, "I think you mean Sir". I explained that in the Second Battalion, and I understood the First too, the colonels disapproved of officers Sir-ing each other except on the parade ground.'

'What did he say to that?'

'He harrumphed. Then he told me not to be insolent.'

'Good God.'

'I told him I was not being insolent, merely sharing a little local knowledge. Then I stared him down with a big smile like Colonel Guy does sometimes.'

'You've made an enemy.'

'I was trying to be friendly but you could be right. Isn't it getting rather cold out here?'

We made for my hoochie, where Maxwell had the chuffer going well.

'I hope you enjoyed the concert, Maxwell?' I said.

'Very much. The *corps de ballet* was remarkable and, for

some, I thought a little over-exciting. It was fortunate the men were sober, Sir.'

'Which reminds me. The RQMS telephoned this morning to say he was sending up a case of claret and some champagne. You'd better find it before the sober soldiery do, Maxwell.'

'Then I'd better do that now, Sir.'

Burgo and I sat down on two old ammunition boxes in front of my chuffer.

'Do you want me to brief you on the duties of an ADC?' I asked him. 'I sent a message to Hugh to ask him to join us here. I thought we might do it together.'

'Plenty of time for that. I'd like to hear what happened after I was wounded. It seems I had the easy part.'

I told him about the battle for Hill 220.

'I must go and see Dermot and Serjeant-Major Budd. Now I'm sorry I'm going to Hong Kong. I'd really much rather stay here.'

'It doesn't look as if Hugh is coming,' I said. 'Doughty can take you up in my jeep. Don't be late back for dinner.'

I lit a Turkish cigarette and was thinking what a happy day it was turning out to be when Maxwell came in with a long face.

'Grave news, Sir. I've found the champagne and the claret and I fear they've been subjected to the elements.'

'Are you trying to soften the news, Maxwell? Could you be a little more specific?'

'They were frozen. The corks of the claret are all pushing out of the bottles and the champagne bottles have all smashed.'

'Oh, no!'

'I fear so. The champagne was Australian,' he said in a deprecatory voice.

'What was the claret?'

'The claret *is* Chateau Mouton d'Armailhac 1936. It's thawing out well.'

230

'Do you think we'll be able to drink it?'

'I once heard that wine hates heat but doesn't mind being frozen.'

'Maxwell, what would I do without you?'

'I'd prefer not to know, Sir.'

'What am I going to tell the colonel?'

'Nothing, if it thaws out as I think it will.'

'Be careful of the labels.'

'I'm afraid I might lose those. I shall decant it.'

We sat down to dinner. Colonel Guy placed Jack Trench on his right and Burgo on his left. Opposite him were Percy Smythe, me and the padre, whom the colonel asked to say grace.

'I hear we've champagne for your birthday, Miles,' said Colonel Guy. 'I'm looking forward to this.'

Jack Trench looked astonished.

'We're not having much luck with our cellar again, colonel,' I said. 'The champagne has frozen and burst its bottles.'

'Good heavens,' Colonel Guy said. Turning to Jack Trench he said, 'Miles is full of surprises. In October he produced claret that had been boiled in Japan and now his champagne has frozen. What about the claret, Miles? Has that frozen, too?'

'It did, Colonel, but Maxwell has saved it. Maxwell, would you serve the claret?'

Maxwell poured the claret out of the aluminium water bottles he used as decanters and into the glasses we'd got from Japan in October. Colonel Guy sniffed his glass.

'Not bad,' he said. He took a gulp and rolled it round his mouth. 'Not bad at all. A trifle warm but not boiled. What is it?'

'Mouton d'Armailhac '36.'

'How many bottles have we got?'

'A case.'

'So that's one each tonight and one each for Christmas day?'

'Yes, colonel.'

'Excellent, Miles. You'll be mentioned in despatches after all.'

'Thank you, colonel.'

Jack Trench drank little and not everyone drank a bottle. After dinner Colonel Guy took Trench and Smythe away to his bunker to drink whisky and talk. Burgo sat on with Frank Parsonson and me in the mess tent to finish the wine and chat.

'How's your chapel?' I asked Frank.

'The Regimental Chapel, Miles. You must come and see it. Serjeant Body can turn his hand to anything. Can-can dancers, chapels. You name it. He can do it. I'm really pleased.'

'Do you have the regimental plate and chalice and things?' asked Burgo.

'Those were left in Hong Kong. I have the necessary in my case, which I keep at A Echelon. It's been sent up. I've got a fine cross, too. You can see it if you come to midnight mass.'

'Midnight mass?'

'It's Christmas, Burgo. We celebrate communion at midnight. I wonder if I could have what's left of the wine for communion?'

'Of course,' I said. 'Burgo brought a bottle of Remy Martin with him from Japan. At least that won't have frozen. Would you like some now, padre?'

'Brandy? Please.'

I handed the last decanter of wine to Frank. It was a third full. Then I opened the bottle of brandy.

'Do you really believe Christ lived?' asked Burgo.

'I've no doubt he lived.'

'And you believe in him?'

'I believe the gospels are genuine.'

'Do you believe in him?'

'He was an amazing man. You don't have to believe every-thing to realise that he was amazing. I believe in him.'

'Do you believe in God?'

'That's another matter.'

'Tell me.'

'Jesus is an inspiration. I find him tangible and credible. He is a model to us all. God is more abstract. What do you think?'

'I find it difficult to understand he could exist in all the misery we see around us.'

'So do I, sometimes.'

'You mean you don't believe he does?'

'I didn't say that. I don't know. I pray, but I find him difficult to reach.'

'Why are you a clergyman?'

'I like what I do. I help the men – and officers – in any way I can. I give them hope and the example of Christ.'

'Is there a life hereafter?'

'I doubt it.'

'But you go on being a priest?'

'I think I do some good.'

'You do immense good, padre,' I said. 'What do your superiors think of your beliefs?'

'I don't discuss them. When I was finishing at theological college I began to have doubts. Then I decided I believed in Christ and that was enough, so I went ahead. I haven't regretted it. I think I have a more realistic attitude than most priests, and I understand more and I can help more. It's not that I want to do good. I find that suspicious. I want to help people where I can. This is good brandy, Burgo.'

'Do you think Tom Body's can-can dancers were salacious, padre?'

'Christ never said anything about sex. You might say it's

god-given enjoyment. So long as it doesn't hurt anyone I can't see it matters. Nothing in excess.'

'That's Greek.'

'I was a classicist. The Greeks got a lot of things right.'

'Can I come to midnight mass?'

'Anyone can come. Have you been confirmed?'

'We were all confirmed at school without thinking.'

'Not that it would worry me if you were not. I'd give you a blessing.'

'I'd like to take communion from you. I've a lot to be thankful for.'

The regimental chapel, the Chapel of St Birinus, was full for midnight mass. Burgo and I went, much to the surprise of most there. We were the only officers. Twelve took communion. Serjeant Body got a blessing. Frank Parsonson gave a powerful, and mercifully short, exhortation. He certainly had a following. On Christmas morning he visited every company and gave short services. The service he gave at battalion headquarters was attended by all the officers and most of the men. We sang carols with fervour.

When we had moved into the reserve position the cooks were able to cook on a company basis. They decided to make their cookhouses, which had to be out in the open, as comfortable and warm as possible. The Battalion HQ cooks had built a hut of straw on three sides of the cookers, which protected them from the worst of the weather and retained much of the heat. Now, on Christmas morning, they were preparing a feast. There were turkeys and chickens, potatoes and green vegetables, Christmas pudding and mince pies, gravy and custard. The supply services had worked hard to provide the raw materials and the cooks were working their hardest to produce the meal on rudimentary cooking equipment. There was Asahi beer, too. Beer was generally rationed both to restrict excessive consumption and to meet the administrative problems of supplying it in the line. As we were in reserve we had been able to build up considerable stocks. At midday the bar opened and free Asahi beer was dispensed to anyone who wanted it.

This was, of course, after the traditional officers versus serjeants football match held on the parade square, which the RSM had had bulldozed out of a paddy field and was now more like a skating rink. In a short, dangerous game the bugle major, as referee, called it to a close when the score became three all. The players, and those officers and serjeants who had been watching, retired to the serjeants' mess where the bar was opened.

After a quick drink Colonel Guy and Percy Smythe went off to visit the rifle companies. The rest of us stayed and drank the serjeants' beer. Few therefore noticed the problems the cooks were having in preparing the meal, or the abandonment with which the soldiers were attacking the stockpile of Asahi beer. The dinner hour went by. Only the cooks noticed. They pumped up their burners to greater heat and worked more furiously to get Christmas dinner on the table.

I was talking to the bugle major, who was keen for another pheasant shoot to be organised, when we heard shouts and cheering coming from the cookhouse. We took little notice. After more shouting and cheering we turned to look. The straw hut round the cookhouse was on fire. Flames were leaping skywards as the cooks danced around trying to save the meal. The fire was already too far gone to be put out by the meagre fire-fighting equipment to hand. The cooks darted in and out, helped by a few reckless souls. Most of the men, Asahi beer in hand, were surrounding the fire, cheering on the cooks and the few who had gone to their help to save the Christmas meal. Turkeys and chickens were being hurled out like large grenades, pans of vegetables were being passed from hand to hand like batons in a relay race, mince pies were being thrown like cricket balls and Christmas puddings were being carried in two hands like rugger balls in the effort to get them away from the inferno that was the cookhouse. Slowly the RSM and bugle major managed to get some order into the scene. When the straw had burnt to the ground the remnants of the Christmas meal were collected together in a small pile. It was too late. The men, drunk now with the beer and the excitement, had helped themselves to the food as it was saved. The cooks had over-provided so there was more than enough. Here and there were groups of men sitting on the ground with a turkey or chicken between them, tearing it apart with their hands, gobbling it down with a mince pie or a piece of pudding and washing it down with more Asahi beer.

'It's disgraceful,' said Jack Trench to the RSM. 'I've never seen such indiscipline in my life.'

'The men are enjoying themselves, Sir,' said the RSM. 'They're best left to themselves. It's Christmas. Not their fault the cookhouse burnt. I'll just go and have a look at my ammunition dump and see that's in no danger.'

Burgo was spending the day with his old company and was returning before nightfall when the officers at battalion HQ planned to have their Christmas dinner. Colonel Guy and Percy Smythe were still visiting the companies, as was the padre. I had to fall back on the company of Jack Trench and failed to heed Burgo's warning.

'In my first twenty-four hours here I've seen nothing but laxity, indulgence and indiscipline,' said Jack Trench. 'I find it hard to believe. They told me there was no finer battalion in the division. Aren't you ashamed, Player?'

'I'm proud of the battalion. It's just letting its hair down after coming out of the line. We had a hundred casualties.'

'I'm not surprised at the casualties.'

'I don't know what you mean by that. We had twenty-three

killed and sixty-six wounded, excluding the missing, and we took all our objectives on time and held them.'

'Nothing to the casualties we had at Arnhem.'

'Arnhem? What's that got to do with it?'

'Arnhem was a great battle.'

'The trouble with you paratroopers is you cream off the best of the officers, NCOs and men from the good regiments and then waste them, throwing them into disasters like Arnhem.'

'How dare you say Arnhem was a disaster.'

'Arnhem was a defeat. Badly planned, badly executed. I accept some of you fought like lions. You had to. A disaster.'

'You don't know anything about it. You're as insolent as the other young officers round here.'

'I object to that, Major Trench.'

'I shall report you to the commanding officer, Lieutenant Player.'

'I'd be happy if you did. But you won't. He'd laugh at you.'

I thought Trench would explode. He didn't. He got up and walked out of the tent.

I went to my hoochie, lay on my bed, lit a Turkish cigarette, started to read Tolstoy's *Tales from the Outposts* and its vivid stories of the Crimean War and fell asleep.

'Wake-up, Sir.'

Maxwell was shaking me.

'Officers' dinner in quarter of an hour.'

'Let me sleep, Maxwell.'

'You'll miss the dinner, Sir. You can't do that. You've already missed the best theatre of the day.'

'I saw the cookhouse burn down.'

'Not that, Sir. Serjeant Body's *corps de ballet*. Clever pun that, not that many will have noticed it. Did you have anything to do with that?'

'I suggested the name. I saw the performance yesterday, Maxwell.'

'They gave another performance this afternoon, with audience participation.'

'Was it as good as yesterday?'

'Better. Hilarious. The troupe returned from their tour of the provinces in their truck as the men were looking for another distraction after their dinner. They enjoyed their dinner. I did too, Sir. As soon as they saw the troupe they shouted "It's the can-can dancers. Let's have the can-can" and things like that, but a bit more explicit. So Serjeant Body, who likes the limelight as you know, Sir, fits up the stage and the piano. By this time there's quite a crowd. The pianist starts up and on come the troupe, all high stepping and looking gorgeous, though I say it myself. The lads can't contain themselves, shouting and whistling and cheering. Then one lad jumps on to the stage and starts dancing too. Oh, the shouting, Sir. Several more run on the stage, not so much to dance but to carry the dancers off. I wouldn't like to think what they had in mind. Then the RSM appears with the provost serjeant. They must have seen it all from the serjeant's mess. Order is resumed, not without a few sore heads. I'm told the RSM has banned the troupe from ever appearing again. Some poor sods will never see it now. Quite a Christmas one way and another, Sir, and not quite "All Sir Garnet". You're going to be late for your dinner if you don't hurry.'

Colonel Guy and Percy Smythe were in an excellent mood. They had drunk their way round the companies and were slightly pissed. Burgo was hardly sober and the padre was catching up fast. Jack Trench was looking stony and sober. They were standing around, drinking and waiting for dinner to be announced.

'Did you see the can-can again this afternoon, Miles?' Colonel Guy asked me as I came into the tent.

'I missed it but Maxwell gave me a vivid description. I wish I'd been there.'

238

'I'm told it was a riot, in more senses than one. I'm rather glad I wasn't there. The RSM has told me he's banned it. What do you think, padre? You're here to advise me on such things.'

'I missed it this afternoon, too. Under control it was harmless enough. I'm told the men were in exuberant spirits, which is why it got out of hand. They were looking for an opportunity for excitement.'

'And I hear the cookhouse burned down. That must have been a sight. Nothing like that happened in the companies. I only have to turn my back and you have all these excitements. Was it dangerous? Was anyone hurt?'

'Disappointing for the cooks,' I said, 'but no casualties, not even the food which the men said was very good even if they ate it rather unconventionally.'

'It was a disgrace, Colonel.'

'What's that, Trench?'

At least Jack Trench was calling Guy Surtees 'Colonel' and not 'Sir'.

'The conflagration in the cookhouse and the can-can dancers were a disgrace.'

The Colonel stared at Jack Trench.

'Come on, Jack,' he said. 'The men have had a hard time. Let them relax a little and have some fun. No one's been hurt. When we're in the line we fight hard, When we're out of it we play hard. That's the motto of this battalion. We'll be back in the line in the new year. Let's enjoy ourselves while we can.'

He gave Jack Trench a long look. Everyone was silent.

'Gentlemen,' Roberts announced in a loud voice, 'dinner is served.'

'Padre,' said Colonel Guy, 'come and sit on my right for Christmas dinner. And would you give us one of your engaging graces?'

## Chapter 16

# Back in no man's land

On Boxing Day, Doughty drove Burgo to B Echelon in my jeep, on the first stage of his journey to Hong Kong.

'Avoid Trench Foot, if you can,' he said in farewell. 'I doubt there's a cure for this new para strain.'

I went to Percy Smythe's tent and asked him if we could talk.

'What, now?'

'I'm afraid I had a *contretemps* with Jack Trench.'

'You, too? Oh dear. What happened?'

'We were sitting in the mess tent yesterday afternoon and he said he thought the battalion indisciplined. I defended the battalion and told him what I thought of the paras. He said I was insolent and that he would report me to Colonel Guy.'

'Is that it?'

'In a nutshell.'

'Why are you young officers all so intolerant? You didn't have to get into an argument with him. You want to be careful about saying things about the paras. Colonel Guy commanded a parachute battalion in the war. I know they've changed since then and their ways are different from ours but they're good troops even if they are a little too keen on publicity. Colonel Guy won't tolerate differences between the officers. You go and find Jack and apologise to him for insulting the paras. He hasn't said anything about you to the colonel or me. I think he'll be civil to you. He got the message last night. He's going to command A Echelon later today. You'd better catch him before he goes.'

I found Jack Trench in the officers' mess tent.

'Major Trench,' I said, 'may I have a word with you, outside?'

'Yes,' he said.

We walked out of the tent and out of earshot of Roberts and Maxwell, who were preparing lunch.

'I apologise for insulting the Parachute Regiment and I'm sorry for what I said yesterday,' I said.

'That's decent of you, Player. I was a little hasty myself. Let's shake hands and forget about it.'

We shook hands.

'Would you like a briefing on the situation? We've an up-to-date map in the intelligence tent.'

'I'd like that a lot.'

We walked to the intelligence tent where I personally briefed him on the map. He asked good questions. He knew his trade. He thanked me and walked away. I wondered if his earlier behaviour was nervousness or whether he was really as pompous and self-opinionated as he had appeared. I hoped the former but feared the latter.

We did not return to the line until mid-January. We were called on to do more patrols, which were unpopular as they came under the control of the forward battalions and disrupted our own work and training. One patrol was ambushed and we lost three men. The cold became intense. We had to make getting frostbite a military offence. If you got wet socks from sweating, which you could, you had to change them or they would freeze on you. An hussar put his bare hand on the side of his tank and lost the skin as he pulled his hand off.

241

When we returned to the front line we took over the position from the Canadians that we had held for a week before Christmas. We found the Chinese, not just the winter, had changed the nature of the war. They had been digging their way forward, zigzagging down their hills into no man's land with long communication trenches reaching almost to the paddy. Off the communication trenches they dug deep positions, which they manned both as observation posts and as bases from which to patrol. They developed a honeycomb of tunnels to serve these positions. They used their increased artillery more frequently, employing it in hate sessions in which they would bombard a company furiously. There was no pattern to this. They included battalion HQ in these sessions. As soon as they started you ran for the nearest dugout. Occasionally someone was killed. More often someone was wounded. The Chinese also brought up self-propelled guns on to the forward slopes of their hills. They would fire directly at our positions for a few minutes before withdrawing, and were difficult to detect.

During this time they never attacked us, just patrolled against us mercilessly. All work on our forward slopes, such as wiring and improving the position, had to be done at night. Coupled with patrolling nightly, we were slowly being worn down with tiredness. In the morning we would some-times find the Chinese had left propaganda material on our wire, leaflets denouncing the Yanks as capitalists and profiteers and promising us safe conduct if we surrendered.

We retaliated. We set ambushes. We laid more mines between the companies. Our artillery harassed theirs and our tanks brought direct fire to bear on their positions. We sent patrols to take out their dugouts, which had been directing fire on to us during the day. We had our successes and we paid for them.

Our first attempt ended before it began. Tim Seymour, who commanded a platoon in Dermot's company, ran straight

242

into an ambush from which he was fortunate to extricate himself with only two men killed, and himself wounded.

Then a subaltern from W Company, who had led some successful patrols, took a finely planned patrol unnoticed up to an observation post and was severely wounded when he was placing the charge to blow up the dugout. A Chinese sentry darted out of a tunnel and sprayed him with a burp gun, catching him in the legs. He told his men to abandon him. They were fearless, disobeyed him and carried him safely back. The NCO won the MM and the officer the MC, but he lost a leg.

The next day we borrowed an American Persuader. It blew the dugout to pieces with twenty rounds.

Then Hugh Jermy and Serjeant Foxton attacked a dugout. Dermot and I debriefed them on their return.

'All went to plan,' said Hugh, 'as we crossed the paddy. I dropped Serjeant Foxton and the Bren gunner to cover us and I led the attack group straight up to the dugout. I lay down and shoved the charge into the gap. There was no one around. We retired twenty yards and I blew the charge. All hell let loose. They mortared us and machine-gunned us. The artillery fire you retaliated with, as arranged, quietened the machine-guns and the mortars stopped. We rejoined Serjeant Foxton and retraced our steps in bounds. First Serjeant Foxton led while we covered him. Then Foxton covered my group as we went ahead. We leap-frogged each other until we were quite close to our lines. Serjeant Foxton was twenty yards ahead of me when he walked into an ambush. His Bren gunner was wounded immediately. Foxton threw a grenade, then picked the gun up and started firing. The Chinks hadn't noticed my group. I fired a Verey light. We could see them all clearly. We charged them and they fled. They left two dead and one wounded. We left the dead where they fell and brought the wounded one back with ours. We were lucky.'

Lucky, or not, Hugh had brewed up the dugout and brought back a prisoner which was a rarity. He won an immediate MC.

Others were not so lucky. Chris Worthington, a young regular officer who had joined with Robin Brett at the time I became intelligence officer, took out a fighting patrol. An ambush was waiting for them at the bottom of our hill. He shouted to his patrol to run and stood to shoot it out. The rear marker group of a corporal and three men got out and observed. There was furious firing then silence. When he thought it was safe the corporal led his group forward and found Chris and his group dead. In the morning Hugh took a patrol to collect them.

'I found them immediately,' Hugh said. Dermot, Robin Brett, Hugh and I were sitting in Dermot's dugout. 'They were lying where they must have fallen, stripped of everything except their clothes. The Chinks took everything off them. We searched the area. It was clear the Chinks had casualties too, how many we could not tell. I felt sick. They were badly shot up. Chris didn't have a chance walking straight into an ambush before he'd hardly started. When you're out there you don't know what you're going to find.'

Dermot was talking Hugh through it, getting at the facts and damping down the emotion. Hugh may have felt sick. He did not show it. He spoke calmly, if hesitantly.

'I can't believe it,' said Robin Brett. 'Oh, no. Not Chris. We were at school together, went through Sandhurst together. I can't believe it. Not Chris.'

He sat in the corner of the bunker, almost paralysed, saying, 'Oh, no. Not Chris. I can't believe it.'

Dermot poured out whisky for everyone. It was ten o'clock in the morning.

'To Chris,' he said, 'and his brave men. We must be as brave as they were. Robin, I want you to take out an ambush patrol tonight. We're not going to let the Chinks get away with this.'

244

Robin took out an ambush patrol for several nights. It froze so hard they could not stay out for long and the Chinks knew better than to return.

The Chinese patrolled and patrolled. One night, a mile behind battalion HQ, a truck was ambushed and the driver captured. A Chinese patrol had crawled through our mine-fields and roamed behind the lines. This explained the so-called guerrilla activities against which we had operated before Christmas. There were no guerrillas behind our section of the line, though they operated elsewhere. The Chinese were patrolling deeply.

We laid more mines and more wire to prevent the Chinese moving so freely between the company positions. The Chinese still seemed to move at will around us.

A draft of National Servicemen left us to return to England to be demobilised, their two years' service expired. This, coupled with constant casualties, reduced our numbers further. Some platoons, which had arrived from Hong Kong thirty-five strong, were down to sixteen or seventeen men. Men went without sleep. Patrolling had to be curtailed. To boost our firepower the machine-gun platoon got two more Vickers machine-guns, making eight in all. A small draft of fresh soldiers was formed into the Browning platoon and issued with eight Browning machine-guns. Both these platoons were positioned on the edge of companies to shoot with immense firepower across our front, and across the front of our neighbouring battalions. One night the Australians, on our right, were heavily attacked. We watched the sixteen machine-guns firing tracer across their front. With the mortar and artillery fire being brought down too, the Chinese could not get near the Australian trenches.

This was the beginning of what came to be known as the static war when the onus of the fighting fell completely on the shoulders of the platoon commanders and their NCOs, who carried the remorseless weight of patrolling and being bombarded daily. Every night, while the war raged around us, we could see the balloon, lit by searchlights, flying over Panmunjon to indicate peace talks were still under way.

Colonel Guy and I were studying the map in the command post discussing patrolling when Percy Smythe came in.

'The king is dead,' he said.

'Not unexpected, I suppose,' said Colonel Guy, 'but a sad day for England. He was a good king. One of the best we've had.'

'We have a beautiful young queen now.'

'Yes, a new era. I wonder what it holds for us?'

'A bright future surely, colonel?' said Percy.

'Maybe, Percy. Certainly a different future. The world has changed and England is tired. I sometimes wonder if we haven't shot our bolt. Perhaps a new queen will give us a shot in the arm.'

'I've never heard you talk like that, colonel.'

'When I was Miles's age I was at the king's coronation. Since then we seem to have had crisis after crisis. We came through the war by the skin of our teeth. We've been over-stretched all my life trying to meet our commitments. And here we are in Korea, under strength and fighting a new enemy.'

'I thought we were doing rather well. We won the last war and now we're putting out the fires that keep bursting out.'

'America and Russia won the last war, Percy. We don't recognise that. We may have saved the free world by standing up to Hitler alone but I feel we were mortally wounded.'

He paused. Then he said, 'The king is dead. Long live the queen.'

For a while we were silent.

'Now, Miles, where exactly was that last ambush?'

246

Colonel Guy held regular O groups for the company commanders at battalion headquarters to co-ordinate patrolling and defence, and to share information. We all gained from the camaraderie of the meetings. The company commanders led lonely lives, sitting in their dugouts alone at night waiting for their patrols to come in and praying they would. I often went and sat with one of them to relieve the unbearable tenseness of the night.

One morning Colonel Guy, Dermot Lisle, Ben Wildbore, Rex Topham and Jack Trench were sitting in the battalion HQ bunker. Colonel Guy was waiting for Hadji to arrive before he started. They were joshing each other when Percy Smythe came in with an ashen face.

'I'm very sorry to have to say, colonel, that Hadji has been killed.'

'Killed? How? I heard no gunfire.'

'After stand-to one of his platoons reported the Chinese had left propaganda leaflets on the wire. Hadji went down to have a look. He picked the leaflets off the wire. They were booby-trapped. He was blown up. His men got him back to his lines. He died thirty minutes later.'

There was silence. No one looked at anyone else. Each of us was deep in his own thoughts. What had just happened to Hadji could have happened to any one of us. Then the death of dear, lovable, eccentric, brave Hadji sank in.

'Not Hadji,' said Rex, in a whisper that burst the silence.

I looked at him. Tears were glistening on his cheeks and his eyes had a faraway look.

'Not Hadji,' he whispered again. He was weeping.

There was another long silence.

Then Colonel Guy said, 'We are soldiers. We live on the edge of life and death. We have to bear these things, however hard. Miles, would you ask the padre to join us.'

I found Frank Parsonson immediately. He was waiting outside the bunker, probably expecting to be called. Hadji

247

had asked for him and he had been with Hadji when he died.

'Ah, padre,' said Colonel Guy. 'You know the terrible news about Hadji? Would you say a prayer for him.'

Frank constructed a beautiful prayer.

'Thank you, padre,' said Colonel Guy.

A week or two later I was sitting with Dermot in his bunker. Robin Brett was out with a patrol and we were waiting for his return.

'You know how terrible they say it was in the trenches in the Great War?' Dermot asked.

'I've seen *Journey's End*, read Sassoon and Graves and know about Passchendaele and the Somme.'

'This is far worse.'

'Are you sure?'

'Except in the great attacks, and they were dreadful, a battalion was only in the line for an average of four days at a time. We've been here for six weeks and still no notice of being relieved.'

'Only four days?'

'Then they went into reserve in the villages behind the lines and trained and ate decent food and poked the girls in the brothels.'

'And caught VD?'

'Probably. Have you heard of any brothels around here?'

'The Yanks have some. Unofficially. The Korean girls come up in a group and find a ruined village a mile or two behind the lines. Pretty grotty. The word goes round and they're inundated with custom. Then the authorities get to hear and the girls are moved on. So Captain Kim tells me.'

'I like Captain Kim.'

'He's a very decent, intelligent and funny fellow. He's my friend. What about Anzio? How does that compare?'

'Anzio was worse, far worse. It was a beachhead. We never

248

got properly dug in. We couldn't. It was too low lying and wet. Two foot down you hit water. Out of the line we were still in range of the German guns. They shelled us mercilessly. Anzio was unbelievable. Rather like here we were saved by the artillery breaking up the German attacks.'

'No one in the battalion ever talks about Anzio.'

'We had terrible casualties. We lost over half the battalion.'

'Half the battalion?'

'Almost three-quarters. Others had worse.'

'What's that noise?'

A scratching sound was coming from somewhere in the dugout.

'That's Curly.'

'Who's Curly?'

'Curly is my friend. He's a rat. Look. There.'

'He's big. How do you put up with him?'

'I don't. He's bloody cunning. Watch.'

Dermot got out a bayonet and started shadow-boxing Curly, lunging at him and missing.

'See? Too cunning.'

'Let me try.'

I took the bayonet and tried to get Curly. I lost my balance and ended up on the floor. Curly disappeared through a hole.

'Is this a new dugout?' I asked as I got up. 'It looks different from your old one.'

'I couldn't stand the old one. Someone who'd had it before used to piss in it. The stink got me down. So we filled it in and built this. Curly prefers it, too.

'Why are we forbidden to shoot the rats in the bunkers?'

'Accidents, mainly. It's not effective either. I'm not inviting you to prove me wrong but neither of us is good enough with a revolver to shoot a rat. It's difficult enough to shoot a man with a revolver.'

'I thought you were an Olympic shot?'

249

'That proves my point.'

There was a noise outside the bunker.

'That must be Robin,' said Dermot.

Robin came into the dugout. In his blackened face there was a grim, tense look. He walked in hesitantly and, without a word, slumped on to an upturned ammunition box. His head dropped on to his chest. Slowly he raised it. His eyes were glistening. A tear fell down his cheek, ploughing a clean furrow through his camouflage.

'I can't go on, Dermot. I'm shot to bits.'

'Where? Where are you shot, Robin?'

'Shot to bits.'

'Where? Where are you wounded? I can't see.'

'No, no. Not wounded. It's my nerves. They're shot to pieces.'

No one spoke. Robin was weeping now, his head dropped forward again, his shoulders shaking and his arms hanging loosely and jerking as he shook. After a bit he quietened. Dermot poured a mug of tea from a flask, adding rum.

'Drink this,' he said.

Robin held the mug in his hands, spilt some and then drank.

'I can't go on, Dermot.'

'Are all your men safely in?'

'Yes.'

'Then what happened?'

'Nothing happened. That's the trouble. Nothing.'

'Tell me about tonight.'

'Not just tonight. Every night.'

'Tell me.'

'Every night I go out I pass the place where Chris was ambushed. I can't help thinking about it and wondering if they're waiting for me. I sometimes sit watching the place for half an hour just listening. I can't sit there any longer. It's too cold. When I go on I still don't know. I'm terrified.'

'Exactly what did you do tonight?'

'I went out with Corporal Truss and Jones 45 and Owen. After half an hour we went on and we set up a position on the river. No one came. They never do because they're waiting for me somewhere. Then we came home and, as we got close to where Chris was killed, I had to go through it all again.

'You did very well. Just what you had to.'

'No I didn't. I was terrified. If it wasn't for Truss I would still be out there.'

'What did Truss do?'

'He said, "Come on, Sir. We've got to go on or we'll freeze." I would have liked to have frozen to death. He coaxed me back in. He thinks I'm very brave sitting there. I'm terrified. I can't go on. I can't do it again.'

'Yes, you can. We're all frightened. It's controlling it that counts. You're doing very well. You're just very tired. We all get tired. We've been in the line too long. What you need is a good rest.'

'I want to die.'

'No you don't. You're just very tired, Robin. It happens. I understand.'

'Yes. I'm so very tired.'

He looked at Dermot beseechingly.

'I can't stop thinking about Chris.'

'I understand, Robin. Life has to go on.'

'I can't go on.'

'You have to. We all have to. Think of Chris, then. What would he say? Don't you have a duty to him?'

'I wish I were dead like Chris.'

'No, you don't. You've everything to live for. Your parents, your friends, your soldiers. They all depend on you and are looking to you.'

'I know, but I can't.'

'Yes, you can, Robin. I know you can. Of course you're upset

251

about Chris. We all are. We're soldiers. That doesn't mean we don't feel. We just know life has to go on. We have duties and responsibilities to others. You can do it if you want to.'

'I don't want to.'

They went on talking like this: Dermot gentle, encouraging and firm; Robin dejected, despondent and played out. I wondered what I would feel like if, night after night, I had to go out on patrol into no man's land past the place where my best friend had been killed, wondering who was waiting for me in the dark.

'Look at it like this, Robin. You've run down your bank of courage. I've asked too much of you. It's my fault. You'll get your courage back. You need rest and time. You've had it harder than any of us.'

'Do you think so?'

'Of course. You've overdrawn your courage. After a rest it will come back.'

'Do you really think so?'

'I know it.'

Slowly Robin calmed down.

'Yes, Dermot,' I heard him saying. 'You're right. I must try and do my duty.'

'That's more like you, Robin. Now I want you to go and get some sleep. You need a good rest. We all do from time to time. You've been overdoing it. You're exhausted. No more patrolling for a bit. You get your sleep back.'

'Thank you, Dermot,' he said.

'You're a brave man, Robin. We're all afraid. The trick is mastering it. You are. Well done. Now to bed with you.'

Robin left. I don't think he ever noticed I was there. I looked at Dermot. Our eyes met.

'Will you send him to the doctor when he wakes up?'

'No. We can't do that. It would be the end. Let's see what he feels like when he's had a proper rest. He needs time to get over it.'

252

'He'll have to go out again,' I said.

'Not yet. I'll tell the colonel, not you. I'll do it when Robin's ready to go out again. We'll have to think up a good task for him to get his confidence back.'

Jack Trench took over Hadji's Y Company. Hugh Jermy and Serjeant Foxton were transferred to strengthen it as it had lost two subalterns. A serjeant was to command Hugh's old platoon until a new officer arrived. Several platoons in the battalion were now commanded by serjeants, such had been the officer losses. Hugh was as seasoned and experienced a subaltern as any now.

I still had a nagging feeling there was something wrong about Jack Trench and was concerned that Hugh should be with him. Hugh wasn't worried at all.

'It's good to have a change,' Hugh said to me. 'Trench Foot is a bit of an old woman, fussing about, but I'll be able to manage him. It's a subaltern's war now.'

We were in my intelligence bunker at battalion HQ. Hugh was passing through on his way between the two companies.

'There's something wrong with Jack,' I said, 'and don't get over-confident yourself. You're not a god. We're all mortal.'

'True enough.'

'Have you heard from Burgo?'

'No, but Sonia says he's doing fine. They're very pleased to have him.'

'Sonia says?'

'She writes to me from time to time. Now show me your famous map and brief me on what's going on. This place is the lap of luxury. What about one of your Turkish fags? I've run out of my Egyptian.'

'Do you miss Hong Kong?' I asked as I handed him the tin.

'Of course. But I wouldn't be anywhere else but here. Have you got many of these?'

'Corporal Low has a standing order with the Turks.'

'Could you spare me some?'

'Keep the tin.'

'Do you remember, when we were first commissioned and at the regimental depot, how we stank the anteroom out with our Egyptian cigarettes?'

'I suppose we could get some Gyppo fags sent from London. Don't you think these are better suited to Korea? They're much cheaper.'

'And stronger. They hide much of the stink, too. I'll take two tins a week if Corporal Low can get them. Does he take a cut?'

'Probably. This is a trading battalion.'

'Anyone else fancy them?'

'Frank Parsonson. Percy's not too keen on us smoking them in the command post. Colonel Guy doesn't seem to mind. Look, let me brief you on the map.'

We studied the map and Hugh had asked a few questions when we were interrupted by explosions outside.

'They shell you, too?'

'No one escapes now. You'll have to sit tight here until it's over. They won't be long.'

There were more explosions. Then they stopped.

'Not too hairy,' Hugh said.

'You didn't seem at all frightened.'

'I was terrified. I'd far prefer to be out in no man's land than sit in a bunker being shelled.'

'When we first came they didn't have much artillery. It's much heavier now, especially in the front line.'

'That's what Foxton says. It's the indiscriminate shelling that gets the men down.'

'You never seem to be down, whatever happens,' I said.

'Do you remember when we capsized all those years ago at Burnham?'

'It was my fault.'

'No. I did an uncontrolled jibe. It was my carelessness.

When we were both in the water with our boat full to the gunwales and I saw the other boats sailing away I felt really down. Then someone inside me said "get back in the boat, you can't just lie in the water. You've got to try. Don't you want to win?" I can see us now, bailing like Trojans, then setting sail and catching the fleet. Not being last across the finishing line was a great moment.'

'I always thought I had capsized that boat.'

'No. I made a Horlicks and then I did my damnedest to put it right.'

'You've had that sort of determination as long as I can remember.'

'Have I?'

Dermot asked me to join him when he told Colonel Guy about Robin Brett.

'Oh, God,' Colonel Guy said. 'I hope the battalion isn't losing its nerve.'

'No, colonel. We're just tired. Robin was exhausted. I'd sent him out on too many nights. He's had a good rest. Now Miles and I have worked out a plan for him to lead a successful patrol.'

'Take me through it.'

We took him into the HQ bunker and explained our plan on the large-scale map there. The key to the plan was for Robin to have a tank in support so that he would be able to call for fire any moment he wanted it. The tank was dug in on the company's hill and commanded the ground over which Robin was to patrol. Robin wouldn't feel he was completely alone knowing he could do this. He was to work out a fire plan himself with the tank commander and see the targets registered. The objective was to blow up a Chinese observation post that had been troubling us for some days. It was exposed and should not prove too difficult. There was always the danger that he could be ambushed or run into trouble on the objective. He was to take an experienced corporal and ten men with him.

'It's a good plan,' said Colonel Guy. 'Go ahead.'

Robin took his brief from Dermot, worked intently on a fire plan with the tank commander and saw the targets registered. He briefed the patrol. They had their last meal, blacked their faces, equipped themselves and hung their ammunition and grenades round them. Then they stood around having a last smoke until Robin called them together and took them down the hill and through the wire in the dark.

Dermot and I retired to his bunker where we listened to Robin's progress on the wireless. For a long time nothing happened. The first we heard was the explosion when the charge went off to blow the enemy OP.

'He's done it,' Dermot said. 'Let's see if he can get back safely.'

On his way back, Robin called for the tank to fire twice. We could not tell whether he was running into trouble or not. He arrived back and walked into the bunker. Through his black, grimy face his eyes glinted. He broke into a smile.

'We did it,' he said. 'I just hope I brewed up the right dugout.'

In the morning we examined the OP through our field glasses. He had blown up the right bunker.

A week later the tank commander was standing by his tank when a mortar bomb fell through the open hatch and killed the three men inside it. The same night, Robin extricated a patrol that had wandered by mistake into one of our minefields. He got them all out. Then he stepped on a mine himself and was killed.

The next day we were relieved by the Canadians. The balloon was still flying over Panmunjon.

# Chapter 17

## Commonwealth Games

Late in March we came out of the line into the reserve position we had occupied at Christmas. It rained, it snowed, it froze, it thawed and froze again. Then, slowly, the snow and ice melted into a sea of mud. We slid round the position, vehicles careered off the tracks, in places trenches collapsed and some of the bunkers subsided. We became a battalion of renovators and repairmen. As soon as we had stabilised the position we were ordered to a group of virgin hills to build another reserve position. Spring was about. The days were longer. We shed our winter clothing, rolled up our sleeves and dug.

'The Aussies and the Kiwis have challenged us to an athletics match,' Percy Smythe said to me one morning.

'Pity Burgo's left us,' I replied.

'We must have some other athletes. Colonel Guy has appointed Jack Trench athletics officer and told him to train a team. Jack's asked me what the officers can do. I seem to remember you can throw something?'

'The discus.'

'Haven't I seen you hurdling, too?'

'Yes. I like hurdling.'

'No hurdles in Korea. Well, no sporting hurdles. Any ideas about people who might perform?'

'Tom Body can throw the shot.'

'I know that.'

'Why doesn't Trench call for volunteers?'

'The Battalion would volunteer *en masse* to escape digging.'

'Why not hold inter-company sports to find the best athletes?'

'We can't do that. We're holding an inter-company boxing tournament. That's enough for the time being.'

Jack Trench did call for volunteers. If Dermot or Ben or Rex had called for volunteers the whole battalion might have come forward. Jack was an unknown quantity in the battalion. Only a few of our experienced athletes were still with us. Most volunteered. The teams we had fielded so successfully in Hong Kong were severely depleted and we had not had the opportunity to identify new talent in Korea or the time to train. We were in for another drumming at the hands of the Aussies.

The day came for the contest. A large paddy had been prepared beside the Imjin. It looked more like a motor show than an athletics meeting. Rank after rank of serried jeeps surrounded the sides of the field. Behind them were parked the trucks that had brought most of the men of the three regiments. It began as an exciting day and ended in our humiliation.

Tom Body narrowly won the shot. I came second in the discus. In all the track events we were soundly beaten, as we were in the other field events. The Aussies won, ahead of the Kiwis. We trailed a bad third. Jack Trench took the blame.

'If Serjeant Body can win and Mr Player come second why didn't our fucking runners do better?' I overheard Private Rumble, of the intelligence section, ask Corporal Low.

'It's that new major's fault, the one they call Trench Foot,' Corporal Low answered.

'What about him?'

'He was in charge. He was the fuckin' athletics officer.'

'So what?'

'The officer is responsible for training the team and seeing they fuckin' win.'

'Are you saying this Major Foot didn't run it proper?'

'Trench, not Foot. Looks like it.'

'What's he like, this major then?'

'He came from the fucking paras.'

'Wasn't Serjeant Body a para?'

'No. SAS.'

'What's the difference?'

'SAS has got brains. Cloak and dagger stuff. The paras just jump out of aeroplanes and get fuckin' slaughtered.'

'Sounds as though Major Trench is going to get fuckin' slaughtered by the CO.'

'They say Y Company's not what it was when old Hadji commanded it.'

'Perhaps this Major Trench should eat some curry?'

'No. The fucker's fuckin' fiery enough as it is.'

Corporal Low's was an understandable judgement. I was quietly pleased that Jack Trench should take the blame, though I knew it was unfair. He had not had the right men or the time to train them.

The approach to boxing was more scientific. First, every company held bouts to select the most promising boxers. No one was excused, subalterns included. This resulted in some able boxers emerging. In the battalion tournament W Company narrowly defeated Headquarter Company but all the companies had their successes. W Company's team had been led and trained by Hugh Jermy and Serjeant Foxton, who had now rejoined Hugh. Foxton was a fine lightweight and an experienced trainer. Hugh gave the overall direction. Foxton was tactician, goad and task master.

I had thought that W Company's triumph would have pleased Jack Trench, its company commander. The kudos went to Hugh and Foxton, not Jack, and Jack knew it. Jack was mean spirited, too. Worse was to come.

After Colonel Guy had presented the prizes, a few of us were standing around chatting about the bouts and the boxers.

'Colonel,' Hugh said, 'why don't we challenge the Aussies to a boxing match?'

'That's a thought,' replied Colonel Guy. 'You think we could win? We must if we challenge them. I can't have us humiliated again.'

'We've as good a foundation for a team as we've ever had, in every weight too. Foxton can train them up. We're all much fitter now than when we came out of the line. The problem with our athletes was they weren't fit. At boxing we could beat any battalion in Korea.'

'If *you* say so, Hugh, I think we could. There're no racing certainties but the odds are more in our favour than they were in the athletics. I can see the talent. Will you and Foxton train a team?'

'Delighted to, colonel.'

'When shall we fix the match? Two weeks today?'

'One week. We don't want to give the Aussies too much time to train. I will want our team to concentrate on training and exempted all duties.'

'How many?'

'Fourteen and Serjeant Foxton.'

'You've got them. I'll issue the challenge tomorrow.'

Hugh went off to find Foxton. Unfortunately Jack Trench had been there. Not only had he heard Hugh and Colonel Guy criticising the athletics, he felt he should have been consulted as Hugh and Foxton were in his company.

The battalion turned out for the boxing match *en masse,* as did the Australians. A ring had been built in the middle of the athletics ground. Serried ranks of jeeps and trucks surrounded it. Both sides started throwing invective at each other long before the first bout. Colonel Guy had bet the

Australian commanding officer an even tenner we would win. When this was announced the Australians roared with laughter. Many started to offer odds on the outcome and individual bouts that were too good to ignore. An Aussie captain gave me two to one we would lose. I bet a fiver. Then he offered me five pounds to one we'd lose every bout. When I looked doubting he gave me ten pounds to one. I took it, more out of bravado than sense.

There were to be seven bouts. The New Zealanders provided the referee and timekeeper. The hussars and the sappers provided the two umpires.

The first fight went the three full rounds. Our man was clearly the better and he won. This enlivened our men, who had been much quieter than the Australians. The Australians paid their bets. Some took more bets and lengthened the odds they were giving. Pound notes were fluttering around.

The second fight went three full rounds as well. We won. The Australians were not downhearted, shouting 'Luck' and 'You wait, you Poms'. They took more bets, though I noticed they were not offering such favourable odds. Our men, emboldened by two wins, accepted more bets.

Serjeant Foxton stepped into the ring for the third fight, hailed by furious shouts of encouragement from our boys and jeers from the Australians. He knocked his opponent out in the first round. A stunned silence was followed by a roar from our men. The Australians paid up and took more bets both on the next bout and on the final outcome. We had won three fights out of seven. We only had to win one more to take the match. I took another bet we would win from an Australian subaltern.

The fourth bout started in total silence. Occasionally a voice shouted encouragement to one or other boxer, but both sides were hushed. This was a critical bout. For two rounds our man pursued his opponent round the ring, battering and bloodying him until, in the third round, the referee stopped the fight and held up our man's arm as the winner. The noise was indescribable. I thought the Australians would rush the ring and lynch the referee. They said they would. The threats seemed ferocious but they were made in good spirit. The Aussies paid up. More bets were laid on the following bouts. We won the fifth and sixth. Surely the Australians must win one bout, everyone asked. The Australians emptied their pockets.

Into the ring stepped a tall, young National Service officer, a most unwarlike figure called Jeremy Last who was in Ben Wildbore's Y Company. I hardly knew him. Opposite him a fit and swarthy Australian, not quite the same height but full of bounce, was showing off his muscles and his torso to his backers who screamed encouragement.

'Can we win this, too?' I asked Hugh.

'You watch. He's one of our best. Last but not least.'

The Australian captain offered me double or quits. I took it.

Jeremy Last outreached his opponent and boxed with textbook skill. The Australian, clearly the stronger, pushed him round the ring. Jeremy was quicker on his feet and landed, I thought, more punches. At the end of the first round the outcome seemed uncertain. The second round was much the same and I thought Jeremy was ahead on points. The third round started to tremendous shouting. The Australian came rushing in. Jeremy landed a straight left on the Australian's jaw and he went sprawling. He got up immediately but he had lost heart. Jeremy out-boxed him for the rest of the round and was declared winner.

'Remarkable,' said Colonel Guy to the Australian commanding officer as he took the bundle of notes that were handed over. 'I should have bet the regimental funds. You gave us excellent sport.'

'We fight better without Queensberry rules.'

'You trounced us at athletics. Justice is done.'

'Justice be damned,' the Australian said. Then, turning to Hugh he said, 'I gather you're the smart young kangaroo who arranged this. What about a transfer to the Australian army?'

We all laughed.

Colonel Guy handed his bundle of notes to Hugh.

'Take these, Hugh,' he said, 'and look after the team. Now, let's go back to the mess and celebrate. Don't forget to collect your winnings, everyone.'

The mess was jumping. Most of the officers were there.

'How much did you win?' I asked Dermot.

'I didn't bet,' he said.

'Why not?'

'I didn't have any money on me,' he said, laughing. 'What about you?' he asked.

'Rather embarrassing. Thirty pounds.'

'That'll come in handy in Tokyo.'

'If only I was going on R and R.'

R and R, short for rest and recuperation, was the term we used for the spell of leave to which everyone in the battalion, and the Commonwealth division, was entitled after six months in Korea. Mine was long overdue.

'You are.'

'Am I?'

'Yes, next week.'

'I didn't know. How do you know?'

'You're going with me and Jeremy Last.'

'Goodness at last. Are you sure? You're not teasing?'

'Percy told me before the boxing. I'll want a copy of your *Tokyo Tips*.'

'As many as you like.'

*Tokyo Tips* was the dossier that, as intelligence officer, I had been asked to compile for officers off to Tokyo on R and R. Based on the debriefing of my fellow officers on their return, it had already run into several editions.

Ben Wildbore joined us, a cigarette hanging out of the corner of his mouth.

'Did you notice something odd about the RSM?' he asked Dermot.

'Hasn't he just returned from R and R?' said Dermot.

'Yes. I thought he didn't quite look his imposing self.'

'Now you say it,' said Dermot, 'yes, he did look different. I know. He's shaved his moustache off.'

'That's it,' said Ben.

'Why on earth would he do that?'

'Japanese girls don't like being kissed by men with moustaches.'

'How do you know?'

'I had to shave mine off.'

'Is that in *Tokyo Tips*?' Dermot asked me.

'*Tokyo Tips* has to be discreet. Supposing it fell into the hands of Lady Mountbatten?' I replied.

'Your head would roll.'

'Not just mine. The colonel said essential information of this nature should be included but not explicitly.'

'How does one get this essential information, then?'

'You'll find the bars and restaurants mentioned in the guide are graded by stars. A few are underlined. The guide says those underlined are strongly recommended.'

'What does that mean?'

'It means,' said Ben, 'that the girls are clean, perform at a price and are unlikely to give you flowery, willowy sickness.'

'How do you know they're clean, Ben?'

'As they work in restaurants they come under the Tokyo City Health Authority and they get their hands and fannies inspected weekly.'

'What about the geishas?'

'They won't sleep with you. They're sophisticated entertainers of great accomplishment who dance and sing. They may live in geisha houses and entertain in restaurants but they're owned by Japanese businessmen, who treat them as business wives and concubines. See them if you want. They're no more than a pretty sight, and not always that. You won't get a tumble there.'

'Are there brothels?'

'You don't want to go near them. Full of GIs and very *déclassé*.'

'What if someone wants something a little different?'

'I'm told you can get anything in Tokyo.'

'Can you recommend a place?'

'Try Mimosa's. It's in *Tokyo Tips*.'

## Chapter 18

# Rack and ruin in Japan

Dermot took Jeremy Last and me in his jeep to Kimpo airport, fifteen miles west of Seoul. We caught an American Constellation to Tokyo. In the plane I sat next to Dermot.

'Do you understand this war?' I asked him.

'Sort of. Do we have to talk about it now?'

'I'll ask you in Tokyo, then.'

'If you have to. I want to sleep.'

Dermont went to sleep. I looked at Jeremy. He was asleep as were most of the soldiers in the plane. I was too excited to sleep.

We land and check our weapons and ammunition into the armoury at the trooping centre. Then we strip, shower and are issued with a complete set of new uniform. We retrieve our regimental flashes and badges of rank from our old uniforms. Those and our berets are the only pieces of clothing we now wear that we have brought from Korea. We change money into Japanese yen. Then we walk out and check into the Marounichi Hotel, where a charming WVS lady looks helpful.

'What does the editor of *Tokyo Tips* advise first?' asks Dermot.

'The barber,' I say, and ask the WVS lady if she can direct us.

'That's where all the Prince Regent's officers go first.

There's an excellent barber just outside the hotel. Two minutes' walk. Come back when you've finished and I'll help you make a plan, if you like.'

I sink into a chair at the barber's. The feeling of release from Korea overcomes me. The barber throws a white covering over me and ties it tightly, stuffing towels and wadding round my neck. He puts a hot towel round my head, then another. I relax, semi-comatose, only half conscious of what's happening. The barber washes my hair, massaging my head deeply with his fingers and the heel of his hand. He dries it with a towel and starts clipping away. I lie there, eyes closed. He lathers my face with a brush and shaves my cheeks, my chin, round my lips, my neck, round my ears and between my eyes. He clips my eyebrows. Then he massages my head again, harder this time, with deep, long, stimulating strokes. A girl comes and rakes out my ears with a spatula. Then I get another head massage before the barber tilts back my chair and puts a hot towel on my face. He works on my face with lotions: my chin, my jaws, my cheeks, my nose, my forehead, behind the ears and round the neck again. More hot towels. He sits me up and works on my shoulders with his wrist and the heel of his hand. My back and neck cry with pleasure. He holds my head in both hands, squeezes it until it's clamped in his grip, lifts it and drops it. It cracks.

I get up a new man. I've been in the chair for an hour and a half. Worth, almost, twelve months in Korea. I pay the barber the equivalent of half a crown.

'Please come again,' the barber says.

Dermot and Jeremy stand before me, looking years younger.

'What next?' asks Dermot.

'The Japanese eat early. Why don't we get a taxi to take us to a *tempura* restaurant off the Ginza and eat? Then, if we want to, we could go on to a bar, like the one Ben recommended.'

We are made welcome by countless men and women who

help us off with our shoes. We follow a maid along a passage, stepping on wood so polished I can see myself reflected. We are shown into a small sitting room where we are offered whisky or martinis.

'Martinis,' we all say. We have not seen a martini for a year. We drink.

In a few minutes a girl comes and escorts us up a flight of stairs into another small room. This one has a low, crescent-shaped table. We are asked to sit on cushions arranged on one side. A chef enters through a sliding door with an assistant carrying bowls of food. The chef sits on his haunches on the opposite side of the table, switches on an electric ring and starts to cook. Bowls of delicacies are placed on the table with chopsticks. We know how to use them and what to do from Hong Kong. First we are handed prawns. We dip them in soy and start to eat.

'Heaven,' says Jeremy. 'I would be happy if we only ate prawns.'

'They would be offended,' I say.

More prawns come, followed by a variety of fish.

'Do you really want to talk about the war?' asks Dermot.

'Not now,' I reply.

We eat more fish. It's very fresh.

'What shall we do tomorrow?' asks Jeremy.

'I suggest we go and sign the books first,' I say.

'Books?'

'The visitors' books at the embassy and at the commander-in-chief's. Colonel Guy likes us to do that. We will be asked to a party if they have one while we're here and we might learn something. They entertain regularly.'

More fish comes and vegetables. We drink green tea and little cups of warm *sake*.

'My father was at the embassy here before the war,' says Jeremy, 'before I was born. He has given me the name of a Japanese general long retired who was in Korea and made an exceptional collection of Korean ceramics. My father says it is better than any collection in Europe or America and I should see it if I can.'

'How are you going to contact this general?'

'I've got the address. I hoped the embassy could help.'

'All the more reason to go there.'

We drink some *sake*.

'These cups and plates are rather beautiful,' says Dermot.

'The Japanese learned how to pot from the Koreans,' Jeremy says.

'It's difficult to believe the Koreans were so cultured from what we've seen,' I say.

'You said you didn't want to talk about the war.'

'It was only an observation.'

Soup arrives in lacquer bowls.

'We might look at one of the department stores. They say they are as good as Harrods or Selfridges,' I suggest.

'If we've any money left after this meal,' says Jeremy.

'I've a wallet full of winnings, so let me pay for this.'

'Do you think they've got geisha girls here?'

'I'm sure we'll be asked if we want one to join us.'

'Why waste our money on geishas here?' asks Dermot.

'We might as well see what a good geisha girl does while we're here,' I say. 'I really have got a lot of money on me.'

'That's very generous but I'll go halves on the bill,' says Dermot. Now rice is served.

'Some rice,' says Jeremy.

'Some *sake*,' I say.

'Some meal,' says Dermot.

We are asked if we would like to be joined by a geisha. We have eaten and drunk too well to refuse.

The geisha is neither beautiful or young. Swathed in robes, she only shows the nape of her neck. Her face is coated in white paint. She is expressionless. She sings plucking a

269

*samisen*, which is a Japanese guitar of three strings, with a plectrum. Her song is pleasant. She appears to be trying to please, bending towards us and moving her body languorously. The song is over. She withdraws, bowing.

'Rather sad,' says Jeremy.

'Rather a disappointment,' I say.

'Perhaps she's not a top geisha,' says Dermot. 'Let's go to that bar Ben mentioned.'

We walk into the street. It is dark and a fairyland of lights. The bar is quite near. We are welcomed by modest looking girls wearing western dress. Mimosa herself, an ex-geisha who owns the bar, comes to greet us.

'We have been recommended to come here by Major Wildbore,' Dermot says.

'Major Ben,' she says. She speaks quite good English. 'How is he? You are most welcome. We do not normally welcome military but if you friends of Major Ben's I am happy to serve you. I will ask my girls look after you.'

They do.


In the morning at the embassy Jeremy finds a third secretary who speaks Japanese. He, too, would like to meet the Japanese general who is famous and a recluse. He telephones the general's house. Jeremy's entrée works. We are asked for that afternoon.

The third secretary drives us to the general's house, which is hidden behind a long wall. We enter, walk through courtyards and gardens white with cherry blossom and are shown into a room that, by western standards, is severe with only a few chairs grouped together.

The general enters. He is ancient, tall and stoops a little. His straight white beard and hair fall from his face. He is dressed immaculately in what must be a Savile Row suit, old and fitting perfectly. He leans on the arm of a military-looking servant. We bow. He bows. He welcomes the son of an old friend and the brave British officers. We all sit. Tea is served. The third secretary translates.

'How is your father?' asks the general.

'He is well and sends you greetings and trusts you enjoy good health, Sir,' Jeremy replies.

'I can expect no better. What does your father do? Why does he not come to Japan?'

'He is at the foreign office in London, Sir.'

'He must be nearly the same age now that I was when we met in 1929. How old is he?'

'He was born in 1898 so he is fifty-four.'

'A young man still. I was born in 1872 so I was fifty-seven when we met. Has he a collection of ceramics now?'

'He has some he has collected in his travels. Chinese, Mayan, European but not Korean. And not a great collection like yours.'

'I was fortunate to be in Korea on and off for thirty years with much leisure. The Silla and Chosun dynasties built great settled civilisations long before we Japanese.'

'Did you enjoy your years in Korea, Sir?'

'Immensely. It was a beautiful, feudal and agricultural country, which we helped to modernise in a sympathetic way. The economy and population of Korea grew remarkably under our guidance. What is happening now is a tragedy. That's because Japan lost her way, became over-ambitious and the wrong men took power. It was suicide to attack America. I told them so.'

'May we see your collection, Sir?'

'I talk too much. My servants will show you. Forgive me for not showing you myself but I no longer walk that easily. Tell your father to come and see me. We have a lot to talk about. Thank you for coming. You have given me great pleasure.'

We bow. He bows. He goes out on the arm of his servant. Another servant guides us along a passage to a rectangular room, about forty-five foot by twenty, with shelves on all sides and tables running down the middle. Even I, who know nothing about ceramics, can see it is an exceptional collection of great beauty. Jeremy asks the servant questions, through the third secretary, and gives us a commentary. We leave. In the car on our return journey the third secretary reports the servant to have said we were most honoured to see the general and the collection. He sees no one nowadays.

Dermot and I are eating lunch in a sushi bar. Jeremy has found a National Service officer with whom he trained. They are exploring the shops.

'Dermot, can I ask you about Jack Trench?'

'You can.'

'Has he ever served with the regiment before?'

'He was in Normandy with the first battalion and wounded. When he'd recovered he volunteered for the Parachute Regiment.'

'Why isn't he still with them?'

'I understand the colonel of the regiment wanted him to make up his mind whether he became a regular parachutist or stayed with us. He opted to do a tour with us.'

'Why?'

'Haven't you noticed how ambitious he is? I expect he wanted to see if there were better opportunities for him. Besides it was a chance to get more ribbons on his chest. Why are you so interested in him?'

'I had a brush with him when he first arrived. So did Burgo. I think Percy did, too. He just doesn't seem to fit.'

Dermot does not answer. He picks up a piece of raw fish with his chopsticks, dips it in soy and pops it into his mouth.

'It isn't really that,' I say. 'I'm worried about Hugh Jermy being in his company.'

Dermot pops another piece of fish into his mouth and says nothing.

'They're so different,' I say. 'They're bound to clash. Hugh is becoming over confident. It's all going too well for him. Trench won't like that. Trench is a shit. Trench will try and trip him up.'

'Good fish this,' said Dermot. 'Miles, I hope you're wrong. I didn't want Hugh to leave me. Colonel Guy thought Jack Trench needed an experienced regular subaltern. I can see why. There's nothing we can do. Hugh has been lucky. He may even have a charmed life. He can look after himself. Some people think he can be a bit of a shit, too. Anyhow Colonel Guy won't let Trench bugger Hugh about.'

'It worries me.'

'Why worry? What can you do about it? It's in the lap of the gods. I do like this fish.'

'You're heartless.'

'Far from it. I've rather fallen for my new little friend at Mimosa's. I understand what you're saying. I've been thinking about it myself. Miles, it's time you learned not to concern yourself or worry about things you cannot affect. In this case there's nothing you or I can do.'

'Your battalion's making quite a name for itself, Dermot.'

'Sounds bad,' says Dermot.

We are at the commander-in-chief's house. About twenty-five people, many in uniform, are in the room drinking the general's gin and whisky. A lieutenant-colonel, clearly on the staff, is talking to us. He is wearing a lightweight service dress. Dermot knows him.

'No, good. Your general told my general that he has no finer battalion in his division.'

'What about the Australians, colonel?'

'He's never met a finer fighting battalion.'

'And the Highlanders?'

'The stoutest battalion in defence he's ever seen.'

'And us, then?'

'He says he can rely on you to do anything. You're the best

273

all-round battalion. Whatever you're asked to do you get on and do it in your own quiet way.'

'Not so quiet sometimes, colonel.'

'You've had a lot of casualties.'

'We had heavy, not excessive casualties in the big battle for the Rock. It's this static war with the constant patrolling and bombardment that's leading to a constant drip, drip of officers and men. We were in the front line for eight weeks, you know, and we're under strength.'

'How long have you been in Korea, now? A year, isn't it? You'll be going home soon.'

'Anything definite about that?'

'It will be announced pretty soon.'

'What's that? What will be announced soon?'

The commander-in-chief joins us. He's a lieutenant-general and commands all the British forces in the area. He is dark, six foot and has four rows of ribbons on his chest. He is clean-shaven. I wonder if he enjoys Japanese girls.

'I was saying, Sir, that the PRLI will be relieved soon. They've been in Korea for a year.'

'Very good of you to come,' says the General. 'I know how many attractions there are to keep you away.'

Dermot introduces us.

'You've done very well, very well, in Korea. I'm sorry about the heavy casualties. How's morale?'

'Very good, general,' says Dermot.

'I'm glad. I often wonder if you all know how important what you're doing is in defending the free world. I cannot emphasise enough how vital it is we contain the communists in Korea and how impressed I am by the forces we have there. That very much includes you.'

'Do you think it will go on much longer, Sir?'

'That's a good question. The closer you are to the firing line the less you know about the war. The Chinese at the peace talks are being tricky about the repatriation of

274

prisoners. They want all the Chinese and Korean prisoners back. We're saying the prisoners should have the right to choose. The Chinese also claim the lists of prisoners we provide are incorrect and incomplete. To be frank, the Americans haven't been too clever in running the prisoner-of-war camps. In some the prisoners have taken over. We're having to send some of our troops to help clear up the mess. Oh dear, your glasses are empty. We can't have that.'

The general beckons a soldier who brings a tray of drinks. We help ourselves. The general moves on.

'Hello, Miles.'

I turn and find a familiar face from Sandhurst. He's a captain in a Scottish regiment, with an MC and wearing an aiguillette on his shoulder to indicate he's the general's aide-de-camp.

'I didn't know you were here, Michael,' I say, 'or I would have contacted you.'

'I saw you were here from the book. I missed you when you came to sign. I fixed this party. We weren't going to have one this week. The general likes parties. Enjoying yourself?'

'You bet. It's all so different we won't believe it when we get back.'

'You're a smart lot in your regiment. I've seen your *Tokyo Tips*. It boxes the compass and is very discreet. It always takes a visitor to tell you about your own city. I've found it useful myself. For briefing people, of course.'

'Does the general know about it?'

'I did show it to him. He asked me if I knew any of the places recommended?'

'What did you say?'

'I said I'd heard of some of them. He chuckled and said he hoped Lady Mountbatten wouldn't be able to decode it. Then he told me a story about serving with Monty when Monty commanded a battalion in Egypt before the war. Monty had one of his subalterns on the mat, suffering from fatigue caused by overdoing his nightlife. Monty rationed him and told him he had to get his permission to have a woman. Monty always put the telephone on his dining-room table during dinner in case there was an emergency. One evening it actually rang during dinner. It was the subaltern ringing to say he was desperate and had to have a woman. Monty barked back, "All right, then. Permission granted. But mind, only one."'

We are on the aeroplane flying back to Seoul. I'm sitting between Dermot and Jeremy. We are silent.

'I think I'm going to fall asleep,' Dermot says. 'Now's your last chance to talk about the war if you still want to.'

'No,' I say. 'The general answered my question. This war has nothing to do with the Koreans. It's between the west and communism. It just happens to be fought in Korea. Poor Koreans.'

'There you are. You've got the answer. I often find if you put a difficult question in the pending file it solves itself or someone else answers it for you. You sound sad.'

'I am. I'm thinking about how quickly the last few days have slipped away.'

*'Omne animal post coitum triste est.'*

*'Post ferias tristissimus sum,'* adds Jeremy.

There's more silence.

'I'm thinking,' says Jeremy, 'of chucking Cambridge and going to university in Tokyo. What do you say?'

No one replies. Dermot is asleep and I am miles away thinking about Kitty.

## Chapter 19

# *Last patrols*

'I hate giving you this order but I must,' said Colonel Guy.

We were sitting in Colonel Guy's tent, which served as his new command post, in the position we had taken over from a Canadian battalion. It was the best-prepared position we ever occupied and it was in the quietest part of the line. The forward companies were dug in on hills that overlooked a vast, flat overgrown paddy running 2000 yards across to the Chinese lines. Through it flowed the Samichon River.

'General Jim doesn't like the order any more than I do but he says we must do it.'

Colonel Guy and Percy Smythe had taken one look at the enormous, dank and deep command post in the new position and had immediately pitched a tent behind the top of battalion headquarters' hill, saying they had become allergic to living in continuous artificial light. Being summer there was no longer any problem about keeping warm. The issue now was keeping cool.

'The corps commander has ordered us to check all our minefields and to update the maps recording them.'

Next to the tent they had dug a new, smaller bunker into which they retreated when shelled. The Chinese sent over a daily quota of shells. Like the mail, the shells could arrive at any time of day. Colonel Guy and Percy liked to sit in the sun outside the tent, which overlooked the approach road to the battalion, watching visitors puffing and panting their way to the top of the hill. Even the grumpiest senior officer was speechless when he reached the top.

'He knows, as we do, that there are unrecorded minefields along the front that are a hazard.'

Colonel Guy looked at us. Dermot Lisle, Ben Wildbore, Jack Trench, Percy Smythe, Michael Harrington and I were sitting on canvas chairs listening to him. Michael Harrington had taken over Z Company from Rex Topham when we had been in reserve. After three years with the battalion Rex had returned to England to a staff appointment. Michael was charming, relaxed and full of good humour. He had been accepted by Z Company immediately. He was the opposite, I thought, of Jack Trench.

'The corps commander is concerned at the number of *our* casualties caused by *our* minefields.'

'That's sensible,' says Jack Trench. 'I don't see a problem, colonel.'

'Wait till I've finished.'

Percy Smythe and I knew what was coming. I turned so I could see the others' faces.

'Here comes the sting. The checking is to be carried out by company commanders and no one else.'

Everyone showed surprise, even shock. Jack Trench sat up in his chair and the map he was holding on his knees fell to the ground.

'What do you think of that, Jack?' Colonel Guy asked.

'Well, well,' Jack stammered, 'Well, colonel, well, we'll have to do it.'

Colonel Guy looked at the others. They were all silent, thinking about the obscenity of the order.

'I suspect,' Colonel Guy said, 'that the order is directed at the American divisions, where he can't trust the battalion commanders to carry out the orders without stipulating who is responsible. But those are his orders and we must obey them.'

278

The extreme tenseness in people's faces faded. I could see they had all begun to think what carrying out the order entailed.

'I want you,' Colonel Guy continued, 'to carry this out with the greatest care. I cannot afford to lose one more officer, and certainly not a company commander.'

They all knew the problem. It was partly due to the pickets and wiring marking the minefields falling over when the snow and ice had melted. More serious were the inconsistencies in marking the minefields on the maps and the absence of information. In the early days some of the American battalions had laid minefields without marking or recording them.

'I want you to take your time doing this,' said Colonel Guy. 'We have to report in a week. Don't hurry it. Do as much preparation as you can before going out. Think through every move carefully. Miles has made the most accurate map he has been able to compile from all the records. He's going to give you the latest trace for your maps. Miles, will you brief us now.'

'How did that go, Sir?' asked Serjeant Savage.

He was waiting for me in the intelligence section bunker.

'No one fainted.'

'I should hope not, Sir.'

'Captain Smythe is going to inspect the minefields round battalion headquarters.'

'Did he volunteer?'

'He didn't want the colonel doing it.'

'I don't think there're any problems around battalion headquarters apart from fallen pickets.'

'Where do you think the big problem is, now that you've studied all the records so closely?'

'On the flanks. Major Trench and Major Harrington have the most dangerous jobs. The maps record nothing. I can't believe there're no minefields there.'

There was a scuffle at the entrance to the bunker. Corporal Low and Rumble came tumbling into the dugout.

'Incoming mail, Sir,' said Low.

There was an explosion. A shell landed a hundred yards away. Then another. Snowball tumbled into the bunker.

'Early today,' said Serjeant Savage.

'Count them,' I said.

The next explosion seemed closer.

'One day they'll get the colonel's tent,' said Snowball.

'Never,' said Corporal Low. 'Not with a shell.'

Dug in on the reverse of our hill we were well protected from enemy shellfire. Only the enemy mortars could lob bombs on to us with any success. The Chinese did not mortar battalion headquarters as often as they shelled it. There were more explosions, none close. Sitting in a bunker being shelled or mortared was the most terrifying experience of the war. Nothing compared to it.

'Where are Corporal Witney and Doughty?' I asked.

'Down with the vehicles. They'll be all right,' said Low.

Doughty was looking after me now, as well as being my driver. Maxwell had left to be demobbed. Percy Smythe had apologised for not replacing him due to our being so under strength.

The explosions continued.

'I hear we're to get a new draft, Sir,' said Savage.

'Correct,' I said. 'Seventy strong. They'll all go to the rifle companies.'

'That's only six per platoon,' said Low. 'They'll still be under strength.'

We waited for more explosions.

'That was fifteen, Sir,' said Low.

'That'll be it for the day,' said Savage.

There was a low roar of guns behind us.

'Outgoing mail,' said Low.

Our own guns were now returning fire.

'Go and find out if there's any damage or casualties, Corporal Low,' I said. 'And check on Doughty and Corporal Witney.'

The companies were sending out patrols, mainly listening or reconnoitring to get to know no man's land. Occasionally they heard Chinese patrols but there had been no clashes. One night Jeremy Last, leading a reconnaissance patrol back in, walked into an unmarked minefield next to Jack Trench's company. He lost a soldier and was lucky to escape with his life.

I thought I should go and have a look at the area myself. Late the following afternoon, when the fierce heat of the sun had declined, Doughty drove me up to the jeep head behind W Company. I climbed the hill to company headquarters and found Hugh Jermy outside Jack Trench's hoochie.

'Hello, Miles,' he said. 'How lovely to see you. What've you come about?'

'I've come to ask Jack if I can view the minefield that Jeremy walked into last night.'

'Jack's asleep. I've just brought him back from my position. Come with me.'

We walked across to his position where we sat by ourselves in an observation post.

'Jack's been a bloody fool and is lucky to be alive,' he said.

'What happened?'

'He went to check on the minefield Jeremy stumbled into. I watched him go out. You know how hot it gets here in the middle of the day. He was stripped to the waist and wasn't wearing a hat. He had a revolver but no water bottle. He was alone. I hoped he wasn't going to go out for long, forgot about it and went to sleep. One of my corporals woke me, saying, "Company commander, Sir. He's here. He's in a bad way." I hardly recognised Jack. He looked as though he'd

281

been in the desert for a week and was completely dehydrated. He couldn't talk, he could hardly stand and his eyes were popping out of his head. He was trying to say something. No more than a dry gasp came out of his quivering lips. I sat him down and got my water bottle and a spoon. For half an hour I spooned water into his mouth. Very slowly he began to regain his strength and return to sanity, that's if you could ever call Trench Foot sane. He told me what had happened.

'He had gone out to inspect the minefield. He'd been walking around for a while when he suddenly realised he was in it. It was midday and the sun was at its hottest. He must have been terrified. Very slowly he retraced his steps, being careful only to walk in his footprints. Sometimes this was obvious. Sometimes he had to take a gamble. How he got out alive I do not know. He was found crawling up the side of our hill, gasping, almost delirious. After he'd rested a bit I took him back to his hoochie. He's had quite a shock. He'll be all right in the morning. I'll keep an eye on him.'

'Don't you think we ought to send him back for the doctor to see him?' I asked.

'And humiliate him? I think he's had punishment enough.'

'I'd better tell the colonel.'

'Don't tell anyone. Let him recover. If there's something wrong with him in the morning I'll see he's looked after.'

'Aren't you taking on too much responsibility?'

'Who else will? Give him a break. He hasn't any confidence. He knows he's not liked and has made a fool of himself. He's taken to the whisky. He needs encouragement. Let him be.'

Hugh was senior to me. It was his decision.

'What are you going to do about that minefield?'

'I'm going down with a team now and we're going to map it and mark it.'

I was lying on my bunk, half asleep, when two men came into the section bunker. My hoochie, as usual, was built off the main bunker, separated by a blanket as a curtain.

'That was a good swim, Snowy,' said Rumble.

'Best part of the day, going down to the Imjin to swim,' said Snowball. 'Lucky it's out of gun range for the Chinks. We'd look right tits if they caught us in the river naked.'

'They don't call you Snowball for nothing then, do they?'

'What do you mean?'

'I saw you bollock naked.'

'So what?'

'I like your tackle, Snowy.'

'My what?'

'Your tackle. Lovely pair of balls you got down there.'

'Sod off,'

'I could do something for you with all that, Snowy.'

'Sod off, you fucking poofter.'

'I was only trying to be friendly.'

'Not like that you're not. I'm getting out of here. You fucking keep away from me.'

I heard Snowball leave. Then there was a loud sigh and Rumble followed him.

I had often wondered if that went on.

Colonel Guy called an O group to take stock on checking the minefield. Each company commander reported in turn.

'I cannot be completely sure, colonel,' said Michael Harrington, 'that I've found all the minefields. We've re-staked and signed the known minefields and one minefield I've found. Without walking every inch of the ground between here and the Samichon River I cannot be one hundred percent sure.'

'I understand,' said Colonel Guy. 'One can never be a hundred percent sure in these things. At least you've marked everything you know about. Jack, what about W Company?'

'I found an unmarked minefield, too,' said Jack Trench. 'I wandered into it and, when I realised, I retraced my steps. I identified the limits and then staked and marked it. I believe it was the only unmarked one in my area.'

'How can you be sure?'

'I spent a lot of time out there reconnoitring.'

'I see. Anyone else have anything more to report? No? Then let Miles have your traces.'

As I took the trace from Jack Trench I looked him in the eyes. He looked away. He did not have to report with such bravado. Was it fear or pride? Probably both. I wished I had told Colonel Guy after all.

The intelligence section was sitting outside its bunker cleaning its weapons in the morning sun. I still carried the Lee-Enfield rifle to which the armourer had attached a telescopic sight I had got in Japan. The pheasant season was long over and I wanted to go on shooting. Sometimes in the afternoons I would join Dermot and we'd shoot at targets together from his hill. The front lines were too far apart to do any sniping, and Colonel Guy disapproved of us doing that.

'How much longer are they going to keep us here in Korea, do you think Sir?' asked Corporal Low.

'There are rumours this is to be our last tour in the line,' I said.

'Has any other battalion been here so long?'

'We're the most experienced battalion in Korea, now.'

'Any other battalion had our casualties, Sir?'

'One or two, about the same.'

'More than the Gloucesters?'

'The Gloucesters didn't have many casualties. Half ours, I should say.'

'I thought they lost over five hundred men.'

'They were captured. They had fewer casualties because

the Chinese hadn't developed their artillery then. A lot of our casualties have come from artillery fire.'

There was a low crump from the Chinese lines.

'Here we go again,' said Serjeant Savage. 'Take cover. Mortar fire.'

'Incoming mail,' shouted Corporal Low.

We made for the bunkers fast. Half the section had got under cover when a group of mortar bombs whistled down and fell on the rest of us. We threw ourselves to the ground. I put my hands over my head. Four bombs exploded in a circle round us. A piece of metal plopped into the ground beside me. Another flew over my head. Then I saw Rumble hopping round unevenly, holding his arse and sobbing.

'They got me!' he cried. 'They got me in the bum! I've lost me trade! I've lost me trade!'

Serjeant Savage and I caught him, carried him into my bunker and lay him down on my bed, face down. His trousers were badly torn and he had a nasty gash in his buttocks which was pouring blood.

'Field dressing, someone,' I said.

Corporal Low ripped Rumble's trousers and underpants apart and slapped a field dressing on the wound. Rumble was shaking and crying.

'You'll be all right, Rumble,' said Low. 'It's only a flesh wound. Nothing serious.'

'I've lost me trade,' said Rumble. 'Lost me trade.'

'Let's get him down to the doctor at the RAP,' I said.

'I've sent Snowball for a stretcher,' said Savage. 'The mortaring's stopped.'

Snowball arrived with two buglers carrying a stretcher. They took Rumble down the hill to the stretcher jeep. He was still muttering.

'What's he on about?' said Snowball.

'He's a poofter,' said Low.

'I know that.'

'He thinks his wound has fucked up his chances.'
'Daft bugger. Up 'im!'

Colonel Guy called another O group.

'Thank you,' he said, 'for carrying out the corps commander's order to check the minefields so efficiently.'

He looked round the tent and everyone nodded.

'He has now issued a new order that, once again, I dislike giving you.' I looked at the faces. They were alert and resigned.

'I don't like this order any more than you will. He wants a prisoner.'

Anger and disquiet appeared on every face.

'I have remonstrated with General Jim and General Jim has protested to the corps commander. The corps commander is adamant. The front has become very quiet all along the line. He wants a prisoner to find out what's going on. He's awarding five days immediate R and R to anyone who captures a prisoner.'

'Some fool will try for it,' muttered Ben.

'What's that, Ben?'

'I said, colonel, that we'll have to try for it.'

'That's what I thought you said,' Colonel Guy replied and smiled. 'I have some good news.'

Everyone looked disbelieving.

'In six weeks' time we are to be relieved and we return to England.'

'About time!'

'I don't believe it!'

'It's unbelievable!'

'Home for Christmas!'

'We'll be home before Christmas,' Colonel Guy said. 'First, we have to capture a prisoner. Let's talk about how we're going to do it.'

Elation died.

'The fairest way is for the companies to take turns. I've decided we'll draw lots to choose who goes first. If the company that wins gets a prisoner, that will be it. If not, the three remaining companies will draw again and so on until we get a prisoner. Everyone agree that's fair? Right, Percy, where's the pack?'

Percy Smythe produced a new pack of playing cards, unwrapped it, took out the two jokers and started shuffling the cards expertly. He cut them and laid the pack on the table.

'Please draw,' he said, 'in reverse order of companies. Z first. Aces high.'

Michael Harrington got up, walked to the table and drew the knave of diamonds. Ben followed and drew the ace of spades.

'You can't beat that,' Ben said. 'I'll capture a prisoner myself. I claim the five days R and R now, colonel.'

We all laughed.

'All yours, Ben, if you can. Come and tell me your plan when you've made it.'

Jack Trench looked put out. Could he, I wondered, have wanted to have first go himself?

'I hear we're to be relieved in six weeks,' Serjeant Savage said when I got back to the intelligence section.

'How on earth do you hear these things? The colonel only told the company commanders five minutes ago.'

'Grapevine, Sir. The RQMS hears everything at B Echelon. He told the RSM. The RSM told the bugle-major. The bugle major told Serjeant Body and Body told me. I presume it's true?'

'True as can be. Do you know about the order to capture a prisoner?'

'What, Sir?'

'The corps commander wants a prisoner'

'Captured by us?'

'Anyone. There's an immediate reward of five days R and R.'

287

'The RSM will go for that.'

'He's too late. Major Wildbore has already volunteered.'

'How's he going to do it?'

'He hasn't told anyone yet. We'd better prepare a new "Get a Prisoner" map.'

'Corporal Low,' Savage said, 'you heard what the intelligence officer said.'

'I've got a prisoner.'

We had been watching Ben Wildbore with one of his soldiers and what appeared to be a Chinese soldier climbing the hill behind battalion headquarters. They walked straight up to the command post tent where Colonel Guy was talking to Percy Smythe and me.

'I caught him myself, colonel.'

'Congratulations, Ben. How *did* you do it? I don't remember you telling me you were going out on a daylight patrol.'

'Spur of the moment. After stand-down this morning one of my platoons reported there were two Chinks caught in the minefield below it. I went to have a look. Sure enough there were. The platoon commander wanted the soldier who had spotted them to go into the minefield to collect them. I said no. I knew the minefield best, which I did, and I'd made some tracks through it so I could get in and out easily. I said, no, too dangerous, I will capture them.'

'What happened to the other, Ben? You've only brought one,' said Colonel Guy.

'He's dead. No, I didn't shoot him. He hit a mine and nearly took me with him. I caught this one quite easily. He just sat waiting for me and gave himself up without a struggle. I then saw the other one was wounded. He started crawling towards us and blew himself up on a mine. Great pity. I had hoped two prisoners would mean ten days R and R.'

The prisoner had sat down meekly, head bowed as if awaiting execution.

'Miles, you'd better tell Captain Kim of our great fortune. Ben, you rascal, I'm glad you didn't catch two. Ten days R and R would kill you.'

The news spread and a crowd collected round the prisoner, including Corporal Low and Snowball, whom I ordered to guard the prisoner.

Colonel Guy took Ben and Percy into the tent to celebrate. More people came to view the prisoner, who seemed cowed but made no resistance or attempt to end his life. Snowball gave him a mug of tea which he drank with difficulty but gratefully.

'You'd better get him into the bunker,' I said to Low. 'We don't want him killed by a sudden enemy bombardment.'

'What about the smell?' Low asked.

'Better a smelly bunker than no prisoner.'

'Righto, Sir.'

The Chinese did not fire on us that morning. After an hour Captain Kim arrived. I took him into the bunker and watched him interrogate the prisoner, who spoke quite freely. After a few minutes Captain Kim laughed.

'He's a deserter,' Kim said. 'He says he gave himself up. They'd been trying to give themselves up for two days. His comrade was killed crawling towards the officer to surrender, too. Of course he'll give us some useful information but deserters don't count as prisoners.'

Ben sent out strong fighting patrols three nights running. The patrols lay in ambush at the crossings on the Samichon River, which we knew the Chinese used. They were not using them that week.

'Take a card,' said Percy Smythe. 'Companies in alphabetical order. Aces low.'

Jack Trench drew a six of clubs and looked disappointed. Then Dermot Lisle drew a ten of diamonds and Michael Harrington a two of spades.

'Congratulation, Dermot,' said Colonel Guy. 'Let me have your plan later today.'

'I've made it already, colonel.'

'Good man. Let's hear it now. It'll help having everyone here.'

'May I use the map?'

Dermot stood next to the large map of the front always displayed and kept up to date in the command tent. He picked up a pencil to use as a pointer.

'I've studied what we know about the Chinese position. There are some communication trenches here and here. I propose to send out a thirty-six-hour patrol. On the first night half the patrol will drop off at a crossing point on the Samichon River here, as a covering force. The rest of the patrol, under its leader, will find this communication trench, here. It will lie up during the day in the trench and capture the first person that moves along it. Then it will get out. If they fail to take a prisoner and remain undetected they are to return at nightfall. I will need pre-selected tank and artillery targets that the patrol can call for.'

'Daring plan. Who will lead it?'

'Tim Seymour.'

'He's your most experienced subaltern now. Good. The dangerous bit will be getting a prisoner out in daylight.'

'That's why I want the patrol to be able to call on the pre-planned artillery support to keep the Chinese heads down in the patrol's neighbourhood.'

'When will you do it?'

'Tomorrow night.'

'OK, Dermot. It's a good plan.'

Dermot asked me to join him the night the patrol went out. I went up with the colonel, who came to see the patrol off. He fell into conversation with Tim Seymour.

'Three months from now, Tim, we'll be in the saddle in England, riding to hounds.'

'That's something to look forward to, colonel. I missed last season.'

'I've missed two.'

For ten minutes they told each other hunting stories. Then Colonel Guy talked to every man in turn, giving each his full attention. He knew most of them well. They all had a last cigarette and moved off silently in the dark. There were no 'goodbyes' or 'good lucks'. They went out as if it was a routine, daily event.

After the colonel left us, Dermot said, 'I don't expect any fun and games until tomorrow. You never know though. They should be in position within three hours. Until they make a contact there's wireless silence.'

'Why don't you get some sleep,' I said. 'I'll wake you if anything happens.'

'I've never been able to sleep until my patrols are in. Sometimes I fall off and then I'm woken up. I have standing orders to be woken every quarter of an hour.'

'Not all company commanders are so fastidious.'

'Oh?'

'Trench Foot, for example.'

'I don't want to hear anything I would be embarrassed to know.'

'Aren't you curious?'

'Yes.'

'Not only does Trench Foot sleep while his patrols are out he nearly died of dehydration inspecting his minefields.'

'I heard him say he'd walked every inch.'

'He got lost in a minefield in the middle of the day and was lucky to live. Hugh saved him.'

'Didn't he say he'd inspected them all?'

'I wonder if he did. Only Hugh knows. I wanted to tell Colonel Guy but Hugh told me not to.'

'I think Colonel Guy knows something.'

'How do you know?'

'I've heard this before. Word gets out. Trench's serjeant-major told Budd. They're old mates.'

'That's not the colonel knowing.'

'Apparently Trench's serjeant-major also told the RSM.'

'So?'

'The RSM will have told the colonel. Colonel Guy would far prefer to hear this sort of thing from the RSM than from you.'

'Why?'

'Officers don't tell on each other. The RSM can say what he likes.'

'Have you noticed how Trench Foot didn't like it when Ben drew the ace and you drew the highest card in the last draw?'

'He did seem miffed.'

'I cannot understand him. I try. Hugh seems to get on with him. I cannot fathom him.'

'It's his ambitiousness, Miles. He is ridiculously ambitious and will do anything to get on. He's also not quite as good an officer as he thinks he is. He came here, as I told you in Japan, for the opportunities. He wants to win a medal and get a good report. He'll do anything to get them.'

'Isn't that dangerous?'

'You're right. It's dangerous and it's selfish. You put yourself and your desires above all others. Ambition is fine. Hugh has ambitions. So do you. So do I. Ambitions are necessary to get on in life. Ambitiousness is another matter. Jack Trench, I have come to believe, has it in spades. In Tokyo I told you not to worry about Hugh. I have to say I am a little concerned about Hugh now, though there's nothing I can do about it.'

'Hugh says not to worry about him. He says he can manage Trench Foot.'

'I'm not sure I quite trust Trench. That's a terrible thing to say about a brother officer.'

'What about the colonel? Does he trust him?'

'I don't think the colonel does either.'

'Don't tell me Percy Smythe has fixed that pack so that Trench Foot always draws a low card?'

'No. That's going too far. Colonel Guy is watching him very closely, I can tell. Remember, Trench Foot was sent here by the colonel of the regiment. Colonel Guy needs a very good reason to act.'

Serjeant-Major Budd came into the bunker with some hot drinks.

'Very good to have you with us, Mr Player,' he said, as he handed the drinks round. 'Tomorrow could be exciting.'

'I'm honoured to be invited, serjeant-major. I miss the company and wouldn't want to be anywhere else tonight.'

'This company is the best billet in the army,' he said.

We chatted for a time. Then Dermot showed me where I was to sleep and I dossed down.

In the early hours when Dermot believed that the patrol was in its positions he went to bed. He woke me well before dawn so that we could be ready at stand to. Nothing happened. We sat around all day and nothing happened. We heard nothing from the patrol until it returned to our lines about eleven o'clock.

'It went like clockwork,' Tim Seymour reported. 'We dropped off the covering party on time. We found the communication trench and lay up. We waited for daybreak. No one came. We waited all day. We saw and heard some Chinese but no one came down the trench. I thought about waiting through the night but it wasn't in the plan and, if no one came by day, why should anyone come by night. It seemed to be an unused trench. So we came back.'

'I'm so sorry, Tim. What rotten luck. You did well, very well.'

'Jack, it's between you and Michael,' said Percy. 'You draw first. Aces low.'

Jack walked up to the table and drew the Queen of Spades. He smiled. Michael drew the King of Hearts. Jack pulled a face.

'What's your plan, Michael,' Colonel Guy asked.

'I'd like to follow Dermot's plan with modifications. I thought it an excellent plan. Tim Seymour returned apparently undetected. It's a matter of choosing the communication trench in which to lie up. Miles has got some fresh air photos and I've had a long session with Tim.'

Michael went up to the map.

'Tim says he saw and heard activity here and here. This is borne out by the air photos. I'd like to go tonight.'

'Who will lead it?'

'Jeremy Last.'

'One of our boxing champions. Very good, Michael. Make the arrangements.'

Jeremy ran into an ambush at the river. He told us that he heard the click of a burp gun being cocked. He shouted to everyone to get down and hit the ground firing his sub-machine-gun in the direction of the click There was firing everywhere. Quite quickly the enemy fire petered out and stopped. Jeremy thought the heavy fire of his twenty men had overcome a smaller enemy patrol. He had four Bren guns. He searched the area and found one dead Chinaman whom he left. Jeremy had had three men wounded and decided it was too dangerous to continue the patrol.

A sombre O group met to hear Jack Trench's plan.

'You may say,' he started, 'that there's been a lot of bad luck. There's no doubt the enemy is more alert now with the attacks he's getting from our patrols all along the corps line, and all unsuccessful. I think we have to have a better plan. My plan is more aggressive and has two prongs. I'm going to put two fighting patrols in position. The first attacks a known enemy position to create a diversion and withdraws immediately, as

294

fast as it can. Then the second attacks another known enemy position and snatches a prisoner. I can fill in the details. That's the broad plan.'

'Very daring, Jack. How many casualties do you expect?'

'We've got to expect casualties, colonel.'

'Not unnecessarily. Who leads your two patrols?'

'Hugh Jermy leads the diversion. I lead the snatch party.'

'You can't do that.'

'Why not?'

'You are a company commander. Your responsibility is to lead your company, not a snatch party.'

'But I want to, colonel.'

'No buts, Jack. Think again.'

'Then Hugh Jermy leads the snatch party and Serjeant Foxton leads the diversion.'

'Have you discussed this plan with them?'

'Hugh Jermy and I developed it.'

'And Hugh is happy with it?'

'Definitely, colonel.'

'All right, go ahead. And Jack, remember, your role is to command your company.'

Jack Trench asked me to sit with him in his bunker. I learned it was Hugh's idea. I was surprised that Jack agreed. Maybe he thought it would be a good idea to have a witness to his heroics, someone who would verify how well he had conducted the operation. Then Colonel Guy told him he had to have David Sartorius, the New Zealand forward observation officer from the gunner battery. The artillery fireplan was a vital part of the operation.

Colonel Guy came to see the party off. It was a strong group. Hugh had developed a detailed plan, leaving little to chance. A strong covering party was to guard both sides of the river at a point we had not crossed before. After crossing the river the two fighting patrols were to divide. There were RVs and check points for each patrol. Serjeant Foxton had a party of nine, as did Hugh. They went off into the night cheerfully. The men had great faith in Hugh and Serjeant Foxton.

Jack Trench was excited.

'We're going to pull this off. I know we are,' he kept on saying.

'You buggers deserve a break,' said David Sartorius. 'You've tried hard enough.'

'Not hard enough yet,' said Jack. 'We will tonight.'

Wireless silence was to be kept until contact was made with the enemy. We heard nothing for the first few hours. Jack had opened a bottle of whisky. We watched the clock following their progress by the timetable. They would have crossed the river now, we said, and the patrols will have parted company. The first attack was to be timed for ten minutes to one in the morning, preceded by a short artillery bombardment. The second was to go in at five minutes to one without a bombardment. Serjeant Foxton's orders had been adjusted so that he could snatch a prisoner if he saw the opportunity. His main purpose remained diverting attention.

Midnight came and went. I drank nothing, but the whisky bottle seemed to get lower. The patrols would be lying up now, waiting for H hour. We waited. So far, so good. At twelve minutes to one the artillery regiment's guns, all four batteries, poured fire on to Serjeant Foxton's objective. For two minutes salvo after salvo landed on the objective one hundred yards in front of Foxton's patrol. At ten to one he led them in, throwing grenades and firing automatic weapons. He saw no one. The sentries must have retired to the bunkers when the bombardment started. He retired immediately, running down the hill before the enemy could bring down his defensive fire. Within two minutes it came down on them. They moved as fast as they could out of and

296

away from the belt of exploding shells. One soldier was wounded in the shoulder. They strapped him up. He could still walk. All this Foxton told us afterwards.

We heard the firing but we couldn't tell what was happening. A coded message was tapped out over the wireless. It told us Foxton had attacked, did not have a prisoner, had one wounded and was returning as planned.

The Chinese defensive fire was still coming down. This now mingled with the crack of small-arms firing and grenades from the direction of Hugh's objective, which was a mile from Foxton's. We waited. The fire died away. Then we heard the Chinese defensive fire exploding from Hugh's direction. We waited ten minutes. A message came through tapping out Hugh's news. He had a prisoner and two of the patrol were wounded.

'There you are,' said Jack Trench. 'I knew we'd do it.'

David Sartorius was on his wireless direct to his guns. Within seconds they began to fire a series of prearranged targets to protect Hugh's retreat.

We waited. We waited a long time. The whisky bottle was half full. Only Jack had been drinking. A voice came up on the wireless. It was Foxton. They had all crossed back across the river but Hugh was one of the wounded. Hugh had ordered Foxton to return with the prisoner. A small party was bringing Hugh back. There was nothing we could do but wait.

Serjeant Foxton arrived with the prisoner and two walking wounded.

'Let's get the wounded back to the doctor now,' I said. 'We'll keep the prisoner until it's light when it will be more difficult for him to escape.'

Jack appeared to be drunk from the whisky and the success of capturing a prisoner. He only seemed to be interested in the prisoner, who looked terrified. Jack sat him in a corner of the bunker and stared at him. Serjeant Foxton told me and David Sartorius what had happened.

'Where is Mr Jermy wounded?' I asked.

'In the leg and body, Sir. They're having to carry him. I'm told he caught a spray of bullets from a burp gun after he had nabbed the prisoner. He's conscious but he doesn't look good, Sir. We shot him full of morphine when they got him to the river.'

'Why did you leave him?'

'He ordered me to. He said we must get the prisoner back at all costs, before we were intercepted or caught in a bombardment. He had to order me.'

'Where is he now?'

'They're bringing him back through the minefield. It's the quickest route.'

'I hope they know it like the back of their hands.'

There was an explosion from the flank of the company.

'What was that?' I asked.

'A mine, Sir.'

'Where's Mr Jermy's wireless operator?'

'With Mr Jermy.'

I got on to the wireless and called him. He replied immediately.

'Where are you?' I said.

'We're in a minefield.'

'Are you all right?'

'No. We've lost the path. Corporal went looking for it and a mine's just exploded. I can't get the corp to answer.'

'How's your sunray?'

'Unconscious.'

'Stay where you are. Don't any of you move. We'll put some star shells up and come and find you. Do you understand?'

'Yes.'

'What are you to do?'

'Stay here and not move until you find us.'

'Don't move an inch.'

I put the microphone and headset down.

'Jack,' I said. 'Hugh's party is lost in the minefield. You know the minefield. Don't you think you should go and find him.'

'I'm staying here to look after my prisoner. When it's light I'm taking him to the colonel.'

'You mean you won't go and rescue Hugh?'

'Hugh knows the minefield. He'll get out. I'm going to guard my prisoner.'

'Hugh is lying unconscious in the minefield.'

'He's clever and lucky. He'll get out.'

'Jack, Hugh is seriously wounded, unconscious and his party has lost its way in the minefield. What are you going to do?'

'You go if you're worried about him. My job is to command the company. You heard the colonel say that.'

'You mean you won't go and find Hugh and you know the minefield.'

'I'm not going into that minefield.'

David Sartorius and Foxton had watched this. I turned to Foxton.

'Do you know the way into the minefield?'

'Yes, Sir.'

'Will you lead me?'

'Of course, Sir.'

'We need bayonets.'

'I'll find you one, sir.'

'And tape.'

'That, too.'

'David, can you put up a continuous umbrella of star shells to light us?'

'We can do that.'

I looked at my watch. 'In five minutes from now?'

'Of course.'

'When I've found Hugh I'll tell you on the wireless.'

Foxton and I left the bunker and I followed him across the hill, down through the wire to the side of the minefield. We waited for the star shells to light our way. The first one broke.

'This way, Sir.'

We walked over the marker fence and slowly followed a path in the minefield.

'Can you see anyone?'

'No, Sir.'

We walked on very slowly. There was a shout to our left. We turned. There was a body lying quite close to the path. About twenty yards from it were four men lying on the ground. The shout came from the group.

'Don't move,' I shouted. 'We can see you.'

'Fucking hell, Sir. They missed the path all right.'

'How do we get to them?' I asked.

'We'll have to probe. They're in the middle of the minefield.'

'Have you got your bayonet?'

'Yes, Sir. Have you?'

'Yes. I'll lead, serjeant. You follow and check I haven't missed a mine.'

'We'll have to make a wide path to carry Mr Jermy out.'

The star shells kept bursting. I unsheathed my bayonet, lay on the ground and started probing. Slowly we moved in a straight line towards the motionless body, clearly the corporal's. I unearthed a mine before I reached him. He was dead. I crawled on towards the others, probing and probing. I was covered in sweat and it was not that warm. I unearthed another mine and prayed David Sartorius could keep the star shells bursting. It must have been ten minutes since they started. I reached the group and crawled all round them probing. It seemed safe where they were.

I looked at Hugh. He was breathing but unconscious. The wireless operator and the two men who had been carrying Hugh were shivering with fright. I took the wireless and talked to David Sartorius. The star shells stopped. I was worried that they would attract the Chinese and expected a bombardment at any moment.

Foxton had laid a white tape from the path we had left, round the body and on to us.

'How were you carrying Mr Jermy?' I asked the group.

'Under the arms, Sir.'

'See that tape? All you've got to do is follow it. Pick up Mr Jermy and carry him along that tape. You'll be safe.'

They picked Hugh up.

'Serjeant, you lead. I'll bring up the rear.'

'What about the corporal?'

'He's dead. We'll collect him in the morning.'

We got Hugh out of the minefield and lay him down on the ground. Foxton went to get a stretcher party. I took Hugh in my arms, poured water on his face and stroked his forehead.

His eyes opened, then closed. It was difficult to see him clearly. He looked very tired.

'It's me. Miles.'

His eyes opened again.

'What are you doing here? I capsized.'

'I've come to take you back.'

'I don't think I can swim. I can't move my legs.'

'Lucky I qualified as a lifesaver. I can get you back.'

'I won't win the race now.'

'You've won it.'

'Have I really?'

'Yes. You won.'

'That's grand.'

He was silent for a moment.

'How's the boat?'

'The boat's fine.'

'I don't think I can keep afloat, Miles. I feel I'm drowning.'

'You'll be all right. I'll get you back.'

'You've always been my best friend, Miles.'
'You're mine, Hugh.'
'I'm drowning, Miles.'
'No, you're not.'
'Miles, tell Sonia I won.'
'I will.'
'And Miles—'
'Yes, Hugh.'
'Tell Sonia—'
He was silent.
'Tell Sonia what?' I asked.

He didn't answer. I passed my hand slowly across his eyes. They were wide open and did not blink. He was dead.

# Chapter 20

## Last post

'I'm surprised he lived as long as he did,' said the doctor. 'What did for him was a bullet in the lungs. Even if you'd got him back to me, it would have been touch and go.'

'And the others?' I asked.

'They'll be fine,' he said. 'He was a brave man and will be much missed.'

A wave of sorrow had hit the battalion. Hugh had been popular and many felt his loss. A noticeable caution crept into everyone's actions. People began looking over their shoulders and saying, 'The next one to go is not going to be me, if I can help it. Only three weeks and we'll be out of the line and off for home. I must stay alive.'

As long as we were in the line we had to continue to send out listening patrols and set the occasional ambush. The fighting patrols were called to a halt. We had captured our prisoner though we never heard if what the prisoner revealed had been worth the cost. The Chinese left us alone bar shelling us occasionally.

Serjeant Foxton brought me Hugh's belongings.

'Major Trench asked me to give you these,' he said. 'I told him you were Mr Jermy's best friend and I thought you'd know what to do with them.' He handed me Hugh's pack.

'I'm very sorry about Mr Jermy, Sir. He was a fucking good officer. All the lads are sorry, too.'

'You're a bloody good serjeant,' I said. 'Mr Jermy often spoke to me about you. He thought the world of you. And he loved his platoon. You've a fine lot of lads there, serjeant. It was wonderful how you brought him back.'

'I'll never forget him, Sir.'

I was looking through the contents of the pack.

'Nor will I,' I said.

I held up a dozen or so letters tied with a piece of string.

'Has anyone read these?'

'Not to my knowledge, Sir.'

'Major Trench?'

'Major Trench didn't look in the pack. Just told me to bring it to you. There's a photo, Sir. Do you know who the lady is? She's very beautiful.'

I looked at the photo. It was Sonia.

'I don't know,' I said.

I cannot recall much about coming out of the line except the palpable relief of knowing that we were not going back in. A haze of alcohol clouded any memory. Party after party followed in celebration coupled with a series of presentations. First, we gave a silver bugle to the Indian Field Ambulance who had saved so many of our wounded; then to the Kiwi gunners who had been our most valued support; to the hussars who had become a virtual part of the battalion; and to the other two battalions in the brigade who had fought alongside us.

The band had joined us from Hong Kong. The bugle major exchanged his rifle for his display stick and trained his buglers to bugle once more. We were relieved to hear the regimental fanfares and marches again and to have the band and bugles enliven our parades. This was an easier way to soldier.

A violent storm heralded the rains. The Imjin had been a placid pool in which we swam daily. Suddenly it turned into a furious torrent, rising hourly until it broke its banks and threatened to break the bridge which we had to cross to leave the battlefield. The bridge held, though we were delayed for two days. At Seoul we boarded a train that took us down the railway the Japanese had built at the turn of the century from Pusan, where we paraded in Korea for the last time. For in Pusan was the United Nations Military Cemetery.

On a sad, late summer day the band and bugles led the battalion to the cemetery. We formed up in a space below the rows of graves. Frank Parsonson took a short service in memory of those whose bodies we were leaving in this foreign soil. The bugle major himself played the last post followed by reveille. Then, as the battalion stood to attention, the band and bugles played our grand regimental march *The Trojans* in a minor key. The parade was dismissed. We split up and walked round the cemetery, searching for the graves in which so many of our comrades lay, to pay them our last, personal tributes.

A little behind Robin Brett lay Chris Worthington, together in death as in life. There was poor, lost Private Flint who had fallen under a tank and Hadji who had been so kind to me. Too many faces rose in front of me. Then I found Hugh. A small plate, just like the others, gave his rank, name, decoration, regiment and date of death. I stood and was lost in my thoughts when Doughty took my arm and told me everyone was leaving.

The troopship carrying us to England took us to Hong Kong in four days. There we were met by Ivan Blessington, accompanied by Burgo and another ADC, and a new commander-in-chief.

'Sonia wants to see you,' Burgo said. 'I'll take you to Government House. The boat is here for forty-eight hours. We'll go to Shek O afterwards and have a blow out.'

Sonia was in her sitting room.

'Oh, Miles, darling,' she said. She gave me her hand and gazed at me. Then she kissed me softly on the cheek. 'Thank God you're safe. I couldn't have borne it if you had been killed, too.'

'I'm terribly sorry, Sonia.'

'You wrote us such an understanding letter.'

'I've brought you these,' I said, and took the package of letters out of my pocket.

'You know, of course?' she said.

'Yes.'

'Don't give them to me. I'd cry if I read them. Burn them for me, Miles.'

I nodded and put them back into my pocket.

'Tell me how he died.'

I told her what I had not been able to write in my letter.

'What do you think he meant by his last "tell Sonia"?' she asked.

'Just that he'd won and he thought that would please you.'

'He always had to win. Ambition killed him.'

'No, ambition made him,' I said. 'It was the tyrant chance that killed him.'

# Main characters in order of mention or appearance

| | |
|---|---|
| Major George Bulman MC | Commanding X Company |
| Captain Dermot Lisle MC | 2i/c X Company |
| Lieutenant Burgo Howard | X Company |
| Lieutenant Miles Player | X Company |
| Major Horace Belcher | Commanding Y Company |
| | |
| 2nd Lieut Toby Errington (Manky) | X Company |
| Serjeant-Major Budd DCM | CSM X Company |
| Colour Serjeant Crum | CQMS X Company |
| Serjeant Whettingsteel (Big Steel) | Miles Player's platoon serjeant |
| Corporal Whettingsteel (Little Steel) | Section Commander in Miles's platoon |
| | |
| Sir Ivan Blessington GCMG, GBE | Governor of Hong Kong |
| Lady Blessington (Sonia) | Wife of Ivan, cousin of Miles |
| Captain Hugh Jermy | ADC to the Governor |
| Lieut-Colonel Guy Surtees DSO OBE | Commanding Officer 2 PRLI |
| Miss Kitty Fisher | God-daughter of Sonia Blessington |
| | |
| Lance Corporal Rothwell | X Company marksman in Miles's platoon |
| | |
| Captain Percy Smythe | Adjutant 2 PRLI |
| Lance Corporal Tidmarsh | Mortarman in Miles's platoon |
| Captain Tony Strickland | Commanding MMG Platoon |
| Private Maxwell | Miles's soldier servant |

| | |
|---|---|
| Corporal Foxton (Foxy) | Section commander in Miles's platoon |
| Corporal Wildman | Section commander in Miles's platoon |
| Private Flint (Neolithic) | Private in Miles's platoon |
| Serjeant Tom Body | Commanding Assault Pioneer Platoon |
| Captain David Sartorius | FOO New Zealand Artillery Battery |
| | |
| RQMS Quartermain | Quartermaster's right hand |
| Captain Ben Wildbore | New 2i/c, X Company |
| 2nd Lieut Tim Seymour | X Company |
| Brevet Major Fred Player MC | Miles's father |
| Mrs Player (Evelyn) | Miles's mother |
| | |
| Major General Sir George Fisher Bt CB CMG DSO | Kitty's father |
| Private Ellis | Dermot Lisle's driver |
| 2nd Lieut Chris Worthington | Y Company |
| 2nd Lieut Robin Brett | X Company |
| Captain Pat Bussell | Intelligence Officer |
| | |
| Serjeant Savage (Monty) | Intelligence Section Serjeant |
| Corporal Low (Lofty) | Intelligence Section |
| Lance Corporal Witney (Blanket) | " |
| Private Snowball (Snowy) | " |
| Private Rumble | " |
| | |
| Private Doughty | Miles Player's driver |
| Major Arthur Hickey (Hadji) | Commanding W Company |
| Major Rex Topham DSO MC | Commanding Z Company |
| Major Tom Warburton | Commanding Y Company |
| Private Roberts | Colonel Surtees's soldier servant |
| | |
| Captain Kim In Sup | ROK Army Interpreter |
| Major Henry Hammersley MC | Commanding Hussar Squadron |
| Major Desmond Dennis | Commanding New Zealand Artillery Battery |

| | |
|---|---|
| Captain Revd Frank Parsonson | Regimental Padre |
| Lieut Roddy Kington | Commanding Hussar troop |
| | |
| Mrs Knox (Verity) | Widow of Major Knox, Jasper's father |
| Jasper Knox | Schoolboy son of Mrs Knox |
| Mrs Jermy | Mother of Hugh |
| Mr Jermy | Father of Hugh |
| Major Jack Trench (Trench Foot) | Takes over HQ Company, then W |
| | |
| 2nd Lieut Jeremy Last | Platoon Commander Y Company |
| Major Michael Harrington | Takes over Z Company |

## 2 PRLI in Korea 1951/52

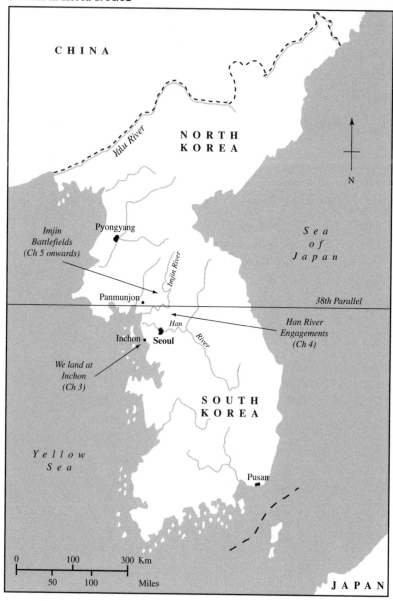

## 2 PRLI operations across the Imjin, 1951

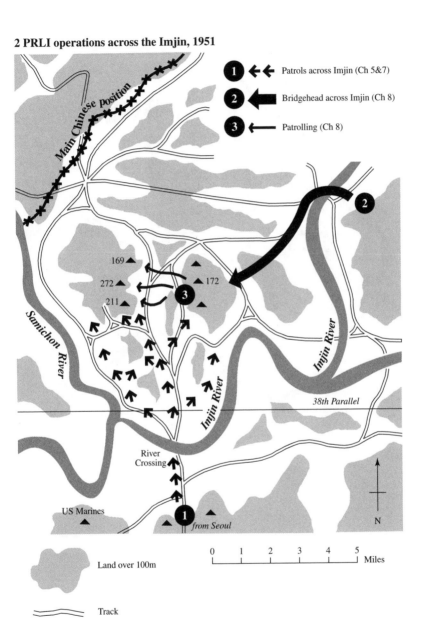

**1** ←← Patrols across Imjin (Ch 5&7)

**2** ← Bridgehead across Imjin (Ch 8)

**3** ← Patrolling (Ch 8)

Main Chinese Position

169

272

211

172

**3**

**2**

Samichon River

Imjin River

Imjin River

Imjin River

38th Parallel

River Crossing

US Marines

**1** from Seoul

N

Land over 100m

0 1 2 3 4 5 Miles

Track

## 2 PRLI in the battles of 'Mansok San and 'Hill 220' and later patrolling

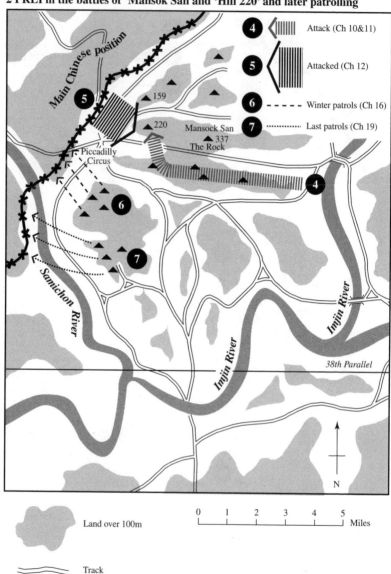